(R)EVOLUTION

(R)EVOLUTION

PJ MANNEY

47NORTH

This is a work of fiction. Names, characters, organizations, places, events, and incidents are either products of the author's imagination or are used fictitiously.

Published by 47North, Seattle

www.apub.com

Amazon, the Amazon logo, and 47North are trademarks of Amazon.com, Inc., or its affiliates.

ISBN-13: 9781477828496
ISBN-10: 1477828494

Cover design by Megan Haggerty
Cover illustration by Adam Martinakis

Library of Congress Control Number: 2014955046

Printed in the United States of America

To Nathaniel and Hannah:

The future is yours to create.

PROLOGUE

Ready or not, revolution comes, thought Emma Lancaster. Bodies flowed past a coffee shop in the grand lobby of the Las Vegas Convention Center. Emma sipped a tall cappuccino, watching them with resignation. She was small boned and slender, with long, honey-hued hair pulled back in a high ponytail that lent her the perky charisma of a cheerleader. Or class president. She'd been both in her short life. But this morning, she was subdued.

Next to her, a pale, wispy teen, with watery blue eyes open so wide a puff of reality might blow him away, nursed his soy chai latte. Donovan Katz had to brush his unruly ginger hair out of his cup every time he sipped from it. On Emma's other side stood Brandon Tellmer, black buds firmly in ears. His brown buzz-cut head bobbed and his legs twitched in time with his personal soundtrack, aided by two extra shots in his café mocha. Green Day's "American Idiot" leaked through his headphones, the headbanging polluting a Muzak version of Elton John's "Tiny Dancer" that pumped through the ceiling speakers.

All three seemed no more than overgrown children: clean-cut collegiate types, dressed in their mall-bought clothes, armed with large, techno-friendly, solar-powered backpacks. They radiated competence, seriousness, and dedication. Had they worn suits, you might have mistaken them for Mormon missionaries.

The Las Vegas Convention Center was packed with over one hundred thousand people, distributed among its three main halls. They were there to attend IAM—the International Association of Media. Media shrunk the world into its common needs and goals regardless of nationality, and IAM provided everything that multicultural buyers and sellers needed, sharing the common language of money in the largest gathering of electronic companies on earth, a convergence of broadcast and cable television, motion pictures, radio, gaming, music, news, and mobile phones to feed the ever-hungry maw of the Internet.

The Smart Badges that hung from the three young people's necks identified and linked them as collegiate casters from Brigham Young University in Provo. But their identities were forged. For instance, Emma posed as Sally Dunbuster of Mt. Pleasant, Utah. Each had come from a different college, a different background, and had only met six months earlier to train for their common goal.

Emma looked at her watch. It was five minutes to twelve. Discreetly, the boys also checked their watches. Then they stared a moment too long into each other's eyes.

Emma offered her hand to shake. Donovan playfully knocked it away, smiled, and opened his arms. She stepped into his hug, then hugged Brandon. He was damp, trembling, but his expression remained stoic. Without a word, Emma stepped back from Brandon's embrace, scooped up her backpack, and strode to the central hall.

Brandon headed for the north hall while Donovan took off at a jog, cutting quickly through the crowd, for the more distant south hall.

A herd of conventioneers crushed Emma in the chute of the central hall doors, offering a suited man in his forties the opportunity to brush his hand against her breast. She drew back, but before she had a chance to look at his face, his dangling Smart Badge buzzed in automated greet mode: "Hi, Sally Dunbuster! I'm Bob Grant—Network Sales. Let me tell you about product placement and promotion opportunities for your faith-based programming!" Bob's bleached, toothy grin aimed to impress, suggesting, "I practically run the network": whereas, in reality, he sold *Still Keeping Up with the Kardashians* to Kazakhstan. He glanced at his own badge for preprogrammed information to use as a conversation starter. Like many conventioneers away from home, he was desperate to get laid. Emma disappeared into the crowd, forgiving his clumsy come-on.

Once inside the central hall, she disabled the Smart Badge and stood on tiptoe to survey the enormous room. Its six hundred thousand square feet were filled with almost a thousand trade-show booths. They hawked hardware, software, services, and an endless variety of content, all aimed at the blessed convergence of multimedia information technologies to be delivered through the one-two punch of the GO/HOME, a handheld and wall-sized all-media system. In this brave new world of information technology, the GO/HOME was all people needed. The choices made by owners of the systems reflected their passions and habits, and this valuable marketing information was sent back to the companies so they could provide what the public wanted. Of course, that presupposed the public knew what they wanted, or could favor nonexistent choices. It was hard to tell who believed this innovation was more heaven-sent: entertainment addicts, techno-geeks, or media conglomerates.

Emma cut quickly through the hall, past "Content Creation Village," "Satellite Site," and "Internet Services," to the far corner where "Technologies for Worship" was housed.

Shucking her backpack, she propped it against the wall between "Event-gelicals" and "VC Cubed: Viewer Content for Virtual Catering of Virtual Communion." Again, she checked her watch:

12:00:17. With smooth, swift moves born of countless practice runs, Emma knelt and pulled a nylon bag from inside the backpack. Quickly removing some plastic and ceramic pieces, she fitted them like a K'nex set, until the object in her hands was recognizable as a drone aircraft, about a meter long. A tiny video camera peeked from beneath its nose, and a miniature directed-thrust engine with four nozzles was cradled inside the skeletal fuselage. Emma skinned the frame with tightly fitted black fabric. Finally, she clipped a preassembled pod resembling the passenger cabin beneath a dirigible to the bottom of the craft. Together, the belly and pod created a sign in bright, cheerful letters: "Smile! GOD'S Watching!"

Emma placed the tiny craft on the floor and powered up the remote, pressing "Collect," which initiated a collection of spatial information from two scanning laser sensors on its belly and dorsal. When her remote's light turned green, she pressed "Start." The miniature Harrier jet rose into the air. Several exhibitors and attendees clapped as it climbed above their heads to the ceiling and away.

She tossed the remote into the backpack and slipped into the crowd to find the nearest ladies' room.

Inside the restroom, two leggy spokesmodels complained about frequent costume changes as they washed their hands and reapplied makeup. Emma locked herself in a stall and unzipped her backpack on the toilet seat, quickly removing three clear ziplock bags. One contained nonpermeable polymer nose- and earplugs, rimmed with a nano-superadhesive protected by pull strips. She ripped off the strips and shoved the plugs up her nostrils, high enough not to be seen, and squeezed her nose around them, forming a tight, gap-free seal. Then she stuffed the other pair in her ears. She pulled off her ponytail band and fluffed her thick hair around her ears to obscure the plugs.

The second bag held a nonpermeable polymer mouthpiece connected by a tube to a small steel container. She yanked off the strip and bit down hard, locking her inner lips around the adhesive seal.

Two small tubes emerged from the left side of her mouth. She took small breaths, keeping her mouth shut to conceal the mouthpiece, and stuffed the container and extra tubing into an inner pocket of her jacket. Ripping open the last bag, she removed a pair of adhesive-rimmed plastic goggles designed to look like wraparound sunglasses and fitted them around her eyes.

Entering the hall again, Emma looked up. The drone skimmed one meter below the ceiling, almost thirty-five feet above the crowd, maintaining a precise distance from the rigging, its laser guidance enabling it to avoid displays, signs, banners, and lighting equipment that hung from the rafters and catwalks.

Emma permitted herself a satisfied smile as she strolled past a display for super high-definition cameras, and tossed the remote beneath the display's large skirted table. No one noticed. And there would be no fingerprints. All three of them had dipped their hands in clear, fast-drying acrylic that created an invisible glove, preventing incriminating fingerprints or sloughed skin cells.

Just ahead of her, a man in his sixties with a huge gut stopped to catch his breath. He had the pallor of someone about to pass out. Or worse.

Emma quickened her pace. With fourteen acres under this roof alone, she still had serious ground to cover. As she breathed more deeply, the tiny tank under her jacket struggled to provide her with sufficient air.

At the Panasonic booth, a twentyish intern with black spiky hair suddenly fell to the floor in what appeared to be an epileptic fit. Concerned patrons immediately surrounded him, dialing GOs for medical aid.

A burst of adrenalized panic overwhelmed her. Sprinting down the aisles, she dodged attendees like a football running back. High above, the plane flew ahead of her, reaching the front doors, only to turn around in an ever-widening loop.

More people looked ill. A few squatted in the aisle, head between the knees, to prevent passing out. An elderly woman in a motorized chair stopped by a squatting teenage podcaster and offered him her oxygen mask.

Sucking limited air through the regulator made Emma woozy. She burst through the glass doors of the grand lobby onto the sidewalk, trying not to faint, convincing herself she just needed more oxygen. She scanned the parking lot. They had parked their getaway cars in different areas, all within a block of their buildings. Her car was the farthest from the halls, beyond the lot and across Paradise Road at the Courtyard by Marriott.

Cold sweat made her shiver in the sweltering heat. A shuttle bus pulled up to take conventioneers from the center to surrounding halls and hotels. Two people got off, but a crowd was lined up, ready to board. As Emma got on, the itinerary taped to the dashboard listed the Courtyard by Marriott as the first hotel stop. She found a seat in back.

Adrenaline coursed through her body, so to slow her racing heart, she practiced the controlled, deep breathing her trainers taught her. As seats filled up, a ruddy-faced blond man in his fifties paused by her seat and politely gestured "Do you mind?" before settling in. His Smart Badge read, "Anders Sandberg—Satellite System Technician." He tried to maintain a polite distance between them, but the bodies crushed together in the aisle shoved him closer. Soon, over seventy people filled every available standing or sitting space on a forty-seat bus. The babble of many languages—Hebrew and Arabic, Mandarin and Spanish, Hindi and German—created a polyglot white noise. The Smart Badges' proximity sensors went into overdrive. "Hello Japendu! I'm Benicio—Segment Producer. Let me tell you about geriatric media opportunities for healthcare providers!"

Peering out the window, Emma saw Brandon dash outside the north hall for the nearest parking area, his loping stride revealing a long-distance runner. Reaching his anonymous Ford Escort, he fumbled for the keys. They hit the ground and he dived out of sight behind the car to find them. When he popped back up to unlock his door, he caught a glimpse of Emma in her shuttle as it pulled away. They traded a relieved look. He jumped into the driver's seat, turned the key . . .

. . . and a white light enveloped the parking lot, burning the retinas of all who witnessed it. A high-pitched hum became a whooshing sound that sucked all other sounds up and away.

The shuttle driver slammed the brakes. Passengers shrieked, and a few lost their balance, falling into seated laps in confusion.

Emma froze, hands pressed against the hot window glass, the screams around her muffled by the earplugs. Satellite Man burst out, "*Herre Gud!* Did you see that . . . that . . . What the hell *was* that?" His accent was Swedish.

As eyesight and hearing slowly returned, everything looked washed out, overexposed. The blinding light was gone. Along with the car. And Brandon. All that remained in their place was a hole in liquefied tar, strewn with chunks of molten metal and a sprinkling of ash.

This was not the plan. None of the team was supposed to die.

The stunned driver came to life. Grabbing the microphone, he yelled over the passengers' babble, "What do you want me to do?"

"Go! Go! Go!" was the unanimous reply. If the center was under attack, no one wanted to stick around. He hit the gas pedal, sending more standers off balance. Terrified now, they clutched at each other. A few cried.

Emma stared fixedly at the south hall doors, willing Donovan to come out. Moments later, he emerged. His casual but purposeful saunter told her that he hadn't seen Brandon wiped off the earth. Intent on his goal, he paid no attention to the gathering witnesses.

Trapped on the bus, with the regulator glued into her mouth, Emma couldn't scream a warning to him. The bus rapidly pulled away. She twisted in her seat and tried to wave at him, but it was impossible for him to see her.

Anxiously, she glanced around at the rest of the passengers. The din had quieted. Several people looked ill. Two men, an Indian at the back and a German at the front, began to shake uncontrollably. A new, higher-pitched babble broke out.

An Israeli-accented voice screamed from beside an Indian, "Stop the bus! He is ill!" It took only seconds for other passengers to look around and realize many were sick.

Another accented voice shouted, "Out! Everybody out!" prompting more panicked entreaties to the driver.

The bus driver flicked terrified glances in his rearview mirror and quickly turned into the driveway of the Marriott.

Satellite Man wheezed, left hand clutching his chest, his shaky right fumbling madly for an asthma inhaler in his front trouser pocket.

The moment the shuttle stopped and the doors flew open, the stampede began. No one was more desperate to escape than Emma. Unable to rise, Satellite Man gasped like a landed fish and clutched her arm. She tore his clammy, grasping hands off her as she crawled over his lap to plunge into the mass of passengers in the aisle. She forced her way through the twisted, convulsing bodies to the bus's front steps. Those who realized she was unaffected clawed at her to carry them to safety. But she slapped them off fiercely, helping no one. Bursting out of the open door, she half stumbled, half ran down the steps and onto the pavement. Fixated on reaching her white Ford Escort, she shut out the sights and sounds of her dying bus mates.

The few who made it out of the bus and collapsed set off their Smart Badges' reoriented proximity sensors. In virtual conversation, the same dispassionate, female compu-voice kept repeating on dozens of badges, "Hi Gunther! I'm Mingmei . . ." "Hi Jorge! I'm François . . ." "Let me tell you about . . ." ". . . writing the . . ." ". . . shooting with . . ." ". . . starring as your own . . ." They would be the last words the badge wearers would ever hear.

Feverishly fishing out keys from her pocket, Emma paused. Could Brandon have triggered something? If she unlocked the door, would she die, too?

The sirens were getting louder. And her options fewer.

Her trainers were adamant: don't deviate from the plan. Slowly, she slipped the key into the lock. It turned easily. The door opened . . . Nothing happened. Maybe it was the ignition. She got behind the wheel, fastened her seat belt and gently put the key in the ignition. The car turned over, and the engine hummed. No white light came to extinguish her existence. She breathed a constrained sigh of relief through her mouthpiece and carefully backed out of the space, following the arrows to a far exit, turning right onto Paradise Road and immediately crossing over two lanes to make a left onto East Desert Inn Road, tires squealing below the suspended corridor created by the hulking convention center above her.

The sirens were close.

The authorities would close the largest arteries first, so Emma avoided Interstate 15—the usual route through Las Vegas—to escape on surface streets and back roads. The plan was to meet up 150 miles away. Only she and Donovan would make it now.

Within ten blocks, traffic slowed. As the overpass for the 515/95/93 loomed before her, she saw it. A smoking hole in the asphalt at a stoplight, blocking a lane. People surrounded it, staring into its wet, inky blackness.

Emma began to cry.

Traffic freed up after the overpass. Word of what happened had not yet reached the local drivers. She careened right, turning the corner of the first street she saw, Backstage Boulevard, and made a quick left on Florrie Avenue. She was in a residential neighborhood, full of one-story, 1960s ranch–style homes. She parked in front of a gray house with white trim peeling in large flakes from the relentless Las Vegas sun and left the keys in the ignition, in case removing the keys might trigger an explosion.

She bolted down the street, gasping for air. There wasn't enough. It could have been her weeping, or maybe her air filters had failed and she, too, was infected, but she couldn't stop. Through the fogged lenses of her goggles, she searched for an escape route. In one direction there was a dead end into railroad tracks. She dashed right into a cul-de-sac.

Suddenly, Emma felt as if her head might explode. Her ears rang and she experienced a sensation of her body being peeled inside out . . .

After the burst of blinding white light faded away, the center of the cul-de-sac had an oozing, tarry hole in it. Emma was gone.

It would be over six hours before a cruiser from the Las Vegas Police Department came to examine the hole after receiving a housewife's hysterical 911 call.

PART ONE

CHAPTER ONE

I t hadn't sunk in yet.

Peter Bernhardt caught sight of his reflection in the glass of a framed photograph: a scarecrow sagged over the Biogineers conference room table, raking fingers through unbrushed shoulder-length brown hair, staring back with blue bloodshot eyes, chalky pale skin taut with stress. Was that him? Or was a ghost floating in front of the photo of California's governor shaking hands with a different Peter Bernhardt: six foot, broad shouldered, crooked nosed, cleft chin paired with a single cheek dimple in a smile that was a little too eager to please, dressed in his daily uniform of a black T-shirt and jacket, blue jeans, and black running shoes? Other specters bounced off framed articles about Bernhardt and Biogineers in *Wired* ("Is Peter Bernhardt Going to Change Neuromedicine Forever?"); the *Economist* ("Biogineers: The Super Small Will Soon Be Super Big!"); the *Wall Street Journal* ("Conquistador Capital Explores Brave New World of Nanomedicine with Biogineers"); and the *New York Times* ("While My Guitar Gently Reaps," about how he came up with a nanorobotic structure while playing "Mother's Little Helper" by the Rolling Stones on a Gibson Firebird, and the idea for Biogineers while playing "Bad Brain" by the Ramones on a Fender Stratocaster).

He had thought these mementos represented a level of success that could never be taken away. Would he burn them now? Peter was in shock, obsessing about bullshit, having just been axed from the nanobiotech firm he created. Because of Biogineers, he was being blamed for the biggest mass murder in history. And he didn't even know why.

Bruce Lobo stared unblinking across the table, pale gray eyes devoid of emotion. Short, muscular, he looked like any number of wealthy Latino businessmen in Silicon Valley. But he wasn't just anybody. Lobo was the most powerful man in the biotech business. For two days, he had been Peter's boss. Now, he was Peter's enemy.

"Because the government believes nanorobots were used to perpetrate the attacks," said Bruce, "you and Biogineers are under suspicion. To protect ourselves, Lobo Industries' board of directors has decided to terminate your contract—with cause—for gross negligence, or willful misconduct, or terrorism, or any other damned thing we can prove. Biogineers and Lobo Industries will distance themselves from you personally, using any means necessary. Amanda will tender her resignation immediately by signing this resignation letter written on her behalf." The letter lay in the middle of the table. Bruce rocked back in his seat. Silent. His stare penetrating Peter's skull like a bone drill bit.

No amount of homework could have prepared Peter for this morning. Lobo was a challenging business colleague with a ruthless and monopolistic reputation. But Peter had thought that two poor-but-smart Catholic boys who had made good in the same industry might have a lot in common and be able to bond. They had both used intelligence and ambition to climb to the top of the biotech field. A field that daily changed how humanity dealt with illness. Peter's technology was on the brink of making Alzheimer's obsolete. Depression a thing of the past. Brain diseases something that only happened to those who didn't receive treatment. People would live longer and healthier lives than ever before. He'd thought he was creating happiness for millions, if not billions, of people.

By teaming with Lobo, Peter had hoped to synergistically work with other Lobo enterprises to create something bigger than the sum of their parts. He had thought the buyout would be the best thing for everyone. But apparently, everything he knew about Lobo was wrong.

Just two days ago was no ordinary workday. A welcome-to-the-evil-empire party was in full swing as Biogineers's team celebrated their big payday. By 10:00 a.m., Dom and Raging Bulls flowed and everyone was having a great time. Amanda even pulled Peter into a storeroom for a congratulatory drunken make-out session, her long limbs wrapped around him.

Even after eleven years, Peter marveled how this woman could be his wife. He kissed her impossibly high cheekbones that slashed across copper-colored skin. Glossy black lashes and thick eyebrows framed almond-shaped eyes—the right, blue-green; the left, brown. Her long, straight black hair fell over her face, stroking his cheek, and she absentmindedly pushed it back up behind her ear, where gravity would prevail again in a minute. He often fantasized she was descended from a famous Indian chief. His own Pocahontas. Her family history included a sizable chunk of Cherokee, so it was possible.

The only thing that stopped them from having sex right there was a few equally drunk coworkers who opened the door screaming "Surprise!" moments before they were in flagrante delicto. Everyone thought it was hilariously funny. At the time.

Just two days ago, Peter was glad-handing employees, telling them this was the beginning of great things. He hunted down the chief engineer, Chang Eng, surrounded by his exuberant team down in the manufacturing lab. Chang quietly nursed a beer as the jokes flew around him. Everything about Chang was condensed to its essence, from his slim physique to his perfectly fit chinos and oxford shirt that allowed for no more fabric than was absolutely necessary, to his hair buzzed weekly at a number two. Biogineers would never have achieved half its success without Chang's extraordinary engineering and problem-solving skills.

Peter pulled him aside. "You know this is all because of you. And it's just the beginning . . ."

Chang's head bowed. "It wasn't me. It was our team. They allowed me to do all the hard work."

Peter slapped him on the back. "Stop being so Chinese! You're now part of the Microsoft of biotech! You have unbelievable benefit and stock packages. Just say, 'Thank you.'"

Chang shyly stared down the barrel of an empty beer bottle. "Thank you."

Just two days ago, they had been on top of the world. Then the bad news arrived from Las Vegas.

By 12:04 p.m., reports spread to Biogineers. Employees' GOs demanded attention like a gaggle of screaming toddlers, since every modern communications device and self-aware brain paired with an opposable thumb was marshaled to spread the news. Employees ran for cubicles, looking at monitors. Someone in the bullpen screamed, "Turn on the big screen!" and the 3-D 156-inch was fired up.

Every media feed switched to the Las Vegas Convention Center halls. All unfiltered. All live. In all its empathetic horror. No censoring the gruesome or graphic by fearful news producers. Even though September 11 had been more spectacular, with its fires, collapsing buildings, and ash-covered survivors, this was far more horrifying. The intimacy of their deaths destroyed denial, with only the screen preventing you from sharing their last breath.

On the screen, a tanned, buff marketing exec sat on the ground, confounded by his inability to stand because his legs flopped like dying fish beneath him.

A leprechaun-like ISP exec grabbed on to his Amazonesque display designer and, unable to unclench his fingers from her arms, shook them both with convulsions so violent, the designer screamed in panic.

A fat, jowly DJ staggered like a cartoon drunk on a bender. He grabbed the flimsy booth of porn provider "Hot Pockets" to buoy him up, but toppled through the cheap, homemade display of foam core and flat screens. Images of moaning naked men and women crashed down with him in a tangled orgy of men and machines.

Saint Vitus's dance brought Saint Anthony's fire. Hundreds of digital camera–screen systems aimed down aisles to grab the egocentric attention of strolling attendees instead captured images of helplessness. As the first victims fell, spokesmodels grabbed the cameras and began filming, each their own Robert Capa, if only for minutes. The big screens, 3-D screens, laptops, and GOs revealed different parts of the action. It was the biggest multicamera shoot in human history, recording the largest unscripted drama of all time, and the horror was multiplied by video's virtual reality. Footage was both evidence and media clips, delivered electronically to our stunned world. Although hysteria gripped the crowd, it would not be for long. Most exposed to the high-tech plague were too busy dying.

Mediacasters like Apple, Univision, and NarcisCity went live to their portals. The webmasters and editors knew extraordinary footage when they saw it and shared the moment in a way every news department dreams of. "Breaking News," which came of age chasing white Broncos and watching Twin Towers fall, reached its apotheosis.

Peter shivered before the big screen, holding Amanda protectively. She bit her fingernail. "My God," she whispered. "The whole world is watching."

Many of Biogineers's employees wept, alone or huddled together. Several rocked, arms wrapped around their ribs. Others froze in silence, unable to comprehend the enormity of the vision. But none could tear themselves away.

On the NBC feed, north hall exit doors were hidden by a cresting tsunami of bodies. As people tried to escape and failed, they piled high, with the swell diminishing back down the aisle toward the cameras. Beyond the horror, it indicated a repeated behavior of the dying: a panicked run, loss of control of limbs, convulsions, inability to breathe, sudden death.

Peter had the sickest thought of all: What if it was a nanoagent, like Biogineers's nanoviruses or nanobots? Refusing to make assumptions, he asked loud enough for the room to hear, "What could have killed those people in that way, based on what we can see right now?"

A tiny Korean personal assistant named Jae choked back a sob and asked, "A biological weapon?"

"Of what sort?"

"Bacteria?" she continued.

"They died too fast."

"Virus?" yelled out a nanoengineer.

"If it's a classical virus, same problem. Not enough time to replicate," said Peter.

"Chemical?" said Amanda's right hand, Ernesto.

"But what kind?" asked Amanda. "Each person goes haywire in a similar, yet personal way, then dies."

"And there's no sign of the bodies' rejection of the agent," Peter added, "like blood from the eyes, nose, lungs, even vomit. They just shudder, like a machine, then stop."

"Attacked the brain directly?" said the nanoengineer.

Everyone stopped talking. No one wished to voice the next logical step: it took nanoparticles to pass the blood-brain barrier that fast.

Chang stood next to Peter. His look of appalled recognition, paired with something else—an irrational sense of responsibility, perhaps?—reflected Peter's feelings. Maybe their technology, created to help mankind, was responsible for this.

Jesse Steinberg, a giant, shambling, shaggy bear of a code jockey, spoke their thoughts aloud in his basso profundo to get everyone's attention. "What about bots?"

Someone shouted, "Shut the fuck up, asshole!" Another sobbed loudly. Amanda's fingernails dug a hole in Peter's arm. If Jesse could come up with that assumption so quickly . . . Peter's stomach did a flip-flop and settled somewhere near his larynx.

He couldn't watch anymore. "Everyone?" he shouted. "We're closing the offices for the rest of the week. If any of you have friends or family . . . involved . . . Amanda and I give you our deepest sympathies, and please let us know what we can do to help." Chang turned to go, and Peter grabbed his arm.

"Get your team," said Peter. "We need to find out who did this. And how to stop another one like it."

Chang nodded.

In the days that followed, the media force-fed the images until viewers vomited up terror with chunks of guilt and revenge. News anchors wept on cue behind their desks as they rewatched their dying friends and colleagues. The images were society's collective consciousness made digital. Memories preserved forever, byte by byte, so not only could we never forget, but we would be reminded when we least expected it, like the visceral, knee-jerk PTSD horror that gripped New Yorkers when they unexpectedly saw an image of the Twin Towers. The media flashed them with the subtlety of a sledgehammer. Only after death might there be peace, because the memories lodged in their brains would be gone, finally and forever.

Or would they?

No one yet grasped that everyone was a victim of the newly dubbed "10/26." Some died. Some didn't. Some wished they did. Peter Bernhardt would soon discover which type of victim he was.

"So now what?" Peter asked.

Lobo sighed. "Only three companies in the world have technology like this, and Biogineers is the only US manufacturer. The FBI assumes the nanobots came from here. You are a suspect. Is that simple enough for you?" He rocked back in his chair. "As of now, you and Amanda will leave immediately and be barred from entering any Lobo facility, unless requested to do so by either me or the federal government. You may not take anything with you. You may not delete or destroy anything. The authorities have demanded everything be left as potential evidence. Biogineers will comply with all government requests and cooperate to the fullest extent possible, including Congressional, DHS, and DOJ's criminal investigations. If you resist, Biogineers will be obligated to remove you by force."

Peter flushed in rage and tried to still his shaking hands.

Lobo's eyebrow cocked in amazement. "I'm offering a dignified exit. What more do you want?"

Peter pounded the tabletop. "This is my company!"

"No! It's *my* company! And you sold me a worthless, murderous piece of shit! And I'm going to make sure you rot in jail, pal."

"We didn't kill anyone! How could you think that? Why isn't anyone accusing the Koreans? Or Singapore? Why aren't we finding out who did this?"

Lobo rose, a smirk spreading across his lips. "Are you that stupid? The whole world is investigating this." He headed for the door with his trademark limp, where two security guards in black suits and ties loomed. The meeting was over.

Peter leapt from his chair and grabbed his arm. "Bruce! This is insanity. We should be working together to vindicate ourselves! Why are we even fighting?" Peter stood a head taller and had forty pounds on Bruce.

The guards instantly spun, ready to fight, but Lobo raised his free hand to heel them and glared at Peter's white-knuckled grip on his French-cuffed shirt with disdain. "Because it doesn't matter who did it. There's always a fall guy. And since it's never me or Lobo Industries, it might as well be you."

Peter hadn't hit anyone in twenty years. The last time, his teenaged opponent broke his nose, but Peter had done much worse to him.

His straight punch to Lobo's head was deflected as the smaller man grabbed Peter's arm and twisted it, along with Peter, to the ground, following with a powerful uppercut. Peter dropped. Lobo kicked his face, and blood spewed from Peter's nose. As a parting gesture, a boot to the ribs, complete with audible crunch, was executed with the same economy and practiced ease as the rest of Lobo's dealings.

"Wrong league, fuckwit." Lobo limped out the conference room doors, security murmuring in their mouthpieces in his wake. Down the hall, he yelled over his shoulder, "Hey *Católico*, you got fifteen minutes. I'd start praying to the Holy Virgin if I were you!"

CHAPTER TWO

P eter staggered to his office and grabbed handfuls of tissues
to stem the nosebleed. Then he grabbed a 1972 Gibson Les
Paul from the row of vintage and contemporary guitars that
rimmed the room. It was the first guitar Amanda bought him when
they were still Stanford undergraduates. Many guitars followed, but
this one had special meaning. It was when they realized they loved
each other and there would never be anyone else. He refused to
leave it behind and wanted her to remember its meaning while he
told her what happened.

There were no days off for Amanda. Peter found her where he
had left her, in her office fielding query after query. As Biogineers's
vice president of public relations, she supervised media information
24/7 for months before the Lobo acquisition. The formal announce-
ment of the closed deal had been disseminated to all major news outlets to break two days before, but their news was eclipsed by a much
more important story. Instead of handling the usual post-merger
requests for press releases, photo ops, and expert quotes in business
and trade journals, she waded through voice mails from national
press asking for interviews with Peter to discuss the terrorist attack.

Two days ago, she had been as devastated as anyone about 10/26 and cried in his arms for hours. But the next morning, she was hard at work saving the company from death by public opinion.

Only it wasn't their company anymore.

"So I'll need the public statement from our counsel to you when? Arnold? God damn it . . . Arnold! Shit." She slammed down the receiver as Peter reached her door. "And where's the Internet?" She tapped her keyboard. "What's going on?" She heard Peter, but didn't look up. "Of all days, my e-mail's frozen, phone's on the fritz . . ."

"We have to go. Now."

She saw his blood-smeared face and T-shirt. Then the guitar. "What happened?"

He kissed her cheek, careful not to get blood on her.

"I can't leave," she said. "Arnold was setting up a media step-list with handpicked outlets . . ."

"There is no company left to save, Mandy. At least not for us. Please, you have to come with me." He tugged at her hand and she rose, uncomprehending, to follow him.

"But you're bleeding!"

"I forgot this wasn't the schoolyard."

"You need X-rays," she said.

"I know." He led her into the elevator. "Lobo says I'm under suspicion for 10/26 and we're out. Executive summary: Forced resignations. No severance. No stock. A criminal investigation from Lobo and the shareholders and the feds. Probably millions in debt for legal fees."

Amanda was speechless for the first time in her life. And shaking.

As they exited the elevator in the main lobby, their longtime security guard, Francis Bullock, moved from behind his desk to stand directly in their path but started at Peter's condition. "I'm sorry, Mr. Bernhardt, but you . . ."

He wasn't alone. Two more black-suited Lobo security men stood at the exit doors, looking as menacing as the first pair.

Known to all as Saint Francis of Sand Hill Road, the guard was about seventy and white haired, but still spry and twinkle-eyed.

"What's the problem?" mumbled Peter. His face was swelling.

"I gotta check you out, Mr. Bernhardt. Pat you down. Make sure you take nothin' outta the building. And you can't take that either." He pointed at the Gibson slung around Peter's back.

"Francis. It's just a guitar."

"I know that, Mr. Bernhardt, but I gotta do it. Even though we both know this is dumber than a picnic in a hurricane, you know me losin' my job over somethin' stupid be wrong, too."

One of the gorillas by the doors stepped forward. "We'll handle this."

Saint Francis spun on them. "No you ain't. I know my job." He turned back, eyes fierce. "Better me than them," he whispered.

Amanda turned away, trying not to get emotional. She chewed her thumbnail as Peter pulled the Gibson's strap over his head and handed the guitar to Francis.

"Please put it back in my office. And be careful with it. It's a special one."

"Yes, sir. You know I will."

Saint Francis laid the guitar against his desk so softly that it made no sound. He then proceeded to pat Peter down. Peter had only a billfold in his pocket and handed it to Francis, who made a show of looking through it carefully. Then he checked the contents of Amanda's purse.

When he was done, a guard said, "Pat her down, too."

"I know it!" snapped Saint Francis. "I'm old, and I'm gettin' there!"

Amanda stood with her arms in a T as he patted her as lightly as a butterfly. His downcast eyes were damp, and he began to recite quietly, "'I will incline my ear to a proverb; I will solve my riddle to the music of the lyre . . .'"

She stared at the ceiling, trying to ignore the guards' leers. Peter wanted to kill them.

Francis continued, "'Why should I fear in times of trouble, when the iniquity of my persecutors surrounds me, men who trust in their wealth, and boast of the abundance of their riches?'"

One of the guards smirked, "You missed her back pockets. Inside."

Francis avoided Amanda's infuriated eyes. He carefully pulled back the tight fabric of her jeans' pockets and pretended to look inside. "'Truly no man can ransom himself, or give to God the price of his life, for the ransom of his life is costly and can never suffice, that he should continue to live on forever, and never see the Pit.'"

Finished, he whispered with deep embarrassment, "You're clean."

"We know," Peter whispered back.

CHAPTER THREE

Biogineers was housed in the last building of the last anonymous industrial park before Highway 280. Peter pulled his LeMans Blue 1968 Corvette Stingray out of Biogineers's parking lot in a daze and onto empty Sand Hill Road. Rush hour usually inched, but the malls and buildings were mostly empty and the roads clear of traffic, like a zombie movie. The public feared the new plague.

On mental autopilot, he followed El Camino Real north. No longer the Royal Road of the Spanish Empire, it was now the high-tech highway through the world's greatest technological empire of Silicon Valley. Peter had fancied himself a Spanish grandee in that brave new empire. Until today.

Today, the Inquisition had begun.

Amanda tapped her GO, checking e-mail and news. She avoided answering the phone, not knowing what to say.

The CNN feed was grim: a hitherto unknown group called ATEAMO—American Terrorists End American Military Occupation—was taking responsibility. They wanted an end to foreign occupation and opportunistic wars and were willing to spill their own blood and that of their fellow Americans to do it. Three young people were named as perpetrators, and their identities were confirmed by security footage and DNA analyzed from saliva left on their disposable coffee cups thrown in trash cans.

"My God . . . children inspired by bad TV reruns!" gasped Amanda.

"No," sighed Peter. "'A-Team' is a Special Forces nickname for their fighting units. Shit."

The FBI said their deaths were a radical form of suicide bombing, designed for maximum shock, awe, and elimination of evidence. An investigation to find the creators of both attack and suicide technologies was ongoing, but there was evidence to suggest a Californian company had the capabilities to make this new plague. The government's failure to prevent the tragedy was blamed on insufficient security and intelligence funding, and law enforcement agencies were asking Congress for authorization to protect our nation with private security contractors, unfettered by federal law enforcement regulations. Congress would agree to provide this and more in the months to come. They acquiesced without debate, because fear was a budget line item.

CBS televised the martyrs' final videos, and Amanda watched, mesmerized, on her GO.

"I don't understand," said Peter. "How did three undergrads get this tech? It's so specialized. And who knows how to attack with bots?"

Amanda exited the video tab to read headlines aloud. "Senator Mankowicz Urges Special Panel to Investigate Nanotechnology Industry."

"What industry? Everyone does nanotechnology."

Like many scientists who worked on the nanoscale, Peter didn't think of himself as doing "nanotechnology." That simply meant he made things on an atomic scale. He could manipulate atoms and molecules like LEGO bricks, making structures so small, a million nanotubes twisted together would be the width of a human hair. He was a bioengineer curing diseases by building tiny machines, only molecules big, as drug delivery or therapeutic structural systems. Others doing "nanotechnology" were chemists building labs-on-a-chip to diagnose diseases or identify pollutants; physicists making renewable fuel cells; biochemists making water filtration systems; or electrical engineers designing quantum semiconductors. Nanotechnology only applied to the scale of the efforts, a new arrow in their technological quiver and not an objective in itself. Yet "nanotechnology" captured the public's attention as a discrete borderline of technology, thanks to the media. It was a good sound bite and headline: "The Atom as the Final Frontier." But there were numerous final frontiers over the years. Space, thanks to JFK and *Star Trek*. The sea, thanks to Jacques Cousteau. Some said the brain was the final frontier. Now the atom. In his opinion, there was no final frontier. If there was, humanity was screwed.

Amanda continued, "President Stevens condemns terrorists. Swears to root out and bring ATEAMO to justice." Her messages chimed.

"All I want to know is where the hell did those kids get the tech? And why does everyone assume it's me?" His first calls would be to his Asian counterparts to see if they had any clues about the Korean or Singaporean companies.

"Carter called. Maybe he could help?"

"He's *your* best friend. You call him."

"He's your best friend, too," said Amanda quietly.

"We both know that's been in name only, for a while."

Amanda expelled an exasperated breath. "Would you stop being such an ass about this? So he didn't invest in Biogineers. That was ten years ago! He didn't abandon you. He made a business decision. When are you going to let it go?"

"I don't want to see the 'I told you so' in his eyes. How is he always right about everything?"

"Enough," said Amanda. She flipped the AM button. Newsreaders hammered home the repercussions and collateral damage of 10/26: the tent city of quarantined convention center victims; the collapse of financial markets and shoring up by the government; possible confiscation and banning of all nanotechnology. It was only two weeks before the elections, so the pundit parade sucked down the controversy with the enthusiasm of mosquitoes draining a pregnant woman. Politicians made hay over biotech's cowboy ethics, calling for tougher domestic security measures and nanotech regulation. The incumbent president had run in a dead heat with his challenger. But polls shifted in the president's favor overnight.

"Fucking assholes!" Peter stabbed the radio's off switch. "It's their fucking fault!"

"Why?"

"We warned them! Remember? There are two ways to cure Alzheimer's with nanotech: hardwiring with nanowires or ingesting nanobots. I wanted hardwires, because bots could be mass-weaponized. But everyone else, including you, wanted bots. And when I wanted strict international protocols for the bots, everyone—investors, competitors, the FDA—had a fit."

Amanda shook her head. "Hey, it wasn't me or the investors. The focus groups want a pill to cure their mental illness. Not brain surgery."

"Bullshit!" he spit. "You can't get brain surgery in some corner store whenever you want it from a guy who took a weekend seminar on brain-machine interfaces, like Lasik or cosmetic surgery. At least not yet. Only patients who were supposed to get the therapies would get them. Not millions of people looking for a quick mental pick-me-up."

"Well, I'm sorry, but when people think 'hardwiring,' they think 'Frankenstein.' Or 'cyborgs.'"

"We *are* cyborgs! We've got pacemakers, cochlear and retinal implants, deep brain stimulators and insulin pumps. We've built artificial hearts, lungs, kidneys, livers, tongues—even an artificial anus! And what about prosthetic limbs? We're not afraid of those guys. They're either veteran poster boys or Olympic heroes." He snatched her GO and waved it. "And what about this? It's our brain on a chip! We don't have to know or remember anything anymore. Just look it up on the GO/HOME. It's the World Wide Mind, and we're all hooked up to it!"

"Why are you yelling at me?"

"Because if you don't agree, you still don't get it!"

She grabbed the GO back. "Other people have different points of view," she said in a softer tone, "but let's face it—a pill's more likely to be taken. They wanted to make it easy."

"The bastards promised me there wouldn't be any risk. So I took their money and gave them their Goddamned nanobots and now look—I'm a mass murderer!"

"That's not what's really upsetting you."

"What the hell's upsetting me then?"

"You're upset you let yourself believe them!" she said.

That shut Peter up. His self-deception was disturbing, but worse were the implications.

Exhausted, Amanda dropped her GO in her purse and stared blindly at the buildings on El Camino Real's transition from workaday Palo Alto to upscale, leafy Atherton.

After a minute, Peter placed a hand on her thigh. "Mandy? I don't understand why this is happening, but I swear, if we get through this in one piece, I won't let anyone hurt us again."

She squeezed his hand in response. But her expression said she was not convinced he could keep his promise.

CHAPTER FOUR

I f hell exists, it will have television news crews stationed in front of the fiery gates to broadcast your arrival.

Perdition Brothers, Brimstone and Hades Circus rolled into town to welcome Peter home, and Patricia Drive in Atherton was the center ring. White trucks and vans—splayed with satellite dishes and rigging, and cheerfully painted with station call letters and network affiliations—ferried a hellish host of hair-sprayed, camera-ready talking heads and their indefatigable cameramen to his front yard. Still photographers and print reporters double-parked along the street. Neighbors crept out of houses to see the serial killer who had made their quiet little enclave famous.

The Bernhardt house was a solidly built neo-Georgian, red brick and white trim with neoclassical columns framing the front door. It sat between a mini Norman château on one side and a Tudor manor on the other. When he saw this house a year and a half ago, it was everything his deprived fifteen-year-old self had ever wanted. So he bought it.

Everyone recognized the Corvette the moment Peter turned onto the street. They ran toward it. Had the authorities put out an APB?

"Don't talk to anyone!" screeched Amanda. "Just keep them off our property!"

"Why?"

"If we allow them on it, they can claim implied consent to trespass. They can stay indefinitely."

It was one of the rare times the First Amendment didn't sound like a great idea.

Peter's finger stabbed the garage remote and he turned into the driveway. Video and still cameras and reporters' microphones rushed the car, jostling for position closest to his window. More bodies crowded the hood. If he rolled forward, he might hurt someone. Through the gray noise of screamed questions, Peter could pick out words: "nanobots . . . murder . . . terrorist . . . responsible . . ."

He laid on the car horn, but it wasn't enough, so he popped the hood to up the decibels. Amanda covered her ears. The TV folk all went for their headpiece volume controls, and the earsplitting sound instinctively drove the few diehards on the bumper out of the way.

Peter thought he'd feel better being home, but he didn't, even as the V8 engine growled loudly in the garage, a sound he usually relished. They were under siege. He turned off the ignition.

"What about your X-rays? We have to go back out there," said Amanda.

"Tomorrow. I know what to do for now."

He unlocked the kitchen door and shuffled right by the HOME console on the countertop, but Amanda paused in front of it and hesitated.

"Mandy? You're kidding. Don't."

"But we don't know . . ."

"And I don't care. We've got a lynch mob with unlimited rope out there!"

"I don't believe it . . ." As soon as she pressed the speaker button, the six degrees of separation game began. Their accountant's secretary returned their call. "Uh . . . hi Mr. and Mrs. Bernhardt. Mr. Nelson's brother attended IAM and hasn't . . . um . . . turned up yet, so our office won't be returning any more calls until the situation . . . resolves itself."

Peter rested his head on the refrigerator, but didn't bother to open it. He had no appetite. "Is 'resolves itself' a euphemism for 'shows who to sue for wrongful death reparations'?"

"Stop it," said Amanda. That message ended, and the next began.

"Hey, Pete, it's Kevin. Remember Clarissa Brouchard? On our freshman hall? I'm guessing you know she was president of Narcis-City . . . and was at IAM. Her funeral service is next Thursday . . ." Suddenly, six degrees dissolved to one.

Amanda turned on the HOME's TV feed. Serious, pointed voices of news anchors drowned out the insistent yapping outside. She pulled up five news channels at once. CNN took up the main screen, and four open windows in the screen's corners showed a selection of local, national, and international news. CNN was finishing a report about the attacks. FBI, CDC, and DHS's forensic tests confirmed that nanobots had killed the victims of 10/26. The only bots made in the US were by Biogineers. Two other stations mentioned Bernhardt and Biogineers as the only US manufacturer capable of making bots of this complexity.

One of the screens had a live feed, with a reporter doing his stand-up. There was their house. On TV. And if they opened a curtain, they'd be on it, too. Peter headed toward a window.

"Pete! Don't!" begged Amanda.

He ignored her and peeked between the curtains to see two dozen reporters parked on the front lawn. All armed with headphones, GOtooths, and other assorted devices, it was hard to discern who might be surveilling them for media, as opposed to government, purposes. And was there a difference anymore?

Amanda picked up the HOME phone and dialed a number. Peter recognized the button notes. It was Carter's number.

"Mandy, not now!" said Peter.

She ignored him. "Hi . . . Yeah, we're watching . . . Tapped directly into the satellite feed. They're transmitting for broadcast later . . . Really? I'll ask." She covered the mouthpiece. "He wants to help. I think he can." Peter's eyes narrowed. She muttered into the receiver, "Sweetie, can I call you back . . . ? Uh huh . . . Yeah . . . Bye." She sighed and hung up. "He wants to see you. He also said you'll be picked up for questioning soon, so cooperate and keep your chin up. But lay low otherwise. He would have said more . . ."

The press crept closer to the house.

"Fuck these assholes!" Peter stormed out of the media room and passed a mirror. The sight made him stop: bruised face, nose swollen to the size and color of a plum. He could only imagine the bruises on his ribs. "Jesus . . ." It was time to get tough.

He hustled through the house, opening windows to the mayhem outside. This appearance of accessibility only drove the media to greater heights of trespassing. They couldn't see him positioning movable speakers to face the windows. In his home office, he synchronized all the speakers, except those near Amanda's kitchen monitor, on a single input. Then he plugged his Roland GR-33 guitar synthesizer into a Roland-ready Stratocaster he kept nearby for synth doodling when he needed to think.

Firing up the MP3 library, he clicked Jimi Hendrix's immortal Woodstock improvisation of "The Star-Spangled Banner" as he turned all volumes to "11." So much for laying low. He'd be on the evening news for sure.

Hendrix started conventionally enough, finger picking until the phrase, "And the rockets' red glare . . ." Then Jimi and Peter slammed into hard feedback-filled improv. A measure later, Peter hit the waterworks. Sprinklers rose from the lawn and soaked the few reporters not driven back by the wall of sound. Cameramen may have had rainproof equipment, but the stand-ups' hairdos couldn't withstand the deluge.

Peter played a countermelody over, under, and around Hendrix, weaving through the classic performance with surprising skill. Any musicians watching the news would at least be impressed by how Peter's melodic thread became a second voice of protest. With a lead foot on the synth's sustain pedal, and fingers wailing the whammy bar, he barely heard Amanda screaming, "Peter? What are you doing?"

CHAPTER FIVE

The press retreated to the street. Some left to bring rein-forcements. It wasn't over yet.

Exhausted and bone sore, Peter wandered from his study, through their living room, toward the loggia at the back of the house. He had had enough.

The huge glass-enclosed space, designed like an eighteenth-century horticultural conservatory, enclosed an Olympic-length lap pool. Amanda had had it built especially for him. Its Enlightenment Age icing was excessive and a classic Valley indulgence, but he jus-tified the pool as necessary for his sanity. Through the enormous greenhouse windows, the sun set pink and purple over the red-, yel-low-, and orange-colored leaves of the maples, sycamores, and oaks that separated their yard from the neighbors'. But they wouldn't appreciate the view much longer, given the size of the mortgage.

Peter swore to himself he would never assume anything in life, ever again. Nothing was safe.

Amanda had returned to the backlog of phone messages in the kitchen, which he could still hear playing faintly in the background. "Hey Amanda, Joe Vauxhall's memorial service is Tuesday at noon. We're meeting at the *Chronicle* offices, then walking to the Yerba

Buena Gardens, like Joe did every lunch hour." And then he heard a new message.

"Um . . . Hey . . . It's Kevin again. Pete? Um . . . I don't think it's a good idea you come. Clarissa's family doesn't want you there. Sorry, dude . . ."

Clarissa's family had just watched the news.

Peter stabbed at a HOME entertainment console, searching for music to drown out the dead. Maybe it was on the nose, but he needed some focus. Talking Heads' "Once in a Lifetime" blasted from the speakers. Shucking off his clothes at the water's edge, he stretched his arms and torso. His ribs made him flinch where a bruise spread down his left side. He dived naked into the deep end and expelled all his air to sink to the bottom. The music's burbling bass notes wove through the water. He held his breath as long as possible.

He watched dried blood liquefy and slowly cloud the water around his face. His lungs ached for air and his chest throbbed. He thought about breathing in to let the water equalize the pressure for good . . . but instead surfaced to Australian crawl the pool's length. He concentrated on strong, rhythmic strokes, lap after lap, willing his body to swim past the pain. As he hoped, the song made him wonder: How in hell did he get here?

Poor boy raised by single, fuck-up dad, but made good—check. Did everything to not become his father—check. Stanford on a full science scholarship, which brought him to Palo Alto, never to leave—check. Married his college sweetheart—check. Created a successful biotech start-up—check. He'd been a good husband, hadn't he? Done everything on the checklist to achieve the American Dream, hadn't he? Except for the fact they hadn't had children yet, of which Amanda never ceased reminding him—and he was now unemployed and accused of a crime against humanity—life was great.

Like most men, Peter believed work defined him, and he never paused in the process of accomplishment for fear of . . . what? That he wouldn't be satisfied? Afraid he hadn't done enough or done it well enough? Wasn't part of the American Dream committing to a course of action and never deviating until all goals were accomplished? Well, had he done it or not?

Until today, he believed he had. But after today, his goals felt as hollow as the Tin Man's chest. His life's work was called evil and taken from him. Game over.

Swimming's physical effort and repetitive motion kick-started the more rational, objective parts of Peter's brain. They spoke insistently over the pain, the emotions, the doubts and the unanswerable questions that still chattered away, but were getting quieter lap after lap.

Rationality ruled because the chaos underneath was too terrifying: Sell everything . . . and don't dwell too much on the fact he was losing the armor he had built up against his impoverished past. Cooperate with the government, help find the bad guys, and stay out of jail, if anyone would believe him. Find allies in as many fields as possible. Let Amanda spin it. Cut losses and move on. But move on to what? Would it be the "same as it ever was" again?

Todd Rundgren's song, "Born to Synthesize" played on shuffle. It stopped him, and he listened. He had a soft spot for psychedelic music and played it a lot, which amused his wife and annoyed his friend Carter, who loathed the aural indulgences of the genre. But Peter was bizarrely stimulated every time he heard "Born to Synthesize." The high-frequency scintillations of the synthesizer jiggled his neurons like a massaging showerhead. There was something there to figure out . . .

Amanda yelled down the stairs, "I'm going to bed."

Peter padded along plush carpeting up the half-circular grand staircase in the central hall to their bedroom.

Amanda watched CNN in bed. There was their house, with sprinklers and reporters running. She glared at him. He ignored her and showered off the remaining blood and chlorine, bandaged and taped up his playdough nose, downed a handful of ibuprofen, brushed his teeth, and climbed in beside her. He rolled away, lying still, hoping she wouldn't talk. But she turned off the HOME and scooted over to wrap herself octopus-like around his back. He accepted the warmth of her body. But that was all.

She kissed the back of his neck and ran one hand into his hair while the other hand reached around his front to trace spirals on his chest with her fingernails. He tolerated her for a few moments, then gently removed her hands.

"Honey?" she whispered.

He grunted.

"Please, Pete, look at me."

He didn't move.

"Don't cut yourself off from me. I love you."

He rolled to look at her. "Mandy, my dick's on sabbatical."

"Okay. I get it." She grinned. "Maybe you should hang a sign from it, saying 'Gone to France,' or something, so I'll know when to ignore you." He didn't laugh. She prodded. "Any plans for your dick's resurrection?"

"It's not exactly Frankendick, is it?"

"Hey, you're the bioengineer." She rolled on her back and stared at her own patch of ceiling. "You know, I'm ovulating."

He was so foggy from the abuse of the day, he didn't understand at first. "What?"

"I stopped taking the pill," she said.

"When?"

"A month ago."

"You're shitting me."

"No. I am not shitting you. I love you, and I want to have our child."

"Everything's unstable . . . too up in the air. And especially not now!"

She teared up. "And you always promise that in some near future we will. But we don't. It's been ten years. This is your neurosis. Not mine."

"Were you not here today?" he yelled.

"We need a baby *because* of today!" She yelled back, her cheeks wet. "Because we can make life in spite of it!"

"Mandy, I can't handle this right now." He fought back his own tears. "I thought I'd made it, but I can't give you a job or a house or a baby or even take care of you. I've failed you. I've failed everybody. And on top of it all, I'm being blamed for something I had nothing to do with!" He punched his pillow in frustration.

"How did you fail?" she sniffled.

"Only a nanobot could have done this! And I'm the only guy in the US who makes them. Just the fact the technology exists . . ."

She wrapped herself around him again, even though he resisted. "You are not your father. This is not going to destroy you. It's going to make you stronger. This is the first time I've ever seen you eaten alive by doubt. I know you're innocent. And I will always be here for you. For God's sake, if I could escape my parents' commune and make myself into someone entirely different, you are more than capable of getting over this."

"But we're losing everything!"

"This is one of those trips the universe throws you, so you don't get complacent. I know it sounds cruel, but it's an opportunity to do what you always wanted. And you know what I've always wanted."

He grabbed her and buried his face in her long silky hair. The delicious, spicy smell of her wrapped around him like a warm, soft life preserver. But it was not a sufficient aphrodisiac. As he drifted off to sleep, he hoped he wouldn't dream about his day.

CHAPTER SIX

The next day, against Amanda's better judgment, Peter insisted he leave the circus that had been his home and make his twice-a-week pilgrimage to see Paul Bernhardt. He was lucky that vintage American muscle cars were fast, the roads empty, and the police otherwise occupied.

In a cozy nursing home room in Menlo Park, Peter's father slumped in a floral-upholstered armchair, dressed in an old plaid flannel shirt, a worn "Mr. Rogers" cardigan, sweatpants, and shearling slippers that Amanda had bought him for Christmas last year. His once-broad shoulders curled forward from lack of use, but a strong cleft chin, ruddy cheeks on fair skin, vivid blue eyes, and a crooked nose gotten in a fight were still common Bernhardt traits. There were other traits Peter was grateful he hadn't inherited or acquired: addiction, rage, isolation, irresponsibility, and apathy.

In his youth, Pop's hair had been almost black. Now it was pure white, giving his reflective pale skin a gray cast. Paul Bernhardt's identity disintegrated as his brain was attacked. That living, breathing person was not Pop anymore. Alzheimer's would claim another victim unless Peter could figure out a way to stop it.

Biogineers had been so close to a marketable cure, developing a nanorobotic drug delivery system the FDA had fast-tracked to approve. They had created several types of ingestible bots to perform different jobs to halt the spread of Alzheimer's. One bot fit like a lock and key to receptors in brain cells to stop the production of beta amyloid proteins outside the neurons, which were a key component to Alzheimer's lesions. Another nanobot system could raise levels of acetylcholine, which when deficient, caused neurofibrillary tangles, insoluble twisted fibers inside the neurons of Alzheimer's patients. And another could deliver stem cells to repair the damage. Adding insult to injury, the FDA believed Pop didn't qualify for human trials because of medical technicalities and his relationship to Peter, so Pop had to wait like everyone else. Hope wasn't only gone for Alzheimer's patients around the world. It was gone for his father. And would it be gone for him, too, since the disease appeared to have a genetic component?

Losing one's mind was the most horrific thing Peter could imagine.

His previous idea, abandoned a decade before, surgically implanted an alternate brain system, like a cochlear implant. But venture capitalists and the feds nixed it at the research stage. As far as Peter knew, no one pursued that line of research to completion, because of the limited ethical commercial applications. Maybe DARPA continued exploring it for the military, but that research was hidden, if it existed at all. Congress stopped funding anything that smacked of the words "revolutionary" or "groundbreaking" years ago. No one would get something off the ground quickly enough to benefit Pop. He didn't have much time left.

Peter lightly fingered the strings of an acoustic archtop.

He often played for other residents. Music elicited a greater response for Alzheimer's patients than any other stimuli, because music traveled different neural pathways than did other perceptions—pathways that remained intact. Still, it never ceased to amaze when a room full of the living dead came alive as he played. He discovered patients were particularly responsive to this guitar, a 2001 Manzer Paradiso he was lucky enough to pick up secondhand, since he'd never top Linda Manzer's waiting list filled with performing legends. Its tone, of such clarity and brilliance, pierced through the fog of rotted cortex to touch a fundamental part of their remaining selves. Heads bobbed, feet tapped, hands clapped. Previously silent lips sang verses. Faces smiled. It was beautiful to watch.

Pop heard Peter's doodlings and rocked back and forth slightly in his chair. That meant "Get on with it." He began with the Beatles. Pop loved the Beatles.

Peter strummed the chorus to "With a Little Help from My Friends." Paul stopped rocking, but after a few measures, slowly shook his head. That meant "try another." Peter played the opening of "Norwegian Wood," which sounded particularly lovely with this guitar's piercing voice. This brought vigorous head shaking. Peter knew what dissatisfaction meant. There was only one song Paul wanted when he got this way. And Peter hated it. To his generation, the song was so obvious, so banal, so simple, it descended into cliché. And it so accurately described his father's life, the son shuddered in filial pain. Pop used to say that's what made it a perfect song. Everyone thought it was about them.

Peter broke into the opening chords of "Yesterday," afraid to tell his father he'd lost his company, even though Pop was too far gone to hit or insult his son like the bad old days. Alzheimer's only gift was that the old man's monumental rage was snuffed out.

But Pop's stare wasn't vacant as the song continued, and something between a smile and a grimace played on his lips. Was the glimmer of love in the rheumy old eyes for Peter, or for the memory that still remained of love lost, against all neurological odds?

Pop swayed happily to the music. Peter was free to play anything from now on. Rundgren's "Born to Synthesize" still preyed on his mind, and he played it to recall thoughts he'd had earlier. On one hand, the song's message could be quite literal. Todd Rundgren was one of the first musicians to use a synthesizer in unorthodox and groundbreaking ways, and it could have been about the creation and manipulation of sound waves on a synth to make music and the creative process in general. But it felt like it should have meant more. Like there was a nugget of inspiration couched within the lyrics. Rundgren sang that creation was based on such simple and opposing building blocks. All alone, they were meaningless. But add and subtract and combine and multiply and bingo—the birth of the new. The emerging pattern and how we interpreted it *was* the message.

If that wasn't a good description of how the brain worked, Peter wasn't sure what was. But what happened when it didn't work? Like Pop. What was missing? What could be replaced?

Replacement parts for the human brain had been fraught with difficulties for decades. The brain did not process information like a computer, digitally, using ones and zeros. It was an analog memory system, made of specialized cells called neurons. But bridges between the two were possible. Scientists learned how to make computers "talk" to the brain's auditory cortex for cochlear implants for the deaf, and to the visual cortex for retinal implants for the blind. Prosthetic limbs could be controlled by the "thoughts" of the motor cortex. All by figuring out the computing algorithms necessary to communicate with the brain.

So instead of a computing model of brain biology, scientists reversed the idea and pinned their hopes on the biological model of computing to not only create artificial intelligence, but to unlock the convoluted cortex's secrets.

Rundgren referred to the Hindu idea of "orbits of consciousness" spinning, but getting nowhere until you combined them. And then . . . cognition happened. So what if the orbits of consciousness were two different types of cognition in two different types of cortexes: biological and digital? As of now, "thinking" couldn't go anywhere, except within its own organic or machine system. How could thoughts migrate back and forth, from the gray matter between the ears to a computer processor? And could he make one small enough to implant, yet big enough to hold our thoughts, now collected by the artificial memory of a prosthetic hippocampus and shuttled around both the human cortex and the mechanical cortex? But how would the mechanical cortex affect how we thought?

And the combinations of consciousness creating your reality led you where? Rundgren said, "to . . . the center"—but what and where was the center of the orbits of consciousness? Could it be where you blended both your biological thoughts and your mechanical thoughts? That might be a better model of reality than what our meager brains could create with our faulty senses and a hope for Alzheimer's sufferers everywhere.

In the song were the seeds of his new brain prosthetic. One he could build. Peter knew a Eureka moment when he had one. But what could he do with it?

"'You . . . born . . . synthessssss . . .'"

Pop spoke! And remembered the song! But was it a message? That Peter was born to synthesize, to put things together that had never been put together before? Tears welled in his eyes, even though Pop never tolerated them, despising self-pity. God, he could be a tough bastard. The son struggled to hold them in, afraid tears would break the connection.

It took intense concentration to reach the end of the song. Peter pretended to study the silent strings; raising his eyes would reveal wet proof of his uncontrollable emotions. Instead, worn and knotty hands turned palms up and lifted arms to the son. Peter swung the guitar around his back and fell to his knees at his father's feet. Old man arms gently encircled him, as though afraid the younger man might break from a caress. The bricklayer's bandy, toughened muscles, work-knobby bones, and calloused skin had degenerated into soft dough and brittle glass under baggy clothes. The last time they had hugged was at Peter's bachelor's degree graduation fourteen years before.

Pop's fingers ran through Peter's hair. The last time that had happened was elementary school. Young Peter's teacher assessed him as unintelligent by virtue of his boredom and poverty, and stuck him in a special education class. The rich, "smart" kids mercilessly tormented him, and he gave up believing he was gifted or capable. And for once, his father's anger was turned not on him, but on the bullies and the school. Pop had fought for him and been so loving and told him not to believe them, not to quit . . .

The floodgates opened, and the son sobbed into the father's shoulder, "I won't quit, Pop . . . I won't . . . I promise you I won't quit."

Human connection tired Paul out. The brief window that had opened into his mind closed as suddenly, and he slipped back into the dark room of his own private reality. Peter wiped his face and crammed his emotions down as he packed the archtop back into its case.

As with the rest of the citizenry, the 10/26 attacks had gotten under Peter's skin, calling forth primal protective instincts he couldn't shake off. He checked the battery on Pop's medical alert station and ensured it was securely fastened to his belt. Then he made sure the floor treads in the bathroom were slip free, counted all Pop's pills, and moved the emergency evacuation bag to a prominent position so the nurse would see it in case of fire or worse.

He glanced above the door's lintel. There was a new smoke alarm, still shiny and with a brand tag he'd never heard of. He assumed the facility had modernized their system.

Peter stopped at the nurses' station to check out. A tiny Filipino nurse, Mrs. Manela, swiveled on her chair away from her HOME screen to shine her very big, very bright smile. Probably in her fifties, but with the energy of a twenty-year-old, she was efficient, missed nothing, and didn't take unnecessary grief from patients or their families. His kind of woman.

"How . . . was your father today?" she asked. Her hesitation teased with the unmentioned knowledge she had seen him on the news last night.

He wiped his eyes. "Better, thanks. Are you updating the smoke detectors?"

"Not that I know of."

"Well, did my dad's detector die? He's got a new one."

"I don't think so." Mrs. Manela's eyebrow raised and her grin vanished. She opened a filing cabinet and pulled Paul's file to scan the paperwork. Then she went into a different cabinet and pulled out the smoke detector maintenance schedule. "Nada. Nothing new in his room. Nothing fixed or changed anywhere. Smoke detectors are serious business here. We keep a record of it for the state."

"Well, Pop's definitely got a new one."

"I don't know what to say. But nobody messes with my systems and gets away with it. I'll find out . . ." Her knitted brows implied heads would roll.

The unit still tickled Peter's curiosity and not in a good way. "Mind if I go back in for a sec?"

"Not at all. Need me?"

"I'll call if I do."

Pop dozed in his chair, little wheezy snores puffing out his nose. Peter grabbed the guest chair, placed it in the doorway, and balanced on the squishy seat as he unclipped the front cover of the detector. Instead of a simple circuit board, an ionization chamber to sense smoke, a horn to sound an alarm, and wires to connect it to the building's main fire system, this unit was self-contained, with no connecting wires. It held a circuit board attached to a tiny fish-eye lens. And a tiny microphone. With a tiny transmitter. There were two other small components that weren't obvious. One was a nanotech lab-on-a-chip that monitored environmental data. He assumed it was taking air samples and searching for specific chemicals. The other he couldn't recognize at all. What other surveillance could possibly be necessary?

He ripped the unit from the wall and flung it to the linoleum floor. Jumping down, he stomped and ground it under his heels. He didn't need to call Mrs. Manela. She came running.

CHAPTER SEVEN

P eter was afraid to use his GO. He wanted to call Amanda and his lawyer, but the reason not to was scattered in pieces over Mrs. Manela's desk. Peter kept the GO off, using the car's obsolete digital player to listen to music. He assumed the Corvette was jacked already. He should have gone straight home, but he needed to think, and driving helped.

What the hell did the feds expect to capture in Pop's room? Some teary bedside confession of terrorism to his mute father? Fuck the feds. He was in a fight for his life and reputation. But how could he keep his promise to Pop and not quit?

Driving aimlessly on Junipero Serra Boulevard near Stanford Hospital, he turned onto Campus Drive into the university. Then it hit him. But he wondered if she'd see him after everything he had done to her.

He had no choice. He'd make her see him.

Stanford University is one of the greatest institutions of higher learning in the world, and its campus is one of the most impressive.

Not in the magnificent and ancient way Cambridge, Heidelberg, or the Sorbonne are, but in the way that individuals in modern times, with more money than God, can create monuments to themselves and their loved ones.

Leland Stanford Junior University was founded by railroad magnate and California governor Leland Stanford and his wife, Jane, to honor their only child, Leland Jr., who died of typhoid at age fifteen. After their tragedy, Leland said to his wife, "The children of California shall be our children." The university's motto, *"Die Luft der Freiheit Weht,"* means "The wind of freedom blows."

Peter wasn't headed for one of the slick buildings surrounding William Hewlett, David Packard, or Bill Gates's generosity, but instead entered the last remaining 1950s concrete bunker, which once housed the physics and chemistry departments, built in the Cold War rush for scientific research to fuel the newborn military-industrial complex. Two types of research were housed there: the potentially hazardous and the financially impoverished. Neither justified shiny glass-and-steel towers.

Dr. Ruth Chaikin's research fell into the latter category. Most of her nanobiotech compatriots toiled in the state-of-the-art Geballe Laboratory for Advanced Materials that housed the Stanford Nano-characterization Lab, or the Stanford Nanofabrication Facility housed in the Paul G. Allen Center for Integrated Systems. But Peter had to pick his way through a basement hallway, whose peeling paint was at least two decades past due, and around an obstacle course of abandoned and scavenged lab equipment donated by fellow researchers and department coordinators all beholden to the Chaikin family in one way or another. The hall reeked of rodent dander and feces, meaning animal testing rooms filled with mice and rats were nearby. Peter knocked on a door. A high-pitched woman's voice yelled from behind it, "Bhupal? Get your *tuchus* in here!"

Inside, the windowless lab was as unorganized as the hallway. If it wasn't for Ruth occupying it, the room would be mistaken for storage. Ten years had aged her in the normal ways, but she didn't fight the passing time as other women might. Her once dishwater-brown hair was graying rapidly. And it was as short and frizzy as ever, creating a misty halo around her face. Even though her pasty skin only saw the sun on her bike rides to and from the lab, wrinkles abounded, and she didn't try to hide them. Her coke-bottle glasses were bifocals. She wore an old dark green turtleneck and stained chinos cinched around her waist with a piece of webbed nylon strapping used for securing crates. Electrical wire replaced shoelaces in her ratty black Converses. She was still too skinny from nervous energy and disdain of food. A poster child for a technical geek, the only thing missing was a breast pocket with a pocket protector. And a penis. It was impossible to believe she was only a couple of years older than Amanda.

She was already flapping in a dither, darting quickly from table to table, moving small lab items to and fro, still unaware of Peter. "How can I find anything? Such a *hekdish! A foiler tut in tsveyen!* You want I should lose my research?"

"My Yiddish is a little rusty. It's a long time since your dad cursed me." Peter started counting. She pottered for a full five seconds before she looked at him with incredulity. And suspicion.

"A lazy person. Has to do a task twice," she hissed. Her eyes narrowed. "What are you doing here?"

"Nice to see you, too. Who's Bhupal?"

"Grad slave. Instead of studying for midterms, he made a *hekdish*." His expression betrayed ignorance. "Horrible, messy place!" she insisted, arms waving around her.

"And now?"

She scrutinized her room. "Finally, some kind of order."

It still looked *hekdish* to him. But that was a Chaikin family trait: making exquisite sense out of chaos. Ruth backed herself up behind a far table piled high with computer printouts. He could only see her from the shoulders up.

"What's wrong with your n-nose?" She tried to stare Peter down, but her eye twitched, and it wasn't a come-hither wink. She couldn't control it. Especially when she was nervous. The more stress, the more things twitched.

"I had a little accident. Is this a good time for a visit? I wanted to talk to you."

"What if I don't want to be seen? Or talked to?" Her left shoulder jumped to her earlobe. He couldn't tell if the tremors went farther down than that.

"Then I'll leave you in peace. But I made a New Year's resolution to try and see my old friends once every ten years. Today's your lucky day."

"Az a yor ahf mir," she muttered. Peter looked confused. Ruth sighed, "I should have such l-luck . . ."

He tried to make sense of a mess on a table. "What are you working on?"

"What you should be! If you hadn't dumped me for richer pickings! You might be poor. But you wouldn't be a *shandeh un a charpeh*." She ducked a little lower behind the papers.

He remembered that phrase: "A shame and a disgrace." It was a favorite of her father, and it stung. Peter wanted to say "Shove your sanctimonious trip where solar photons don't reach" and storm from the room. But instead he said, "Ruth, answer me honestly. Regardless of what happened between us, I loved your father. Would you say that's a correct statement?"

Ruth made a funny little humming noise. That was a new tic. He assumed it meant agreement.

Placing his right hand on his heart and his left hand in the air,

Peter declared, "Then I swear on Nikolai Chaikin's grave, and may he come back to haunt me if I'm lying. I had nothing to do with the attacks. Neither did my company. Regardless of what you think about me professionally, you can't think I would have anything to do with that. Can you? Really?"

"Irrelevant. Papa would never haunt you. Neither of you believe in ghosts."

Peter laughed. "Damn straight." He poked around the lab. A hodgepodge of old mismatched computer components fought for table space with piles of technical papers. He scanned the cover of a failed grant proposal. "Still working on brain-computer interfaces?"

More humming.

Screen-saver aliens bombed exploding planets. He hit the space bar. A detailed graphic of a molecular machine popped up: a man-made cell. "And you've concentrated on theoretical work; I'm assuming because you couldn't get funding for experimental models."

Her arm flew up and another pile of papers fell to the floor. *"Schlemiel!"* she said under her breath as she picked them up. Peter approached her to help, but she barked, *"Nein!"*

"Why didn't you snuggle up to DARPA? They would have funded you, like they funded Nick."

"Not interested in building Universal Soldiers. That's all they want from me. Perfect killers. No more pain. No more hunger. No more sleep. No more bleeding. Faster killing. *Feh! Zol es brennen!"*

"So where's the money come from?"

"What money? I get five grand a year from some *alter kocker* crony of Papa's. He feels bad for me. And an alum from Des Moines. Thinks for twenty-five grand a year, he owns all my work. The Next Big Thing."

"Does he?"

"No. But I let him think it."

"That's pocket change."

PJ MANNEY

"P-p-pocket change to you, Mister Sand Hill Road. I'm not *ongeshtopt mit gelt*. I don't suck on the teat of VC. Or Big Pharma, NIH, or DARPA. To me, it's oxygen."

Peter slowly worked his way closer to her as he peered at a molecular model displayed on a monitor. "Let me guess. Still get a little royalty money from Nick's designs? And you spend it here, instead of banking it like he wanted you to."

More humming. And more averting of eyes.

He rounded her table to see all of her backed into a corner like a mouse. He continued, "And the hallway of tribute out there? Stanford's hand-me-downs to their most famous Nobel laureate's progeny? So they can keep your last name on the website?"

The humming stopped and the twitching recommenced. "P-P-Peter . . . *Bite* . . . G-g-g-go away." He had noticed years before she only stuttered in English. She hung her head to avoid eye contact, and it swung back and forth in a subtle movement.

"I can't, Ruthie. I need your help. I just saw Pop."

Ruth said nothing, and her muscles quieted down.

"I wish he'd told me to say 'Hi.' But he doesn't know who I am most of the time. And I promised him no matter what happens to me in this mess, I wouldn't give up trying to help him. And I thought you might want to help me, too. Because I was lucky enough to have two men in my life I considered fathers. Pop was one. And Nick Chaikin was the other. Nick's been dead, what, eleven years? And Paul might as well be, unless I can do something."

She finally looked him in the eyes, but she couldn't keep the derision from her voice. "Because your t-t-t-terrorist research won't fly anymore? I should hand over all my hard work? To you? To exploit me? You ab-bandoned me!"

"You're right. I did. But for what it's worth, it seemed like the right thing to do. I never did research out of pure curiosity, like you and Nick. It was more than solving the big intellectual problems

54

for me. I had other reasons. I won't lie to you, making money was a big one."

But she felt abandoned for more than that. Carter had told him a year after Peter left the lab that she nursed an unrequited crush for him. Ruth knew she was a *mieskeit*—an ugly person—compared to Amanda, but she also knew she could kick Amanda's intellectual ass. And in her mind, that should have counted for something. But she couldn't have acted on her sexual impulses, even if Peter swept her off her feet in her lab coat. She couldn't even let him hold her. Only her parents had held her, and that was as a child and under duress. She had a hugging machine at home, built by Nick, just like the one created by the famous animal behaviorist and autist, Temple Grandin, to calm her in stressed moments. Peter knew all this, but would never insult her by saying it aloud.

She sighed. She knew what he wasn't saying, too.

He'd softened her up. Time to talk fast. "I want to go back to our old work. Invasive brain-computer interfaces, but specific ones that act as prosthetics. Like a prosthetic hippocampus. And a wearable or implantable hard drive as a separate cortex, that, eventually, can translate the algorithms of thought, while helping move the information back and forth between the prosthetic hippocampus and the real and prosthetic cortexes."

"Hold it, Genius Boy." Genius Boy had been one of Nick's favorite monikers for uppity grad slaves like him. "Translate the algorithms of thought! Why not just make it read minds?"

"Someday it will. You know it's not impossible. We've decoded aural, visual, and motor brain algorithms. Why not this?" Her stepping back-and-forth motion indicated she needed to wander around. "Concentrate on the input and the output, Ruth. Forget I said anything about translation. We're not building an entire brain. Just replacing tiny parts of it . . . building a bridge to make sure the signal gets from one place to another in one piece, from analog to digital and back to analog. You don't need to understand music theory to fix a GO's music player."

"Shouldn't you concentrate? On staying out of prison?" Her hums buzzed between her sentences as she puttered around the lab. "So what about power? You're talking center of the brain. Not periphery like cochlear implants. You've got to minimize heat generation. Create constant, dependable energy supply . . ."

"What about biothermal?" suggested Peter. "Or glucose-run fuel cells? Or externalize it?"

She paced, thinking. "Not enough thermal gradient in a deep implant for biothermal. Glucose fuel cells are possible. Maybe externalize the whole thing? Or . . . electricity from existing mechanical energy? Like blood flow? A nanogenerator, like a hydroelectric plant in a vein?"

"That's brilliant."

"Not my idea. Wish it was." She buzzed some more, then, "So you'll want to see my neuro-compatible nanowires. And my biotransistor. Uses protons, not electrons. And my designs for a synthetic-neuron . . ."

It was hard to keep the excitement out of his voice. "Yes!"

"Farm out the cognitive computing. To some *shaigitzes* in Allen I know. They do interesting stuff . . ." That meant their work was groundbreaking. However, the fact they weren't Jewish lessened the accomplishments in her eyes. Before Nick died, he dubbed Peter an honorary Jew, so Ruth let him slide.

She stopped scurrying and vibrated in place. "There is a price for my help."

"I'm willing to pay." He wasn't sure how.

She grimaced a smile, lurched past him and out the door. There was the sound of tables shoved and boxes falling in the hallway. She returned with a cardboard box labeled "C&A Scientific." Peter peeked inside. It was filled with glass microscope slides and blood-drawing lancets, probably for the mice down the hall.

"You must swear a blood covenant. We will be bound together. You will not leave me again."

Peter was stunned. "Ruthie, I'm married."

She sneered. "This is not m-marriage. There is no *Get.* No divorce from this. You are committed. Regardless of circumstance. We work together now. We work together forever."

"Can't you just ask for fifty-one percent of the company? This is crazy . . ." Behind yet another pile, he noticed a photo of Nick, Peter, Ruth, and Carter, back in their graduate school days. Nick had his arms around the boys. Ruth stood apart. There was so much detritus piled near, it seemed she obscured the image on purpose.

"Tokhis oyfn tish."

He remembered that phrase, too. "Put up or shut up." She extended her own index finger to demonstrate.

He did the same, and she stabbed his finger with a lancet, but since she would not touch him, she mimed squeezing the fingertip. He milked a drop of blood onto the glass slide she held.

"Swear that you are bound to me. In a blood covenant. To work with me forever," she said.

Peter couldn't believe this was happening. "I swear I am bound to you . . ."

"And I swear I am bound to you. In a blood covenant. To work with you forever." Then she did the same to her own finger. Her blood drop splashed on top of his. She sandwiched the specimen together with another slide and held it up for him to see. "So what help do you need?" She dug around in the box for a slide clamp.

He chuckled ruefully. "Everything . . ."

With her back to Peter, she asked, "Have you asked Carter Potsdam to help you?"

"On this?" He let her scurry past to put the slide in a drawer.

"The whole *megillah*. Your position after the attack. This idea. The rest of your life."

"Well, he wouldn't help me with Biogineers, so I'm not expecting anything."

"Such a *macher*, that one. If Carter helped me. I shouldn't be in a hole in the ground. I thought he would. He and Papa loved each other. So much."

"But he's stayed friends with us. Amanda and he are still like siblings. They talk every day."

"Lucky for you, he's a *faigelah*." Ruth's face said more of her lack of luck, than Peter's luck.

He wanted to change the subject. Above a counter, another photo of Nick and Ruth hung crookedly on the wall. Nick had just received the call that he'd won the Nobel Prize. Nick hugged Ruth, aged twenty-two, with one arm and raised a spectrometer's eyepiece with the other like an Oscar statuette. Ruth appeared to tolerate his touch. Maybe her happiness at the prize overcame her wiring for once. As the "father of bionanotechnology," the Nobel committee acknowledged his controversial research into the very small was important. Only years later would people accept his crazy prognostications of human life forever altered might come to pass.

"I remember that," said Peter.

Ruth stopped humming.

"I really miss him," said Peter. He hoped she'd speak.

She migrated away in a small, sideways shuffle. "What part? The part where he complained you were a *schlemiel*? Or a *schmegegi*? Or where you proudly showed him your work? Where you thought genius doesn't fall far from his tree? And he blew a hole through it. Like buckshot against a spider's web. Then took a few of the strands. Tied them together. In some different, mysterious way. Made it all work better to catch flies than you ever could."

"Both," said Peter. "But you're forgetting the best part. The part where he loved us and protected us like he was a lioness and we were his cubs, from all the bullshit of the outside world, so we could get on with our work."

"I miss that," Ruth conceded.

"Did you ever find out what he was working on before . . . ?"

". . . he died?" She stared at the photo, wondering if that happy girl could really be her. "Something with nanowires. Papa asked me to mind my own b-business. I didn't have security clearance. He didn't want me to have it . . . which was strange. Then he died . . . then DARPA was here, making a *hek*— mess . . . cleaning out the lab. Then all kinds of spooks, agents, bureaucrats. *Shnooks, shnor-rers*, all of them. Nothing came of it. After twelve years. The trail is absolute zero."

"That's cold."

"Nanowires are yesterday's news. Everybody uses them now. Government research . . . work for *schmucks* . . ."

"You won't have to work for the government. It's purely thera-peutic to start . . ."

Ruth raised a hand and her eye blinked. "*Shoyn genug*! You had me at prosthetic hippocampus." She turned her back to feverishly dig through piles of paper. Had she added obsessive-compulsive dis-order to her list of mental idiosyncrasies? "Ten years. Living hand-to-mouth in this dump. It's enough. Unlike the rest of you, I missed all my *tchotchkes*. From the last two tech bubbles. My big screens and ergonomic chairs . . ." She was gathering research journals from all over the room and making a new pile. "We're not going to suc-ceed unless you find a pot of *gelt*. So go find it. Repeat after me: *"Gelt is nisht kayn dayge* . . ."

"*Gelt is nisht kayn dayge* . . . which means . . ."

" 'Money is not a problem.' Your new mantra, Genius Boy."

"I'll find it." He wasn't sure how.

"And don't forget, you and I. We are together. Forever."

Peter shivered. "Okay . . ."

"You've got a lot of catching up before we talk." She presented him with the pile of papers. "Bloodstream nanogenerator's at Georgia Tech. Read Berkeley first. Then Duke, Rice. You'll figure it out. And keep outta prison. Now scram, *bubeleh*. I got thinking to do."

CHAPTER EIGHT

Dealing with Ruth made Peter hungry for the first time in days. He ate a turkey sandwich outside the Packard building café, catching the fleeting autumn rays and flipping through the pile of research papers. Undergraduates scurried by, laboring under heavy backpacks. Terrorist attacks couldn't stop the pursuit of academic excellence, because these kids calculated the odds of getting hurt and realized the trade-off of getting a lower grade for a false sense of security wasn't worth it. They could have been Peter over fifteen years ago, speaking the multi-culti polyglot of English and Asian languages on top of the universal language of science necessary to communicate with their fellow students. He had gained many valuable skills here, including the ability to say unspeakably rude things in Mandarin, Japanese, Hindi, and Korean.

Peter tossed the plate in the recycling bin, and while balancing the paper pile, a distracted student bumped him with his backpack. Hopping back quickly, both lost their balance. Peter torqued his body around to catch the sliding articles. The boy reached out to help, but tripped into him instead. He grabbed for Peter's arm, landing on the older man's left leg as they both sprawled to the pavement, papers flying.

The clean-cut, brown-haired preppy yelped, "Crap on a crêpe, man! You okay?"

Peter sat up gingerly. The concrete had bruised his hip. "Yeah . . ."

"Sorry, man, really I am . . ." The kid gathered the scattered research papers, but fidgeting, stole a look at his watch.

"Late for . . . ?"

"Myerson. I'm in deep shit as is."

Professor Myerson in chemistry was a legendary prick. Peter waved the kid away.

He threw the papers at Peter, yelling, "Thanks, man!" over his shoulder as he ran.

As Peter picked up his mess, the preppy disappeared behind the Packard building.

He was going the wrong way to Myerson's class.

It didn't make sense. Peter stumbled to his feet to follow the boy, but he wasn't visible until Peter cornered Ruth's bunker. A navy-blue Lincoln sedan idled on a custodial access road. The kid jumped into the backseat, but not before spotting Peter.

"Go!" he screamed to an unseen driver. The door slammed as the driver stomped on the gas.

The Lincoln skidded around a corner, gone. Who the fuck was this kid? A federal agent?

"Mandy, this is one fucked-up day."

Peter had rushed home to tell her about the surveillance in Paul's room, his visit with Ruth, and the mysterious kid at Stanford with the getaway car. The reporters were still outside, but maintaining a foot of distance from their property line.

Amanda sat on a sofa in their den, watching her half-dozen news feeds again, taking notes. She was stunned by his story.

"The kid only stayed as long as he needed to. So what did he do?" wondered Peter aloud.

"Did he touch you? Or your things?"

"Yes." He tried to remember the fall in detail, but it was hard. Peter flipped through and shook all the paper he had brought home. Nothing was evident. Then he methodically stripped off all his clothes, looking carefully in pockets and along the fabric. He found nothing.

He remembered the student had actually touched his legs, so he studied them closely, running his fingers along the thighs and calves, to feel for something that might not be seen.

As he bent over, she kissed his cheek. "It's a waste to leave you alone like this . . ."

Peter pulled back. "Is it safe?"

"What do you mean, 'safe'?"

"Jesus Christ, Mandy! Stay away from my dick! We are not having a kid right now!"

Her eyes welled up. "'Wait until my PhD . . .' 'Wait until the start-up . . .' 'Wait until we sell Biogineers . . .' It'll never be the right time, will it? You might go to jail!"

"Exactly! I might go to jail. *We* might go to jail. We need to deal with all this! And I've just been attacked!"

"I don't see any attack! Only a bruise where you fell."

"You don't think he tripped me on purpose?" He looked at the bruise more carefully, but couldn't distinguish it from a regular bruise. "I need a scalpel."

"For what? You think you're under surveillance inside *and* out? Please . . ." She started to cry. "You need help . . ."

He glared at her, insulted.

"Okay! *We* need help. We can't do this alone . . . I'm calling Carter . . ."

CHAPTER NINE

S keletons, colorful tissue-paper banners, and flowers decorated Tito's Taqueria, a taco stand down a back alley in East Palo Alto, known to dayworkers and dot-commers alike for its excellent burritos. It was November 1—the Day of the Dead. Sheltered under the tin roof and sitting at the only table, Peter nursed a Coke. He hadn't chosen Tito's for its culinary delights, but because, after a few evasive maneuvers, he could drive backstreets and alleys and avoid the paparazzi.

It was neutral territory to meet with his "best friend."

Peter had met Amanda and Carter at Stanford their freshman year. The two men shared many classes because of their common science pursuits, and everyone used to stare at the elegant young man as he strode into the lecture halls. Peter recognized that the prep-school perfection of his shaggy blond hair, brightly hued polo shirt, and perfectly slouched khakis was a little too studied, too slick. But he still ached to look and act as carefree as Carter Potsdam and elicit that admiration.

One day, Carter sat next to Peter. After a few classes, Carter judged him sufficiently intelligent and socially trainable. They became study and lab partners and bonded over a mutual love of Warren Ellis's comic *Planetary*, David Bowie, and open-source microcontrollers called Arduinos. And after Carter told Peter about Dr. Nikolai Chaikin, both dreamed of working in the famous lab. Peter still didn't know how Carter managed to get them both in as undergraduates.

Meanwhile, Amanda lived in Carter's freshman dorm and developed a painful crush on her handsome hall mate. While Carter adored her as a friend, he was gay, and mindful of her feelings, guided her in the direction of his new lab partner. They became the Three Musketeers. Ruth was right: Peter was lucky that Carter was gay, because Amanda's choice would have been different.

Carter was the best man at their wedding, and they all shared a large house right on Stanford Avenue that Carter bought with trust fund dividends his junior year. At the time, Peter thought the house was the biggest extravagance a college student could contemplate. But Carter had always been one of a kind. They stayed through the boys' masters, doctorates, and postgrad work in Chaikin's lab, while Amanda learned the PR and marketing game, working her way up big Valley companies like Apple and Hewlett-Packard.

After finishing his doctorate in biophysics, Carter sank his East Coast fortune into the minds and bodies of Silicon Valley, becoming one of the most successful venture capitalists in the world.

But when Peter first conceived of nanobots and Biogineers, the tension in the house from Carter's lack of interest drove the Bernhardts out of Stanford Avenue and on their own. After all these years, Peter felt more distant from Carter than ever.

A pristine white convertible Aston Martin One-77 pulled into the parking lot next to the Vette, a sight which didn't faze the locals, who saw more exotic wheels than in Beverly Hills. Carter eased out of the car and sauntered toward the taco stand, making Peter smile in spite of his conflicted feelings. He still got a kick out of Carter's style, because Peter didn't have any, following the 'anti-style' endemic of Valley geek-boy culture: plain or geek cartoon T-shirts, jeans or cargo pants, sneakers or five-toe footwear, hair in whatever style you could manage to remember to groom. Or not.

However, in a business environment where a polo shirt, V-neck sweater, khakis, and sneakers was "business formal," Carter remained immaculately East Coast and proud of it in beautifully fitted slacks and a groovy, superbly tailored button-down, with a perfect sports coat thrown just so over his shoulder, and elegant Italian loafers. He could as easily have gone to tea with the Queen or posed for a fashion shoot as chowed down at a local dive. Valley geeks chalked it up to his being an eccentric queer. Carter raised a "wait a minute" finger and leaned on the counter toward the middle-aged Latina taking orders. She melted as he asked for two of the house specialty, *carnitas burritos*. But Carter never acknowledged the reaction, except to be gracious for the attention.

The two men bro-hugged, then holding Peter at arm's length, Carter took a good long look. Peter's taped-up nose had blossomed angrily. Lower eyelids sagged. "Jesus, Pete, Halloween was yesterday. Slept much?"

"Not really." Admitting it made him more exhausted.

"How long's it been?"

"Mandy thinks six months. Not since the Khosla party." He left unsaid they had argued at the Khosla party, and sagged on his stool.

Carter left it unsaid, too. "Too long." He sat tentatively. "How was your meeting with the feds?"

"You mean the interrogation? Which one? FBI? NSA? Or Homeland Security?"

"Any . . . all . . ."

"No matter how much you cooperate, they pull every psychological trick short of waterboarding. Great fun."

Carter sighed. "Sorry, buddy. Talked to the old gang?"

"Phone's dead. Can't you see the 'scarlet P'?"

"P?"

"'Pariah.' Even Valley blogs, which you would assume represent a higher IQ, equate me with Bin Laden. Someone called me the 'McVeigh of the Valley.' Nice . . . Changed my GO/HOME address and numbers this morning because of death threats. Springing that trap on reporters didn't help . . ."

"No, but I laughed . . ."

"I've been unfriended by just about every contact on social sites and uninvited to funerals. And I can't figure out where those kids got the tech to kill everybody. Total dead end . . ."

"Shit . . ."

"And Mandy's pissed at me."

"Please do us all a favor and knock her up. Not that I don't enjoy whining women."

"You don't get to say that. Our life's not a bed of roses like yours."

"Bullshit. This is all *your* security head trip. Make a baby and move on."

"You, of all people, are preaching reproduction?"

Carter glared at him. "You asked for my help. Do you want it?"

Peter didn't at the moment, but he kept quiet.

"And by the way," continued Carter, "I'm not in such great shape, either. 10/26 was a wake-up call. Time to clean up my act and be with the people I love. And since Nick's gone, that leaves just you and Amanda, you asshole. The rest is bullshit. And I've got some ideas how to neutralize your problem and avoid the worst-case scenario, where you join the martyr's club, doing time and coming to represent everything that was ever wrong about nanotechnology. We don't want you to go down just because our country has some fucking crucifixion complex."

"Who's 'we'?"

"I know . . . some people . . . who are not happy about this . . ."

"But you work in nano. What are you doing to distance yourself?"

"Consolidating or selling where I can, emphasizing that the rest are either benign or indispensable. In my position, it's really just spin to the right people. Most importantly, I don't make bots."

Peter shifted uncomfortably. They were close to the taboo subject. Carter knew Peter needed permission. "Go ahead. Ask me."

"Okay . . . Why did you never help me or Biogineers before?"

"Because I always believed bots might be manipulated given the right circumstances. You did, too, but you got over your reservations . . ."

"But . . . !"

"I know, I know you tried to fight your VCs and the feds, but by the time I felt strongly about it, you didn't want to hear it anymore, you were so desperate to move on and make a success of the company. And I wasn't up for another fight with you. And now . . . nanobots are dead."

Peter sighed. "Next question: You've backed so many companies. Did you stay away from Bruce Lobo on purpose?"

"Oh Jesus, yes."

"Why?"

"Because I know what he is. And how he thinks. I don't need that kind of grief."

The Latina brought over the meals. When she placed Carter's

steaming plate and Smart Water down, she gave him her most special smile. The one she reserved for her boyfriend, but not her husband.

"*Gracias, Alma,*" gushed Carter. "*¡Que delicia mas impresionante has cocinado! ¿Y quién se puede comer un burrito tan grande? ¿De verdad hicistes la salsa de Chipotle solamente para nosotros?*"

Alma nodded, giggled, and ambled away.

Peter rolled his eyes. "Did you ever have to go head-to-head against him?"

Having taken a big bite, Carter nodded vigorously.

"And . . . ?"

Carter finished chewing, swallowed, and dabbed his lips with a napkin. "I beat him every time," he said with relish.

"How?"

"By being as ruthless as he was and never presenting a vulnerable side. He's a fucking animal." He took another big bite of burrito. With a full mouth, he garbled, "Eat. It's great."

Peter never thought of Carter as ruthless, but then Peter had never been on the other end of a deal with him, either. The burrito looked tasty enough, but his appetite had waned since the attacks, and his baggy clothes showed it. Peter took a bite, chewing on thoughts before speaking. The enormous burrito made a mess of his hands and face. But Carter was untouched by the salsa and juicy *carnitas* meat that squirted from both ends of the tortilla.

"How do you eat so neatly?" Peter asked.

"Breeding."

"Asshole."

They grunted with laughter, and Peter spit a bit of burrito out.

"My dear, I can't take you anywhere." Carter handed him a napkin to mop up his dripping chin.

"Okay . . . ever since we met, you've hidden your business from me. Even when we were both starting up. Did you really not trust me? You know me well enough to know I'd never divulge anything, never steal from you, never betray you."

"You're right. I was paranoid. But I was also a kid. And I apologize. So even though I wasn't there before, I am now. I'm going to get you out of this mess, because there's still some life in that carcass of yours."

Peter couldn't avoid feeling the aristocrat was being patronizing. "Noblesse oblige?"

Carter sighed with annoyance. "And you're going to need more than just my help. There's a . . . group I want you to think about . . ."

"Group? What's a 'group'?"

"A club."

"I'm not a joiner, you know that."

Carter appraised his mood, changing tack. "Well, you need to get your hands dirty."

"Dirty? How?"

"Nobody's getting reelected without making heads roll over 10/26. You're part of the investigation and it's your head on the chopping block. They'll go after all the top execs, including Amanda, because they can. And she can't get pregnant if you're in separate prisons. There's a bit of cabinet and agency reshuffling going on, and they need to know who's got the job to nail you. If I do nothing, you'll probably be whoever's first meal to make his— You grew up with the Italians. What's the Mafia phrase?"

Peter's former playmates would not appreciate the cultural stereotyping. "Make his bones?"

"Right. Make his bones with the administration. In the meantime, I have some friends I want you to meet, so hopefully, you won't be a meal at all."

"Who?"

Carter smiled. "Ever been to an inaugural ball?"

"Nope."

"Then consider me your fairy godmother."

Peter snorted. "That's not too hard."

"You'll meet the right people there. The kind that can help."

"But I'm not voting for the guy!"

Carter glared like a stern schoolmaster. "You roll with the punches and play with the big boys now. Or it's over, and Amanda and I learn to love the drive to Lompoc for visiting day."

"So how am I getting my hands dirty?"

"Make every president your president; and every administration and their associates, hangers-on, and cronies will be there when you need it. And you couldn't need it more." Carter pushed his empty plate away. "Look. Once they've strung you up as the patsy, the anti-nano bill will be presented for a vote by Senators Mankowicz and Davidson as a bipartisan salvo right after the inauguration. The president promises if he wins, it's the first thing he'll sign. It'll pass overwhelmingly, and by the beginning of next year, the US will be under full restrictions and sanctions regarding all nanovirus and bot supplies and research. The EU sanctions will immediately follow. And they need their scapegoat to make it happen. We've got to stop the bill and stop them from slaughtering you. You will do whatever it takes, to whomever you have to, to save your ass. Don't forget, everyone has their price."

"I don't," said Peter quietly.

"How can you still be that naive? It's a vicious world out there. You're up against the wall, Pete. And they're loading their rifles."

"After all these years, you still don't know who I am?"

Carter snorted. "You got over your reservations about nanobots. And you will make the necessary choices when you realize how much you're threatened now. I'm telling you, Peter Bernhardt will survive this. And I'll prove it."

"Has anyone ever told you 'no'?"

Carter laughed. "No."

"And everyone's telling me 'no . . .'" The world felt very heavy. Peter wasn't sure he could hold up Amanda's needs, society's acrimony, and the brunt of the government's legal might, alone. He looked across the street. A ten-year-old Mercedes had parked, and a man in a baseball cap and sunglasses pulled out a long-lens camera. It was too obvious to be a fed. A paparazzo had found him. He shuddered, feeling the firing squad take aim.

"Help me, Carter. Please . . ."

CHAPTER TEN

During the two and a half months before Inauguration Day on January 20, the Bernhardts lived under continued surveillance. Biogineers took a beating in the media, but while no links between the company and the attacks had been proven, they didn't have to be. Peter cooperated during continued lengthy interviews with the FBI, DHS, and NSA, but he was still treated like a terrorist. Their assets were seized and their house foreclosed upon, but Carter made sure they didn't starve. Meanwhile, Ruth and Peter focused their research and brought on Chang Eng and Jesse Steinberg as consultants. They had no job prospects with Biogineers on their résumés and hoped this long shot might resuscitate their careers. But it was no coincidence they were also the only former colleagues willing to speak to Peter. He remained persona non grata to the entire high-tech world.

When the team was ready, they pitched the full brain-computer interface concept to Carter. He loved it, and asked to partner with Peter. But the amount of funding needed was very large, and Carter couldn't cover it alone. And Peter's name scared any investors away. Carter told him to take one thing at a time: Peter had to save his ass before starting another company.

Carter helped immediately in more fundamental ways. Their old Stanford Avenue college house was to be vacated. So he gave the Bernhardts their old digs back, rent free, for as long as they needed it, and Peter traded his glorious lap lane for Stanford's Avery Aquatic Center. Peter resented being back in the old neighborhood. It meant he had failed. And the looks and comments he got at the pool from students angered him daily. There was no more idealistic, righteous, and misinformed mudslinger than a university undergraduate. However, he was a short walk from Ruth's house, so they could discuss work at any time. And being surrounded by busy young people, even scolds, made him more optimistic about the future.

Meanwhile, Carter arranged invitations for them to the most exclusive inaugural ball for face time with people who could help. He spent days briefing the Bernhardts on what to say, and tested them while flying from California to Washington on his Gulfstream VII. They had everything riding on their presentation. The powers that be would either release Peter from purgatory or send him straight to hell.

The main ballroom of the Washington Convention Center held the American Ball. It was only one of ten official balls that evening, with names such as the Freedom Ball, the Democracy Ball, and the Independence Ball, each celebrating the reelection of President John Stevens in the greatest landslide in American political history. Attendance at the balls was based on the state one hailed from or whether one fulfilled a special role, like active military personnel. But the American Ball was special. It was for the inner circle of the president and by invitation only. All its attendees had been invited to another ball, many of which were in different ballrooms created within the convention center, or in separate hotels; however, this was the one they arrived at by the end of the evening to show deference and loyalty. The American Ball would have been the hottest ticket in town, if tickets could have been bought.

Standing at the ballroom doors after running several security gauntlets, including a vigorous and intimate manhandling of Peter's genitals after being X-rayed, the Bernhardts took in the remarkable display of national and personal power. It was beyond the million-dollar necklaces on the couture-gowned ladies or the tables heaped with caviar, lobster, and oysters and the free-flowing champagne. What made eyeballs pop was the over-the-top set dressing. The huge, institutional space was transformed into a neoclassical, Jeffersonian pastiche. Presidential portraits from the National Portrait Gallery lined the blue velvet damask-covered walls, installed to hide the convention center's industrial design. Dozens of crystal chandeliers, each one worthy of *The Phantom of the Opera*, hung overhead, suspended from a false ceiling of tented and draped red-and-white-striped silk. Tables were set with real linen, real sterling-silver place settings, real lead-crystal glasses, and real porcelain. Enormous silver centerpieces from the Smithsonian and White House collections held hundreds of thousands of dollars of flowers. White columns festooned with red-rose garlands divided the space. A rotation of the best dance bands in America played off to the side next to the parquet dance floor.

Amanda couldn't help but catch her breath at the outrageous display. Carter smiled indulgently at her, like a parent at a child's delight over a just-lit Christmas tree. He leaned over and whispered, "Now remember, girl. Their rocks may be real, but the faces and tits ain't. And if some old broad gives you the cold shoulder, give 'em a few 'Om Shantis' back. That'll shake 'em up." She whacked him nervously with her evening clutch.

Carter had dressed them with the same degree of care, and cash, lavished on the ballroom. Peter wore his first tuxedo, handmade by

Carter's tailor, and even cut his hair to a socially acceptable length. Carter wanted to make sure there was nothing about Peter that read "irresponsible" or "immature" to the people they would meet. Amanda's long black hair was piled on top of her head, and she wore a beautiful barebacked, sleeveless gown of draped pale gold satin. She looked otherworldly, like Galatea come to life from the pages of *Vogue*, and every man that evening admired her as she passed. She had never looked so beautiful. Not even on her wedding day. To level the playing field, Carter had borrowed a pair of spectacular canary diamond drop earrings from his mother to go with the gown. She kept touching them to make sure they were still there.

"Don't worry so much," Carter whispered. "They're insured."

"How much?" she asked.

"Two million."

Amanda stiffened, more nervous than before. With her arm linked through Carter's, and Peter dutifully following behind, Carter said, "Now don't wander off. Security's tight, and we might get separated."

These weren't Peter's people, and they would smell a fraud. Perspiration trickled down his back. Which meant he couldn't take his jacket off without looking like a wreck. That made a new rivulet of sweat break out and head south. He wedged himself between Carter and Amanda and whispered in her ear, "Mandy, don't let me drink champagne, or I might not stick to the script."

"It's not the words I'm worried about, Pete. It's your eyes. You never hide how you feel. I love that I always know what you're thinking, but not now. Please, honey. Just for tonight."

"I'll try." He studiously ignored a passing waiter with a tray of cool bubbly.

The waiter stopped and served a glass to a guest. In a room filled with men hanging on to their wives, and their wives desperately hanging on to body parts mismatched to their carcasses, she was a vision. Wild, bright red hair hung in long ringlets down her shoulders and back, framing languid eyes and a dancer's posture. She was very curvaceous, in a long, black body-hugging dress that emphasized every taut inch of her, like an old-time movie star. "Bombshell" was the word they would have used back then to describe her. Or later, "Jessica Rabbit." No one else in the room, except Amanda, looked as lovely. But what set her apart was the intelligent intensity that shone from her eyes. She looked like a woman you wouldn't want to cross, because she'd get even in ways you couldn't imagine. She regarded Peter over the rim of her champagne glass and smiled.

Carter scanned the crowd, catching someone in his sights. "Perfect. Two o'clock. Senator Patrick Davidson. Pennsylvania. Friend of the family. Chairman of the Health, Education, Labor, and Pension Committee. He was a vocal critic of nano from the get-go. Coauthored the anti-nano bill. Wife's name is Mathilde. She's French. Professor at U Penn. Now he's got the bit between his teeth. Excellent practice. Let's roll."

As they made their way through the crowd, Amanda said, "I could handle Mathilde if we need to divide and conquer. What's she a professor of?"

"Oh God. I don't remember," said Carter. "What are the French professors in? Postmodernism? Semiotics? Jerry Lewis?"

Davidson looked to be about seventy years of age. The same age as Peter's father, but they couldn't have been more different. Here was a man who took great pains with himself, who would be pleased to be called "fighting fit" like the ex-marine he was. Mathilde had long gray hair, but done in a tight, chic chignon that emphasized the severe simplicity of her floor-length silver sheath, like a slender surgical blade.

They were in conversation with another couple. The woman had a blown-tight face only a wind tunnel could love and the hands of a crypt keeper. The man had his own plastic surgery to keep up, his skin looking like a slick pickle recently removed from its jar.

Carter approached at a discreet distance and caught Davidson's eye. After a bit more banter, Davidson subtly brought him into the conversation and introduced him.

Carter put out his hand. "Pat! How's the elbow?"

Davidson shook hands gingerly, then reflexively rubbed his right elbow with his left hand. "Last surgery was two months ago. Doc promises me I'll be whipping your ass with my serve by May."

"Then I'd better tell Father to get the court in shape. He doesn't pay attention to the grounds staff if we're not around to harass him." Both men laughed. Carter smoothly maneuvered Peter in, leaving Amanda to handle Mathilde and the other couple. "Pat, I want to introduce you to my dear friend, Peter Bernhardt. Pete, this is Senator Patrick Davidson from Pennsylvania."

Davidson caught sight of the "scarlet P" with a grimace. "I'm surprised you've got the nerve to be here, Mr. Bernhardt."

He shook the senator's hand, trying not to pump hard. "It's a pleasure to meet you, sir."

Davidson winced in pain. "Carter, I assume you're introducing us because we all know he's in a heap of trouble and you think I can help. That's an unusual miscalculation on your part."

"Yes, sir," Peter jumped in. "I know I'm in a lot of trouble. But it's also unjustified, sir."

"How can you say that? Over seventy thousand people died because of your nanotechnology. I watched them, young man!"

"Neither I, nor my company was responsible. We simply manufactured a technology similar to what was weaponized. Two other companies in Asia did, too, and I hope the government is investigating them as well. However, for what it's worth, I tried to convince the government ten years ago this might be a problem. And I was told by the administration at the time that they didn't want to ruffle business feathers with overregulation and that I had an overactive imagination. I still have copies of all the correspondence to prove it. Regardless, Senator, I never want this to happen again, and I am prepared to do whatever it takes to protect the public."

"That's rather after the fact."

"I appreciate that, but here's my dilemma, Senator. I want to save people's lives on both ends of the debate. Not only from becoming victims of weaponized technologies, but also from brain diseases we can cure. This is very personal to me, sir. My father suffers from Alzheimer's. And I was producing a cure for him, and millions of others, before this disaster happened."

Carter winced behind the senator, making a subtle throat-slashing sign with his hands.

"But aren't there other techniques available that we've got a better handle on? Where we know about the dangers and pitfalls more thoroughly?"

The senator seemed engaged, and Peter was midexplanation with no way out, so he ignored Carter. He caught sight of Amanda charming Mathilde. Whatever she was a professor in, Amanda was holding her own.

"Well, to someone," said Peter too quickly, "every one of them has pitfalls, be they genetic, robotic, nano, or pharmacological in nature. Some of the objections are moral. Some are social or economic. Some have undesirable side effects. And some just suffer from a yuck factor."

The senator shook his head. Peter thought he didn't understand and plunged ahead, speaking faster still. "That's when you think, 'Yuck! Why would I do that?' but you don't have a better reason not to embrace the idea. Historically, the yuck factor has been a deterrent in technology development, but only temporarily. It's also a moving target. What we thought was offensive a generation ago is not offensive now, like in vitro fertilization. Or recycling technologies that purify sewage. And what we think is icky now, won't be to our children and grandchildren . . ."

"Mr. Bernhardt . . ." interrupted the senator.

"Senator?"

"We don't want your nanobots . . . or nano-anything . . ."

"I'm not trying to convince you about nanobots, sir, just how we should respond to this crisis . . ."

"You are not the man to deliver any 'gifts.' No one wants what you're offering." Senator Davidson turned to Carter. "My boy, we're done here. Please send my regards to your father." He returned to Mathilde as she was introducing Amanda to two distinguished gentlemen. They kept ogling her, while casting glances at Peter with a smirk. They weren't even waiting for his dead body to cool.

Even Carter shivered. He caught Amanda's eye and beckoned her back. "Pete . . . I'm sorry, I had no idea he'd be so negative. And slow down, man! Use a little finesse." He took a deep breath and looked for another target. Congressman Salvatore Amendola of New York was passing with his aide. "Congressman!" said Carter jovially.

"Mr. Potsdam! How ya doin', buddy?" He slammed his meaty paw into Carter's manicured hand.

Carter introduced the Bernhardts.

"I grew up in your district, Congressman," said Peter, smiling.

Amendola went pale. "I can't help that . . ." He turned to Carter. "How'd he get in? You bring him?" Amendola looked furtively to his right and left, then pulled Carter in close. "You hear the rumor? They might have a warrant for him, right?"

Carter looked stunned. Peter felt sick.

The aide tugged on Amendola's arm. The congressman ducked and weaved. "I can't be seen talking to him. Good luck, buddy!"

Carter was contemplating their options when a bellicose fireplug with a mean comb-over waddled up to the trio: Senator Herbert Mankowicz of Illinois. "Davidson said you were here. You got balls. Both of you." He wagged his finger at Carter. "And you should know better!"

"Herb!" beseeched Carter, "please just hear us out. That's all we're asking."

Peter went into his song and dance again, finishing with, "But here's the most important thing I can tell you: no laws stop the juggernaut of technological progress. At best, we only delay it slightly. Now that humans know how to make nanobots, they will make them again. Even delayed, we can't know everything up front, even though we desperately want to, and we ride out the unexpected the best we can."

"It's easy to be glib when it wasn't your family members who died at the hands of the unknown," scolded Mankowicz.

"I'm not being glib, sir. And that doesn't make it less of the truth. Only more painful. But here's the point: If ATEAMO hadn't used nanobots, they would have used something else. Terrorists use whatever works. They don't stop being terrorists because you take away one of their weapons. And they don't become terrorists because they find a new one. The objective is to create tools and prevent them from being used as weapons, because for every stick we dug up the ground to plant food with, we could have used that same stick to bash in someone's head. Swords into plowshares, sir . . ."

Mankowicz looked at him with sudden contempt. "You don't think anyone buys that ATEAMO is just three snot-nosed kids! Who supplied them? You?"

"No! Of course not! And I want to help find who did! But no one will let me."

"You're damned lucky you're with Carter. Or I'd have kicked your ass myself!" The fireplug stormed off.

Peter couldn't stop shaking. "Please, Carter. Let's get out of here." Amanda squeezed his hand for support.

"No," said Carter as he gestured for a waiter. "That's just blood in the water for these sharks. You've got to rough it out. Nanotech scares a lot of people, and they want someone to blame. If we can change even one or two of their minds, it's worth staying all night." He handed Peter and Amanda flutes of champagne.

Peter couldn't drink his. "Why are you damaging your relationships for me?"

Carter looked surprised. "I want what's best for you."

"That's your insecurity talking again, Pete," said Amanda quietly. "We need you to keep trying."

Much of Peter's fear came from misunderstanding the power dynamics of the room and how he did or didn't fit in. He assumed he was the only victim. The truth was every person there was on the make as much as he. Along with them, he burned with the envy of the perpetual outsider, a peculiarly American schadenfreude. Money, power, or beauty were supposed to mystically confer insider status in American society, but rarely did to the extent the possessor wanted, because no one believed they'd finally arrived at the magic circle's center.

Through it all, Carter's performance was smooth as silk. He held chairs for women, entered and exited conversations without a social ripple, and made everyone feel good in his presence. Peter tried to emulate him, but fear overwhelmed his synapses. His clumsiness only made matters worse.

And so the evening went. Carter introduced them to more members of Congress, cabinet officials, corporate tycoons, even religious leaders and entertainers; and Peter did his best to convince them. No one's opinion seemed to budge, and Peter was tossed out of the magic circle time and time again.

Four hours into the evening, there was a commotion, and many men dressed in tuxes, sunglasses, and earpieces filtered through the crowd. With chants of "Four More Years" ringing around them, President John Stevens and First Lady Elizabeth Stevens made a grand entrance. This would be the couple's last stop of the night after making an appearance at each of the official balls in their honor.

The band struck up "Hail to the Chief." The usually unmusical Carter sang the lyrics under his breath, loud enough for Peter and Amanda to hear.

"I didn't even know there were words," said Amanda.

Carter smirked. "You think he's the only human GO player in the room?" jerking his thumb at Peter. "Learned it in the womb. Family's had a rep at every inaugural ball since the first. But it wasn't played until James Polk's in 1845. We must have heard it then."

After shaking hands and slapping backs for half an hour, the president stood at the podium to speak. He told them the nation chose once again to place awesome responsibility into his humble hands and that the overwhelming voter support was a powerful confirmation of his policies. He pledged, with God's help, to avenge the deaths of the innocent Americans of 10/26, and he gratefully accepted the mandate of the people. The words life, liberty, the pursuit of happiness, democracy, America, family, values, justice, and pride were rung like bells throughout. Deeply uninspired, everyone expected this speech and could have written it on their cocktail napkins between drinks. Yet his audience responded like it was the Good News from Heaven.

Peter stood behind Amanda and Carter, so they couldn't see the devastation in his face. That's when he saw Jessica Rabbit again. Her gaze took all of him in and savored it, making her grin mischievously. He found it hard to believe his makeover was *that* successful, and he watched her from the stronghold behind his wife. The speech seemed to go by more quickly than before, until an elder statesman stopped to speak to her in passing and the two quickly went their separate ways, each disappearing into the crowd.

By the early hours of the morning, the party wound down. A few diehards slow danced. The three slouched in their seats around a table. Amanda had kicked off her shoes. Then the band kicked into one last song: "American Pie."

Amanda, exhausted only moments before, perked up and grabbed her husband's arm. "I want one dance. Just one. Something has to be salvaged from tonight."

"Don't you mean one last dance on the *Titanic?*" said Peter. He didn't get up.

"Come on, Amanda," said Carter. "I'll do it."

Her face lit up, as though Prince Charming had asked her to dance. Carter handed her back her shoes. "You're going to need these, Cinderella." She grimaced, but slipped them on anyway before curtsying to him. He took her hand and waist and they spun away. Peter had never seen Carter dance like this before. He twirled her around the floor, and in his arms Amanda became Ginger Rogers. It was easy to imagine her fox-trotting into Carter's aristocratic class. Formal dance lessons were not a part of either Peter's or Amanda's childhoods, but he used to watch the rich kids go to the Presbyterian church at the top of Main Street and Broadway for their lessons every Tuesday night, all decked out in suits, dresses, and polished shoes. He never had the opportunity to join them. On Tuesday nights, he washed dishes at Benny's Restaurant to help his dad pay the rent.

He wondered if observers thought Amanda was Carter's wife.

The song ended, and the two dancers tripped the light fantastic back to him.

"God, it's been years since I've done that," panted Carter. He gave Amanda's hand a squeeze. "I'll make a society matron out of you yet."

"Lemme guess," Peter deadpanned. "Kiddie dance classes."

"Every Thursday night for four fucking years," said Carter. "Complete with navy suit, red rep tie, and buffed black oxfords. And acne."

Everyone applauded as the band said good night and the recorded music kicked in. As they walked to the garage, Peter absentmindedly said a prayer, even though he didn't believe in them, that they could have the opportunity to start again. Dear God, that's all he wanted. A fresh start.

CHAPTER ELEVEN

C arter led them underneath the convention center to the parking lot and the toasty warm limo he had hired for the evening. They sprawled in the back. Peter was afraid to speak.

"Carter, do you really think Pete will go to jail?" asked Amanda quietly.

Carter couldn't bring himself to respond.

The three were silent as the limo joined an endless procession that crawled past security, street closures, and demonstrators, including "Remember 10/26" supporters and anti-nano activists, all the way back to the Hay-Adams Hotel, where they shared a lavish two-bedroom suite, again courtesy of Carter.

The limo pulled up to the canopied hotel entrance, and Carter turned to Amanda. "Do you mind if we abandon you to take a walk? I need to talk to Pete."

Normally, Amanda would complain about being left out of the threesome. But tonight was different. Maybe it was the cold weather. Or maybe she needed to be alone.

"Do what you need to do," she said.

Peter helped her out of the limo and walked her to the lobby.

She kissed him and said, "Never forget how much I love you. And don't keep me waiting too long . . ." As she walked away, three different men appraised her while she crossed the lobby, as though they knew she'd be available soon.

Carter and Peter wandered in the stingingly cold night air, crossing H Street and entering Lafayette Park toward the bright lights of the White House and the Washington Monument rising like a sentinel behind it. Painful scenarios ran through Peter's mind. He'd go to jail. Amanda would divorce him in prison, and some other rich man would marry her. They'd have the child she always wanted. Maybe a house full of children . . .

Carter was silent, too, hands stuffed in overcoat pockets and head bowed. Peter hoped he'd get on with it, because his nose was numb, his stomach was spurting acid, and his bones ached from fatigue.

"I don't get it," Peter finally blurted out. "I'm smart. I've worked hard. Done everything right. And I'm about to lose . . . my life. It's over." The iconic columns and front door of the White House were visible at the end of the allée of naked trees they passed, branches heavy with ice. "How does it all come so easily to you? Was it because you were loaded to start with? Or knew how to get what you wanted?"

Carter snorted, steam belching from his nose. "That's not half wrong. But that's not everything." He was silent again.

"Well, are you going to tell me?"

"Yes. But are you ready to hear me?"

"Haven't I been following your orders all night?"

Carter looked unconvinced and stared at the White House. "When I was at Stanford, I knew I wasn't going to make breakthroughs and be one of the people up on the dais in Oslo when they handed out the Nobels. But I know how to read people. And I know what they want. Even before they do. That was a way that I could make myself matter. I could see the miracles nanotechnology would bring to us were just about to break, and I was determined to be a part of it. As much as I wanted to do this, I needed help from people more powerful than myself. So I joined a club. I trust them like I trust you. And they made my dreams come true."

It sounded simplistic and overwrought, but Peter couldn't help asking, "What club?"

"The Phoenix Club. Ever hear of it?"

"Yeah. But I thought they were just a bunch of rich old farts playing Iron John games in the woods. Isn't that passé? And didn't the Sun Valley Conference and Davos eclipse all that?"

Carter nodded his head. "It's what everyone would like you to think. And some of them are rich old farts in the woods . . ."

"Why would I want to be a part of that?"

"Like everything in life, it's more complicated than that." Carter began walking toward the White House again.

"Why are we talking about clubs again? You know it's not my scene. I've made my own way the hard way," said Peter with resentment choking his voice.

Carter's voice dropped with gravitas. "Forget everything you think you know about clubs. This is not a country club. Or even a fraternal organization or secret society in the traditional sense. This is an echelon of society, the engine in the country's machine. I can't explain it all to you right now. It's too fucking cold. I want someone else to do that. Just do me this favor. Come to lunch with me tomorrow. It's the last chance you've got, Pete."

"You're kidding . . ."

"These are the only people who can help you now. 'If I have seen further, it is by standing on the shoulders of my club brothers.'"

Peter shook his head. "Okay, man, now you're just fuckin' goofy. And who'd want *me* in their club? And why?"

Carter's mouth formed a small, tight grin. It was too cold to smile any bigger. "A couple of weeks ago, I went ahead and put your name up for membership. Just in case. Tomorrow, you can meet the president of the club and ask him anything you want. The bigger question for you is: How much did you value your old life? What's it worth to you to avoid jail? Get your company back? Save your marriage?"

"And what do I have to sacrifice to do this?"

"Trust me."

"I'm innocent. The truth will set me free."

"I hope Amanda's next husband is smarter than you." Carter turned away and walked quickly back to the hotel.

Peter had never felt so cold in his life.

CHAPTER TWELVE

Amanda was under the covers on the far side of the bed, breathing softly and evenly. Disappointed, Peter quietly shut the door to the suite's living room and tiptoed in, taking off his overcoat and gloves and throwing them on a chair. She purred and rolled to him with a heavy-lidded smile.

"What was that about?" she murmured.

"What?"

She turned away, mumbling into her pillow, "If you're going to be that way . . ."

He crawled onto the bed and rolled her toward him. "I'd rather be this way." She was warm and inviting. He kissed her deeply, afraid to let it end.

She pulled her mouth away and laid her hands on his jacket lapels. "Your tux is still freezing. So, do I have to play Mata Hari and sleep with you to find out?"

"Yes. Most definitely."

"Okay, so why's Carter all secret squirrel?"

"He wants me to join a club."

"And . . . ?"

"If I agree, I meet the head guy tomorrow. Carter thinks this is my last lifeline. That it might somehow solve our problems. I've never done anything like this, never asked for this kind of help before. And I don't know what the price is. There has to be a price. After a whole life of doing things the right way, I'm not selling my soul for a sin I didn't commit."

"You and your damned integrity are going to destroy us. Carter put his reputation on the line for you tonight. Your ego is more important than him? And our family?"

She had taken apart her elaborate updo, and her still-lacquered hair spread across the pillows, framing her face in waves of shiny black silk.

He knew she was right. He had to save himself. And her. "I can't resist you both," he said.

She stroked his face. "No, you can't, my love." Then she kissed him. And he kissed her back.

CHAPTER THIRTEEN

At the Capital Grille, a DC restaurant frequented by the denizens of Capitol Hill, Peter and Carter met Josiah Brant in a small private dining room. Peter was not meeting Brant in his capacity as secretary of state of the United States of America. Brant was there as the president of the Phoenix Club.

The men's club–like interior of the restaurant was everything Peter thought it should be for this kind of conversation: dark with mahogany and leather and old paintings, the smell of charred cow flesh and expensive wine. On his way through the packed main dining room, Carter stopped to say hello to a number of people Peter didn't know, as well as several he had met last night. The day after an inauguration was always busy.

But in their private room, the sound of deal making between government employees and lobbyists muffled behind closed doors into Washingtonian white noise.

"Thank you for meetin' me back here in Siberia, gentlemen. I'm an old dog who can't kick the trick of smokin' these things with my meals, and they are gracious enough to humor my vices and allow me to break the law in private." Brant turned to Peter and waved his cigar. "I'd ask if you minded, but I'd smoke 'em even if you did. Maggie says it's my most unpleasant characteristic."

Short, stocky, and white haired at seventy-two, Brant had a pleasing face and cherubic demeanor, like a clean-shaven Santa Claus, using his infamous Southern Comfort charm as the velvet wrapped around his iron will. Peter would proceed carefully. After the trio deconstructed the previous evening's festivities, received their drinks, and ordered their meals, Josiah got down to business. "So Carter told you exactly what about the Phoenix Club?"

"Not much. It's a men's club, and it helped him become successful. That's about all."

"Is that all you feel about your brethren, Carter? We gave you a leg up?" Josiah's eyes twinkled in jest.

Carter gave Peter a grimace as thanks. "No, Josiah. I thought you could explain the club better than I. You being so colorfully articulate and the club's president and all."

"I love this boy! He gives as good as he gets, even to his elders." Josiah cackled, but his smoker's cough got the better of him. When the coughing subsided, he said, "Fair enough . . . fair enough. I will only give you a general idea of the club till we can gauge your interest as serious. As you can imagine, we like our privacy and don't share our laundry outside our intimates." Josiah sat back in his chair and puffed on his cigar to gather his thoughts. "The club was founded by our nation's foundin' fathers to take care of the best and the brightest and nurture them to become the leaders of tomorrow. It's a simple mission, and yet one we've taken very seriously for over two hundred years. Think of us as national talent scouts. We look for people who not only conceive of positive change, but know how and when to implement it for everyone's greatest benefit. If I gave you a list of members, which I hope you'll forgive me if I don't at the moment, you would see the Who's Who of American business, government, culture, academia . . . You name it, we got it."

"Does the club have a specific agenda?" asked Peter.

"Only to keep the country safe and strong and movin' forward by makin' sure the cream rises to the top and gets to accomplish their goals. To say there was a more specific and permanent agenda would mean we were not open to the shiftin' winds of change, which are so important to heed in times like these. In fact, I'd say our agenda is all about chartin' change and . . . surfin' it, as you California boys say."

"Josiah thinks that all Californians are surfers," Carter countered. "I keep telling him that's a stereotype."

"Maybe not on literal waves, but on figurative waves, you sure do. That's what I love about Californians. You're always lookin' for what comes floatin' in on the global trade winds. You got your fingers on the pulse of the planet in ways most other states don't. My fair state of Alabama, for instance. Best people in the whole world. Salt of the earth. Trust 'em with my life. But my neighbors in Mobile—hell, my own family—ain't gonna be tellin' me what the world will be doin' in five, ten, twenty, a hundred years from now. Or at least not be right about it!"

The waiter arrived with their meals. Steaks, rare, all around. Peter took a deep breath and asked the question that needed asking. "So why me? Why now?"

Josiah smiled. "Smart boy. Thanks to Carter, we know what you're developin'. We want it to succeed. All this nano-nonsense will blow over eventually, and I'm not gonna let China run away with the biggest technological advantage since the computer."

"You really think it's that important?"

"Son, put all those ideas you've got in your head together, and I think you can change the world. We want to see that happen. Here. At home . . ."

Carter interjected, "And I brought it up before. And you shot me down."

93

Josiah laughed. "We got plenty of members who don't think they're club-types. They learn the club is what you make it."

Peter hadn't eaten since hors d'oeuvres last night, and he dug in with zeal. "So if I join, how do you nurture my supposed talent?"

"What do you perceive as your biggest disadvantages?" asked Josiah in return. His T-bone was still sizzling, and he patiently waited for the meat to cool.

"Well . . . right now it's a two-front war: my reputation and my finances."

"Let's start with your reputation. It's no surprise that I know everythin' about you. You figured out mighty quick you were under surveillance. But I think you can appreciate why the government had to do it. So, it should be equally unsurprisin' that I've read your FBI and NSA files in preparation for our lunch. Forgive my bluntness, but I know your past, your present, and most probably, your future. And given everything I've seen, I know you're . . . all right. It wasn't your fault. Certain parts of the government know that, too. However, let me be clear: That doesn't mean that you're out of the woods. People have been made scapegoats for far less. Politics is a brutal game, and you're just pigskin for our football."

A chill ran through Peter's body. Being spoken of so arbitrarily, as though his life and the truth didn't matter, reminded him why he had never liked politics.

The older man finally dug in to his steak. He enjoyed it tremendously, chewing with noisy gusto. "I won't lie to you, son. You're screwed. You've got good legal counsel, but that doesn't mean squat against the DOJ. And even if you are acquitted, you know your Psych 101. If I see a headline that says, 'Terrorist Suspect Found Not Guilty' and your picture's next to it, all I remember is 'Terrorist . . . Guilty' and your face." Josiah paused and took another mouthful of meat.

"So how would joining the club help me?"

Josiah noticed his cigar was near its end. He stubbed it out in the ashtray and removed a cigar storage tube containing another from his inner breast pocket. "Simply put, most of the people who'd mess with your life would do so for no other reason than to boost their own approval ratings back home. They see you as a steppin' stone to higher office. We can stop that 'cause you're a Phoenician now. I hate to be so bald about it, but there it is." From his hip pocket, Josiah removed a guillotine cutter and quickly and cleanly snapped off the head of the new cigar and flicked it into the ashtray.

Peter's meat didn't look so appetizing anymore.

Josiah lit his cigar and drew deep with great satisfaction. "Now on the financial end, the advantages to all of us are simple. Carter here tells me you two are goin' to buddy up on a new venture. I hope you don't mind, but he's told me a little bit about your idea, and I think it's just dandy. So one of the ways we reward our members for havin' dandy ideas is by financin' them ourselves. As you can imagine, the club has been around for a couple hundred years of staggerin' economic growth and amassed a substantial endowment of its own, which it invested into the companies of its worthy members from the very beginnin', not only allowin' some of the most successful corporations in history to come into bein', but bringin' back dividends into the club coffers."

"So would you compare yourself with, let's say, Harvard's endowment? What's that now, about fifty billion?"

Josiah cackled and coughed. "That's gimcrackery, son! Let's just say whatever you need, we can provide."

Carter leaned into Peter. "This is why you needed to talk to Josiah. It's one thing for me to say that I've benefited from this. It's another for him to offer it to you officially."

Carter's mysterious business history became clear. Why he wouldn't discuss his plans. Why he acted paranoid. Everything had been a big secret. Because it had to be. Carter's charmed life was courtesy of the Phoenix Club.

"Look at Carter. Look at all of us. Without the club as financial partner, moral support, or ideological guide, we might be midlevel bureaucrats. Or unsuccessful entrepreneurs. Instead, we're the Fortune 500 and the nation's leaders. And we stay that way. We believe you have what it takes to be one, too—if you're still interested in joinin' our little endeavor."

"It's an amazing offer, sir, really amazing, but with investment and ownership comes control. How do you control your companies? I've experienced being owned by someone else, albeit for a short time, and that loss of control and the subsequent loss of my company was a terrible experience. I never want that to happen again."

"The best thing that ever happened to you . . ." sniffed Carter.

"I have to agree with Carter, son," said the older man.

Carter leaned forward. "This is the kind of opportunity that rarely comes more than once in a lifetime, Pete. But I don't want you to think you're relying on our promises. It's all written in a proper contract, which you and your attorney will examine, and you'll see that the club is strictly hands off. And for good reason. If you're special enough to be asked to join, we believe you are more than capable of running your company as you see fit. Granted, some mistakes have been made in the past . . ."

Carter and Josiah shared a look, and Josiah sagely nodded and said, "You've read about them over the years. We do our best to mitigate the damage, but a train wreck's a train wreck. Even though we start off with the best information available, any organization can be taken advantage of from time to time. But ninety-eight percent of the time, we're correct in our assessment."

Carter leaned forward and spread both hands on the table. "You and I both know that we have what it takes to do this right. And the club is a silent partner, because they know after years of investing that groundbreaking, out-of-the-box innovation rarely comes from a committee process or anxious overseers. It still usually comes from individuals like you who experience the 'Eureka moment' and have the ability to see it through."

"Are the companies public or private?" Peter asked.

Josiah said, "Depends on the situation. Not only does the club invest its endowment, but individual members can invest in whatever business opportunities interest them. It's a remarkable investment pool."

"But if the company is public, isn't that considered insider trading?"

The two Phoenicians shared a laugh. "First of all," Brant pointed out, "few start out as public companies, so SEC laws do not apply. If they get so big or have a need for funds so large that it makes a public offerin' necessary, the chairman of the SEC is a member. Problem solved." Brant leaned over the table and winked at Peter. "But you didn't hear that from me." His eyes twinkled again. He was Saint Nicholas with the world's biggest checkbook.

Peter sat back, his jaw slack and his eyes slightly out of focus. The Phoenicians looked at each other, and Brant guffawed.

"I think we poleaxed our boy, here!" Brant said and slapped Peter's shoulder. Hard.

Josiah Brant was right. Peter's head spun. If he joined this club, what could be possible? And there was Carter. He was happy. He was successful. He had never indicated that the road he took was a difficult one. Just one he had to keep secret. If Peter could only make the choice to join and ignore what he perceived as questionable practices, he would be saved. They could start their family. And be happy. But what was the cost?

Brant stubbed out his cigar. He'd only smoked a third of his second one. "Maggie only lets me smoke two a day. Gotta ration these precious jewels out." He slipped the partially smoked cheroot into the tube and back into his jacket, patting his chest where the cigar lay. "A man must protect his petty vices from those who would relieve him of them."

"So what do you think?" Carter asked Peter.

"This has been a most . . . remarkable lunch. But I need to think about it."

"Such a careful man," said Brant. "That's no bad thing in this crazy world. Carter will speak to you tomorrow about it, and if you're still interested, he'll give you the time and place of your initiation, and he'll be there to hold your hand as your sponsor."

That stopped Peter. "What kind of initiation?"

Both men gave sly glances at each other and snickered, acknowledging an inside joke. Carter replied, "Don't worry. We haven't lost anyone."

Brant rose from the table and the young men followed. He shook Peter's hand with real warmth and sincerity. "Son, I'm sure by the end of the week I'll be sayin', 'Welcome to the club.'"

As Josiah and Carter strode through the room, the palpable power they exuded was enviable. Both made a couple of stops and waved or acknowledged others, but moved quickly to the front doors to collect their coats from the maitre d'.

Carter grabbed Peter's arm. "I'm tagging along with Josiah to a State Department meeting, as an industry expert. Not so coincidentally, it's about nano, and you'll be a topic of conversation. Do you mind getting a cab back?"

"Oh God, no, you both do whatever you have to. We'll see you at dinner. And Carter? Thanks, man."

Carter gave him a heartfelt smile, and Peter watched through the glass door as he escorted the secretary out to his limo and joined him in the backseat.

The maitre d' approached Peter. "Will you be needing a cab, sir?"

Grainy snow blew in gusts off dirty snowbanks, and the few hardy souls walking looked like they'd prefer a root canal.

California had made him soft and forgetful of East Coast winters. "Definitely. The Hay-Adams, please."

"I just called one for the Hay-Adams. It's right outside. Would you mind sharing?" The maitre d' nodded to someone behind Peter.

"Of course, it'd be a pleasure," said a female voice. He turned to see a beautiful, redheaded woman smiling enigmatically at him. It was the bombshell. From the ball.

CHAPTER FOURTEEN

They sat in the backseat, his hands kneading his overcoat's fabric until he saw his clenched fists and relaxed them. It wasn't only her beauty that made him tense. Sitting side by side, it was hard to look her in the eyes, but he had a great view of her legs. They were hidden last night under her long gown, but today she wore a short, fitted black skirt suit. Her ankle-length fur coat, which looked like sable, slipped open to both sides. Her legs, silky in sheer black stockings, crossed at the thighs. They were splendid legs: long, slender, and curvy, ending in high-heeled black suede pumps with girlish bows at the toes. But it wasn't just the sight of her that made his heart race. This woman crackled with energy. Cut off from the driver by foggy and scratched bulletproof Plexiglas, her vibe rattled around the claustrophobic confines of the backseat and stunned him.

She followed his line of sight and looked back up at him. Moving close, she whispered, "I can read your mind." Warm breath tickled his ear in the chilly air of the taxi. Hair on the back of his neck stood on end. And that wasn't the only part.

"You don't have to. What I'm thinking is obvious," he surprised himself by saying. "That's not mind reading."

She smiled. "But I *can* read your mind. For instance . . ." She studied him for a moment. Her frank gaze virtually undressed him. "You're . . . a . . . scientist or technologist of some sort?"

"So that proves you have ESP?"

She clapped her hands excitedly, like a little girl. "I was right!"

Was it possible she had never seen any news item on Biogineers or Bernhardt's involvement? "You're sure you've never seen me before?"

"Positive. Last night was the first time."

"Not even on CNN?"

"Nope."

"So how did you know I was in science or technology?"

"Elementary, my dear Watson." She scrutinized him carefully. "You're trying to fit in to DC, but you don't. Wrong shoes. Wrong shirt and tie. Wrong suit. It actually looks good on you, so it wasn't bought here. Your hair's too perfect—you had it cut for last night. And you run your fingers through it in a way that meant it used to be very long, very recently, so you'd work where long hair was acceptable. You don't believe in the paranormal. You're an observer, not an instigator. You have the remnants of a Tri-State New York accent. Maybe time on the West Coast? Oh, and I've seen you two days in a row in the company of a biotech venture capitalist who lives in San Francisco. But you're too old to be his type. And you've got a wedding band. So if I go for the cliché, you're a Silicon Valley biotech something or other who had to scrub up and make nice with the newly appointed natives. Although I'm still trying to figure out how Secretary Brant fits into the picture."

Peter twitched nervously, a fresh sweat breaking out. "That's definitely not ESP. You're a detective. Who *are* you?"

She raised her right hand in an oath, putting on a solemn expression. "I'm not a detective, I promise."

"And how do you know . . . ?"

"Carter Potsdam? Everyone inside the Beltway knows him. He makes sure of it," she said. "You seem to know him well."

"Yeah."

"Lucky duck. So . . . biotech . . . as a biologist . . . no, you're probably one of those interdisciplinary guys, like a biochemist or a biophysicist or something . . ."

He nodded. "Bioengineer."

"And what does a bioengineer like you do?"

"I can't discuss any details, but it involves a machine to decode and recode thought patterns. So I know a lot about how the brain works. And why ESP doesn't exist."

"You need multiple, double-blind experiments that confirm the same findings before you'll believe anything exists. I'm guessing angels are out."

He laughed in relief. "Damn straight."

"Then you must be missing out on an awful lot of reality because they haven't proven it exists yet to your satisfaction. Is it really acceptable to discount millions of people's personal experiences if they haven't been reproduced in a laboratory?"

"Yes, because unfortunately, the brain isn't a recorder to record reality. It tries to make sense of it, even if the input is completely random or, in some cases, doesn't exist. Déjà vu, synchronicity, telepathy, clairvoyance, are all the brain's attempt to make sense of chaos after the fact. You only think it happened before the fact because your brain needs to think so."

"And you have proof you're correct?"

"To be fair, no. It's impossible to disprove anything. But there's enough neuroscience research to build an adequate case for my hypothesis, in my opinion."

She recrossed her legs toward Peter. Her skirt slipped higher, garters peeking out. "Well, as long as it's enough proof to make you happy. It's going to take an awful lot of proof to convince me that I didn't experience what I think I experienced. Because what else do we have but experience?"

The way she said "experience" made him think not of the supernatural, but of something sensuous, tactile, naked. And involving a bed. More sweat surged out, and he twisted away in discomfort. A stranger might have a little flirt in a cab on a snowy day, but this woman was aggressively seducing him. His neck hairs stood up from fear, not attraction. The hotel loomed ahead, and he grabbed his wallet. She thanked him for paying.

Jackrabbiting from the cab, he helped her out of the seat and onto the icy pavement. She took his hand and locked eyes, not letting go when he slammed the door behind her.

"Would you like to continue our conversation somewhere private?" she asked. Apparently, more than scientific inquiry would be involved.

"Uh . . . mmmm . . . that's . . . a really . . . generous offer. I'm flattered . . . but, no, thank you. I'm . . . I'm very happily married, and my wife is upstairs waiting for me." He tried to shake off her hand, but she wouldn't let go. "Right now."

"By the way, I'm Angie Sternwood."

"Peter Bernhardt." It slipped out before he could stop it.

His name registered no pariah reaction in her face. Her full red lips made a lopsided grin, her eyes rueful. "Your wife's a lucky lady." She let go of his hand. "Good-bye, Peter Bernhardt."

Before he could say good-bye, she spun on her high heels and sashayed through the lobby into an open elevator without a backward glance. The doors closed. He caught his breath before taking his own elevator. Angie had gotten an awful lot out of him, while telling him nothing about herself, except her name and that she had a penchant for psychic mumbo jumbo.

Back in their suite, Amanda was working on the room's HOME, surfing the news between IMs.

"Hey, honey, how'd it go? Where's Carter?"

"He'll catch us at dinner." He flopped on the sofa, winter coat still buttoned. "Mind if I check something out?"

"Sure." Amanda handed him the handset.

He googled "Angie Sternwood." Nothing. "Angela Sternwood," "Angelica Sternwood," and "A Sternwood." Nothing.

"Who's Angie Sternwood?" she asked, as she curled up and laid her head on his shoulder.

"Some woman I met. Can't find anything about her."

He called the front desk. "Angie Sternwood's room, please." Moments later, the hotel operator said there was no one registered in the hotel under that name. He thanked her and hung up, reclining back on the cushions.

Amanda tousled his short hair. "Should I be jealous?"

"You? Oh God, no." There were a number of possibilities. The most benign was a bored DC trophy wife trolling for casual sex under a pseudonym. But she could have been an investigator, either governmental or corporate. Or an industrial spy. Or . . .

Amanda threw a leg over, straddling him, and grabbed his coat lapels. "Are you going to tell me, or do I have to torture it out of you?"

It took a moment for him to realize she meant the lunch meeting. "Yes . . . I mean, no . . . No torture. I can't believe it, but it seems most of Carter's success has been due to this club. We didn't talk specifics, but if I'm reading them right, they're offering me the full six hundred million dollars of investment as a private company, immediately, with offers of more money if needed and with Carter as my partner, with no interference. And somehow, miraculously, the government is off my back. Just like that."

Eyes wide and watery with relief, her hands covered her mouth, muffling her "Oh my God . . ."

"But these guys are talking about manipulating the SEC, insider trading, almost a government within the government!"

"How has that hurt Carter? And what about me? They'll send you to prison otherwise."

Peter sighed, kissed her forehead, then grabbed her GO, dictating a text to Carter as his wife kissed his face over and over. "Tell Brant 'Yes.'"

CHAPTER FIFTEEN

At eight o'clock sharp the next evening, Peter stood in his good suit and overcoat on the doorstep of a Federal-style mansion in the middle of Washington and rang the doorbell. The building blended in with the other white-columned, neo-classical buildings in the area that housed libraries, government offices, NGOs, and museums. This one had no sign in front, so Peter hoped he had read Carter's message right. A gray-haired butler, complete with wingtip-collared shirt, long black tie, gray waistcoat, and long black jacket with pinstriped pants came to the door. Peter introduced himself and was escorted to an early nineteenth-century library, where Carter waited in a wing chair with a glass of scotch. Volume-packed bookshelves rose on all sides, ending a few feet from the sixteen-foot ceilings. Around the room, a hand-painted frieze circling below the ceiling read, "'What's good for the Phoenix Club is good for America, and vice versa.' Henry Ford."

Carter stood and embraced Peter. "Are you sure you want to do this? It's . . . not easy."

"Yes. I'll do whatever it takes."

"Want a quick tour before the festivities?"

"I'd be a fool not to."

They strolled the ground floor. Portraits of past members looked down to chastise all who would dare enter the inner sanctum: club founders George Washington and Thomas Jefferson. Teddy Roosevelt and his cousin Franklin. Generals Patton and MacArthur. Jay Gould, Leland Stanford, and Henry Huntington. Booker T. Washington and W. E. B. Du Bois. William Randolph Hearst and Thomas Edison. Judge Learned Hand, Supreme Court Justice Thurgood Marshall, and Colin Powell. Albert Einstein and Henry Kissinger. Cole Porter and Irving Berlin. Every president of the United States. In a nearby hallway, there was a more subdued wall of photographs. Here, he saw women—Eleanor Roosevelt, Margaret Thatcher, Madeleine Albright, Hillary Clinton.

"I thought men's clubs were for men," said Peter.

"We award the women honorary memberships—especially a Brit like Thatcher—so they can use this clubhouse and get invited to various functions, but they're not initiated or invited to the annual campout. With over two thousand male members, it's such a bad boys' week, they wouldn't put up with our shenanigans, and boys do need an occasion to be boys. So don't worry. You can make as big an ass of yourself there as you'd like."

The diversity of the portraits was impressive. "So this wasn't a 'straight white man's only' club?"

"No. That's the beauty of secret societies—the membership is secret. In the case of the Phoenix Club, it was the only way for people on opposite sides of issues, or from differing backgrounds or lifestyles, to come together and talk and get to know each other without racists, bigots, or zealots using it against them. Political deals brokered, companies brainstormed, ideologies argued or conceived. More real history has happened here than probably any place in the country. Except maybe the Oval Office. Only no one knows about it, except the members."

"So what about this initiation no one wants to tell me about?"

Peter goaded. "Is there some little rite of passage or a speech for me to memorize?"

Carter sighed and repeated by rote, "As your nominating member, I'll lead you through the process and make sure you come out in one piece by the end."

"Yeah, you said that yesterday, but I thought it was a joke." Carter didn't answer. "Well, there can't be much to it. Hell, I can take anything that pussy Edison could've . . ."

Peter chortled heartily, but Carter didn't. They walked past the grand dining room. On its wall was a huge painting, done in the neoclassical style of Jacques-Louis David, of the Founding Fathers in Greco-Roman garb, set in the amphitheater of the Roman senate. Washington stood, in imperial toga, right arm raised, declaiming to the assembly. There was Jefferson, head resting in his left hand, appraising George with a cocked eyebrow. And Madison to Jefferson's right, dutifully taking notes on a parchment. And that was definitely the diminutive and choleric John Adams stewing in the corner.

Carter came up behind him. "It's by Charles Wilson Peale. Again, no one knows it exists. Not even Peale scholars. He was a member, too." Carter pointed out other faces. "That's Alexander Hamilton"—he pointed at a young, elegant gent posturing behind Madison, then indicated another diminutive man in the opposite corner from Adams—"before he shot him."

"Aaron Burr."

"Right." Carter continued pointing. "That's John Jay. Dr. Benjamin Rush. Richard Henry Lee. John Hancock. Oh, and there's Peale's self-portrait." Carter led Peter back out to the hall. "Do you know about the Masons?"

He meant Freemasonry, the international fraternal organization often thought of as a secret society. "Of course," said Peter. "But I thought they died out. And really, how seriously can you take a bunch of old geezers wearing fezzes, driving around in tiny clown cars in

Fourth of July parades while claiming they have the exclusive handle on Universal Truth? That's right up there with UFO abductees."

"Be nice. They're not dead. They're still around, and I'll bet a small but significant percentage of our membership are also Masons. The Phoenix Club has a kinship with the Masons because so many of the Founding Fathers were Freemasons. They created this club with certain structural similarities in ritual and values, but with very different mythologies and purpose. If I had to compare the two, I'd say our traditions are like . . . the Masons on acid. The initiation can be a bit . . . strenuous. But that's all I can say. I've said too much already." Carter stopped by an old elevator with a hand-operated cage. He opened the cage and gestured for Peter to enter, following behind to close the cage with a big brass handle.

"I'm sure I'll manage."

Carter pressed an old Bakelite "B2" button, and the elevator descended slowly. They passed a basement floor and continued descending. "You'll find what's under this building . . . extraordinary. When the builders of Washington DC were digging the foundations of the city, they found out not everything was a festering swamp. Jefferson was shown what you're about to see and decided the club would rest on this spot. It's one of the most important archeological finds of all time. And it will never be shared with the public. Our own members have done several archeological studies over the centuries and we've self-published them, but only club members can read them here in the library. It's a shame. Consider yourself fortunate."

After a surprisingly long time, the elevator opened into a large wine cellar, floor-to-ceiling bottle cubbies on all sides. Carter walked to a cubby and grabbed a bottle of wine, but instead of lifting it out of its diamond-shaped slot, he yanked and pushed it back like an organ stop. The wall of wine swung open. The B-movie stunt should have been goofy, like Carter leading a tour of Disneyland's Haunted Mansion, playing on countless movie memories of mysterious walls opening into dungeons. But this felt creepy and real. And if everything was over two hundred years old, this was built before those horror stories were written.

"Carter, was Edgar Allan Poe a member?"

"Yeah. But I hear he was a handful."

They passed into an anteroom with walls that contained the narrow doors of many closets and one half-sized door opposite the entrance. It reminded him of a hobbit door or *Alice in Wonderland*. Carter opened a closet, picking out a white bundle from a shelf to hand to Peter, who opened it. The fabric didn't make any sense to him.

"It's a toga," said Carter. "I'll show you. Take off everything, including shoes, socks, underwear." He opened another closet, which had a pole with hangers on it. He handed a couple to Peter, then began removing his own clothes. When Peter was naked, Carter handed him a long white linen tunic to pull over his head. He folded, draped, and wrapped the plain white fabric of the toga around Peter and tucked the end of the fabric in front. Then Carter put on his own costume. His looked like a Roman senator's toga, more regal and flowing than Peter's, but instead of the white with purple trim of Imperial Rome, his was black with red trim. Like the Founding Fathers' portrait in the dining room. His friend looked like an escapee from a production of *Julius Caesar*.

"*Et tu, Brute?*" joked Peter.

Carter put his finger to his lips and beckoned to follow through the tiny door, which was eighteenth-century woodworking on one side, but opened into rock and dirt on the other. They crouched through the small opening, and as Peter slowly rose, he beheld the most remarkable place he had ever seen.

The cave was limestone, with a natural domed arch through the ceiling's center. The sides had a few stalactites and stalagmites, but not many. Whatever water had seeped into the cave in antiquity was long gone. The ground had been leveled for ease of walking, and it formed a space approximately one hundred feet long by seventy feet wide. The center of the cave ceiling disappeared about thirty feet into the air into what looked like a dark hole. He couldn't tell if it was a geologic or man-made chimney. The natural cathedral was lit dramatically with torches along the perimeter. And it was very cool, around fifty-five degrees Fahrenheit. That was a bit chilly to have one's balls blowing in the breeze of the toga's updraft.

Peter moved to view the ceiling and walls. They were covered in ancient cave paintings of sacred rites. The slaying of the bison. The hunting of the bear. A hunter mauled by a giant cat. The death of the warrior. The choosing of the chief. The birth of the tribe. And the megafauna! Creatures that could only be giant sloths, saber-toothed cats, and mastodons shared the walls with bison, bear, and protohorses. These were paintings to rival the caves of Lascaux and Altamira. He moved slowly, his mouth agape in awe. He could barely get out, "It's all genuine?"

Carter grinned and whispered, "Right down to the last bit of ground ocher and charcoal."

It felt like the navel of creation, as though human existence began right here. Its potency shook Peter to his core. And its importance. This cave alone could completely rewrite the history of archeology, anthropology, and art in North America.

"This changes everything!" Peter gasped.

Carter put finger to lips again, pleased to see the cave's effect. He whispered, "I've always wanted you to see this. Jefferson loved his noble savages."

Only then did Peter notice ten men, dressed in the same toga Carter wore, except the last turn of fabric hooded their heads to hide their faces in shadow. The figures said nothing, moving as one to form a semicircle in front of Peter and Carter. Another Todd Rundgren song, "Initiation," flooded his memory, warning him of hidden power and unknown rituals.

"These are the Decemviri, the ten members who have achieved the highest rank of membership," whispered Carter. "Stand right here." Then his friend reached behind him and grabbed a glass goblet from a small wooden table, held it high to the Decemviri, and in a reverberating voice said, "Drink of the Assaratum, blood of brotherhood, and the mysteries of the Phoenix shall be revealed."

With ceremonial flourish, he presented it to Peter, who held the goblet close for inspection. The liquid was dark red and slightly viscous, like blood, and he couldn't help grimacing with revulsion. Carter gave him a "Trust Me" look.

A voice boomed from the center of the Decemviri. "Do you flout and ignore our rules already? Or do you approach this sacred ceremony with the sincerity and reverence it demands?" The Southern drawl was an awful lot like Josiah Brant's.

Carter whispered in Peter's ear, "That's the Praetor Maximus. He's the leader and chief initiator. Do whatever he or I say."

Peter knocked back the goblet in as few gulps as possible. Ghastly taste was followed by a burning sensation down his throat and esophagus. It certainly wasn't a Napa Valley cabernet. He gagged, struggling to keep the concoction down. Carter snatched the glass back before Peter dropped it.

"Step forward, candidate!" boomed the Praetor Maximus.

Peering into faceless hoods, he thought he recognized a face or two from the inaugural ball, but couldn't be sure.

"Who dares bring such an unworthy candidate before the Decemviri of the Phoenix?" accused the Praetor Maximus.

Bowing low and gracefully to the ten men, Carter declaimed, "I do. I am Carter Linus Dickinson Potsdam. Praetor of thirteen years and Quaestor of five years standing."

Peter did the math. Carter went through this same ceremony in graduate school. Could that even be possible?

Carter continued, "I nominate Peter Bernhardt as Praetor candidate and humbly present him for your judgment."

"We accept the nomination and henceforth, you will be responsible for the education and behavior of Peter Bernhardt both within the confines and outside the jurisdiction of the Phoenix. Do you swear to uphold the standards and values of the Phoenix and pass these on to this candidate?"

"I do solemnly swear." Carter bowed again and backed up behind Peter.

The Praetor Maximus turned to Peter. "George Washington, Thomas Jefferson, and Alexander Hamilton saw the transformation of the colonies into the United States of America as a momentous event. The American Revolution held the promise of not only political and social renewal, but personal renewal as well. That is why the Phoenix Club was created; to renew and reinvigorate our nation by nurturin' the best and the brightest. We put ourselves in service of our countrymen and women, regardless of race, religion, or background."

The "in service of our countrymen" sounded great to Peter, although some of the phraseology was a little more nationalistic than he felt comfortable with.

Then he lost feeling in his hands and feet.

The Praetor Maximus continued, "For more than two hundred years, our members have gone to unimaginable lengths to protect this country from all who would harm her. But now we live in a more challengin' time. Empire takes on a different meanin' for us than it did for our forebears. Do you love your country?"

The question surprised Peter, and suddenly the entire scene, surreal to say the least, turned menacing, especially when his rubbery lips resisted obeying his brain. "Yes."

"What did you say?"

Like a soldier in boot camp, his throat still aflame, he yelled, "I love my country!"

"Pledge allegiance to the flag." The Praetor Maximus pointed to the large American flag hung above the altar.

His arms numb and detached from feeling, Peter placed his right hand on his heart with great effort. It pounded fast in his chest. The only thing going through his head was the song, "My Country, 'Tis of Thee." Shit! That wasn't it. He searched dizzy childhood memories. "I pledge allegiance to the flag of the United States of America." Needing oxygen, he took a deep breath. "And to the republic, for which it stands . . ." Could he get the rest out? " . . . One nation, under God, indivisible . . ." His tongue, thick and wooden, stumbled over the words. ". . . with liberty and justice for all."

"You are not worthy!" bellowed the Praetor Maximus.

Peter hadn't noticed Carter holding a wooden staff. His friend bowed to the Decemviri, then swung the staff back like a baseball bat, slamming Peter below the knees.

Peter sprawled on to all fours on the cold stone floor. Torchlight spun around him. Even with numbness, it hurt. The scene went from surreal to terrifying. While Decemviri jeered, he cowered.

Carter's concerned voice whispered in his ear, "Hang on, Pete. It's only a play, and you're the lead. Just roll with it." He dragged Peter to his feet, but the room spun.

The Decemviri's laughter abruptly ceased and the Praetor Maximus asked, "Does Peter Bernhardt still wish to become a Praetor of the Phoenix?"

Between the pain in his shins and the vertigo, everything was fuzzy. He concentrated on keeping vomit down and holding on to Carter's arm . . . Carter . . . Carter was there to protect him. A few old farts humiliating him to make their day had to be the worst of it. Didn't it? His pop always said to finish what he started.

He lifted his head. "Yes."

"Repeat after me," said Praetor Maximus.

While trying to stand on legs that hurt too much to bear his weight and with drugs that filled his system with nausea and numbness, Peter repeated the following:

"I, Peter Bernhardt, do solemnly swear that I will uphold the laws, rites, and traditions of the Phoenix Club and keep all I know of this august body a secret that I will take to my grave. Furthermore, I will, to the best of my ability, preserve, protect, and defend both the Phoenix Club and the United States of America against all enemies, foreign and domestic; that I will bear true faith and allegiance to the same; that I take this obligation freely, without any mental reservation or purpose of evasion; and that I will well and faithfully discharge the duties of my membership on which I am about to enter: So help me God."

The Praetor Maximus replied, "Peter Bernhardt, you have replaced every loyalty you have ever sworn with that of the Phoenix Club. The Phoenix is foremost in your heart and soul. To prove your loyalty to the Phoenix and commit to the death of your old life, step forward to the altar."

How did he just swear that his club was more important than his country? He couldn't remember.

"Ready to let go?" murmured Carter. Peter's head swam, but he nodded. Unsteady, he concentrated on the toga fabric that threatened to entangle his legs at any moment. Disturbingly, cave drawings appeared to move, in a *This Is Cinerama* panorama around the cave. Bison thundered, warriors ran, and chiefs danced. What the hell was in that damn drink?

The semicircle of men appeared to double and split down the middle to reveal a stone altar (or two?) in the center of the room, sitting on a wooden plinth that looked like a Jenga game of railroad ties. On the brown-stained altar's top, a live bald eagle was bound by its legs with a leather strap laced through a metal ring drilled into stone. The bird was a prisoner.

"Take this." Carter placed a ceremonial knife made of iron, with a wrathful Roman god carved in silver and ivory on the handle, in Peter's hands, but his fingers were numb and he could barely hold it. His sight was so drug affected, the majestic bird and its twin flapped before him. If it had been only one, it would have been a damned big bird.

"With the dagger of Jupiter, slit the throat of the eagle and bathe in its sacred blood," ordered the Praetor Maximus, who stood next to Peter.

"Wh-what?"

Carter stage-whispered, "Kill the eagle."

That couldn't be possible, thought Peter, his brain as sluggish as his body. It was so beautiful. And enormous! The eagle, its great yellow eyes darting, and white head weaving, sensed its own demise and flapped wildly in panic. Dodging the animal's tremendous wingspan, Peter tripped on his dangling toga and fell on his ass. Two Decemviri hoisted Peter up.

"Kill the eagle!" roared the Praetor Maximus.

The loud voice disoriented him, and he wasn't sure if the eagle was friend or foe. As he halfheartedly swung the knife, wings kept him at a distance. A Praetor snatched the ceremonial blade. The eagle was still trying to attack Peter when the Praetor Maximus snuck up behind and grabbed its great white head. Before Peter could stop him, the Praetor Maximus slit its throat. Bird blood sprayed from its neck all over Peter's face and chest, covering his white toga in spots and rivulets as red as the Praetors' togas.

"You will suffer the fate of those who break the oath of obedience!" roared the Praetor Maximus. Four men broke ranks and grabbed Peter's arms and legs. Carter tried to help, but the Praetor Maximus and another Praetor restrained him. The altar, with the great bird in its death throes, was covered in blood, and the remaining four lifted the top off. It was a sarcophagus.

The dark interior gaped before Peter. The bottom, which he could barely see in the torchlight, moved and writhed, another hallucination. They hoisted him up and dropped him inside. Peter screamed, "Carter!" as the lid descended with a thud above, the scraping of stone tight against stone as it settled into place.

Peter hyperventilated in the pitch blackness, a hair's breadth from panic. Something slithered against his wrist, and another flicked gently at his cheek, and what he thought was a mattress wriggled. It wasn't his imagination. He lay atop snakes. Screaming, he shoved hard, palms against lid, but the toga tangled his arms, fell on his face, and he couldn't gain leverage to shift the lid. The darkness cleared his mind, no longer confused by lying, doubled sight.

The outer silence was broken by a faint crackling sound. The sarcophagus felt warmer. Snakes grew twitchy and slithered faster. He struggled to free the fabric wrapped around him. And he smelled a faint, familiar odor—burning wood.

They'd set those railroad ties alight beneath the sarcophagus. It wasn't an altar. It was a funeral pyre.

And the snakes weren't happy.

Frantic, he pulled into the tightest fetal position he could, planting palms and feet under the lid. And pushed. Sweat flooded his eyes. Snakes slithered across his face. Air grew thin. He had one good shove left. Or it was over. Mustering every last ounce of control over his numb body, he pushed upward, straining every part to move the stone. Light, air, and smoke seeped into the coffin. He quickly stuffed toga fabric between the lid and the rim. His fingers struggled outside to find purchase along its lip, but drew back in pain. The lid was hot. He wrapped both hands in more fabric and thrust them through the gap. Cupping the edge, his feet gave an almighty shove. The lid slid off and crashed to the floor.

Flames licked around the coffin's lip. He struggled to his feet. Above him was the flag. It was at least four feet out of reach. He bent down and grabbed four snakes, placing a couple under each foot to protect him from the hot stone and flames as he stepped on the rim. The sizzling, exploding snakes squished under his toes were disgusting, but the flag was still out of reach. Balancing precariously on the tomb's slick edge as the flames licked his robes, he squatted, gathering all his energy. He had only one chance. If he fell down, he'd plunge into flames, or break his legs or back on the tomb. He jumped, extending his arms, reaching for the flag . . . reaching . . . and caught the end in both hands. He hung on for all he was worth.

The world spun. His legs baked, the edges of his toga aflame. Hoisting himself up the flag as far as he could, he flailed his legs and arched his back to swing, needing momentum. His burning toga ignited the bottom of the flag. He swung once. The room tumbled in his sight. Twice. Three times. His hands started to slip. He needed one more big swing to arc past the flames below. As he flew toward the center of the tumbling, twisting, turning cave, he let go.

It was a fast crash to the stone floor, still slick with eagle blood. His feet slid beneath him and he fell hard on his ass. Then he rolled around in the blood, slapping down his flaming toga. Extinguished, he collapsed in a heap. Just when he thought his ordeal was over, dark ash fell from the ceiling chimney, dowsing the altar flames and covering him. His robe was no longer white. It was black from smoke, charring, and ash and red from blood, completing his transformation.

The men emerged from their hiding places, applauding Peter, chanting, "Our Phoenix is reborn. Our Phoenix is reborn. Our Phoenix is reborn," but Peter couldn't hear them.

He had passed out.

CHAPTER SIXTEEN

A thousand rampaging elephants thundered past, jolting Peter's bed from the ground. He tried to open his eyes, but the lids were crusted closed. His hands came to their aid, hitting his nose and cheeks before finding eyes. He rubbed, picked, and finally pried them open. His bed was the backseat of a limousine; the rampaging elephants the suspension running roughshod over DC's famed potholes.

Carter sipped a whisky, cool, collected, and amused. "I know I've said in the past that you've looked like shit. I was wrong and I apologize. Now you really look like shit."

Lying as still as the bouncing allowed, Peter took an accounting of his body. Both arms. Both legs. And though he wished it weren't true, his head. At their worst partying, he never, ever, had experienced a hangover like this. Shifting, his shins screamed in pain as pants fabric rubbed against bandaged burns. His arms ached, his fingers and feet felt on fire, and he wouldn't have been surprised if all his lower body hair were singed off.

And the smell. Beyond sweat, blood, smoke, and God knew what else, he reeked of whisky, but didn't remember drinking any.

"What was in the goblet?" croaked Peter. His voice was gravel low and filled with phlegm.

Carter smiled his most devilish grin. "A tasty little cocktail of ketchup, tequila, peyote, a soupçon of Sodium Pentothal, and just enough ketamine to really fuck you up."

He was thankful he was still alive, imagining at least a few candidates over the years had had serious reactions to that brew. "Why didn't you warn me?"

"If I'd told you the truth, your far more sensible brain would have insisted it was stupidly dangerous and not have joined. And if you hadn't acted exactly the way you did—disoriented, afraid, panicked—they would have known I'd spilled the beans and broken the rules. And you don't want to break the rules. Trust me."

Peter tried to nod in agreement, but his head pounded.

"You know," said Carter, "different people solve the 'problem of the burning man' in different ways. Some pass out from the drugs or heat or fear of snakes, or they're too weak to open the box and the fire burns out, and we get them before they suffocate. If they pass out, some wake up thinking they died. Supposedly Bess Truman screamed her ass off to convince Harry this wasn't the afterlife. Could you imagine Amanda? She'd fucking have my ass."

Peter wanted to laugh, but everything hurt too much.

"Some candidates strip off their toga and dampen the fire with it. Common in the nineteenth century, but not so common now, except from former Boy Scouts and firemen. I hear more than a few members tried to piss on the fire, thinking that would put it out. I was pretty proud of your 'superhero' approach. We'd taken bets, and nobody, including me, thought you'd go there. So congratulations." He took another slug. "What made you think of it?"

"Todd Rundgren. 'Initiation.'"

"And what made you think of the brain-computer interface concept?"

"Rundgren again. 'Born to Synthesize.'"

Carter shook his head in disdain, muttering under his breath, "How the fuck do you do that with such shitty taste in music?"

"How'd you get out?"

"My life of excess inured me to the more vicious drug effects. I knew the worst that could happen was I'd pass out from lack of air. I didn't think they'd let me die. And I was right. Anyway, this is important. Your oath of silence is real. You can't even tell Amanda what happened. I certainly won't." Carter smiled to himself and took another sip of whisky.

"Okay, but answer a question: How could you be a member since grad school? You were a snot-nosed research assistant who had his ass wiped by Nick Chaikin, just like the rest of us."

Carter shook his head at the naïveté. "Not everyone comes from a humble manger like you, Pete. Remember that painting of the founders? Well, my ancestors were among them. There've been Potsdams, Reeds, and Dickinsons in the club for two centuries." His glass was empty, so he poured more whisky. "Did you know the term WASP—White Anglo-Saxon Protestant—was coined to describe my family and neighbors? My family knew the 'right' people all over the world. Eventually, a few thought I should join the club early. They considered my contacts, interests, intellect, and ambition and decided early membership was the best way to cultivate my talent for trend forecasting. They felt my access to Silicon Valley could be the basis of a great company for me, the club, and the country."

"Jesus," whispered Peter. "I've known you for seventeen years. Why don't you ever talk about this stuff?"

"Come on," scolded Carter. "First of all, the club's secret. Second, you were raised to believe social class doesn't determine your future. And then there's the California factor . . ."

"California factor?"

"Do you honestly believe that in California, the land of milk and honey and reinvention, a guy like me gets points for being a WASP prince? Only snobs and bigots care about that shit, and if you haven't noticed, they're in shorter supply in California than in other parts of the country . . . Thank God."

"Hey, I would have given my left nut to be you when we met," blurted Peter. "But you're not hiding too well. You're still the best-dressed and most-connected guy I know."

Carter tilted his head and lifted his glass. "Thank you. But the connections? Well, that comes with the territory. Clothes? I don't know if that's about being gay or well-bred, but we Potsdams have style. Whatever it is, it stops with me. I'm no breeder, and I'm not looking for the 'right wife' to continue our dynasty. Hell, I don't even want a househusband, and it's a real pisser my family can't admit to themselves I'm queer. They pretend I'm choosy for all the 'right' reasons. Hey, whatever gets them through the night." Carter looked tired. He took another slug and laid his head back on the leather headrest. "Their rarefaction is a fucking pain in the ass, but I guess it gave me a foot in the door at an age when most guys were still figuring out how high they could get on a Saturday night without dying."

"Are there lots of 'legacies' like you in the club?"

"If you're asking if we're all inbred aristocrats, no. We're not. It's not what makes a person important in this country. Again, it's a foot in the door. But that's it. American royalty is just another celebrity shell game that sells *Vanity Fair* and *Town and Country* and *People*, which sells fashion, transportation, entertainment, and real estate; unless of course, your daddy makes a fortune for the right people and they make you president of the United States. New Money, Old Money, wherever it comes from, still makes this sorry-ass world go round."

"Clearly. But I've got one more question."

"I'm loose. Shoot."

"What happened to the eagle?"

"Stage trick. We drug the bird and use a hidden sack of blood. Pretty effective."

"Bullshit. Josiah killed it. They're endangered."

"Sweetheart, you were so high that bird could have been John Wayne in drag. And they're not endangered anymore. Someone raises them for us at the zoo. Really," Carter soothed, "the eagle's fine. There's nothing to worry about."

"But my snakes were toast."

Carter sighed. "My dear, we can't fake everything."

At 5:00 a.m., the limo arrived at the Hay-Adams, and Carter half carried Peter up to their suite. Amanda was worried sick when they hadn't returned by one o'clock and dozed lightly on the sofa in the living room, waiting to hear the door open. Seeing Peter, she was furious, assuming the obvious: old-boy networking, with too much liquor and not enough sense.

Carter, halfway to drunk, was very convincing. "You should be proud of him! We were in a bar fight, and you should see the three policy wonks he flattened!"

Both men played their guilt-ridden roles to the hilt, and Peter didn't have to pretend he would never do anything as foolish as this again. He swore to her over and over, and Carter apologized over and over. Peter had never lied to Amanda before, but he put that thought aside.

After collapsing on the bed, he almost told the truth. But something stopped him. He liked the secret. Being a giant bruise wasn't fun, and he'd need to recuperate for a few days, but in retrospect, the entire evening had been a great adventure, and if Carter and Josiah were correct, it would save his life. The curtains were closed against the rising sun. Half listening to Amanda berate Carter one last time, he remembered a few more lines from Rundgren's song before drifting off into a well-needed sleep . . . The world revealed . . . Peter Bernhardt finally understood why men join secret societies.

PART TWO

CHAPTER SEVENTEEN

The moment he returned to Silicon Valley, Peter felt like a human cannonball propelled into space, flying high over the crowd. Within days, Carter structured their new company on paper, with a business plan, budget, and timeline the likes of which Peter couldn't fathom. They filled a slick, nameless, glass cube on Sand Hill Road with equipment that existed nowhere else on earth. In addition to former Biogineers alums—Amanda as head of public relations, Chang as chief engineer, and Jesse Steinberg as chief programmer—they let Ruth go shopping for the greatest minds of each link in the intellectual and technical work chain at academic and corporate institutions (including the *shaigitzes* from Stanford's cognitive computing department and the bloodstream nanogenerator team from Georgia Tech), offering salaries no one could match. With experimental results expected so quickly, Peter didn't think the schedule could be met, because it never had before.

Employees needed a mental adjustment to work for Peter, the Valley pariah, destroyer of nanomanufacturing. So he made sure they saw the company's whole, concentrating on Carter and Ruth, and the access each had to the wide variety of specialists necessary in such an interdisciplinary undertaking. There were neuroscientists, computer scientists, cognitive scientists, material scientists, molecular biologists, electrical engineers, biomedical engineers, and specifically, neural engineers. It was biotech heaven.

The next year was a whirlwind of round-the-clock activity, made possible by the largest (and best) biotech team in the world; no government, academic, or industrial oversight; and more money than God. The Phoenix Club gave never-ending support to Prometheus Industries in a Manhattan Project for brain-machine interfaces. And it eliminated all possible impediments by helping to scoot around sticky nano-ban issues with waivers from the Department of Homeland Security and the National Institute of Health to work with nano-sized components, and using Carter's own company's nanowires, which hadn't been banned. In fact, much of their technology was unaffected, since the ban was about nanoviruses or nanobots, not chips and wiring. However, they did have molecular assemblers in a subbasement that fell under the legislation. But no one was going to turn them in. Certainly not to the head of the NIH, who was a Phoenician. While Peter understood that his company was only possible through influence and corruption at the highest levels, he justified its actions as important to humanity. It was the brutal game of politics, finally mobilized for the public good.

Peter decided not to ask exactly how this was possible. He would ignore his squeamishness.

At least Carter let him name the company after his favorite Greek myth. He believed his work would be as beneficial as Prometheus's fire, granting his patients independence. Identity. Life. And so from a dream's ashes, Prometheus Industries was born.

Time was too precious to participate in any Phoenix Club activities. He missed his first Camp Week, embroiled in a technical problem involving proteins that wouldn't bind to polymers like they were supposed to. But Carter told him it was better to wait until they had impressive results. Come to camp a star, not a plebe among thousands.

Prometheus Industries had two goals: a prosthetic hippocampus, "Hippo 2.0," and a prosthetic neocortex, "Cortex 2.0," to replace the parts of the brain destroyed by Alzheimer's. Short-term memories recorded in the Hippo 2.0, instead of the damaged hippocampus, would be transferred, stored, and retrieved in the Cortex 2.0. Like a replacement hard drive for the brain, the Cortex 2.0 was a replacement long-term memory bank linked to the real cortex, so the patient could retrieve both mechanical and meat memories. Both prosthetics would be imbedded in the patient's skull and linked by nanowires to specific neural pathways. Parts of the brain destroyed by disease could be made whole.

Even though work was 24/7/365, the cocoon of Prometheus made Peter feel more in control, more secure. And he finally kept his promise: When the couple realized pregnancy might not be as easy for them as they thought, he was there for Amanda's IVF treatments, injecting nightly hormone shots and holding her hand during implantations. And it had all paid off. Amanda was pregnant. They kept the happy news to themselves, although it was hard making excuses when Amanda ran off to vomit.

Peter would have gotten excited about impending fatherhood if he'd had the time to think about it. Prometheus had succeeded at tissue studies, rat studies, and primate studies. There was no reason to believe that human trials would be any different. After a year of no sleep, all his mental energy was focused on implanting a prosthetic hippocampus chip into the first human subject. It was supposed to be his father.

But the FDA said that was not to be. They rejected all of his prospective patients, pending further investigation of his animal studies. The timetable was ruined. And they didn't seem moved by either Carter's protestations or club interference. Carter heard there was pushback from the pharmaceutical lobby in DC, and he flew back East to handle it. The word from Capitol Hill was Big Pharma would neutralize Prometheus and their revolutionary products, determined to bury the technology in regulatory hell until the pill manufacturers had a product to replace it.

Peter panicked. Screw the FDA. He had to save his father and his company, and he was damned if he was going to stop now.

CHAPTER EIGHTEEN

As soon as Carter returned from DC, Peter tracked him down in the Prometheus rec room. CNN played in the background. A headline banner proclaimed the passage of new anti-privacy laws to root out internal threats from groups like ATEAMO. Peter wasn't paying attention, but Carter watched the screen with a whisky in his hand. It was only noon. Not a good sign.

"Well?" asked Peter.

"I'm working on it. Big Pharma's more powerful than I thought."

"Work faster."

"I'm working as fast as I fucking can. Give it a rest." Carter sounded tense. And pissed.

Peter changed the subject. "I need you to answer honestly. Does anyone spy on us?"

Carter sighed. "Not that I know of. Why?"

"It's eerie. I feel like . . . someone's always behind me. Watching me. I know it's stupid, but it's how it feels."

"Well, you were spied on for so long by the government, either you've fine-tuned your sixth sense or you're knee-jerk assuming the worst."

"Maybe . . . Don't take this the wrong way, but does the . . . you know who . . . spy on me?"

His friend looked at him askance. "Why would they need to? We've got complete transparency with them. That's why I don't understand this FDA bullshit. We shouldn't be back-burnered. I'm here, protecting everyone's interests, and I'm high enough up the food chain to be their representative both ways." He leaned over and whispered, "Trust me, I tell the Decemviri everything. More than I should."

Peter nodded. It sounded reasonable to him, but ever since the mysterious Angie Sternwood, coincidences played on Peter's mind, and he wondered if he was rightly paranoid.

Carter put a finger to his lips and listened to the screen, so Peter listened, too. In a press conference, Senator Mankowicz called for further investigations and sanctions on technologies related to 10/26.

"Fuck you, you Pharma whore!" Carter yelled at the screen. "How many times do we have to do this dance?"

It was rare to see Carter lose his cool. "I thought you said he stopped because he lost bipartisan support since Pat Davidson dropped out."

"I did! But this FDA thing is giving him steam. I am so fuck-ing tired of the same Goddamned fight with this asshole. Just when I think I've got him cornered and cut off like a rat, he pops out another hole with a camera in his face. I've got to get to the Wash-ington press corps. Cut him off, cold-fucking-turkey. See how Pharma likes that . . ."

He might have been naive, but Peter wondered how Carter could do this.

Rattling glass revealed Ruth rummaging in the fridge behind them for a bottle of the latest cubicle speed.

"Hey, Ruthie?" asked Carter, trying to calm down. "Is Peter being spied on, or is he just paranoid?"

"Papa used to say p-p-paranoia was an occupational hazard. Always someone is watching you. Remember the lab pools?"

"Yeah . . . Didn't Nick always assume it was the Soviets or Russians or whatever they were at the time?"

"Or the Americans. He traded one m-master for another."

"Which left the rest of us to bet on the Chinese, Israelis, Iranians . . ." Peter ticked off.

"Now," said Carter, "we'd add the EU, Singapore, Japan, India, Pakistan, Korea—North and South—Islamic Jihadists, the big multinationals, who are as powerful as any country, if not more, and God knows who else. Any money ever change hands?"

Ruth shook her head, adding to other tics. "No way to prove who. Just that it existed. So it's not whether you're paranoid. It's whether you're paranoid enough."

Carter rolled his eyes. "You *are* Woody Allen's cousin."

She twitched in annoyance. "Our p-people have proved throughout history. Better paranoid than dead." She tossed the empty bottle into the recycling bin for emphasis and left.

Peter gave Carter a good-bye punch in the shoulder and followed her out. Ruth always walked very fast. She said it evened out her tics, but Peter suspected she preferred to avoid others through speed. He had to hustle to catch her as she turned a corner.

"You my pace car now?" asked Ruth.

"I need your help. I want to test a healthy subject."

Ruth walked faster. "You have a w-w-war with the FDA. And you want to do something as *meshugeh* as that?"

"I'm not crazy. The FDA is stonewalling us. Nothing Carter does works. I know him. He's pissed because he thinks we're beat, but he won't say it. The FDA could keep us waiting for a decade. We're dead men walking, unless we can show the world how good this is."

"Prometheus cannot operate on anyone without FDA approval."

"Fuck the FDA. We need to prove this works—now. Or Prometheus is dead."

"And who is *meshugeh* enough to volunteer?" She walked right by the elevator.

"Me."

"Your brain is not normal." Ruth burst into the stairwell, climbing two at a time with ease. Nervous energy and a fear of enclosed spaces made her a stairwell champion.

Peter panted behind. "Normal enough for government work."

"Ha, ha. So, what? You think you're Alexander Shulgin? Or Albert Hofmann? Giving your neurons to science? Since already you gave your life? This is no acid trip on a bicycle! And what about Stanford Hospital's institutional review board? You can't have elective brain surgery. *Meshugeh ahf toit!*"

Peter assumed that meant more than just plain crazy. "You know how much self-experimentation goes on. What about Werner Forssmann?"

"*Feh.* That was 1929. Ancient history."

"But the guy had balls! Could you lace a urinary catheter through your antecubital vein and into your heart all by yourself? Then run to the X-ray machine to show the world what you did?"

"You want to lose your job? And your reputation? Like Forssmann? Again?"

"The guy won a Nobel Prize . . . Eventually . . . You know we wouldn't have half our discoveries if scientists didn't put themselves on the firing line first, to prove they're right, before endangering a patient. And who's gonna volunteer for brain surgery if they don't need it?" They emerged from the stairwell and headed for her lab, Peter puffing. He was out of shape from overwork.

"Ach! You said 'endangering.' I didn't."

"And I think I can convince the right people at the hospital this isn't covered by the IRB."

"Why not have Carter do it? He's so good at convincing," said Ruth, badly feigning innocence.

Peter muttered, "He wasn't enthusiastic when I mentioned it hypothetically . . ."

Ruth couldn't raise just one eyebrow. Her entire forehead twitched madly.

"Okay! He said he can't have me dead or incapacitated or needlessly risking myself, and him, and the investors, yadda yadda yadda . . ."

"Even if we did," Ruth interjected, "you have no objectivity. It's your invention. How can you report on results? If you can assume outcomes?" She looked into a biometric eyepiece, and her door clicked open. Peter followed, and the door shut automatically behind them.

Her lab was relatively simple, filled with half a dozen computer workstations. Ruth and her team conceived the individual interface structures in this room. The nanofabricator labs next door worked on building them in reality. It was empty for brunch hour. They had worked all night.

"You'd rather have some poor *schmuck* go first?" asked Peter. "Who knows how many years from now? We have to break the FDA stranglehold! Our patients—and my father—don't have much time left. Or this will all go away!" He gestured around the room.

Ruth's left eye twitched as it followed his hand. "And what will your pregnant w-w-wife say?" Her expression couldn't hide her disappointment that he followed the pleasure centers of his limbic system and not his intellectual cortex when choosing a partner.

"She can't know about this."

Her smirk twitched. "Implant just Hippo 2.0? Or Cortex 2.0 as well?"

"Both. The C-2.0 is programmable-ready. I can activate it later, when we've finished the computations."

"Always *Herr Umgeduldik* . . ." chastised Ruth.

Peter stared blankly.

"Mr. Impatient, P-petulant. If we're gonna do this, you need automatic language translation. In the chips. Ask the *shaigitzes*. They can figure it out. I can't repeat myself all day!"

"'If we're gonna do this . . .'?"

"Yes. We have a blood covenant. We work with each other. Forever. I could not deny you this. But . . . I have conditions . . ."

He was afraid of that.

"You are my partner," she continued. "This is my research." Her index finger stabbed repeatedly at his forehead. "That is mine now."

"I don't understand." For the first time, he wondered if she was mentally disturbed. And what would an unbalanced scientist do, tinkering inside his head? "I'm yours?"

"*Feh*. Amanda can keep your body. I get your cerebral cortex. I decide what gets done. And when."

"I can't give you that kind of power over me."

She tried to shrug fatalistically, but her shoulders bounced up and down. "Then Pharma wins."

"I could fire you!"

It was the first time he could recall seeing real surprise in her eyes. "N-n-no. I am too valuable. And many are here because of me. And we have a blood covenant."

She was right on all counts. He couldn't. "So what would you let me do?"

"Both surgeries. As soon as possible."

"Then why are we even arguing?" he yelled.

Ruth's left leg vibrated. "I like you *verklempt, boychik*." She reached out as if to tousle his hair, but her own wiring yanked back her shaking hand midair. A one-sided grin betrayed the eternal push-me-pull-you of her oddly firing brain. "Almost got me there. But your brain is still mine. And we will not tell Amanda.

I don't want a . . . p-pregnant . . ." she said as though imagining the disgusting intimacy and bodily fluids necessary, ". . . woman attacking me."

"Definitely not. And we can't tell Carter."

"Agreed," said Ruth. "Dozens of people have to know. But they cannot." She sat at her terminal and turned away from him.

"Thank you, Ruth." He would have squeezed her shoulder, but she might have screamed.

Ruth didn't answer him. She was already absorbed in computer simulations of molecular-sized synthetic neural structures. He turned to leave. On the wall next to her, Peter saw the photo from Ruth's old Stanford lab of Nick, Peter, Carter, and Ruth, no longer hidden away. It was clear that Nick was holding Carter more tightly to his person than he was Peter, as though he liked Carter more. Peter had never noticed that before.

CHAPTER NINETEEN

S ecrets can be hard to keep from the ones you love, but Peter persevered. This was the second secret he had kept from his wife during their marriage. When he realized he had degenerated into a husband who kept secrets, it disturbed him, but he rationalized it as necessary for the greater good.

But Peter had bigger issues than whether his wife and partner were opposed. On the news, all over the world, anti-nanotech rhetoric was flowing thick and fast. Some countries, like the United States, had confiscated all nanofabrication equipment and halted all research and development the year before but were still debating all-encompassing perpetual bans or embargoes on nanotechnology of all stripes. Others, like China, Israel, and the Koreas, sent their researchers underground to avoid international pressures. Senator Mankowicz continued to urge a broad nanotech ban in the United States. It looked increasingly as if Prometheus's technology would never pass the FDA or public opinion. Furious at the shifting sands of governmental policy, Carter flew once again to DC to lobby the FDA, club, and congressional members (who were often the same people) and to muzzle the press corps through misdirection and promises of access, to protect whatever nanotech he could.

Before Carter flew off to wrestle the many-headed hydra of Washington, Peter convinced a reluctant Amanda to visit girlfriends in New York City for a weeklong shopping trip. She'd felt depressed about her awkward, changing shape and irrelevant wardrobe. Peter used her need for female bonding time to its fullest extent.

Ruth held up her part of the plan. With Peter's fMRIs and CT scans secretly taken before his wife left, Ruth prepared the components to be implanted with the departments necessary, keeping as many people on a need-to-know basis as possible. It was now or never.

CHAPTER TWENTY

Ruth sat in the waiting room at Stanford Hospital. She had a signed document allowing her the right to remove the Hippo 2.0 and Cortex 2.0, just in case Peter Bernhardt emerged mentally incapacitated. Clutching it in her hands, she watched Peter and his doctors and nurses live on her GO. But she could not keep still, only catching a glimpse of the screen every few seconds.

While brain-computer interface chips would be buried in Peter's brain to fuse with his neurons, the short-term memory Hippo 2.0 and long-term memory Cortex 2.0 receivers would be embedded in his scalp, so they didn't overheat and cook delicate brain tissue. By keeping them just under the skin, they were easily accessible should any changes need to be made. In addition, the Cortex 2.0 prototype would be partially external for easy updating. A magnet connected an outside receiver to his skull and the receiver was attached to a wireless, mobile hard drive the size of a pack of cigarettes. Peter could pocket the hard drive or wear it around his neck. This backup brain's processor and memory was also programmable with Prometheus's computer systems, allowing for easy software updates as the technology evolved. It also held power generation outside the head, because the bloodstream nanogenerator they were using couldn't yet generate enough power for the external processor, only the internal parts of the Hippo 2.0.

Eventually, as the device size continued to decrease and he had proved his concept worked, the hard drive would be small enough to be attached discreetly to the skull and, finally, under the skin itself. Future patients could have the prosthetics and no one would ever have to know.

As they wheeled him into the operating room, the chief of neurosurgery, a gangly man with black hair that stood straight up under his surgical cap, stopped the orderly. "Sure you want this, Pete? You've got nothing to prove." He bent close to Peter. "You, of all people, know the risks involved. But I still feel obligated to give you an out."

"If I'm not willing to walk the walk, I'd never let anyone else do it. And I can turn the damn thing off or have it removed if necessary." He didn't voice his concern that two functioning hippocampi and cortex systems might make him psychotic.

The surgeon gave his team the thumbs up and followed the gurney into the operating room. As they prepped him, every reason why he shouldn't be there flew through Peter's head. But his last thought before chemical twilight descended was he hoped his wife and best friend would forgive him.

An army of activity wheeled around Peter's brain. There was the neurosurgeon, leading the implantation team; a neuroanesthesiologist, who kept him in a painless twilight during the scalp incision and removal of a keyhole in his skull, but otherwise awake; a neurologist to monitor the surgery and make sure no damage was done; a computer engineer to coordinate the robotic and computer-guided systems linking Peter's MRIs to the surgeon's pointer as he operated; as well as nurses, assisting residents, and interns.

Peter's skull was braced by four prongs of a square stereotactic head frame screwed to his scalp, which not only kept it immobile, but helped the small robot sitting at the side of Peter's temple to reference the 3-D coordinate scans inside and outside his brain, finding the perfect location to insert the instruments through the keyhole. The neurosurgery team could rest assured they were working on the correct location for the prosthetic with the help of the fMRI-programmed robot literally leading the way with its own probe entering the brain tissue.

Bundles of nanowires followed, each about one one-thousandth the diameter of a human hair, linking the Hippo 2.0's nano-scaled bloodstream generator in the basilar artery to a chip. The chip's individual transistors would attach directly to existing brain cells through liquid polymer connections formed around the neurons, which would grow onto the chip to integrate into Peter's brain.

They woke Peter after they opened his skull so that if they adversely affected any neural areas, they could spot it in his behavior. Lying there motionless was the most nerve-racking six hours of his life. The only questions he kept asking himself: Am I still sane? Am I still me?

CHAPTER TWENTY-ONE

I t was lonely recuperating without Amanda, Carter, or even Pop at his side. His only visitor, not including his doctors and nurses, was Ruth. For such an unusual woman, incapable of physical contact or affection, she was a welcome sight, tics and all.

After the post-operative inflammation subsided, Ruth said she would bring a *shaigitz* from computing, sworn to secrecy, to help check the neural connections and turn on the unit. In this case it was an Indian American colleague named Bino. Heavyset, with large, expressive eyes and an ever-ready grin, he brought a laptop to wirelessly program the chip and test it thoroughly.

After running the gamut of troubleshooting software, Bino said, "That's it, bro. H-1 locked and loaded. C-2 in snooze, awaiting new programming."

Ruth paced and twitched beside the bed. "So how feels *mein Übermensch*?"

"Not much like Superman. I know I shouldn't have expectations, because I don't have any input, but . . ."

"You expected a bigger bang."

"Yeah. Stupid. Of all people, I should know better."

"No. Just romantic. Come, Bino. *Mein Übermensch* needs rest."

"Ruthie? Will you come back in the morning?"

Peter's plaintive tone almost made Ruth smile. "Of course. You will have things to tell me tomorrow."

Uneventful time passed. He napped. He ate bland hospital meals. He listened to music, checked his correspondence, and returned calls on his GO. He watched the news, but refused to watch movies, since the tiny GO screen reduced anything visually worthwhile to ants on parade and gave him a headache.

Peter had to maintain a fiction with Amanda and Carter as to his whereabouts and remembered why lying was hard: you had to remember all the lies you told before. The chip could help with that! He told his wife and partner that he was at work, doing his normal routine. A handful of Prometheus employees would back that lie up. Carter and Amanda didn't behave as though they thought anything was amiss.

He didn't want to dwell on what might happen if his secret was discovered. Carter would be furious, but he was too invested in the process to abandon Peter. But a pregnant Amanda? Beyond hormonal rage? And uncontrolled weeping? She might walk out on him—at least for a while. Was his little experiment worth losing his wife, even for a short time? He was determined not to find out.

Carter's texts said he was making headway in DC. The *Washington Post* agreed that without additional congressional support, there wasn't much of a story in the Mankowicz nanotech press releases, and they'd move them from the front page to the inside pages in exchange for an exclusive interview with Carter to be determined later, regarding the social and political ramifications of Prometheus's research.

And finally, Peter slept. And dreamed. And that's when it happened.

A functioning hippocampus dumps the day's remembered events into the neocortex during sleep. But the brain doesn't remember everything, because information is prioritized and the hippocampus helps determine what is important. The unconscious decides based on the strength of associations with other things we know, which corresponds with well-traveled neural pathways in the cortex—because the neurons that fire together wire together. That's why you remember the important business meeting you scheduled and the teacher's comments about your child's poor grades, because they are associated with concepts you have already thought about and deemed important and have a strong neural pathway for them, but you don't remember the hairdresser's telephone number or an ignored conversation on the train, because they weren't important and there were no preexisting memories to attach them to. If you remembered everything, your brain would fill up with garbage.

Peter's new hippocampus was taking everything in and not prioritizing it, just as an Alzheimer's patient would need because the prosthetic did not know which pathways and associations were lost, to be created anew. Even though his own hippocampus was sorting and assessing just fine, the Hippo 2.0 kept everything in backup, just in case. He remembered it all, from Carter's verbatim GO texts to the smarmy news anchor's puke-cutesy dialogue with the weatherwoman. And when his Cortex 2.0 was functional, he'd have a place to dump it all.

He dreamed, not reshuffled thoughts dropped into the nonsense logic of the dream state, but huge blocks of real information, cut, shuffled, and pasted like editing a computer document on methamphetamines. He extracted meaning from their juxtaposition, seeing patterns where none existed before. Whether they were relevant to his (or anyone's) life, or simply random, like millions of monkeys striking keyboards and inadvertently typing a Shakespearean sonnet, was anyone's guess. The color of Strawberry Jell-O on his meal tray met the red of the suit the weatherwoman wore, which met Amanda's text about a red, jeweled Indian-style tunic her girlfriend made her buy, and Bino, who was Indian American, had worn red Converses. His dream, which he couldn't forget, was a collusion of redness overlaying other thoughts, as though redness were a clue to his existence. But what did it have to do with reality?

And the music! The GO shuffled all day, from Feist to Nine Inch Nails, from R.E.M. to Johnny Cash, and everything played back in his dreams, a soundtrack over the images and meanings.

When he awoke with complete recollection of the dream trip, he was concerned. If all the information created by processing and deconstructing his one, very boring, nonproductive day occurred every night, then how crazy would his dreams be during important, urgent events? Could he selectively keep some information and dump the rest? If not, would all that information make him insane?

He made sure he discussed it with Ruth the next day before the doctors sent him home. Ruth told him, *"Medarf vartn un zayn."* Wait and see.

CHAPTER TWENTY-TWO

Peter picked Amanda up at Oakland Airport. He was retrieving her bags when she spied a Prometheus-logoed baseball cap on his head.

"What's wrong?"

"Nothing . . ."

"You've never worn a hat in your life."

He knew it wasn't the best moment to break the news about his brain surgery and patted the top of his head. "Oh, yeah, I found a bump, and a dermo at Stanford cut it out. Nothing serious, just forgot to tell you. He said I should be more careful about the sun." The keyhole procedure still had a small bandage over it. He'd keep it covered until some hair obscured the larger incision.

Amanda squinted at him as he put the bags in her Mercedes's trunk.

"How about, 'Hi, honey! I missed you so much!'" He put his arms around her, holding her close as he whispered in her ear, "'Cause I missed you more than you know. Think the baby's up for a little X-rated action?" Her swollen body melted against his, and her head nodded on his shoulder. He'd find the right time to tell her the truth. Just not now. And he'd make sure the bedroom was extra dark, so she wouldn't notice his skull.

Driving home, cumulus clouds cruised the sky overhead. Oddly ovoid in shape, they floated at both low and mid levels of the atmosphere. Higher clouds moved across the sky more slowly than lower clouds, so a nearby cumulus appeared to overtake and consume a more distant one. In his head, he heard the Flaming Lips play "Suddenly Everything Has Changed" and he remembered a conversation with Ruth about future nano-medical applications. Here was the answer, as he imagined a nanobot that could swim through the bloodstream and act like Pac-Man, reeling in bad bacteria, viruses, and other pathogens; consuming them; and destroying them. He could program artificial white blood cells to find specific organisms, like many identical locks in search of the matching keys of disease, to cure a systemic infection within hours. Or even simpler: What if the ovoids were messengers and carried stuff from A to B, like artificial red blood cells, but carrying much more oxygen than real cells. You could administer them to heart attack or drowning victims to prevent brain and organ damage. The medical applications for these bots were so numerous, it made his head spin. Eureka-tingling all over again, he couldn't wait to have Ruth run a computer simulation.

CHAPTER TWENTY-THREE

As Carter promised, Senator Mankowicz and the media went quiet about nanotechnology. There would be no new bans—at least for now. Peter believed if he could show the public his positive experiences, it might turn the tide of public opinion.

First stop on his PR campaign: his own investors. Josiah asked Carter and Peter to present their latest work at the next club Camp Week in July. There was great curiosity about it, even though there were no human trials yet. Peter told Carter he'd handle the club presentation. He planned to hide from everyone that he was the case study until then. The Prometheus programmers were nowhere near reading all his thoughts precisely. But club members would see the potential if he impressed everyone with his own transformation. Of course, it would mean admitting his deception to his partner and his wife, but once they saw his triumph, they'd understand.

Every department worked overtime to get the Cortex 2.0 ready, not realizing the mysterious "investors' presentation" would be for two thousand men at a camp in the Sierra Nevada. Days flew by in a whirlwind of cold coffee, pizza boxes, and bedding on office sofas and floors.

"Why'd you do it?" asked Carter as he closed Peter's office door behind him.

"What?" Peter scanned his daily financial update on his monitor, while Radiohead's "No Surprises" played softly in the background. They had received a cash infusion from the club, and he was double-checking the numbers. The Hippo 2.0 made it much easier to find discrepancies instantly and discuss them with Finance.

"You lied to me. How'd you think I wouldn't find out?" Carter wore a new expression, an odd combination of anger and pity.

A wave of guilt flip-flopped Peter's stomach. "I'm sorry . . . I didn't want to hide it from you. But you were adamant, with every argument nailed to the wall—and you were justified. I had to do it to save the company." He rolled back his chair. "If the FDA guys at camp see how well this works, they'll have to play ball. This will save Prometheus." He loosed an enormous sigh. "I'm relieved you know."

Carter slumped forward on the sofa, devastated.

Peter hurried to his friend to sit beside him. "I've been dying to tell you. We succeeded! The implants are awesome. And I'm working up a presentation that'll blow Camp Week sky high."

"You don't have a fucking clue what you've done, do you? You've jeopardized everything, Pete! Everything! And for what? A little showmanship?"

"Look, I'm sorry you're so upset. I really am. You know this is the only thing I've ever hidden from you, but I had to do it. There was no one else I could do it to in good conscience. You've got to believe me. Just . . . promise me one thing."

"What . . . !"

"Don't tell Amanda. Let me."

"In what part of that motherfucking cyborg skull of yours do you think I'd do something as self-destructive as telling Amanda *you* lied to her and I found out before *she* did! You may not, but I value my fucking relationship with her!"

Carter stood and flung open Peter's door to storm out, slamming it into the wall and spraying plaster dust. Adjacent cubicles went quiet, as employees wondered if they still had jobs.

Peter's GO rang. It was Amanda.

"Pete?" She sounded scared.

"What's wrong?"

"Come home . . . ." She muffled a sob. "I'm bleeding . . ."

CHAPTER TWENTY-FOUR

There wasn't much to do, except make sure the miscarriage was complete. After the D&C, Amanda shivered under the blankets in Stanford Hospital's recovery room, partially from anguish, partially from bodily shock.

Even though he wasn't sure he believed it himself, he kept telling her, "It's no one's fault. We'll try again," on autorepeat, searching his mind for any fault, running through everything she did, said, ate, since her return. And no patterns emerged; no culprit shook its shaggy beast head. At least not yet. He kept running through his memories.

"If you'd been home," she mumbled. "Maybe I could have gotten to the hospital quicker . . ."

"Honey, don't . . ." He took her cold, trembling hand in both of his.

"You're working too hard. You're not yourself," she said.

"What's that mean?"

"You've changed. Ever since I came back from New York. I wondered if you were having an affair . . ."

"Jesus, Mandy, you know me better . . ."

". . . but that wasn't it. Jessica's husband was having an affair in New York, and I had to hear about it ad nauseam. That wasn't it . . ."

He let her talk. He didn't want to say the words first.

"You're just . . . different. So much going on. You talk in your sleep. You never used to. Like you're replaying some mental tape you made." She looked at his hair growing back from the surgery and, pulling her hand from his, ran her fingers over it. Her face fell. The mushroom cloud of understanding reflected in her eyes scorched his. "Please . . . tell me you didn't . . . please, Pete." His guilty expression betrayed him. "Oh, God! Why? Was this Ruth's idea?"

"Baby, I'm sorry, I'm so sorry. This isn't how I wanted you to find out. You know I've never lied to you . . ."

"You lie to me every fucking time the Phoenix Club comes up. You're a fucking liar!"

"But that's . . ."

"All these lies . . . You're destroying us. Destroying our family. And you know what? Ever since Biogineers ended, you made me a liar, too. You know that? I lied to you, too!"

Peter blinked rapidly, as though flicking eyelids could brush away visions plaguing his brain. "What . . . how?"

"Do you honestly think Carter would have come rushing to our aid, guns blazing, if I hadn't told him everything? That day you went to lunch? He knew all about your plans with Ruth. Everything. He knew he could save you with the right business opportunity. And I told him yours. That's why he moved heaven and earth for us! We needed his help, and your big idea was the payment. I thought having him as your partner would stop this stupid shit, like you being a guinea pig! I thought everything was perfect . . ."

Peter spoke, barely within the threshold of hearing. "How many other lies . . . ?"

"You men are fucking eggshells. You've got egos for shit. I knew if I told you, you'd think Carter was doing you a pity favor and turn him down. Or you'd think I put words in his mouth. No, you had to make him do the whole dance . . . prove his loyalty, his belief in you . . ."

Two years spooled backward, during which his wife and his best friend had manipulated him without his knowledge. "How many other lies have you both told me?" Rage exploded. Emotions spun around and around, and recorded memories played at top speed. He couldn't stop the tornado of fury. His new, indelible memories wouldn't let him.

Her strangled laugh surprised him. "Who just got caught having secret brain surgery?"

He shook more violently than she. He hadn't lost his temper like this since Lobo and Biogineers. Disgusted, he sprung from his seat, desperate to escape.

She reached out. "Stop acting like we've betrayed you! We just wanted to help. We love you. Please, Pete. Come over here. Come . . ." She patted the bed, and he reluctantly stepped near her. "I'll forgive you, if you forgive me. Please, baby . . ."

His voice choked with regret, devotion, and pain. He said, "You're the only people I've ever loved other than Pop. And you ganged up on me! I've . . . got to go out . . . for a minute . . ."

He fled, running down the hospital hall. It was awful leaving his wife alone when she needed him, but he had to leave because he was afraid of what he might say. Might do. How could a woman, whom he loved beyond words, manipulate him like that? Was it really so bad? His hurt was knotted up with a nameless paranoia he couldn't release. Had his father's rage been like this? He knew his brain clung to the negativity because of his augmentation. But why? And another question swirled through the anger: Was he being paranoid enough?

CHAPTER TWENTY-FIVE

The repetitive memory of his wife's anguish and their mutual deception haunted Peter. Concentrating on the Cortex 2.0 helped as the work's complexity displaced some pain. Amanda worked from home. She didn't want to face coworkers' questions or pitiable silence, and the combination of antidepressants and anxiety medication made concentration and driving difficult. He also suspected she didn't want to spend more time with him than was necessary. Desperate to have her back to normal, but equally glad for space, Peter begged her to take it easy.

Two weeks before the camp deadline, Peter sat in the lab with Ruth, Carter, Chang, and Bino, as Bino ran diagnostics and tests on Peter's processor. So far, so good. It picked up signals, recording and responding to them from both the Hippo 2.0 and Peter's own neurons.

"*Vi gait es eich, mein Übermensch?*" asked Ruth.

"Got that Yiddish-English dictionary loaded up yet?" Peter joked to Bino.

"Nope, but can I add a Hindi one, while I'm at it?" Bino quipped as he typed and clicked commands. "My grandmother talks to me like I should understand her. You can chat her up for me, least till I get me one o' these."

"Why bother? You'll all be learning Mandarin soon enough." Chang's modestly contained smile couldn't stop the twinkle in his eyes. "Peter will have a head start on you all. He only has to listen to the tapes once."

"I'm waiting for the direct download," said Peter. "Hey! That's our new ancillary business. Direct educational downloads. Just in time for the investors. *School's out next quarter!*" he crooned like Alice Cooper.

While everyone else groaned, Carter snorted derisively, even though the time for protest had long passed. The equipment was working, so what could he say that his body language didn't? Expressionless, he leaned against the wall, arms crossed over his chest, one leg crossed over the other. It didn't take a behaviorist to see he wished he could distance himself from what he still believed was unacceptable risk to both the company and his partner. Peter had tried to warm the chill between them over the last few weeks, and it appeared to be working, until the tiny objects of their disagreement became the focus once more.

"I asked, 'How are you doing, my Superman?'" translated Ruth.

"Good. Again, like last time, nothing momentous to start."

"You've got nothing important to remember or process yet," explained Chang. "Just wait until you've got a lot of information coming at you. Parallel systems working independently, in tandem. Then hang on!"

"Rock and roll . . ." said Peter. His GO rang. "Bino, you done yet?"

"CYA, dude. You're technically locked and loaded, but I'm just backing up. Can't have Superman flying 'round in ripped undies."

Peter checked the number flashing on the GO screen. It was Reception, probably trying to track him down, so he ignored it.

Too much personal capital rode on this working perfectly with his wife and his partner. "By all means, man, cover both our asses." He turned back to Chang. "How much will we have to teach it to work, meaning do we need a rehabilitation protocol? Or will it just pick up neural slack one day when I'm on Mr. Toad's Wild Ride?"

Carter's GO rang and he answered, "Potsdam . . ."

Chang replied, "There may be a functional difference between Cortex 2.0 as a therapy versus enhancement. Given your preexisting, highly connected brain, as opposed to an Alzheimer's patient, I'm guessing you'd need sensory . . ."

"*Shit!*" Carter sprinted out of the room, yelling, "Peter, get out of here! *Now!*"

Everyone was startled. Peter leapt up. "Where are you going?"

The diminishing voice down the hall cried, "Lobby! FBI! They've got a warrant!"

CHAPTER TWENTY-SIX

Running through the offices, Peter couldn't help but wonder if the feds had a warrant for all that "illegal" equipment in their basement. But it didn't account for the fear in Carter's voice. He dashed after his partner, gripping the Cortex 2.0 processor in his right hand, and burst into the lobby to face three FBI agents with guns drawn swiveling toward him. He skidded to a stop and threw his hands in the air, showing them he only held a tiny gizmo.

"It's all right!" shouted a man in a blue suit, wearing a black bulletproof vest with "FBI" emblazoned on the front and back. The agents lowered their guns. Moments before, the same man had been talking to Carter, whose tennis-tanned face looked sickly green. The agent flipped open his badge and said, "Agent Derek Struthers. FBI."

"What the fuck is this?" blasted Peter.

"Where is Chang Eng?" asked Struthers.

"I told you. He's upstairs in the computer lab!" insisted Carter.

"I'm asking Mr. Bernhardt." The agent's laser-like focus never left Peter's face.

He remembered his attorney's advice: roll over and cooperate. "Um . . . yeah . . . I just left him there. Why?"

"We have . . ." but men shouting outside interrupted Struthers.

Peter ran to the glass entry doors.

Outside in the parking lot, a row of six identical black Suburbans created a barrier and shielded a flak-jacketed agent with a megaphone. Next to him were a dozen similarly attired agents lined up with guns and rifles drawn. Megaphone stared at the opposite end of the Prometheus building from Peter, then yelled through the horn to someone unseen, "Stop! Drop the weapon and put your hands in the air!"

Chang ran from the building's far end, holding a gun.

"What the fuck . . . !" Peter burst through the doors onto the concrete path outside, desperate to reach Chang and stop him.

Carter tried to haul him back inside. "Pete, don't!"

"I repeat," yelled Megaphone. "You are surrounded! Drop the weapon and put your hands in the air! Or we will shoot!"

The three lobby agents rushed Peter and held tight as he struggled in vain, unable to see what was happening.

A single gunshot erupted from his friend's direction.

"Chang!" screamed Peter.

A percussive hail of bullets drowned out all else. Then he noticed something strange. While the rounds were firing at the same rate, they seemed drawn out, as though he could hear each shooter choose to pull the trigger and each bullet choose to explode from the barrel.

When the firing stopped, the agents released their hold, and Peter ran into the parking lot. Everyone moved as if under water . . . but why? Chang's bullet-riddled chest gradually leaked shiny-red blood onto the pavement. No one let Peter near. Shooters moved cautiously to the body, guns still drawn, yelling commands, as one of them checked for vital signs.

Chang Eng was dead.

Peter lost sight of the body as agents closed in around it.

Agent Struthers tugged his arm, guiding him back to the building in slow motion. "Mr. Bernhardt. We need to talk."

CHAPTER TWENTY-SEVEN

Peter officially hated conference rooms. Especially his own. But this experience was different from the debacle with Bruce Lobo. There was no bad guy to fight. Instead, one part of his mind was here, present, listening to Agents Struthers and Gualardi deconstruct events for him and Carter. And the other kept reviewing the traumatic events he just witnessed . . .

"We knew fifteen months ago that the 10/26 bots came from inside the country," said Agent Struthers, "after analyzing the design and manufacturing techniques of Biogineers and its competitors in Asia. Which left only Biogineers, or an employee of Biogineers, implicated in the attacks. You, as well as every one of your former employees, have been under surveillance for some time. . . ."

"No shit."

". . . and Mr. Eng was extremely good at covering his tracks, which is why his identification took so long. I'm sure you can understand why we had to be sure. I'm disappointed we couldn't take him into custody, but when arresting a suspect involved in such an unthinkable act, it would be foolish and dangerous to give him the opportunity to do something potentially lethal to our agents or yourselves."

Carter kept shaking his head the entire time. "But why would he do it? Chang was the nicest, most low-key, apolitical guy I ever met."

"And I worked with him for over a decade. I know him. He's not the guy. You killed an innocent man," said Peter.

Struthers continued, "He wasn't innocent. He ran out with a gun. We also established a clear link between Chang and ATEAMO. Apparently, he was sympathetic to their cause and was paid handsomely for his complicity."

"Where and when did he make the bots?" demanded Peter. "How did he transport them? Who were his contacts? Who paid him? Come on, guys, give me something I can get my hands around. Otherwise, this is bullshit."

"You'll have to be debriefed at a higher level than me, sir."

"That's no answer," hammered Peter. "And if you knew fifteen months ago that the bots came from my lab, why weren't we helping you look for the suspects?"

Struthers looked at Peter like he was a slow learner. "Because Biogineers and Prometheus are still under investigation."

"But you claim you caught your guy!" said Peter.

"There may be more conspirators," replied Struthers. "And we have reason to believe there is unauthorized use of technology going on in this building."

"What unauthorized use?" asked Carter.

"If it's here, we'll find it," said the agent.

Peter could have sworn Struthers was looking right at the incision in his scalp.

CHAPTER TWENTY-EIGHT

The partners briefed their staff with what little they knew, then sent everyone home for the remainder of the day, with the exception of the IT department. Unfortunately, those poor bastards had to work with the FBI. Agents swarmed Engineering and Chang's office, taking hard drives, copying company servers, and generally pissing Peter off. Ruth and Bino stayed behind to tell Peter that the moment after Peter ran from the lab, Chang did as well, disappearing down the nearest stairwell like a panicked jackrabbit.

The partners retreated to Peter's office for a private meeting.

"I swear to God I didn't know this would happen. I swear it, Pete." Carter hunched on Peter's office sofa.

Peter paced. "You had the contacts to find out . . ."

"Contacts only work if you know what you're contacting them for. I wasn't wandering around DC asking, 'Is the FBI going to raid me?' Josiah must have known we'd be raided some time before today . . ." This disturbed Carter, and he hunched even more. "But how long did he know? And if he did, I have to believe he kept us in the dark for a reason."

"I don't know how Chang pulled it off. You really think he was a terrorist?"

"Since Waco, the FBI usually don't kill people by mistake. The press is too harsh. And who can cover up a shoot-out in a Silicon Valley parking lot in broad daylight? But . . . he did joke about us all learning Mandarin . . ."

"Oh, please, anyone with half a brain jokes about learning Mandarin," Peter said. "Why shouldn't Chang? My God . . . I can't believe he's dead . . ." He tried to roll his pained neck loose as he paced in ever-increasing spirals. "But why'd you assume the worst? What'd you think was going on?"

Carter didn't reply for a moment. He looked out the window at the hills above Stanford and took a deep breath, apology heavy in his eyes. "Remember the warrant rumor at the Inauguration? I thought the feds changed their minds and were here to arrest you for 10/26. And no one would have told me. Everyone knows if I had any inkling you'd be arrested, I'd have had your and Amanda's asses on my plane to a nonextradition treaty–country so fast, it would make their Beltway blockheads spin. Fuck 'em. Fuck 'em all." Carter lay out on the sofa and threw his legs up on the back. He closed his eyes. "I need a drink so badly, I'd sell my mother to organ harvesters."

Agents stalked the halls outside Peter's door. "I'm going home. There's scotch there. And Amanda's having a freak-out . . . though who knows what kind with the crap she's on. She'll want to see us both."

He shut off the lights and followed Carter down the hallway, past a suited agent rifling a file cabinet. The agent's hair was the same color and cut as the preppy kid at Stanford who may or may not have been a federal agent himself. And what about the others following him? Or could he now add delusional to his list of post-op mental quirks?

That night, his dreams were more intense than ever before. His mind twirled and whirled, drifting deeper into the maelstrom of fantasies.

Chang ran into the parking lot, but Peter stood behind him, pointing a 9mm at his back, riddling Chang with bullets to stand over his body with the smoking gun. Then it was Peter who ran, and Chang who shot him full of holes. FBI agents appeared robotic, free-floating, interchangeable.

Peter awoke in terror, fixating on one detail: the color and flow of Chang's blood. There was so much, so red. Peter knew he was obsessing, reviewing, and rewriting events in repetitive anguish. As he lay hyperventilating, he realized the more his adrenaline surged, the more his extreme stress slowed down his perception of time. Even though this happened to everyone, so their brains could think quickly enough to survive, with the addition of the Hippo 2.0, no perceived detail could be lost. Was this mechanical access to memory like near-death experiences, when victims said they reviewed their lives? What would watching his life pass before him feel like? Did he do the right things? Did he do enough? Was becoming something more than normal worth saving his technology? Peter still believed so. Except for his dreams, being a cyborg felt great. Empowering. More complete. As a neuroscientist, he had to accept that Peter Bernhardt was his brain. His brain's changes meant he changed.

He was not the same man Amanda had married. He was more.

He fell back asleep, but awoke a few times more from traumatic dreams to reach out and grab his sleeping wife, to hold her as a comfort, but even though he wrapped himself around her soft, warm body, she had taken a Xanax before bed and didn't wake up.

CHAPTER TWENTY-NINE

The southbound traffic on the 280 flowed, and the late evening sunset in the July sky cast the yellow hills and dark green oaks with an orange glow that made the dried grasses appear to be lit by fire. The Corvette flew at eighty-three miles per hour in the fast lane. It had been one week since Chang's death. Listening to news on the old Corvette's radio, Peter heard a headline: "10/26 Terrorist Part of Chinese Cell." The report claimed Chang Eng was a long-sequestered mole and covert operative for the Chinese government.

"Oh, for fuck's sake!" yelled Peter. He was fed up with anything the government said on the subject. A White House spokesperson said the government had evidence China was supporting ATEAMO. "Who believes this crap?"

Of course, he was responding to the radio while making mental packing lists he could not forget for the Phoenix Club Camp Week.

At least the news didn't mention the Prometheus connection, unlike earlier reports. Between Amanda's press releases and Carter's contacts, the media dropped the subject. Carter was already at camp for committee meetings to, as he put it, 'prepare the way for Peter'— including multimedia display systems for the demonstration.

In front of him, a Ford Taurus swerved suddenly. Peter slammed his brakes and with his new ability to slow down perceived time when his brain flooded with adrenaline, calculated the rapid deceleration on the freeway's inside shoulder. But the Vette's left wheel well clipped a bent guardrail. Veering to correct, he smashed into the Taurus. Luckily, he had slowed the car enough to avoid injury, and no one was behind to sandwich his rear. He leapt out to confront the Ford's driver, passing his Vette's hood. The front end was shattered, but that was fiberglass for you.

A woman emerged wearing a white diaphanous top with a tiny white camisole underneath, tight blue jeans, high-heeled sandals, and a schoolboy's cap that failed to completely contain her wild red hair stuffed into it. It was Angie Sternwood.

Rage, confusion, and déjà vu swamped him. "Who the fuck *are* you?" He backed Angie against her opened door.

She didn't look threatened. She looked concerned. Pulling a business card from her back pocket and handing it to him, she said, "I'm sorry, but my name's not Angie. It's Talia Brooks. I'm a journalist. Go ahead and check me out. I'm sure you tried and failed already."

He grabbed the card, read it in a second, and threw it back at her.

"I know this is an unconventional way to meet, but you're under constant surveillance at your home and office. And we need to talk . . ."

"Why not pick me up and try to fuck me? That was a pretty effective introduction. Who knows? I might even say yes this time."

She shook her head. Even she knew his bluster was bullshit. "Please. Listen to me. We don't have much time. A traffic satellite's going to pick us up any minute. You're involved with a group of very dangerous people . . ."

"You're nuts . . ." he said.

"Just hear me out! Then write me off. But hear me, first. You're going to the Phoenix Club Camp tomorrow. I know what you're going to do there, and it's connected to why you don't need to keep my card. You'll remember it. And every word and sensation of this conversation."

Peter's face betrayed his shock.

"I know. And I'm telling you that you can't go! Cancel the trip. Tell them this accident injured you. Tell them anything. Just don't go. Or . . ."

"Or what?" he sneered.

"You might not come back."

He stepped away from the woman, as if from a bad smell. "You are crazy."

"I'm not. I promise."

"Why should I believe anything you say? You're some fucking fatal attraction!"

"I tried to meet you several times, but the locations were compromised. This was my last chance."

"I'm calling the FBI."

"Please don't do that . . ." For the first time, she looked frightened.

"Why?"

She didn't speak.

"Sounds like the best reason why I should."

The little ball of redheaded energy exploded. "For such a smart guy, you really are a fuckin' idiot! Trust me, you're all being used."

It was time to humor the crazy lady and get away while he could. "Talia or Angie or Mrs. Claus or whoever the fuck you are, stay the fuck away from me!"

"Idiots like you deserve to die!" she yelled as he climbed into his wreck and threw it into drive. He watched her watching him pull away.

Was it déjà vu all over again if it wasn't déjà vu?

More than ever, he needed some mountain air to clear away the fantasy world he had just escaped.

In the master bedroom of the Stanford Avenue house they borrowed from Carter, Amanda curled up, half sitting on pillows against the large upholstered headboard they brought from Patricia Drive. A big duffel bag for clothes and a small travel bag for papers and electronics lay unzipped, and his stuff spread out in piles all around her as Peter mentally checked them off.

Her blue-green and brown eyes were glazed and her mouth slack, except for the occasional thumbnail chewed between incisors. Images flew by on the HOME monitor as she channel surfed.

"Do you ever wonder if news was designed to keep us afraid?" She felt beyond his grasp, the antidepressants trapping her soul under pond ice.

"When are you seeing Dr. Westover again?" he asked.

"Soon." He waited for more, but there was none.

"I didn't tell you everything about the Vette."

"Hmmm?" She was distracted by a cartoon dog.

"The woman driving the Ford was the one I couldn't identify in Washington. She gave me another name, and I looked it up."

Amanda finally took notice of him.

"And she exists. She's a journalist. I read some articles she wrote for the *Wall Street Journal*, the *Economist*, even *Wired*. I found pictures of her at press events."

"How could that be?" Something clicked behind her eyes. She was present for the first time that evening.

"She tried to warn me about . . . everything that's going on. That we might be in danger."

His wife sat away from the pillows and turned off the HOME. "No. Chang's dead, everything will be all right. They got who they wanted. Carter'll make it go away."

Peter sat down and took her hands to focus her. "Promise me. If anything happens to me, there's fifty thousand in cash in the grocery bag in the safe."

"What?"

"It's been there for the last six months. You never bothered to look. Take it and run. Dump the credit cards and the checkbook and go to your folks and let them help you hide. Oregon's a big, empty place. You can do it. Just disappear. I'll find you . . . if I can."

Even through the icy pond, Amanda loosed warm tears. She shook her head, slowly slipping her hands out of his to turn away, curling tight against the pillows.

He resumed packing.

CHAPTER THIRTY

On a sultry Saturday in July, Peter pulled his rental car up to the legendary Phoenix Club Camp, three thousand acres on the shores of Twin Lakes in the Hoover Wilderness (named after former Phoenix Club president—and, not incidentally, US president—Herbert Hoover) outside of Yosemite National Park. Protected by the US government's Bureau of Land Management, it had been the club's secret retreat for 120 years.

He was grateful for the detailed directions, since there were no signs or outward markings on the road into camp. He even Google Earthed his trip, but an empty wilderness came up on the satellite map. There were trees, streams, mountains, but no sign of human habitation or even roads for the supposed two thousand members and hundreds of staff on hand to serve them. No indication there was any "there" there at all.

Peter found a small parking lot, but it wasn't full. Attendees came from all over the country, and the local airstrip played host to their planes. Others came by limo, but the cars departed immediately. Carter told him it was best to be one of the last to arrive, calling it immersion therapy.

As he hefted his luggage to the front gate, a Hummer limo pulled in front and disgorged a bona fide celebrity. Howard Berger was an action-film star known for his heroic roles on-screen and his hardcore politics off, and if the press was correct, with political aspirations. The driver grabbed Berger's bags—all matched silver Halliburtons on wheels that looked like they never saw the brutal interior of a commercial airport's baggage handling system. Berger was whisked away by a man dressed like the rest of the staff in what looked like a ranger's uniform. They were the Crichtons—named after the eponymous butler of the 1902 play *The Admirable Crichton*. They acted as bartender, valet, personal assistant, concierge, adventure guide; anything the members wanted for the length of their stay. A Crichton approached Peter and very subtly stood in his way.

"Hi, I'm Phil. Your name, sir?"

Peter gave it, and Phil typed at a computer on the check-in table. A file came up, with photo ID and all the information needed to place him properly in the camp.

"Sir, what's the password?"

"Imperium."

"Thank you, sir."

Another Crichton stepped up to him. "Hi, I'm Barry. Do you mind if we examine your luggage?"

"Go ahead . . ."

And another. "Hi, I'm Mel. Do you mind stepping behind the screen?"

Behind the screen sat a backscatter X-ray machine, much more powerful than the standard models at airports. It could see not only under his clothes, but fully inside his body, making cavity searches unnecessary. And that's when Mel noticed some unusual things in Peter that didn't come up as bodily tissues.

"Sir, do you mind if I ask a personal question? Have you had any . . . surgery lately? In the vicinity of your . . . head?"

Phil was typing furiously. "Sir, we don't have you down for surgical provisions . . ."

"Why would you have me down for . . . ?"

Barry radioed for backup. He turned away, whispering.

Peter waved for any ranger's attention. "Excuse me? Hello! Would you please call Carter Potsdam? He's my sponsor. He'll vouch for the surgery."

Crichtons murmured the magical name. "Potsdam . . ."

Within minutes, the cavalry arrived, with his best friend in the back of a small open jeep, driven by a Crichton.

Carter looked disappointed. "You're nothing but trouble. You do know that, don't you?"

Now with his validation, Peter's luggage was whisked away, and Carter gave him a lift to their cabin. As they drove, Peter could see the camp was either based on, or the basis for, every summer-camp fantasy any boy ever imagined. The towering trees and pine needle–covered forest floors in vast groves surrounded hundreds of Lincoln Log–style cabins.

Based on the cabin map, they were halfway between the center of camp, with the choicest accommodations, and Siberia. Carter explained they didn't yet rate one of the really desirable central cabins that heads of state, multinational CEOs, and Decemviri stayed in. But they didn't get stuck out in the hinterlands like the Hollywood types, either.

They arrived at their perfect little cabin, made up of two double bedrooms, a living room, and a bathroom. The cabinmates were already inside, unpacked, and ready to party. Dan Halprin, an attorney from Atlanta, was obese, topping four hundred pounds. Justin Dardanelles, a New York financial analyst, was one of those men so chiseled and steroidally pumped up, he needed all his clothes custom-made, unless they were T-shirts and gym shorts—which is what he wore most of the time. Peter wasn't sure who would drop from a heart attack first, and he prayed it wasn't on his watch. Both drank beer as a warm-up for the night's festivities and seemed pleased to meet him.

It was just a couple of hours before the first ceremony, so Carter asked the Crichton to unpack and took Peter aside, holding him by the shoulders like an older brother.

"Have you taken any mind-altering substances since you had the implants?"

"Nothing since the post-op painkillers . . ."

"Then I'd tell you to listen carefully, but I know you can't do anything but that now. Don't touch them. We don't know your reaction to anything since the implants. Avoid the fountain: It's fruit punch, but it's spiked with Ecstasy, and I know you. You're such a control freak, I'm assuming you've never taken it. If you hate being the only sober person in a fifty-mile radius, just pretend you're high. If you indulge in the other . . . offerings, which I'm sure you won't, use protection. You've got your presentation tomorrow afternoon, so don't stay up too late. We'll go to sleep early tomorrow night, because we've got some ungodly early wake-up call for our fishing trip the next morning. The yacht owner has real pull with the FDA. Might be the pressure point we need to get our tech through approvals."

"Jesus, you sound like Pop. Where are you going?"

"You'll see. I've got a part in our opening night festivities, so I've got to get ready. Dan and Justin will make sure you get there. It's called the Bacchanalia." Carter's knowing smile made Peter's stomach churn. He had worn the same smile before Peter's initiation.

CHAPTER THIRTY-ONE

S eated on a split-log bench in a natural, open-air amphitheater between Dan and Justin, Peter was excited to see so many famous faces, surrounded by the towering redwoods and pines of the high Sierras, all with the same air of juvenile anticipation.

Night had fallen, and the amphitheater was dramatically lit by torches along the periphery, making the underlit trees tower like dark sentinels watching over the crowd. Suddenly, the torches extinguished. A few men flicked open lighters, and more pulled out lit-up GOs and waved them in the air as if at a rock concert, hooting and whistling for the show.

"Silence in the presence of the Praetor Maximus!" boomed a voice over a loudspeaker.

And instantly, the lighters and GOs went dark, and the amphitheater fell silent.

A single arc of light cut through the inky night to reveal Josiah Brant, commanding in his toga, but unlike the last time Peter saw him dressed so, the hood was thrown back so every member could see his aged, impish face.

Josiah threw his hands in the air and exclaimed, "Welcome to the Bacchanalia!"

The crowd cheered and stamped their feet and Peter found himself whistling along with Dan and Justin. As quickly, they were cut off as their conductor dropped his hands.

In his most Praetor-like voice, Josiah intoned, "I call upon loud-roarin' and revellin' Dionysus, primeval, double-natured, thrice-born Bacchic lord. Wild, ineffable, secretive, two-horned and two-shaped. Ivy-covered, bull-faced, warlike, howlin', pure. You take raw flesh, you have feasts, wrapped in foliage, decked with grape clusters. Resourceful Eubouleus, immortal god sired by Zeus when he mated with Persephone in unspeakable union. Hearken to my voice, O blessed one, and with your fair-girdled nymphs breathe on us, your worshipers, in a spirit of perfect brotherly love!"

The stage fell dark, and in the ominous blackness, a sound arose like a million indistinct voices, whispering unknown secrets carried on the breeze. It was perfectly synced with a real wind, whipping through the treetops, and it set Peter's body tingling and hair on edge. The sound came from all directions, and the crowd instinctively searched the dark for the source. Using both cortexes to analyze the sounds, he pinpointed at least three-dozen multidirectional speakers, but guessed there were more.

Suddenly, on stage, a single figure was lit as though from within, behind, underneath, and all around. It had to be some unusual stage lighting effect, but Peter wasn't sure how they did it, except perhaps wirelessly with remote microlamps or mirrors.

Carter was the sun. His blond hair was spun from gold and wreathed in grape leaves. He wore only a mountain lion skin, barely draped over one shoulder and down his front and back to midthigh, exposing most of his long, lean, muscular body. Carter looked more gilded panther than man. And every inch the god of wine, pleasure, and festivity, Dionysus. His festival was the Bacchanalia, a time for civilization's rules and social order to be cast aside, to revel with alcohol, sex, and music. His mythic story represented the cycle of

life, death, and rebirth, like the phoenix, and embodied the mani-
fold contradictions of Dionysus: purity and dissipation, animal and
human, law and anarchy, ecstasy and savagery, freedom and bondage. Ambivalence. Androgyny. The living and the dead.

Dan's fleshy elbow nudged Peter in the ribs. He whispered,
"Some Halloween getup, huh?"

Peter could only nod, jaw slack, leaving Justin and Dan to
cackle at his shock.

The god gazed at the source of the insolent laughter and his
unblinking, preternatural stare cut the two jokesters' guffaws off
dead.

Voice booming, the god spoke. "I am Dionysus. Known to
Romans as Bacchus. A god most terrible and yet most mild to
men. It is I who guide you. It is I who protect you and I who save
you. *I* am Alpha and Omega!" He strode the stage, larger than life,
demanding attention and obedience. And he got it.

"Let us be merry and drink wine and sing of me, the inventor
of the dance, the lover of all songs, the darling of Aphrodite; thanks
to me, drunkenness was brought forth, grace was born, pain takes
a rest, and trouble goes to sleep. In our revelry, I alone make the
humble feel proud, persuade the scowler to laugh, the weak to be
brave, and the cowardly to be bold.

"I, Dionysus, release you from your cares and worries. Cast off
the civilized masks you wear and realize your true nature! Human
and animal! Citizen and anarchist! Alive and dead! Here, in this
sacred grove, you are born again, to live how you wish to live, to be
how you wish to be!

"Go forth from this place and rejoice! *You are free!*" he roared,
outstretched arms raised high to encompass the entire audience.
The crowd rose to its feet in a frenzy of cheering, stomping, clap-
ping, hooting, wolf whistling, and howling at the hidden moon.

The sun was extinguished, and when the torches were lit once more, the god was gone.

Thoughts crashed and banged through Peter's head. The most obvious was: Carter was a star. The performance may have been short, but it was the most intense he had ever seen. Carter held that audience rapt in the palm of his hand, and he could feel the spectators' energy changed from expectation to determined anarchy, all at his whim. The feelings of unworthiness that plagued Peter's life were pricked more sharply. Carter was still in another league, one he could never hope to attain no matter how many clubs he joined.

The civilized perfection of the Phoenix Club in DC, contrasted with the primal cave beneath, had its corollary here. On one hand, the camp was a rustic paradise, comfortably reminiscent of childhood memories. But underneath the fun and games ran a primal psychology deep and dark, almost sinister, and counter to the supposed gentility and sophistication of the participants. And the members' repudiation of their enormous responsibilities, in exchange for the matchless power they held, disturbed him.

But maybe that's how boys could be boys.

Dan and Justin swept Peter up as the audience flooded out and spread among the camp festivities. The Ecstasy fountain sat right in the center of the main party area. The bloodred juice that poured continually from its jets reminded him a little too queasily of the drugged goblet at his initiation. It was already surrounded six deep with men dipping glasses into the fountain's bowl and wandering away. Justin grabbed Peter's arm.

"No thanks, Justin! Not for me!"

"Come on! You don't know what you're missing!" He continued to pull Peter toward the fountain. A very tall man, about six foot nine and recognizable from interview shows as a famous author, grabbed his other arm with a smile and pulled Peter closer.

"You'll experience things you've never imagined," said the famous author.

Justin was next to the fountain, filling a glass. Peter struggled to shake them off. Suddenly, Dan was behind him, pulling.

"Justin! Mike! Let the poor guy be!" The four-hundred-pound man was stronger than he looked. Yanked from his captor's grasp, Peter bounced off Dan's stomach.

"Thanks!" gasped Peter.

"No worries. Justin's great, but he's a pushy bastard!" The two men forced their way upstream away from the fountain. "You're a smart fella to avoid that thing. Follow me." The big man waddled up to a bar and, shoving his way through the pack of thirsty men with his sheer girth, asked the beleaguered bartender for two unopened bottles of forty-year-old scotch and two glasses. He cracked a cap, poured two glasses, and handed a bottle and glass to Peter. Dan held up his own glass in a toast. "To the greatest mancation on earth!" Dan watched to make sure Peter drank.

So Peter took a sip. One little sip couldn't hurt.

Then he took another. And another. Thus armed, Peter Bernhardt made his way amongst the natives.

An enormous bonfire in a clearing drew Peter as it had others. The men gathered were backlit, so Peter could not see their faces, but only heard their drunken voices. As he moved past, their darkened faces saw his well-lit features, then ignored him. One group compared their cloned champion racehorses. Another discussed their bid to buy the entire NFL—every team—although the Green Bay Packers still refused to cooperate. A third surrounded a man convincing his compatriots to move with him into sea-based communities immune from taxes, laws, or social mores and leave society to the schmucks!

And together they ignored him. Peter drank more scotch. Part of him felt like taking a slug at their self-satisfied faces. The other part understood that they just didn't know him. That's when the cogent part of his brain realized that his own hippocampus, which was laying down memories, and his cortex, which was processing information, were drunk. And the Hippo 2.0 and Cortex 2.0, doing the same, were sober. Two states of consciousness—one altered, one not—inhabited his mind at once.

Confused, he entered a torch-lit glen filled with younger members sharing joints, pipes, pills, and powder with amazing openness. One good-looking black man, about his own age, with shoulder-length dreads, a soul patch, and a Hendrix tee broke away from a group partaking of pills to stroll toward a log cabin with a sign above it, painted in the psychedelic lettering of the 60's: "Magical Mystery Store." Pop would have loved the name.

Grateful for an enclosed space to inhabit, Peter followed him in. It housed a pharmacopeia of illegal or simply questionable mind-altering substances, all labeled in glass-fronted rustic drawers, like a serve-yourself general store. And it was free.

The young man, who introduced himself as Andre, saw Peter wide-eyed at the display. "Need advice?" Peter hesitated. Andre offered, "No, really, I'm a biochemist. So what'll it be?" He rummaged through the drawers. "A brother cooked up some primo acid. And I can highly recommend the E. Made it myself." He pulled out a handful of MDMA for Peter to look at. "Love-up-o-rama. Add a little Viagra over there and you've got sextasy on a plate."

"Uh, no thanks."

The good doctor pocketed the pills and pointed to another drawer, "Well, if pot's your thing, this stuff's got the highest level of THC I've ever smoked, with just the right amount of THCV. Real nice shit." When Peter didn't respond, he offered, "Hey, there's harder shit, too. Crystal, crack, smack, but Dr. Andre could not recommend those. It would be unethical." He said this with a straight face, until both guys started laughing.

By now, Peter had practice holding up his whisky bottle and

glass. It was his cross against vampires. "I'm good for now. Not ready to shift gears."

Andre nodded knowingly. "Old school is cool."

Peter pointed the bottle at the psychedelically crazed Hendrix on Andre's chest. It didn't seem appropriate attire for Camp Week. "My main man, Jimi. Irony?"

"Fuck, yeah, brother! Gotta shake it up, ya know?" He fist-bumped Peter again. "You have fun, now. And when you need some fine-tuning, you find me. I'll set you up right." Andre headed out, but stopped. "You just a Jimi fan, or do you play?"

"I play."

"Then get your ass over to the main lodge, man! There's some serious jammin' goin'. How often you get to play with a member of the Grateful Dead?"

Maybe a small part of camp *was* his kind of place.

On his way to the main lodge, he passed the red light district on the camp's eastern edge, with men and women, some looking suspiciously young and dressed in diaphanous togas leaving little to the imagination. Beyond them were tiny, "single" cabins erected for each escort, like the one-room prostitute shacks of the Old West. There were hundreds of them.

A Crichton stood at a gate and asked as he passed, "Anything strike your fancy, sir?"

"Uh . . . thanks, but . . . Not really . . ."

"We have lots more to choose from! Every race and ethnicity imaginable, straight, gay, bears, crossdressers, trannies, BDSM, voyeurs, groups, exotics . . ."

"Exotics?"

"Dwarves, amputees, hermaphrodites . . ."

Peter was thankful animals and children were not part of the sales pitch. But that didn't mean they weren't there. The thought sickened him.

"Come on, sir! Indulge yourself. You deserve it. I promise you'll have a great time!"

Peter's sober self noticed a sense of pressure in the sales pitch's vocal tone, facial expressions, and body stance. Like the Crichton had orders to get as many people into the shacks as possible.

Or was he imagining it?

That's when Peter saw Dionysus, the worse for wear as befitted the hedonistic god. His leafy garland was cockeyed atop his golden hair and missing some grapes. The animal skin, tied hastily around his waist in a knot, scarcely covered his genitals and ass. He leaned languorously against a tree between a pair of "fair-girdled nymphs," two barely toga-clad young men, delicate, dark, and exotic, like a pair of young princes from an ancient Indian or Persian painting, and their beauty befitted Dionysus. It made a mythic tableau right off a Greek urn.

Dreamily, his partner looked up from his charges and glimpsed Peter. Carter's face shifted, betraying a yearning and sadness he had never exhibited before.

Its possessiveness disturbed Peter.

The princes caught their john's change of mood and quickly led Dionysus away to a distant cabin. Peter wondered if either of them had ever screwed a god before.

He wasn't sure if his implants or the place gave him the creeps. All he knew was reality wasn't the same anymore. And he didn't like it. He hurried to the main lodge.

The Phoenix Club hijinks were indeed summer camp for big boys. But for all the freedom Dionysus bestowed, Peter wasn't sure how free they were. While he couldn't begrudge them mind-altering substances or sexual whims, were these freedom? Or simply the indulging of what society deemed vices? Maybe back when social pressures to conform were intense, like the Victorian period, drug consumption or sexual promiscuity might have been interpreted as a sense of freedom. But now? And among men of power and influence, for whom nothing was off-limits, with or without the club? It felt like one gigantic illusion, as much of a stage trick as Carter's sunlight effect.

Looming in the woods, the lodge resembled a smaller version of Yosemite's legendary Ahwahnee Hotel. Music could be heard inside. They were covering one of his favorite bands—R.E.M.—and doing a halfway decent job with "Welcome to the Occupation," one of the rare songs that slayed the violent and avaricious twin dragons of American politics and imperialism.

Maybe there were people here who felt the way he did. He was desperate to join them.

CHAPTER THIRTY-TWO

Hungover and sleep deprived, members had the opportunity to attend a series of seminars throughout the week, led by Phoenicians on subjects like US foreign and domestic policy, the economy, business opportunities, cultural trends, and high-tech developments. But the best-attended presentation was given by Peter Bernhardt in the amphitheater late the second afternoon, where his fellow brothers would witness a club first: a cyborg sales pitch.

With almost all two thousand members in attendance, Peter gazed out at everybody who was anybody. All at once. What the hell was he doing here? It should have been Carter doing the selling, not him.

Carter stood off to the side, watching the crowd to relay the identity of questioners and their question's subtext to a tiny earbud in Peter's right ear. It was important that any government health regulators be identified so Peter could concentrate his arguments on them. Carter had already pointed out FDA chairman James Clement. Peter concentrated on the slender bald man's pate.

Peter took a deep breath and spoke as clearly as he could. "The degenerative cognitive diseases that destroy memory and intellect—Alzheimer's, Parkinson's, and dementia—have had a sharp rise in incidence worldwide. By 2050, one in eighty-five people will have Alzheimer's—that's over one hundred million people. Beyond the excruciating emotional toll on patients and their families, there is another toll as well. Memory lost is wisdom lost, which is value lost, which is money lost, both personally to the victim and economically to society. Over ten million Americans suffer from neurological diseases, which cost this country over five hundred billion dollars a year to treat. The five and a half million Alzheimer's sufferers alone cost two hundred billion dollars a year. And while there are many drugs on the market and in the research pipeline for memory enhancement or to arrest diseases like Alzheimer's, what I'm about to show you is far beyond simple pharmacological enhancement, which can only improve memory up to twenty percent, or at best, arrest the disease midstep. Instead, this is memory restored. And amplified."

The large telescreen erected behind him displayed colorful diagrams of the Hippo 2.0 and Cortex 2.0. He walked the audience through the technology's basics and screened a scene of a patient, whose face was obscured by surgical drapes, but whose brain was exposed through the hole bored into the skull.

"Just in case you were wondering . . . Yes. That's my brain." Gasps and exclamations erupted on cue.

"And no. I don't have Alzheimer's. But I might eventually. My father has it. Because of a mysterious hesitancy by the FDA to continue our research," which Peter said looking directly at the FDA's Clement, "we've had only one patient on the combination of the Hippo 2.0 and the Cortex 2.0 and I think we can count that as a success. I am that patient." He pulled the Cortex 2.0 processor from his back pocket and held it up in his hand.

"I wanted to prove that this therapy is safe and works. There are things I know as a conscious, healthy, intelligent person that I couldn't ask my patients to describe. Communication with an advanced Alzheimer's patient is very limited, especially patients whose families are desperate enough to submit them to experimental brain surgery. And I needed to know . . . what was it like before, versus after? While I could only surmise the inner world of my pre-op patients, I knew my pre-op mental state.

"So I stand here, to show you what the Hippo 2.0 and Cortex 2.0 can do. If you remember Mr. Memory in Alfred Hitchcock's classic film, *The 39 Steps*, you might have an idea what it's like to have a set of these implanted. You remember everything. You can't help it. It's not obsessive or compulsive. It just is. And it's beyond an end to misplaced car keys or forgotten anniversaries. I'll remember each and every thing about my day today. Even if my brain doesn't think it's important, the Cortex 2.0 will capture it, because my own brain might have been mistaken the first time." He noticed a man ducking behind another in the back. He pointed at him. "If you're hiding from me, well, there's no magic. I can't intuit you or see through walls or read your mind or see you in the past or the future. You're safe from Mr. Memory.

"But for those with cognitive degeneration so severe they can't remember their own names or the names of their loved ones without this," pointing up at the screen with one hand and tapping his head with the other, "this is life itself. We are the sum total of all our experiences, our lessons, our successes, our failures, our loves, our hates, from birth to death. And if those memories disappear, what then? Who are we?

"So let's get started. I'd like to go down the first three rows here, so we're not here all day." Peter walked up to the man on the end. "Hi. Please tell me your name and your occupation and then hand the mike to the person next to you, who will do the same, until we complete these three rows. That'll be about two hundred fifty people." He handed the man a wireless mike.

The gentleman cleared his throat and spoke softly. "My name

is . . . uh . . . Michael Fischler. I'm . . . uh . . . CFO of an . . . um
. . . engineering company."

A guy from the back yelled, "Engineering company my ass. It's
Bechtel, for Christ's sake!"

The audience hooted as Mr. Fischler blushed and passed the mike.

And so it went. Man by man, until the first three rows were com-
pleted. The last man handed the mike to Carter.

"I will now repeat the audience's statements verbatim," said Peter,
"and if I make a mistake, I'm sure you'll all let me know, won't you?"
More hooting commenced.

And he did. One by one, but quickly, rattling them off machine-
gun-like. All two hundred sixty-eight members.

After the inevitable wolf whistles and applause, he said, "Now
all this proves is I'm a self-made idiot savant. The Phoenix Club's
own Rain Man." Everyone laughed. "And other than making me
as seamless at introductions as my illustrious partner over there," he
pointed to Carter, who gave a little wave to the audience, the majority of which clapped or yelled his name in return, "it's a cheap parlor
trick. Repetition of information is not enough. What intelligence
requires, especially for the cognitively impaired, is synthesis. The
ability to take the raw data you're given, find patterns, and make
sense out of it. Here's the real trick." Carter rolled out a whiteboard
to the center of the stage. "Mike, since you're a CFO, I'm assuming
you're good with numbers, and you can check my work afterward
and see if I'm right." Mike nodded.

"Of the two hundred and sixty-eight men I just met, the fol-
lowing data becomes apparent: there are eight Johns, seven Jameses,
Roberts, and Williams, six Michaels and Davids, five each of Richard,
Charles, Joseph, Thomas, Christopher, Alex, and Steve." He wrote
the names and numbers quickly on the board. "Four each of Daniel,
Peter, Paul, Mark, Don, George, Ken, Ed. Three each for Brian,
Ronald, Anthony, Kevin, Larry. Two of Jason, Matthew, Gary, Tim,

Jose, Jeff, Frank, Scott, Eric, Andrew, Ray, Greg, Josh, Jerry, Dennis, Walter, Patrick, Phil." He stopped writing. "Then there's only one Harold, Doug, Henry, Carl, Arthur, Ryan, Roger, Joe, Juan, Jack, Al, Justin, Terry, Gerald, Keith, Sam, Ralph, Nicholas, Roy, Ben, Ming, Brandon, Adam, Harry, Fred, Wayne, Billy, Louis, Jeremy, Aaron, Randy, Howard, Eugene, Carlos, Russell, Victor, Martin, Ernest, Todd, Craig, Alan, Sean, Clarence, Nathaniel, Antonio, Rodney, Manuel, Marvin, Vincent, Zachary, Mario, Leroy, Francis, Theo, Cliff, Miguel, Oscar, Dusty, Pedro, Damien, Marcelus, Wolfgang, Jedidiah, Samudragupta, and who could forget Tinsulaananda!" He rattled these last off so quickly, he had to catch his breath. "Based on your own occupation descriptions, fifty-eight of you are in industry, seventy-five are professionals, meaning medical doctors or lawyers, sixty-two are in finance, forty-nine of you are academics, fifty-three are in government, forty-six are in the media and . . . well, thirty-eight of you are lobbyists, and I'm not sure what category that goes in."

A voice yelled from the audience, "Lobbyists don't have a category. They have a species; they evolved from leeches." The audience laughed, lobbyists loudest of all.

"This is the first step in the synthesis of large amounts of raw data. Computers do this all the time, but now I can. The next step in synthesis would be surmising the meaning behind the data, which a computer can't do alone. Do certain names confer higher status in social orders? And if I get some sleep, this little analysis will be much, much better. When I dream, I see patterns emerge that I never would have otherwise, because the two cortexes compare notes.

"Now I told you at the opening that the Cortex 2.0 is still a work in progress, because we haven't completely broken the brain's codes. But we will. Within the year, I hope. So what does that mean? Very soon, you'll be able to read my thoughts."

Peter never stood before two thousand slack jaws before.

"Think about this. People 'locked in' with Lou Gehrig's Disease or brain traumas. Who can't communicate because of cerebral palsy. Or in a coma. Or even in supposedly vegetative states! We could know what all these people, cut off from their families, friends, and caregivers are thinking. Or if they're thinking at all. They don't need to pretend to type in their brain. They don't even need to know how to spell or move a cursor on a screen. They only need to think. And we'll know. We can give the conscious among them fuller, more meaningful lives, through communication.

"Let's take it a step further. If we can translate the thoughts of a human being, then thoughts can go both out . . . *and* in. And we can transfer that information, digitally, anywhere, knowing which thought we're transferring by looking at its code. We can add information to a person's brain, like learning educational models or skills or experiencing scenarios. We'll be getting right down to the elements of what defines consciousness, in a way never possible before. The digital reader will even record the ancillary thoughts that memories attach to. So it will not only record my experience of speaking to you today, but any thoughts I've had that are related to this experience. Like my nervousness at public speaking, which made me flash back to my most nervous moment on a stage, in seventh grade in Mr. Penta's class, watching a girl I had a crush on in the first row watching me. That's all on the Cortex 2.0 now. This is the first step to something that, until now, was only thought of as science fiction—uploads—the copying or transference of all a brain's contents into a computer substrate. The complete thoughts of a human. But in a machine.

"It's extraordinary how far we've come. Everything we've learned about science and technology up to now is converging to produce the most fundamental change yet: taking our machines and putting them in ourselves. Prosthetic limbs, pacemakers, sensory implants, nerve stimulators. They make the unwhole whole. The Hippo 2.0 and the Cortex 2.0 will be key tools in this biotech revolution, bringing the information age to the inside of our brains, which can only lead to a fully-fledged biotech age . . ."

Carter's small voice whispered in his ear. "Something's wrong . . ."

Peter looked into the audience. There was a restlessness, a discomfort that was palpable. He spoke louder, as though increased decibels could win them back. "Never forget, humanity adapts, survives, and evolves. And because of humankind's history of technological advancement, more people today, around the world, experience higher standards of living, better medical care, more security, and less trauma than in any previous time in human history . . ."

"Wrap it up!" the earpiece exhorted. Peter could see the sidelong glances at neighbors. At watches. Peter caught Carter's expression, struggling to look calm.

He plunged ahead. "Some of you might be wondering why I made a presentation that was more 'magic act' than 'investor's pitch.' Well, a man named Arthur C. Clarke, who wrote a book you might have heard of called *2001: A Space Odyssey*, once said, 'Any sufficiently advanced technology is indistinguishable from magic.' And the magic will be here very, very soon. Thank you. Any questions?"

Tepid applause. Rumblings. Carter was subtly shaking his head at Peter. The audience was his until . . . the slack jaws. It was the extrapolation of the technology. But why? Perspiration flushed from his body.

A hand in the audience went up a few rows from the back, but the questioner was short and hidden behind a large man seated in front of him.

"I'm sorry," said Peter. "I can't see you. Can you please stand up?"

The man stood up and only smiled with his mouth, his gray eyes frosty with calculation.

Peter felt the blood rush from his face and flood his gut.

It was Bruce Lobo.

CHAPTER THIRTY-THREE

D o you think you've changed with this augmentation?"
asked Lobo.

"Shit!" said Carter in the earpiece. "I didn't think he was coming."

How could he not have assumed Bruce Lobo was a member? A burst of adrenaline swamped Peter's system. Time slowed . . .

"I . . . um . . . haven't taken IQ tests yet to quantify how much more or what kind of intelligence is specifically involved, but I'm definitely better able to handle multiple and simultaneous information feeds and synthesize data more efficiently. If you're asking if my personality has changed, no, I don't believe so. But you'll have to double-check with my wife. Remembering to take out the trash may qualify as a major personality shift for her."

But Bruce wouldn't sit down. "It's such a subjective question, it isn't fair to ask the patient. Maybe I should ask your partner? Carter, has he changed?"

Carter stared steadily at Bruce. "No. I agree with Pete's assessment. But his wife is definitely happy about the trash." He flashed his most charming smile, getting a big laugh, but Peter could tell he was lying.

His mind, changed or not, couldn't stop spinning. Bruce Lobo. The Phoenix Club. Of course he was a member! A rush of thoughts consumed him: Was there a connection between Bruce's membership and what Bruce did to him and Biogineers and the date of the Lobo/Biogineers merger: 10/26? And why would he be wondering that?

Another hand went up. "How accurate are a person's memories with this device?"

"Usually more accurate, because there's no post-experience reinterpretation of input that doesn't fit your preconceptions. Meaning, even if we don't believe what we saw, we'll still remember it. If I saw a blue bus, it was a blue bus, because the Hippo 2.0 and the Cortex 2.0 are recording the blue bus. I don't change it to a yellow bus later in my memory, because it makes more sense to me to have seen a yellow bus. Humans do that all the time. It's why eyewitness testimony is so flawed. We see what we expect to see and remember what we think we should remember."

From the very back, an elderly man asked, "Do they differ from our memories?"

"Well, the fact they're digitally translated is different. But functionally, only more accurate."

A young man who didn't look too far out of college asked, "Can you put one person's memories into someone else?"

"It's a fantasy, isn't it? To share memories, thoughts. It might create remarkable empathy, to really know what it is to be in another person's shoes. But who knows, maybe not. It's theoretically possible."

A middle-aged man wearing a plain white T-shirt and chinos stood up. He gave Peter the willies. There was nothing concrete that should have disturbed him so. He felt like . . . amorality personified. "Can this machine be used on someone without their knowledge? Or under duress? Or if they're unconscious?"

Carter's voice in his ear was hesitant. "Careful . . . don't know what he really does, but he's with the Pentagon."

Jesus, was the guy a torturer for a living? "If you mean instances against the will of the patient"—and the man nodded—"then I'd have to say you could, but it would be unethical to do so, and I wouldn't. I guess this tech will bring up all kinds of issues over cognitive liberty."

A broad-shouldered man with stick-straight posture and a steel-gray buzz cut two seats over continued the uncomfortable line of questioning, "Can you selectively record or retrieve memories, leaving some information secure and untouched?" He had to be military. DARPA or similar.

The voice in his ear said, "General Padechevsky. NSA."

"I'll have to say, theoretically, yes," Peter replied.

The general continued, "One more please . . . can you tap into a live feed from the Hippo 2.0 or the Cortex 2.0, so it's recorded in more than one location?"

What would the NSA do with this? "Haven't tried it yet. I'll let you know when I do."

A man who looked like a late-night comedy-show nerd stood up. "Can you cross-reference a database of memories for common threads or concepts? And how about in a group of people?"

His earwig said, "Patrick Safire. Head of the GAO." Government Accountability Office. Jeez . . .

"Again, theoretically, yes, I'm hoping to prove you can. Until then, it's only a hope."

Charles, a gray-haired attorney from a white-shoe law firm, stood in the second row. "Could these memories be admissible as evidence in a court of law and, if so, how do you think that will affect jurisprudence?"

"I'm not a lawyer. I don't even play one on TV."

Four seats over, Ronald, a law professor from University of Chicago, stood to reply. "Charlie, I think the questions will revolve around whether recorded memories have any rights at all, since they're digital and can be made external to the human body. For instance, e-mails don't. They are seen as evidence. So will they have First Amendment rights? Or Fifth Amendment rights? Or the right to privacy? Doubtful. It's back to the concept Peter called cognitive liberty. We'll need to define that."

Many heads nodded throughout the amphitheater. There were a lot of lawyers.

Dr. Azziz stood. "I'd like to state something I'm sure my fellow pharmaceutical executives are thinking and that is this technology will really cut into our profit margins!"

"But Dr. Azziz, we can finally make dementia or Alzheimer's a moot point. Maybe this is naive of me to say, but isn't that what everyone wants? Especially you as a doctor? To medically increase longevity, but with a good quality of life, mentally whole? What's the point of a new heart if you have an old, damaged brain to go with it?"

Azziz didn't look convinced.

A bald man with huge, bug-eye glasses stood up in the back row and said, "That's all well and good and altruistic, but what's the killer app?"

The killer application: the use of a technology that would elevate it into more than anyone had conceived. That would make it ubiquitous in society. Like e-mail encouraged people to use computer networks. Or popular gaming titles promoted particular gaming systems.

"I don't know," said Peter, "until it happens. That's the thing with killer apps. It's apparent after the fact. Rarely before. If I had to hazard a guess, I'd say it will revolve around being able to think and communicate more effectively and therefore create increased efficiencies in an increasingly competitive world. Someone will try something, I'm sure."

An older gent rose. "That's what I'm afraid of: the killer app. What happens to society if we allow these things to take over? How do we control it?"

"Control it?" yelled a younger member. "That's not the problem. It already *is* mind control!"

The older gent did not sit down. "Am I the only person here concerned about these 'cyborg citizens' in our midst? This isn't some benign implant replacing a disabled sense—this is a memory implant that could change what you think the world is. And what you think of your fellow, less intelligent humans. Do we all need to get one, just to survive?"

Peter jumped in. "I don't see why you should be concerned. If anything, I remember things better than you, which means I see the world more accurately. I or my father or anyone who has this surgery, are not a threat to anyone. Why would we be any more so than anyone else?"

"Jobs!" yelled a voice from the audience. "You'd get their jobs!" Many heads nodded again.

The older gent turned to his left and directed his question a dozen seats over. "Would the religious right endorse this or oppose it?"

Before Peter could answer, a short man with camera-ready white hair rose slowly from his seat. Peter recognized him even before Carter cursed in his earpiece. It was the televangelist Dill Kenilworth, host of *God's World* and owner of the largest Christian television network on earth. "I can tell you what I and my brethren would say. We'd say this is an evil technology, designed to enslave us to the Antichrist and cease us from being in God's image, as we were created. I'm sure the young man means well, but as surely as I stand here, this contraption is an affront to our God-given human dignity. He's trying to become God Almighty, instead of kneeling humbly before the Lord. He would find no support here." Peter understood Kenilworth's power. His few words were sold by a folksy-meets-brimstone persona. He was as aggressive as a gamecock, with more charisma than any five presidents put together. No wonder people followed him.

"So you would have us do nothing?" asked Peter. "Even as we watch more and more of our loved ones become . . . less and less?"

"It's God's will, to reveal to us our vanities and our arrogance of knowledge. We're all God's children and loved by Him, with or without our faculties."

"Sir, I stand by my work. While you say suffering is the will of your God, I try to help. That's what I was put on this earth to do."

"But we do help them, son. It's called prayer."

The earwig whispered, "Don't go there. Back off."

Peter was dying to tell the reverend where to stuff the hundreds of millions of dollars his downtrodden faithful scraped together and mailed him to have their prayers answered, while he lived like royalty off it. "I'm sorry, but we'll have to agree to disagree on this subject, Reverend. Next question?"

No one stood. No one raised a hand. Peter checked on the FDA chairman. He was frowning.

"May I say one thing in closing? You've opened my eyes today. I'm amazed at the broad range of opinions this group has about what I'm proposing. So maybe this is an opportunity to bring these issues, and the greater issues of science, to the public. It should be the obligation of a citizen scientist like myself to encourage public participation on these issues . . ."

But the uproar silenced the rest.

Voices, not bodies, stood out amidst the din of the arena. ". . . Who's going to get these chips, because they can pay for it? And who deserves them?"

" . . . You don't actually think that 'the people' out there have any idea what in blazes you're talking about, do you? If half of the population is below average, that's fifty percent that you might as well write off right now . . ."

Not all the comments were derogatory. The supporters entered into philosophical fights with their brothers where they stood.

It was difficult to hear Carter's voice in his ear above the pandemonium. "Leave the amphitheater. Now!" Peter looked at him like he was crazy, but Carter was already walking.

Peter grabbed his laptop and hustled out. He chased Carter down the path toward the main lodge, hyperventilating. "What the fuck happened in there? I was ambushed!"

"Ambushed?"

"Well, whaddaya call that?"

"Healthy debate. You present something controversial and these guys'll fight about it."

"It was way more adversarial than that."

"Pete, you're paranoid. Really. Just . . . go away. I've got hands to hold and tempers to calm. And please keep out of trouble for the rest of the day. I'll see you back at the cabin after dinner."

There was nothing else to do. Peter sat at a bar and drank a couple of beers. If Carter was right, it made him even more aware of how ostrichlike he'd been, keeping his head down in Silicon Valley and ignoring the rest of the country and the world. His work touched people at a primal level. Anything that changed the future did that. He wondered if rational discussion between such divergent worldviews was possible. Members filed out of the amphitheater, still arguing amongst themselves, to take up predinner activities of tennis, volleyball, mind-alteration, and escorts, among other diversions. Paul Simon crooned "Boy in the Bubble" in his head, warning of the monied classes joining with technology to create, or destroy, the world.

He unconsciously pulled his hair in annoyance, as though tugging could make the music stop.

No one came up to him afterward. No one engaged him in conversation. Once again, he was the pariah, his invisible *P* emblazoned on his forehead.

CHAPTER THIRTY-FOUR

Peter took a walk around the camp a couple of hours later, because walking alone was less pathetic than sitting alone. A voice called his name.

It was Bruce Lobo, sitting on the hip-high wooden post-and-rail fence that marked the red light district, next to one of the most beautiful women Peter had ever seen. Her long thick hair was the color of pale honey and her eyes the shade of violets. She was not dressed in camp garb, either. Her formfitting designer dress, expensive shoes, and gold-and-diamond jewelry, while inappropriate to the Sierras, led him to believe she was a woman of style and means. Their body language suggested intimacy. Bruce motioned Peter to join them. Since there was no way to avoid either insult or confrontation, he warily approached the pair.

"Excellent presentation, Peter. You've changed the game. Again," said Lobo.

Not sure if it was a compliment, Peter said nothing.

Lobo smiled at Peter's silence. "You're right. I need to apologize. I'm sorry for the brawl. But then, you swung first . . ." Lobo grinned. "Peace?" He held his hand out to shake.

Peter reluctantly shook his hand. "Peace."

"You know I wouldn't bullshit you. Not about this. These idiots are so bogged down in old paradigms, they have no idea the world's moved on. You've moved it on. It's a neurosociety you're building. And it's damn well about time."

Peter wondered who the beauty was. Member? Staff? Prostitute? He held his hand out to her. "It's a pleasure to meet you. I'm Peter Bernhardt."

"Vera Kostina. The pleasure is mine." She had a firm handshake, and her stunning face didn't move much when she spoke, as though the emotions inside were well contained.

Lobo laughed. "Thanks, Bernhardt. You always had better manners . . . when you're not trying to knock my lights out." He turned to Vera. "I'm told he's much more likable than me."

"Attila the Hun was more likable than you," the Russian purred.

Lobo snickered indulgently. Peter realized he had never seen the tycoon laugh at himself, or let anyone get the better of him.

"If we're getting all 'Oprah,' I felt bad for you back there," admitted Bruce.

Vera's deep laugh erupted from the bowels of the earth and struck Peter as the most genuine thing about her. "Well, that's a first!"

"Hey, don't get carried away!" he shot back. "And, by the way," he said to Peter, "I don't apologize for blowing you out of the water at Biogineers. No one knew what the fuck was going on, and anyone who isn't my ally is my enemy. And I destroy my enemies." Lobo smiled. "But that's all over now. You accomplished what I thought would take another decade. Congratulations."

Peter relaxed. Maybe Bruce wasn't bad, unless you did business with him. "Thanks. You get how difficult it was and what it means. The rest of them . . . I understand their concerns, but . . ."

"But they're irrelevant. The future happens whether they like it or not. Life isn't some creationist bedtime story—this is the way life's always been and will always be. It's Darwinian. Life changes. Adapt or perish."

"Exactly!" said Peter.

"By the way," Bruce continued, "now that you've met the lovely Vera . . . she's the best fuck in the whole world. Crazy good. Give her a try. It'll cheer you up."

Vera was completely unfazed.

"Uh . . . thank you, but no. I'm not . . . interested . . ." he stammered.

"Bullshit. Your wife's hot, but Vera . . . Jesus, she's a fucking artist and artwork rolled into one!"

"Too bad." said Vera. "We could have a great time."

Carter was right. Scotch was wonderful. The retox-velvet burn of forty-year-old Glenfiddich cascading down his throat was a cozy amber blanket tucked in around his depression. He didn't care if it made one cortex loopy and the other a critical scold. He had disappointed a lot of people today. People who had invested money in his dream, and having seen it, were unhappy.

Josiah Brant sat between the Prometheus partners on their cabin porch, draining a couple of bottles between them. Owls hooted in the darkness. An enormous shadow, more apparition than bird, swooped past their cabin to scoop up a rodent scurrying for cover from nocturnal food gathering. Peter felt like one of those pathetic mice.

He swirled the scotch in his glass. Tiny amber rivulets ran down the sides, streams flowing to the ocean of gold. Would his Hippo 2.0 and Cortex 2.0 keep recording if he was blind drunk? And how much would he need to swill to pass out?

"Why do I think I'll be the subject of Kenilworth's next sermon?"

Josiah chuckled and sucked deeply on his cigar. "That was the most demandin' audience anywhere. Men who have achieved the highest positions in the most powerful nation on earth. And you told them their time on top of the greasy pole wouldn't be much longer. I think you did well, considerin'."

Peter asked quietly, "What about the FDA? Will they give us the go-ahead for human trials?"

"Doubtful right now," said Carter. "You extrapolated the technology. They don't want to hear that the Alzheimer's cure they approve is going to radically change all of society. That's terrifying."

"And the investors?"

"Who knows? You were preaching revolution. This turns the current power structure upside down."

"It's not preaching," said Peter defensively. "I told the truth. You and I know it. Isn't it time they did?"

Josiah guffawed. "You think they don't, son? They know it better than you. They just don't like it."

"And why should they?" asked Carter. "Haven't you figured out the smart money always keeps the status quo for as long as possible, milking it dry while quietly investing in agents of change, but holding change off, until they're damned good and ready to exploit it? So come the revolution, they're still in the catbird seat. But if you think preparing for that contingency is pain-free, you're nuts. No one likes change. Especially not these guys."

"That's 'cause change hurts. Always has. Always will," said Josiah. "No one likes to have their plans and dreams disappointed. We invest so much in our dreams . . ." Josiah looked far out into the darkness and pulled long on his cigar.

"And yet that's all we've ever done as a species. We change the world around us," said Peter.

"Who said these assholes were any more rational than the rest of humanity?" Carter sighed. "Look, forget about the investment. What happens, happens. You did what you needed to do . . ."

"But you think I've changed," said Peter.

Carter downed the rest of his drink and grabbed a bottle to pour another and top up Peter's and Josiah's glasses. "Did the implants answer those questions you had yet?"

"A couple. Not all of them by a long shot. But a man's gotta do what a man's gotta do . . ."

"You said it, boy." Josiah hoisted his scotch.

They clinked glasses, slung the blessed nectar back, and sat quietly to listen to the night. The wilderness's activity after dark never ceased to amaze Peter. Humans assumed that because they slept, the rest of life on earth slept. So much went on under their very noses that they had no idea about . . .

"You younguns don't know how lucky you got it," blurted Josiah. "Most don't have any grit. Damn it . . ." His cigar was smoked to the end and his holder was empty. Josiah sighed. "You invest so much in children. Teach 'em they need grit and decisiveness and loyalty and passion to succeed. Hope they see the advantages you lay out before them. But do they? No sir, they don't . . . They throw it back in your face. Sure hope neither 'a you boys throw it back in my face . . ." His expression grew dark.

"Sir . . .?" said Peter. Carter subtly shook his head at Peter, but Josiah didn't notice.

"I gave my son the planet on a platter," Josiah continued. "Told him I'd make him anythin' he wanted. Even president. Blindness didn't matter. We had technology to help him. Anything he needed. Only technology he wanted was one he could escape with. Became an addict. Rather live inside a violent computer game than control a violent world. What a waste!" Josiah realized he was talking out loud. "Gentlemen, it's been a pleasure, but I have had too much to drink! Goodnight." The old man waddled unsteadily off the porch and into the night.

Peter waited until Josiah was out of earshot, whispering, "What was that about?"

"His son's a blind gaming addict in a recovery facility somewhere in Nevada. Said he'd rather be a nutcase than Brant's heir apparent. He's been in there for years."

"Brant would lock up his son for not wanting to be the next Praetor Maximus? And there are blind gamers?"

"Yeah and yeah. I told you. Don't cross Josiah. Poor bastard . . . I know how it feels . . ."

"What feels?"

"To be a disappointment."

"Because you're gay?"

"Not my father. Nick . . ." Carter suddenly lurched up. "I need some sleep." And he stumbled into the cabin.

Carter had disappointed Nick Chaikin? To the extent he'd exile Carter? Peter tried to stand, but the porch pitched him over. He grabbed the railing. "Shit . . . Tomorrow . . . I hope I'm not sick on that rich guy's fucking boat." The yacht owner could be the key to getting Prometheus Industries' technologies out of the FDA's clutches.

CHAPTER THIRTY-FIVE

P ete, come on. Get up."
   He opened his eyes. Carter's face hovered above his, concerned. "You're talking in your sleep again. You've got to
learn to stop that."

Ripped from his dream, the length of memory's fabric his mind
wove each night from information's disparate threads was ragged.
Peter's thoughts were incomplete and he felt mentally naked. He
stared at Carter, unseeing for a moment, then confronted by his
friend's worried expression, he yawned, stretched, and scratched
himself. "Sorry if I kept you up, man." He checked his watch. It
was 3:15 a.m.

But Carter didn't reply. He left to use the bathroom.

They flew toward the California coastline in a Bell Jet Ranger. It was
still the middle of the night. Outside their copter, it was hard to tell
the land from the sea from the night sky. There was no moon and
a marine layer drifted along the coastline. With their headsets on
to dampen the rotors' sound, Carter told him about the yacht and

who was on board already. He mentioned names Peter didn't know. The group had slept there last night, but there hadn't been enough beds to include Carter and Peter in the party the night before. Peter didn't care about the guest lists. He hoped that the yacht's owner, Anthony Dulles, might help get the Hippo 2.0 and Cortex 2.0 out of FDA purgatory and into patients. Soon.

Small lights shone ahead in a circle with an X shape. A portable landing pad lit up the beach where they set down. He guessed it must be on the barely inhabited central coast north of Hearst Castle, but south of Big Sur. There were no houselights or streetlights nearby.

Relieved to be on solid ground, he reluctantly followed Carter into a speedboat. Peter noticed the dark-haired pilot's biceps bulge as he was helped into the watercraft. Crewing on a ship probably kept guys like Big Biceps pretty fit. The pilot steered them out into the Pacific, toward the distant lights of a superyacht.

The speedboat was impressive. Silver and sleek as a needle, the four-seater looked like a Porsche and cut through the water like one, too. The speedboat's headlights showed a group of lumps floating in the water. They made an evasive maneuver around it.

"What was that?" Peter shouted over the engine noise to Big Biceps.

"Dolphins. Sleeping," the pilot yelled back.

Within minutes, they approached a state-of-the-art motor-yacht, over two hundred feet long, anchored serenely. On the stern was its name: *American Dream II.*

The launch pulled alongside the stern boarding area at water level. The pilot threw a line to a blond, curly-haired crewman, who secured the line to a cleat. Big Biceps jumped off the bow onto the yacht deck and Angel Hair gave Peter and Carter a hand climbing aboard.

The stern deck was about three hundred square feet and hovered a foot above the sea. It functioned like a beach area on which to sunbathe and jump directly into the ocean. There were large doors flush at the back and below their feet that hid all the toys a superyacht would need: Jet Skis, mini-launches, portable helicopter pads, and more. The two men got a sense of the yacht's lavish size as they made their way from the lower stern, up four floors, to the public rooms on the main deck. Even though it was not to his taste, the ship was extremely impressive from both an engineering and design point of view. But from the moment he stepped aboard, it didn't feel like a boat full of partying Phoenicians. Or even sleeping Phoenicians. The feeling that something wasn't right was particularly powerful.

Peter gently tugged on Carter's arm, halting their progress. "Something's . . . up . . ."

Carter shrugged him off and kept going. "Nothing's wrong. They're all still asleep."

But Peter hadn't said "wrong." He grabbed Carter. "What the hell's going on?"

Carter yanked his arm back. "Stop it, Pete. You're overreacting again."

But Peter wouldn't move. "This is no fishing trip."

Frustrated, his friend circled back. "Would you just calm down? Look, every year the club has a couple of . . . field trips . . . to accomplish certain objectives the club thinks need doing and can't be exposed to public discussion. This year, it's questioning a man on this boat—in a way, it *is* a fishing trip, except we're fishing for information. Your role in all this will become clear very soon. Think of it as part two of your initiation. Just play your part, and you'll be fine. Don't worry."

"The more you tell me not to worry, the faster I want to get outta here." He turned to go.

"Sorry, Pete. You can't," replied Carter. The two shipmates came from behind, grabbing Peter's arms and dragging him forward, while training guns on him. Crushed between the two, Peter noted that neither looked particularly crew-like. More like career soldiers. Angel Hair had a long keloid scar down his right cheek.

Peter struggled in their grasp. "What are you doing?"

"*Shut the fuck up!*" Carter's bellow shattered the silence, and from then on, he ceased pretending it mattered. "And put the guns down!" he barked at the shipmates as he led them along a corridor.

Hustled through a doorway, the three men thrust Peter into the yacht's opulent dining room, done in a Federalist decor that befitted an inaugural ball.

In the center of the room, under a crystal chandelier and two portable surgical lights, an operating table from an Army field hospital stood where the dining table would have been and surrounding it, surgical suction machines, EKG and EEG monitors, and the rest of the bare essentials necessary for modern surgery. An adult male, surgically draped around the head, lay still as two surgeons finished their work. An unmistakable smell filled the air. Peter knew it from experience: bone dust. This was brain surgery.

But it couldn't have been further from Peter's own. There was no stereotactic head frame, no robot, no fMRI, no computer-referenced check to see if they were operating in the right place. There was no team of a dozen medical specialists hovering around the patient. The second surgeon functioned as assistant surgeon, nurse, anesthesiologist, and chief cook and bottle washer for the lead surgeon. But without imaging equipment, there was no way to see if the surgery was in precisely the right place, no less successful. They used basic bone "perforator" drills, and even with irrigation and suction, bone dust and blood covered their scrubs, the surgical drapes, and the expensive Persian rug underfoot. The elegant dining salon looked like a slaughterhouse. The patient was awake, but strapped down, a prisoner of medical torture. It was as primitive and barbaric as anything Dr. Mengele might have dreamed up.

Behind the table stood two more security guards, each beefier than the other and squeezed into navy suits. One had a shiny brown bald head and looked like a brick wall, and the other a black square buzz cut and big square jaw that gave him a blockhead.

Guns pointing at him from all sides, Peter cautiously crept to the patient. The surgeons sloppily closed up, as though technique or aesthetics didn't matter. He knew by the opening's location what procedure they performed. Walking slowly around the drape, he thought he recognized the elder statesman who had briefly spoken to Angie/Talia at the inaugural ball. But since that memory was preimplants, he couldn't be one hundred percent sure. The patient was awake, but gagged so he couldn't speak. His face was wet from tears.

From an armchair in a shadowy corner, a figure rose to greet Peter. It was Josiah Brant. "Let me present to you Mr. Anthony Dulles, Phoenician, owner of this yacht, and traitor to both club and country. We are certain that Mr. Dulles knows a great many things about 10/26 that we need to ascertain to protect national security, so he's been given the gift of a Hippo 2.0 and a Cortex 2.0 by our brothers here."

Anthony Dulles was in no condition to help Peter or Prometheus Industries. He couldn't help himself.

Peter thought he might vomit, and the slowing of time didn't help. "How could you do this and call yourselves doctors?" Neither surgeon would look him in the eye.

"Tony's a spy by trainin', a bureaucrat by necessity, an entrepreneur by inclination, and secretive by nature," said Josiah. "He invented the Cold War interrogation protocols as a young man in the early days of the CIA. Lie detectors are meanin'less on him. And as you know, sodium pentothal is highly overrated as a truth serum, and its anesthetic properties might interfere with any cybernetic information transfer if we required it. And torture takes too long, with unreliable results."

The old man's plaintive face begged Peter to save him. But how?

"That's ridiculous. He's probably brain damaged already," Peter insisted.

"It's a risk we have to take. Could you imagine if the terrorist plot had come from within our own ranks? We need to know what he knows, so we can root out the remainin' traitors to the United States."

"It won't work. Even with the devices, you can't get them to work without the processor synced to his brain and the programs back in Palo . . ." In a flash, Peter understood his role and turned on his partner. "You fucking bastard . . ." he hissed.

Guilty, Carter looked away.

"Yes. You have a workin' processor," confirmed Josiah.

They needed Peter's processor to make the extraction work. While it wasn't synced to Dulles's brain, it was synced to *a* brain. And even if they couldn't upload Dulles's thoughts, per se, their plan to interrogate him with the chip's and processor's assistance made a sick kind of sense. If it worked at all, it would record Dulles's brain activity, like the processor recorded Peter's. Dulles couldn't suppress his neurons' firing and they would eventually learn the algorithm to properly decode the information at a later date. It was only yesterday Peter had boasted they'd decipher thought within the year.

Josiah turned to the surgeons. "Thank you, gentlemen. That's all for now."

The two doctors shared a look of concern, but they weren't going to argue. Angel Hair and Big Biceps escorted them out. Baldy and Blockhead remained.

Dulles continued to stare at Peter as though he knew him. And even a trussed-up patient had body language. The longer Peter watched, the more signals emerged from Dulles, a twitch whenever the subject of his memories came up or Dulles's periodic appraisal of Carter. He also noticed Carter avoided Dulles's gaze. Dulles was afraid of what his mind contained. But did that prove his guilt?

"It still doesn't make sense," insisted Peter. "Even if you extract information, you won't be sure what you've got for at least . . . six to twelve months. And what happens to Dulles in the meantime? This was . . . butchery, not neurosurgery."

"Oh, there's no problem. He'll be dead. You'll have killed him, with this gun," said Josiah, as he displayed a 9mm. "This is the second part of your initiation. To prove your loyalty to the Phoenix Club."

Struggling to hold down the bile that flooded his throat, he looked at his partner in horror. "Mother of God . . . you knew about this?"

"Just cooperate. It's important. It's the most important thing you'll ever do. If you don't, they'll kill you, too."

"You motherfucker!" The last two years swirled madly through his brain. "Was Lobo's takeover a part of this?"

Carter didn't look surprised at the jump in logic. "Yes. We had to separate you from Biogineers to get you to develop this. The timing of the attacks . . . was convenient. I knew if you couldn't make bots, you'd come back to this for your father."

"You sold me into slavery, asshole!"

"And you . . . weren't the man I thought you were."

"What the fuck does that mean?"

"You told me you'd do whatever it takes! And now you won't!"

Josiah separated the young men. "What is it about this younger generation that makes y'all so unable to grasp the big picture?" He looked at Peter. "If you disobey me, we'll kill you, but we'll also kill your wife. If you're so willin' to be disloyal at this crucial moment, who knows how much you told her about the club or your thoughts about it? There can't be any loose ends in a scenario as important as this."

"I swear to God, I told her nothing! Carter knows it's true! Tell him, Carter . . . Please . . ."

Carter said nothing, but at the mention of Amanda's death, he looked like he might cry.

"You youngsters have to grow up and accept responsibility, or this country'll be destroyed within a generation. You don't care about your life, and that's your choice. But do you care about your wife's? Are you willin' to make that choice for her? Please restrain Mr. Bernhardt," Josiah ordered the two remaining guards. Then to Carter, "I believe we'll need that processor now."

Even though he knew it was pointless, Peter struggled in the guards' grasp. He needed every extra moment the adrenaline gave to figure out how he could save himself and Dulles, because, so far, he didn't have a clue.

With the guards' tight grip on Peter, Carter carefully removed the processor's connection from the magnet under Peter's scalp. The moment of disconnection was disorienting. Peter felt . . . dimmer. Less connected. Had he been relying on information within the Cortex 2.0 so heavily, compared to information stored inside his own neocortex, that its removal would feel so immediate? Was his neuroplasticity so malleable that his brain bowed out in the presence of a better model and took a vacation? Panic set in. What if he forgot information? What if his life depended on it? What if he couldn't get it back?

Meanwhile, Carter pulled the cigarette pack–sized box out of Peter's back pocket and placed it on a small table that had been set next to Dulles. He connected the magnetized end onto the magnetic strip under Dulles's sutured scalp to the Cortex 2.0 with a wire for quicker transmission. Then he turned to a laptop on the table and began to type in commands to wirelessly activate Dulles's Hippo 2.0 and Cortex 2.0. Over Carter's shoulder, Peter could see that the implants picked up electrical signals from Dulles's brain, even with inflammation and incomplete neural growth and attachment to the electrodes. It shouldn't have worked. But unfortunately, it did.

"Who else helped at Prometheus? You're not smart enough to have figured this all out for yourself," sneered Peter.

Carter looked hurt, but admitted, "Chang. He was buyable by more than just ATEAMO."

It took Peter a moment more than he would have liked to realize, "You knew about him before he died?"

"Smartest guy in the room, and you don't know shit," Carter snapped.

Peter flinched as though slapped.

No one spoke for several minutes, each man focusing intently on the diagnostics of the chips and processor. Finally, all the components responded to each other.

Josiah asked, "Is he ready?"

"As he'll ever be," sighed Carter.

The secretary of state came face-to-face with Dulles. "What do you know about 10/26?" He paused, giving Dulles time to think his thoughts that the processor could record.

Peter saw the neural firing on the computer screen. God damn it. It was working.

Josiah continued. "Who was the architect of 10/26?" Again, a pause. "Who else knows? Who was involved with you? How long have you been a traitor? Are there any others within the club? Do you have further plans?"

All the while, Dulles kept giving Peter meaningful looks, as though desperate to convey something to him. Josiah couldn't help but notice the silent communication. "You know each other?" Dulles closed his eyes.

"No," said Peter. "We've never met. Until now."

"I guess I'll know the truth about that soon enough," said Josiah. "I still hold out hope I haven't misjudged you, son. I'm tryin' to be sympathetic to the shock you're in and give you the necessary time to reconsider your position."

And what was his position? The club had cornered the world market in his technology, one of global importance in the future for both military and civilian applications, and if they were the only ones to control it, they would have extraordinary power to wield it as both a tool and a weapon. He was sure of that. But there were loose ends to everything he'd seen so far. There had to be a greater agenda, other than a ghoulish interrogation. What else would they be doing with the technology? Was it just this technology? What about the bots?

"Was getting the prosthetics and the bots the plan all along?" asked Peter.

Josiah was about to answer, but Peter cut him off. "No. I want Carter to have the balls to tell me what he knew."

"Yes," admitted Carter. "And frankly, your lack of cooperation isn't reflecting very well on my nomination of you to join the club. I thought you'd do anything to survive."

"You never told me what was at stake! How could you, of all people, think I would do this?"

Carter looked at him with pity. "You still don't know what's at stake."

Amanda's voice played back in Peter's head, even without the Cortex 2.0: *No, you had to make him do the whole dance . . . prove his loyalty, his belief in you . . .*

"Who did you kill to finish your initiation?" asked Peter.

"Many Phoenicians have," Carter replied. "All of us are capable of killing someone, if the good of the club and the country are at stake."

"Who did you kill?"

Carter turned away, ignoring the question.

Josiah joked, "Carter, if your memory's so bad as to forget someone that important to you, then you might need the Hippo 2.0 yourself!"

Who was "that important" to Carter? Were they important because of what the death meant to his membership or important because . . . he and the victim were close? Peter racked his brains. Who could that be? He felt so stupid . . .

"Wait . . . you killed . . . Nick?" The horror of it swamped Peter. "But he loved you like a son. He loved you more than he loved me! Why would you . . . nanowires? You killed him for nanowires?"

Carter was agitated, but remained silent.

"And me . . ." Peter remembered the questions in the amphitheater. "What have I done? You sacrificed me for my tech—to torture, to brainwash—and what will you do with the bots?" The room spun. He lunged at Carter, but the guards held him tight. "And will you kill Amanda? Personally? How will you do it? With your bare hands? Or is it all too dirty for you, and another member does it to prove their loyalty? How will you ever sleep again? There isn't enough whisky or dope or coke in the world to make the memory of us all go away . . ."

Peter could see the questions taking a toll. He turned his venom on Josiah. "And who was your first victim, Mr. Secretary?"

"My initiation? Jack Ruby."

"Jack Ruby died in prison."

"Ruby might 'a technically been a prisoner, but he died of a pulmonary embolism at Parkland Hospital while bein' treated for pneumonia. I dressed as a doctor, walked into his room, and injected fat into his jugular vein. He needed to die . . . loudmouth ass, all hot 'n' bothered about his role in history and ready to blabber at his retrial too much for our likin'."

Carter couldn't take the questions anymore. "For Christ's sake, Pete, just kill the man so we can all get the fuck out of here, get drunk, and go back to our happy lives!"

"Happy lives!" Peter turned to Anthony Dulles on the operating table. "And who did he kill to become a member?"

"Tony?" responded Josiah. "He was initiated before the loyalty test was instituted under club president J. Edgar Hoover back in '63 . . ." He puffed up a little with pride. "I was the first."

The processor was still working, even though Josiah had finished interrogating Dulles. Josiah allowed this continuing conversation to get more information out of the spy. What were Peter and the others saying they wanted Dulles to hear and think about? Why did Peter and Dulles still matter if they claimed they were so willing to kill them?

While arguing, Peter weighed his options for his and Amanda's survival, considering every conceivable scenario and means of escape. Without the Cortex 2.0, he had only one option . . .

"I'll do it. But only because of Amanda. She shouldn't pay for my mistakes, or her best friend's betrayal. But I never want to see your *fucking face again!*" he yelled at Carter, so violently the guards lifted their weapons.

Shaking, Peter took a big, calming breath and turned to Brant. "So what am I supposed to do?" He tried to ignore the expression on Dulles's and Carter's faces. Dulles looked like he was the one who misread Peter. Carter looked unconvinced, but he didn't voice his doubts.

"That's my boy. You'll realize in time you made the right decision." Josiah handed the gun to him. "There's a single bullet, so don't get any heroic ideas, or you're a dead man. One shot to his brain, please. And make it count."

CHAPTER THIRTY-SIX

Gripping the gun tightly in his sweaty palm, Peter circled Dulles's head to face the heavily swagged and curtained picture window. Guns aimed, the guards repositioned themselves, Baldy in front of the window to face him and Block-head to his side. Peter knew the most lethal place to shoot was the temple, the eardrum, or the brain stem. The latter was tricky, given how Dulles's head was positioned on the operating table.

"I'm sorry," he said quietly to Dulles. "I wanted to save your life. But I don't know how."

Dulles looked deeply into his eyes, then closed his own in resignation. Peter placed the gun against Dulles's ear . . .

. . . and yanked the processor off Dulles's head with his left hand, leaving the Cortex 2.0's box swinging in the air by the cord. With his brain in slow-time, he took careful aim at Baldy's gun. But to those in the room, his shot was instantaneous.

BOOM!

The bullet passed through Baldy's hand and partially shattered the window's tempered glass as Baldy's gun dropped to the carpet. Bullet-hole cracks radiated from the pane's center, the glass hanging precariously in place from its sandwich of plastic laminate and metal frame.

Peter stuffed the Cortex 2.0 into his pocket and ducked as Blockhead shot, hurling his empty gun at Blockhead's gun hand, knocking the weapon off bead long enough to let Peter dive for the partially shattered window and avoid the second shot. Baldy grabbed his bleeding hand and ran like an enraged bull for Peter, while Blockhead tried to readjust his aim. The bullet flew toward Peter, but even though he could almost follow its trajectory, he couldn't run fast enough to avoid getting clipped.

It hit his outer thigh, but he hardly felt it with all the adrenaline. Hoping the curtains and rod weren't tacked up for show, he threw himself at the window, grabbed the drapes and kicked both feet at the hole in the glass. The cracked window exploded onto the deck as Peter sailed through. He aimed his legs over the deck railing, twisting around like a midair diver to grab the rail and release the drape. He dropped, scrambling to the deck below.

Blockhead ran to the railing and leaned over, firing multiple shots down at him, but he ran inside the first available door for cover and slammed it behind him.

As bullets pinged outside, Peter limped quickly through the dark room. The iron smell of recent, bloody death stung his nostrils. He found them on the floor next to a bar, their drinks still cold with ice on the marble countertop. Surgeons were expendable, too.

Peter thought faster and time moved slower than he'd imagined possible, even with just his Hippo 2.0. He created a mental map from his memories of the ship and made assumptions about the rest. He had to go down and aft to get to the launch. He cut through a darkened game room, then lounge, and peeked through a door leading to an internal spiral stairwell. He was on the third level. Hearing and seeing no one, he ran down.

Within seconds, a laser pointer flashed near his eye before shots exploded next to his ducking head, embedding in lacquered mahogany walls. It was Angel Hair and Big Biceps. They knew where he was going. He dashed through the first available door on Level Two.

A narrow hallway revealed several doorways on both sides. These were crew quarters. Eerily still bodies of a half-dozen young men and women lay on their bunks. The club must have boarded the ship just after the day shift went to sleep and shot them in their beds with silencers. On a ship this big, they had to eliminate at least a dozen crew, including the captain. The night shift's bodies would be stowed somewhere else.

Angel Hair burst into the hall. Peter assumed Big Biceps would try to head him off. Angel Hair's laser sight glowed dark red on Peter's black T-shirt.

Diving into a room, Peter slammed and locked the door. Bullets blasted at the door and around the frame, but the hardwood gave him a few seconds. The room was internal, with no window or porthole. There were two dead bodies; a young blond woman in a lower bunk and an older brunette in the upper, both shot in the head.

Angel Hair kicked at the door, but the solid wood was tough. Peter thought he heard him speak, maybe into a headset. As slow as time seemed to Peter, he didn't have much of it until reinforcements arrived.

Frantic, he yanked open the closet. A small set of golf clubs leaned in a corner. He grabbed the largest iron and climbed into the top bunk with the older woman's corpse. He burrowed under the bedding and tried to become as small as possible against the wall, arranging the corpse in front of him as though she had not been touched. As he turned her head on her pillow, he saw the entry wound was relatively small, but the back of her head appeared intact. They had used hollow points, which caused maximum internal damage, but would not penetrate far.

Angel Hair shouldered the door open. He looked for Peter immediately behind the shredded door and in the closet. When he bent over to peek under the bunks, Peter pushed the cadaver and bedding in front of him and he and the corpse fell on top of the killer. Angel Hair shot at the nearest body like crazy, but the corpse bore the brunt of the hollow points, sheets and blankets dancing with the impact.

The gun jammed. In the seconds it took for Angel Hair to rack the slide back a couple of times to clear it, Peter leapt, bashing the killer in the head with the golf iron. Angel Hair finally ceased moving, embraced by his victim.

Peter left the jammed gun behind. Brandishing the iron, he dashed down the hall toward the tender.

He burst into a laundry room. There was another door at the end of the line of washers. This opened into an equipment room, filled with wetsuits, inflatable rafts, and other water gear. Another spiral stairway plunged into a dark hall. It was the bottom level, where the beach deck lay astern.

He slid the golf club in his jeans' belt loop head up, like a sword. The stairs were metal and very noisy and he ran down them as quietly as possible. Only at the bottom did he recognize the mother lode hidden in the shadows: cabinets contained scuba tanks, diving weights, harpoons, masks—the works. He loaded an underwater harpoon, grabbed an empty scuba tank and some diving weights, and threw them over his shoulder like a bandolier.

The other wall had mechanical controls, numerous levers, seal wheels, and gauges—mechanisms to open and close parts of the ship's stern.

Feet pounded upstairs.

Not sure what did what to what, he grabbed every lever and switch and moved them to the "On" or "Open" position. The aft wall opened slowly from the top, like a drawbridge. Metal gears ground and rarely opened seals hissed.

Someone outside the opening wall yelled and footfalls pounded down stairs. He dodged left as a bullet ripped through his left bicep and three more missed his head. He whipped around, firing the harpoon gun, and nailed Baldy through the left forearm and into his ribs. Screaming, Baldy dropped his gun. With a hastily tied bandage wrapped around his right hand, now Baldy had a useless left hand as well.

Peter loaded a second harpoon. Outside, Big Biceps' attention was split between aiming his gun at the lowering wall and untying the tender's tie line so the speedboat wouldn't be pulled up out of the water. Big Biceps jumped off the rising deck into the tender to wait for Peter.

Josiah screamed from above, "Get the processor!"

The beach deck rose far enough that the lowering door would soon meet the deck and crush anyone between. Gears screamed as both decks slammed into the other at a forty-five-degree angle.

Peter ran up the twelve-foot hill of the wall toward the tender, lugging the steel scuba tank and the harpoon gun. Josiah ran for the farthest aft rail two decks above. He fired, but missed without a good, clean shot and retreated to the stairs to get a floor closer.

The wall was too steep and slippery to climb just by foot, so Peter used his good right arm. He slid back a couple of feet and tried again. He managed to grip around the side of the dropped wall, using the adjacent exposed wall's left edge for leverage.

Still impaled by the harpoon, Baldy staggered to the control panel to realign the decks—beach deck down and aft wall up. He banged bloody fists and elbows at buttons and levers. Suddenly, the wall started to rise again. Peter scrambled madly, but lost his grip and slid to the metal floor. Baldy's right foot came up to meet Peter's chin, but not before Peter reached up and grabbed the harpoon still in his chest. Baldy knelt in agony as Peter plunged the shaft in and around the chest cavity, between the ribs and below the sternum. Within seconds, Baldy was on his back, mouth gushing blood. Dying.

Peter staggered back to the controls and reversed them. Armed with his tank and harpoon gun yet again, he scrambled up the deck. A bullet whistled past his ear. Josiah aimed again above him on the outer deck. Peter crashed to the metal and slid down the door, holding tight to the tank like a baby. He aimed the harpoon up and fired, driving Josiah away from the rail and back to the spiral stairs. Josiah would be in the control room in moments.

Carter hadn't appeared. Peter wasn't sure whether to be relieved or worried.

Pain only slightly subdued by adrenaline, he built up as much momentum as possible in a few giant steps and leapt off the top left corner of the pitched deck into the waiting speedboat, holding the steel tank vertically in front of his head and heart. But Big Biceps was ready. Bullets pinged off steel as Peter fell upon the shooter into the cockpit of the boat. He slammed the soldier in the head with the scuba tank, while his own legs crumpled in pain under him. Big Biceps toppled and Peter shoved him into the roiling sea.

Behind the wheel, Peter jammed the electronic throttle back as far as it would go and tore off to shore. The boat made a skull-shaking racket at full speed. He turned around. Blockhead was chasing on a Jet Ski, followed by the second high-tech tender, driven by a soaked Big Biceps with Josiah and Carter.

Peter zigzagged, jumping waves to evade Blockhead, but the mercenary was skilled on the military-grade Jet Ski. If the boat was going over eighty knots, the ski was pushing one hundred.

The Jet Ski weaved along the port side. Blockhead pulled his handgun from his shoulder holster. Peter turned the wheel, weaving back and forth and ducking to avoid the shots. He tried to ram the ski, but Blockhead was quicker. Peter was afraid a major evasive maneuver, like a three-sixty, might flip the boat. Blockhead decelerated and followed a safe distance from the rooster tail. Suddenly, he accelerated just in front of the tail, leaping from the ski onto the speedboat's smooth, long stern deck that covered the motor and forward-rolled into the cockpit's rear seats. He raised his gun to shoot . . .

No longer caring if they capsized, Peter spun the steering wheel hard to port, throwing Blockhead off balance as the tiny boat whirled topsy-turvy in the waves but remained upright. The mercenary's arms slammed on the starboard gunnel and his gun flew into the sea.

Aiming at shore again, Peter unsheathed the golf club and jammed it in the steering wheel, braced between the seat, footrests, and the scuba tank to keep the boat on course.

Blockhead leapt over the front seats and threw himself on top of Peter to grapple for the steering wheel and throttle, while the second speedboat gained on them. Blockhead's punches were laser aimed and merciless. A fist to the outer thigh wound, another to the left bicep, his right foot wrapped around Peter's legs, sweeping him to the floor. All of Peter's brainpower could not overcome the brute strength of the Special Forces fighter. With Peter wedged helplessly in the tight floor space, Blockhead reached for an ankle blade . . .

. . . just as the sun rose with a *KABOOM!*

Dulles's yacht blew apart across the Pacific in several explosions. The bursts were so bright, Blockhead squinted into the artificial daylight, distracted. Peter kicked both legs with all his might into the killer's groin.

Blockhead staggered, blinded by genital agony and pupil constriction. Peter scrambled over the seat backs, pulling the dive-weight bandolier from around his shoulder and clutching his golf club. But there were few escape options on a thirty-foot tender.

Doubled over, Blockhead dived for the throttle. Peter swung the club at his hands to stop him from slowing the boat. Blockhead grabbed the club midswing, wrenched it out of Peter's grip, and chased him over the seat back. Peter scrambled for the stern deck. Blockhead leapt on Peter's back, and the two slid across the glass-smooth decking toward the watery rooster tail. To stop his slide off the stern with his palms, he let go of the club and the weight belt, and they slid into the ocean. The killer's hands went around Peter's neck and killer's knee pinned Peter down by his hip. Peter tried to pull the chokehold away, but Blockhead grabbed both his hands and wrenched them up and over Peter's head to meet.

Brant screamed so loudly into Blockhead's earpiece, Peter could hear the order through the wind and engines' roar, "Get that processor—or else!"

It lay stuffed down his front pocket. He pulled his knees to his chest to make access harder. Blockhead tried to rip open the right front pocket, leaving only his left to keep Peter's hands crushed on the deck. Peter wiggled his left hand free from under the killer's single grip and yanked the stern tie line attached to the boat's stern cleat.

The boat jumped a wave and both men's bodies lifted into the air. Peter torqued his body over, wrapping the rope around his middle into a quick knot, while pushing Blockhead away. The killer grabbed for Peter, the rope, the boat, anything, but missed, falling through the rooster tail into the sea.

Peter hung off the starboard stern, bouncing with the rooster tail's high-powered waterspout. Avoiding the propeller, he pulled himself up the rope, back onto the stern of the boat. Safely on board, he yanked open the knot and staggered to the bow to aim again for land.

Behind him, Josiah's speedboat hit a bump. The engine's rpms dropped down several musical tones as the clogged propeller sushied Blockhead into shark chum.

He had only a split second to hear the excruciating sound of scraping carbon fibers traveling eighty knots over unseen jagged rock, before . . .

KABOOM!

A fiery explosion blew his launch into hundreds of pieces, lighting the night once more.

CHAPTER THIRTY-SEVEN

His scalded body sank in frigid water. Searchlights from Josiah's launch ringed the dark hull, like a planetary eclipse surrounded by a corona of light and wreckage. The water above looked cloudier and darker than it should. It was his blood. He sank enough to cease seeing anything but inky blackness. His eardrums ached with pressure.

And he needed air. It was time to strip off his clothing and swim for his life.

He kicked off sneakers and socks and struggled to the surface out of the ring of light for a quick breath.

He dipped beneath the surface again and removed the processor from his jeans pocket. He had to get rid of the heavy, waterlogged jeans and put the processor somewhere. He lashed the processor with its cord to his upper arm. Then he peeled the pants off his legs, but burnt skin ripped away with burnt fabric, saltwater cauterizing the lot. Holding his breath, he held in his scream. Peter left his shirt on, afraid to remove any more burnt skin than he had to.

Pain should have overwhelmed him, but the cold was his friend. He fought tormented nerve endings and swam as hard and as fast from the boat and wreckage as he could. Amanda's life depended on his concentration of body and mind. He had to get to her before the club did. It was the only thought that kept him going as unconsciousness threatened everything. He had no gauge of the passage of time with his internal clock variably slowed. He figured he must be a mile from shore. And the current was with him, increasing with the tide.

Two helicopters rose from behind the dark, empty hillsides to rush the oceanfront, covering the area with searchlights. He guessed they had infrared sights, but hoped they couldn't see him if he was deep enough. He focused on calming his terrified, racing pulse, thus requiring less oxygen and fewer surfacings, so he might evade them. He needed to swim deep . . . Surface, gasp, submerge, swim deep . . . There was a rhythm to it, but he hurt too much to hear music.

WHOOMP! With the impact of an underwater bus, ribs collapsed, lungs spewed air. He folded in two and spun like a gyroscope, with no idea which way the surface lay.

It was a depth charge. Even though his consciousness fought it, his primitive brain refused *not* to breathe, involuntarily expanding his lungs. Seawater rushed into the vacuum. With slow-time, he had the luxury of realizing the big mistake.

It was over. He'd never find the surface in time to expel the seawater from his lungs. Revolving slowly, he was dumbfounded that he had failed Amanda, but was still cursed with thinking. He'd die analyzing his end. To the end.

He felt a nudge. He imagined a gray mass with a fin flashing near his face, but it was too dark to see. More fins bumped him . . .

Suddenly, a zap passed through his head, as though his brain heard an electric shock without using ears. Was he having an aneurysm? Or did his injuries create a short in the implants? The past flickered by: Pop walking with him between the river and the railroad tracks, telling him he wasn't allowed to get seriously involved with his high school sweetheart, Tammi Wanamaker, because a serious relationship would derail him from his dreams. His father's stern voice, the smell of fuel, dead fish, and the funky mud of the intertidal zone gave way to autumn wind chilling him through his thin denim jacket. Memories and moments were jarred from his neurons, like falling fruit from the highest branches of a shaken apple tree . . .

Was this life flashing before death?

Pressured water rushed toward him. A narrow snout poked him gently. It was the dolphin pod. He hoped those rumors that DARPA trained killer dolphins were just rumors.

ZAP!

His brain twinged again, the tingle shooting down his spine . . . After a swish 'n' spit of Listerine while bopping to a decent live-cover of Oingo Boingo's "Dead Man's Party," Carter punched his arm as encouragement during their sophomore Full Moon on the Quad, Stanford's annual mass-kissing ritual. Amanda grooved nearby among the three thousand students, lost in the music. Peter hadn't kissed her yet . . .

The pod closed in, encircling him. At some cetacean cue, they rushed him, pushing his body to the surface. Two dolphins let him use them as floats as he hauled himself over their backs and coughed and coughed and coughed as much of the seawater out of his lungs as he could, gasping at life-giving air. His lungs and ribs seared like frying steak. The pair of helicopters flew away from him as they scoured the water's surface. *American Dream II* was gone—sunk to the bottom. Josiah's launch was beached, and a third helicopter sat on the pad, presumably to take the remaining men to Palo Alto to kill Amanda.

The search copters turned around and headed back toward his savior pod. He let go of the backs and slipped under the waves, but it was impossible to swim again. Between soaked lungs, oxygen deprivation, and injuries, he couldn't get up enough energy to move his limbs.

ZAP! Amanda lay naked in his arms in his dorm-room twin bed, her silky waist-length black hair covering his torso.

His brain felt so jangled and the memories so disorienting, he would have massaged his head underwater if he could. Then it hit him. It was the dolphins' echolocation! Pumped full of adrenaline and endorphins and who knew what hormones from battering and drowning, he still had a corner of his mind clear enough to hope those stories about dolphins cavitating cellular molecules—shaking them so much with their sonar they stimulated chemical production to promote healing—were true. Maybe the stories of dolphins recognizing and helping injured or "different" humans were true, too. He certainly was both.

This time, the dolphins grasped his dilemma. One sidled up, and he grabbed its dorsal fin and let the dolphin tow him quickly toward the shore. The dolphin felt him try to surface for air and helped him up, only to carry him back down again. The pod formed a phalanx, moving at a fast clip and zigzagging through the icy waters. His grip weakening, the dolphin slowed down to let him gain purchase on its fin again.

The pod slowed as they neared a rocky outcropping, and with a gentleness that amazed and humbled him, they nudged him carefully onto the slippery stone. Out of water's weightlessness, gravity did its worst. Any body part that hadn't hurt before cried out in a sensation that couldn't be called "pain." There was no word for what he felt. He crawled on all fours along an outcropping, skinned legs scraping jagged rock, and slipped down into the blackness of a cave.

It was full of water at the bottom, rising with the tide. He felt along the wall for something to climb up.

He needed light . . . Unconsciously, he looked at his watch. He pressed the light of his sports watch to see the numbers display. It was almost 4:00 a.m. The wall was lit ever so dimly before him.

He saw a small outcropping just over his head. Trying to lift his legs to gain a foothold, he noticed the coloration and sediment showed the highest tidemark came to the edge of the ledge. That wasn't good news, because tonight was the new moon. While probably chosen to keep the events on the yacht under the cover of darkness, it also meant it was time for the spring tides, the highest of the month. He hoped the moon wasn't at perigee, the period it orbits closest to Earth, which brought the highest tides of the year.

Dragging his body onto the ledge, he ripped waterlogged hands, knees, and feet against the stone, leaving a bloody trail. He tried to squeeze in as tightly as possible, so if unconsciousness overtook him, he wouldn't fall into the water and drown.

But as soon as he relaxed and his soaked, ice-cold body stopped moving, his heart rate and respiration decreased rapidly. He shook violently while he examined his wounds by watch light. They still seeped blood, but the bleeding slowed with the pulse rate. He could hear his surgeon joke, "All bleeding stops sometime." Yeah, sometimes it all runs out and you die . . . He would have been glad for coagulation, but he didn't want the flow to stop because his body was shutting down from hypothermia. Or blood loss.

Time sped up. The water came in faster, more violent waves. The cave would fill up before daylight.

He fought to stay conscious, repeatedly pressing the watch light to illuminate his corner of the cave, but it didn't help. All he could think about was Amanda. He had failed her. What was she doing right now? She'd have no idea either of them was in peril. Was she asleep? Was she dreaming? The crash and boom of the rising tide made it hard to imagine her . . . hard to think . . .

He could only fight overwhelming odds so long before his body refused to listen to his willful brain, and the void overwhelmed him. The thought that after all this, Amanda was going to die would have made him cry, if he'd had tears to shed and energy to shed them.

"What's wrong, love?" asked Amanda. She was sitting next to him on the rocks, in that pretty white sundress she wore for his last birthday.

"I'm dying, baby. I tried, but I can't help you . . . Mandy? Forgive me? Please forgive me. I love you so much . . ."

"Forgive you for what?"

"I don't know . . . everything?"

He didn't hear her reply. He fell into a warm, black abyss of delicious, welcoming unconsciousness. To die. A tiny part of his mind was grateful for the release. The rest of him fought in fury all the way down.

And then there was nothing . . .

CHAPTER THIRTY-EIGHT

Peter woke moaning, thrashing weakly in the dark water. Men in black amphibious commando gear and balaclavas waded through waist deep, floating Peter out of the cave. With his last bit of strength, he tried to fend off his enemy. It was dark and he couldn't see. His captors were everywhere and innumerable.

A woman's voice came from the smallest commando. "Stop . . . It's Talia . . . Peter . . . It's Talia . . . I'm here to save you . . . Please, stop fighting!"

Disoriented, he felt a stinging in his arm and only had a moment to realize he didn't hear the helicopters anymore before he felt very mellow.

She spoke quietly, but urgently. "Sorry, I had to calm you down. You have to help me. They'll be back in a few minutes!"

At the water's edge, they laid a waterproof tarpaulin under him and half dragged him up the rock side, each bounce and jar into stone an explosion of pain. They carried him to a blacked-out, cam-ouflaged SUV and hefted his body into the back. It looked military grade, with all the bells and whistles of special ops.

Before they covered him with another tarpaulin, he croaked out, "How'd you find me?"

"I'll tell you later . . ." Talia soothed. "What happened to Dulles?"

"He's dead . . ." mumbled Peter.

The tiny figure froze for a moment. But Peter couldn't continue, because once again the void sucked him up into the moonless sky.

CHAPTER THIRTY-NINE

First, there was sound. The beeps of heart and brain monitors, the wheeze of respirators. Distant voices. His right eye opened. His left couldn't, but he didn't know why. A woman with shoulder-length blond hair, wearing a yellow T-shirt, sat at his right.

A man in a white lab coat hovered to his left. Peter tried to say, "Amanda . . ." but nothing intelligible came out. His jaw was immobile. Something was choking him.

The woman said, "Steve," and motioned to Peter's open, moving eye. Peter knew that voice. It had to be Talia. With makeup. And a wig?

He tried to scream again. "Mandy? Carter!" It sounded like gargling.

The doctor moved closer to the good eye. He was of medium height, mostly bald, with a fringe of black hair, large brown eyes, and handsome, like a young Stanley Tucci. He spoke loudly and slowly, as if to a deaf person. "I'm Dr. Steven Carbone. You're at Sacramento General Hospital. I need to ask you some questions. Can you blink once for yes and twice for no?"

He was disembodied, a brain afloat. Was he at Sacramento General? Were those monitors hooked to him? Did they work for the club? Was Carter controlling all this, like he had everything else? Was he their prisoner? He wanted to tell the idiot to stop yelling, he wasn't deaf, but he felt light-headed again and . . .

He opened both eyes.

"Mandy?" he croaked. He tried to clear his throat, but it didn't help. "Mandy?"

Amanda didn't answer. Peter didn't understand. He was sure she was there in the hospital room. His perceptions betrayed, he felt lost, disoriented. He hadn't seen Amanda since . . . since he'd left for camp. Dread crushed his chest. He struggled to get out of bed, but he was strapped in traction. He shimmied a hand free and pushed his buzzer.

The nurse finally arrived. "Are you okay?"

"Where is she?" he rasped. "What day is it?"

"She's right down the hall. I'll go get her." She moved quickly to the door.

"You sure?"

"Of course! I just saw her." And she was gone.

He was so relieved . . . and yet . . . was she really here? Where was here?

Blond Talia walked in, with the nurse right behind her.

Peter panicked. "Where's my wife? What day is it?"

Talia said very clearly, looking him steadily in the eye, "Honey, I'm right here."

"You're not my wife!" He tried to scream, but couldn't say it louder than a raspy whisper.

The nurse shook her head in pity. Talia hustled her out the door and the two women spoke in hushed tones outside. Only Talia returned and shut the door behind her.

"You've got to listen to me . . ."

"Get away from me! Where's Amanda?"

"I don't know."

"She's dead . . ."

"We don't know that . . ."

"Where the fuck's Carter? He said they'd kill her . . . I couldn't save her . . . she's dead! Jesus, she's dead . . . I let her die . . ."

"Calm down. Right now."

"*Who* the *fuck* are *you*?" he raved.

She stepped closer and he thrashed to evade her. "Please, you've got to calm down. You'll hurt yourself again. Please . . ." She sat on the bed, but he shook and stared, wild-eyed, tears rolling down his cheeks. She slowly, gently brushed them away. At her touch, he flinched.

"How'd you find me when the others couldn't?" asked Peter.

"The kid at Stanford."

Peter was stunned.

"He injected a nanochip in your leg. It's so small, you never felt it. It's recorded your location, vital signs, even emotional distress by measuring cortisol levels ever since he nailed you. I've known where and how you are ever since Stanford. Thank God."

"Why are you doing this to me?" he asked.

"I'm saving you. Not hurting you. I tried before, but you wouldn't listen."

That was the last straw. He laid his head back on the thin, plastic-wrapped pillow that crinkled with every move. There was nothing left to do but weep. Talia grabbed a box of tissues and patted his face, catching the tears before they flooded his ears. He had no idea if she and the people who brought him here were part of the club or here for some other agenda. He remembered she knew Dulles, but that raised more questions than answers. She'd rescued him from the copters and shown him kindness, but did that prove trustworthiness? He tried to think clearly. It was hard. He only knew he was completely in her control.

"Have you looked for Amanda?" he finally asked.

"I've tried home, work, friends. I hacked her electronic accounts, but no phone calls, e-mails, IMs, or texts were made since you disappeared. I don't know where else to look."

He was too afraid to tell her about the commune. What if she led the club right to Amanda and her family?

"And Carter?"

"Living his life. Out in the open, at home, at Prometheus . . ."

He struggled in his traction restraints. "Get me out of here." He was desperate to search for Amanda himself. And kill Carter.

She shook her head with chagrin. "You can't even walk yet."

"Why are you helping me?"

"You're a very important person, and we share a common enemy."

"What's that even mean?" he sneered.

"You're not dead yet, are you? You have to trust me."

"Really? Is that why you tried to seduce me in DC?"

"Yes. I was trying to get you alone, where we weren't bugged, to talk to you. And help you."

"If you want to help, find my wife. Bring her here."

"I'm doing the best I can, but you have to help me, too. Can you do that?"

He grunted noncommittally.

"According to this hospital, you're my husband. Terrence McKinley. I'm Beatrice. Terry and Bea."

"Who are you, really?"

"Talia Brooks."

"And what if you're not?"

"You have to take me as I am."

He studied her face. Her eyes looked as truthful as could be, even if they had once been green and now were blue. She could be manipulating him. Just like Carter.

He turned a corner when he stopped passing out. Instead, he slept. He spent more time conscious than unconscious. And he didn't float through the day in a drug-induced haze. He was thinking and understanding. It was a beginning.

Surreality continued and he tried to grasp what he could. The Hippo 2.0 was working, but without the processor, there was no hard drive to dump the memories onto. Or retrieve them from. He had to rely on his own manipulated, battered cortex. Who had the processor now? He assumed Talia, since she had found him, but . . . had she passed it on to someone else?

There were only two sure things based on everything that had happened: He should be dead. And his best friend was responsible.

Had there been hints Carter would betray him? The signs could have gone back to graduate school, when the club first recruited his friend. Only now could he imagine Carter saying, "I'd love to join and I've got two juicy worms to reel in with me: Dr. Nikolai Chaikin and Peter Bernhardt." And why would he think Peter was capable of murder? Peter said he'd do "anything" to save himself, but "anything" rarely included homicide.

Or was it simply those who perform heinous deeds usually assume others capable of immorality as well? And hadn't Peter acted immorally? He'd lied, participated in corruption, acted violently, let an innocent man tortured with his technology die . . .

His head hurt. He found the media remote attached to his bed. With free arms, he turned on the HOME monitor and chose from a selection. The news. He needed to know what day it was, what was happening, so he could figure out what to do next. Yet another interchangeable, blow-dried anchor blabbed about the latest security threat. But that wasn't what shocked him. It was the date.

September 9. He had been in the hospital almost two months.

Blond Talia came in, smiling. "You look so much better. You have no idea."

"Where is she?"

She pulled a chair up close and whispered urgently, while an ad for antiterrorism home security systems played in the background. "I've looked everywhere, checked everywhere, even the morgue and the obituaries. She's disappeared. Would she go underground?"

"I don't know," he lied. Two months and no sign. He felt nauseous. "Give me my . . ."

She smiled. "If you mean the 'gadget,' I've got it. I'll give it back as soon as you're out."

"I want it now."

"No. You'll only expose yourself. You'll get it when you're safely out of here."

"Who the fuck are you?"

She gripped his arm, squeezing until it hurt. "I'm your guardian angel, asshole, so be nice to me. Instead of treating me like the Grim Reaper, how about saying, 'Thank you, Talia, for saving my life.'"

Peter was learning you don't mess with redheads. Even when they're blond. "Thank you," he mumbled.

"Honestly, you're lucky to be alive with everything you've got. You shattered your ribs, your face, broke an ankle, fractured the femurs and tibia in both legs and a few vertebrae, had bullets in several places, burned twenty percent of your body, but that wasn't even the worst of it. You had ARDS . . ."

Acute respiratory distress syndrome; the result of drowning. The lung tissues were so inflamed by saltwater, they couldn't perform the gas exchange of oxygen in, carbon dioxide out. If she hadn't found him, he would have died within a day, suffocated by lungs that didn't work. That would explain the intubations, the ventilators.

"And fifty percent of people treated for ARDS die," continued Talia, "even with all possible medical intervention. And they probably didn't have half as much wrong with them as you did."

"But . . . two months gone . . ."

"They had to medicate you into a drug-induced coma, so you'd stay unconscious for as long as possible to heal. It also makes it easy to starve you. They want you as lean as possible, to lessen the burden on the lungs and heart. You should see yourself."

He held an arm up to examine. His hand was stringy. All knuckles, blood vessels, tendons, and mottled skin. The hospital bracelet around his bony wrist said "Terrence McKinley, O+." He ran his thumb over fingertips. They were smooth. No guitar calluses. He looked at Talia, puzzled.

"Your hands were ripped to shreds, which was good, because they were bandaged for a long time. When they took them off, I had to buff off your prints with an electric sander."

"Whoa . . ."

"Yeah. Glad no one caught me. That would have been hard to explain. 'My husband may die, but he likes smooth fingertips . . .' I also had to make sure they ran no MRIs. Wasn't sure if the implants were metal or not. It was tricky, because you've had a lot of facial surgery, but I told them you had a deep-brain stimulator for depression. Steve knows that's bullshit, but he sold the story to the rest of the staff."

"Steven Carbone."

"That Hippo 2.0 still works. Yeah, he's your lead doctor and a good egg. You can trust him."

Peter trusted no one.

"I've paid your medical bills, as your wife. We've had no insurance since our COBRA expired after your lay-off from the plant, so we've been paying cash, with the help of a generous relative."

"You mean you . . ." His rack-rate bills must have run into the millions.

"Don't worry. It's fine. Now this is important: You can't remember who you are. Or who I am. You've got amnesia from a mysterious boating accident nowhere near your real 'accident,' that may or may not have been an attempted suicide. At some point, local law enforcement may try to question you about it, but we'll be long gone. The point is, once you're able, we keep moving until we get somewhere safe for you . . . and your wife. Because, even though they probably think you're dead, they won't stop until they're sure."

"What about DNA?"

"Good. You're thinking. At first, we used the DNA for lab work from a comatose John Doe. Steve arranged it, but it was risky. The guy had to be enough of a match that they didn't do something to you contrary to your real DNA. You know, treat you for sickle cell or something. Did you have DNA documented or tissue samples anywhere?"

"Sperm samples. For IVF."

"I'll try to see how I can get them back . . ."

"Don't bother. Assume they have my DNA. From my bed at camp, from a drinking glass. My house'll be covered with it. Terry's DNA can't be sampled from me. Or they'll match me."

Talia handed him an old-fashioned cell phone. No one had these single-function electronics anymore with GOs around. "Call the preprogrammed number if I'm not here and you need help.

Don't call landlines. They trace those faster than the mobiles, which use GPS. And don't call anyone else with it. Otherwise, you'll leave a digital trail. Think of this as a one-time, disposable, get-out-of-jail-free card."

There was a knock at the door. Peter palmed the phone and slipped it under his pillow.

"Come in," said Talia.

A head peeked in. It was Dr. Carbone. "How's my patient?"

Talia and Peter just looked at each other.

"Fine. Got it," Carbone said. "Well . . . I've got good news. It's time to take the casts off, get you on your feet. You'll need significant physical therapy, but we'll go over all that later. Ready for a little freedom?"

Peter couldn't wait.

CHAPTER FORTY

After days of physical therapy, this was the first day Peter could move around on his own, although "move" meant a painful, old-man shuffle in grippy hospital socks across slippery linoleum.

Freedom of movement meant he could see himself in the mirror over the sink. As he washed his hands, he looked at his reflection for the first time in almost three months. And it didn't register. He thought he was dreaming.

But this was his face. They had shaved what little chestnut hair remained after the explosion for surgery. It had grown back completely white, like his father's. His hairline was altered, the slight widow's peak he inherited from his father gone. Beneath the hair was a face he didn't know. It had different proportions. The nose was narrower, longer. His cheekbones were more pronounced, and his jawline more refined, giving the face an upside-down egg shape, instead of his squared-off one. His eyes were almond-shaped and had a slight uplift at the outer corners. They also looked much larger on this face. His lips were thinner.

The only familiar things were his azure eyes. Those eyes were his anchors. Struggling for objectivity, he studied the face as though it weren't his. It didn't look bad—in fact, the reflection was handsome in a sickly poet way—but the gulf between meeting that face and owning it was huge. Speaking to Talia and the hospital staff over the last few days, he accepted his voice had changed for good. Dr. Carbone found vocal cord granulomas, developed from extended intubations, giving him a bourbon-and-cigarettes growl that didn't sound like his higher-pitched, clear-toned, clean-living self, either.

It was all too much. He shuffled out of the bathroom and sat on his bed to turn on the monitor for distraction. Finding a news service to surf, he found a story about a yacht sinking off the California coast with its owner, Anthony Dulles, and his guests, Peter Bernhardt, Dr. Jeremiah Vail, and Dr. Larry Zuckermann, as well as twelve crew people aboard. All were lost. Terrorism was suspected, but no suspects named, although the article insinuated a link between the bots from Biogineers and Bernhardt's recent death, as though *he* were the terrorist on a suicide mission. There was a short obituary for Peter in the *San Francisco Chronicle*, but no mention of Amanda or quote from her in any news item related to him, including obituaries.

He turned off the screen and shuffled to the window. He hadn't been outside in three months. It had rained for the past four days, which was unusual. People ran from their cars for the shelter of the covered hospital entrance. Two vehicles looked familiar: a pair of government-issue black Chevy Suburbans, identical to the FBI cars that had visited Prometheus. He was sure they had the same plates, although he'd need his processor to confirm it. Three stories below, a man in a trench coat paced the sidewalk in front of the building. He looked like one of the men in the line of cars who was there the day Chang died.

There was a knock at the door. It startled like a shot. A nurse peeked her head in.

"You look so much better, Mr. McKinley. It's good to see you up and around."

"Uhhh . . . thanks."

"It's good timing. You've got a friend to see you . . ."

For a moment, he imagined it was Amanda.

". . . he might help you jog your memory," she continued.

He. "Who is it?"

She ducked her head into the hall again to ask and back. "Lazlo DiLillo."

Who the hell was Lazlo DiLillo? The combination of a stranger claiming to know an imaginary patient and the presence of two FBI SUVs could mean up to a dozen agents in and around the hospital. But why now? Talia had used his fake DNA weeks ago. He didn't look like himself. Had no fingerprints. All identifiable info had been excised from his record. But he'd been admitted the day of the yacht explosion. That alone may have tagged him. For DNA. They'd want hair, skin, blood, anything to ID Peter Bernhardt. Then they'd kill him and make it look like a medical event. Like Jack Ruby.

He had to get out of here.

A male voice in the hallway spoke. "Can't I pop my head in? Just want to see if I can help."

Peter jammed his foot at the base of the door, wedging the nurse between the door and the frame. He spoke quickly and quietly to the nurse. "I'm sorry, I don't remember a Lazlo DiLillo. And I don't feel up to it today. Can he come back . . . next week?"

The man spoke quickly, smoothly. "Buddy, I know you've got amnesia, but I drove four hours to see you. Just a quick hello, man . . ."

Peter looked meaningfully at the nurse. "Please, it's a lot to handle. Can you give me a few minutes to pee, clean up? I look like hell."

"You let me know when you're ready. I'll make him cool his heels for a few minutes," conspired the nurse.

"You're the best . . ."

She winked and shut the door.

He looked around the room. One door. One window. Three floors up. No fire escape.

He hobbled to the window. Through the rain, he could make out an agent in one of the Suburbans. And the pacer was still at the entrance. He would disappear beneath the concrete portico and reappear under his window. The portico hung out two rooms to the left and one floor down.

Grabbing two pairs of latex gloves from the nightstand, he double-gloved his hands. Then he stretched a pair of gloves as best he could over his feet, still covered in the grippy slipper-socks.

He unlocked the bed's castor brakes, but starvation-weak, rolled the bed with difficulty below the fire alarm to climb onto the mattress and unplug the alarm. Then he wheeled the bed across the room, lengthwise against the front door, and reset the brakes.

He quickly stripped the bed of linens and gathered up anything that he could have left skin, blood, or hair on and threw it in a pile on the floor next to the bed and the door. He placed the cell phone hidden under his pillow on the windowsill.

Unplugging the connecting power cable from the blood pressure monitor, he exposed the internal electrical wire from inside the plastic insulation by rubbing it vigorously against a sharp metal edge of the mirror frame in the bathroom and ripping off the female end. He stripped more insulation from the ragged ends.

All the flammable materials he could find were lumped in a pile: cloth and paper towels, paperwork, and antiseptic wipes. He ripped opened the wipes packets, so the alcohol in them would burn.

Plugging in the exposed power cord to the outlet nearest to the door, he held on to the plastic sheathing and touched the two raw ends together right next to the paper towels, causing a short and spark. A paper towel caught the spark and smoldered alight. A breaker flipped somewhere on the floor, extinguishing the lights in his room, and he assumed elsewhere. He fanned the flame.

There was a sudden commotion in the hallway. People yelled in surprise, but within a second, the building's generator kicked in, while nurses ran for patients' rooms to make sure the most vulnerable were all right.

"Lazlo" tried opening the door to the room. When it didn't, he banged on it. "Open up!"

Peter lit the remaining paper towels as kindling and worked to get his bonfire ablaze, making sure it spread to the bed as well. He grabbed an oxygen hose and stretched it as far as it could reach, aiming directly at the fire to keep it burning hot, then wrapped it around a chair leg to anchor it in place. It made a nice little bellows, and he leveled the tiny flamethrower at the barricaded door.

This was a real blaze. The room filled with smoke.

Coughing, he struggled with the window, but it hadn't opened fully in years. Could his skinny body get through the nine-inch opening he managed to make?

Male voices shouted outside his door and battered their shoulders against it. The bed jerked a little farther from the door with each shove.

Fresh air rushed through the small opening, adding oxygen to the fire. The smoke was getting too heavy to breathe.

An agent's eye peered into the one-inch-wide crack they had made in the doorway. "Fire!"

Peter climbed onto a nightstand and, hoping it would support his weight, reached up to plug in the fire alarm. The siren screamed instantly, and he leapt down on quivering legs as a gunshot hit the wall above his head. Hoping the window was out of range, he grabbed the cell phone, clamping it between his jaws. He stuck his head out sideways to get it through, then shimmied his shoulders and arms out. When he looked down, the agent in the car and the agent guarding the door were gone. They were busy storming his door.

Stabbing pain shot through his chest, his ribs guillotined between the window's lower sash rail and the sill, pinning him like an insect specimen. He was stuck.

Wriggling in agony to get through, the door shoved open another crack. A shot hit the window. Glass shattered. He shut his eyes and ducked, almost dropping the cell phone to the wet concrete below as his jaws twitched involuntarily. He squeezed his mouth down hard.

They were sticking a hand through the crack, unable to aim and shooting wildly. He heard screams in the hall and a bigger commotion at the door.

It was the shot of adrenaline he needed. Utilizing his body's shaking from pain and fear, he shimmied furiously again to work one leg out of the window. It was an old building, with brick facing and old ledge work. Peter grabbed onto the window frame and dragged his other leg out, rubbery toes gripping onto the ledge. It was hard to maintain his quivering hold on the rain-slick building. He crept along the ledge to the adjacent room's window and peeked in carefully. A fed beat him to it. Luckily, they couldn't open that window, either, and couldn't see him. If he didn't get past the window, it was too big a jump to the top of the portico overhanging the entrance. He wasn't sure he could make it.

A white box truck, with panels painted "Driven Snow Linen Service," trundled down the driveway toward the building. It would pass under and out the other side two stories below him.

When the fed ran to another room, Peter crouched and clung to the exterior sill. He scuttled sideways under the sill, inching past. No one inside noticed rubber-gloved fingers skimming the granite outside.

If he didn't jump now, he'd miss the truck. He had to concentrate on keeping the phone in his mouth, no matter what. And not being seen.

Down he dropped, over fifteen feet, landing on all fours on the gravel-strewn portico roof. Hands and legs were lacerated as he scrambled for the end of the overhang and fell onto the large delivery truck's container roof. He hoped the guy in the cab didn't hear the thud. Flattening himself out, he grabbed at his soaking wet hospital gown flapping in the back. No need to have his bare ass smiling at every passing bird. Or copter.

He debated if he should call Talia's number. Logically, he didn't know how she could be working for the club if she was keeping him alive. So who did she work for? There was only one way to find out . . . He pressed the green button.

One ring. Two rings. Talia answered, panicked. "Where the hell are you?"

Shielding the phone as best he could from water and wind, fire alarms rang in the background of the call. She was at the hospital. "Look for the Driven Snow Linen Service truck. White, twenty feet long." He peeked over at a street sign. "We've made a right onto Bruceville Road."

"Shit! If they knew you were there, they may know the car I'm driving. Fuck!"

"Borrow Carbone's."

"He's not here."

"Then hot-wire one."

"What?"

"I'll talk you through it."

"They taught that at Stanford?"

"It's a home-grown talent."

"What do I look for?"

"A vintage Ford, sixties or seventies. They're the easiest. You need an unlocked door or break the passenger-side glass."

"Why passenger side?"

"Do you want to sit on broken glass? Or waste your time cleaning it up?"

"Good point." He heard the splatter of feet running on wet pavement.

She was breathing hard as she raced through the lot. "I don't see anything . . ."

"Keep looking."

More time passed. "I found a Mustang!" she exclaimed.

"Good. Pop the hood."

He heard her grunt, but no shattering of glass. "I'm pulling the hood release, but it won't open!"

"Does it say Mach I anywhere on it?"

There was a pause. "Yes."

"It's high performance. Two clips keep the hood from flying open at high speed. See them on top? Remove them and the hood will open . . . Did you break the glass?"

"It's unlocked."

"A vintage Mach I?"

"Yeah."

"Schmuck. Deserves to lose it."

Peter heard the muffled thud of metal. "Got it," she said.

"The distributor's right up front—that thing with all the spark plug wires coming out of it. See it? Now follow the middle wire to the coil."

"Okay."

"Find the plus terminal on the coil and wrap one end of your wire around that."

"Okay."

"Now string the wire to the plus battery terminal and wrap the other end of the wire around that."

"That's why they call it 'hot wire'?"

"Yes. Now follow the plus battery cable to a little black can thing on the left side of the engine compartment. That's the starter solenoid. The cable is attached with a nut. Pull off the rubber connector closest to where the battery cable attaches, leaving a bolt exposed." He could hear her breathing. "Got it?"

"Ummm . . . yeah."

"Okay. Now place any metal object—screwdriver, earring, anything conductive—across to connect the nut and bolt simultaneously and the car will start."

He could hear the sound of rummaging. Probably looking in her handbag. "Shit . . ."

"What's wrong?"

Another pause. "Nothing . . ."

The engine started.

"You did it! Now haul ass before the owner comes out!"

A car door slammed. The background noise went quiet.

"We're making a right into Kaiser Permanente. Someone will look out a window and see a patient on top of a truck!" He slid left and grabbed a panel seam as anchor. "Shit!"

"No! It's okay. I'll be there."

"Do it soon . . ." He peeked over the side. "Follow the 'deliveries' arrow."

"Got it."

He lay there, counting in his head. In ten seconds, he'd come within sight of the windows of the hospital, and his hospital gown and pale body would no longer blend in with the truck's paint job. By "seven," there was a rumbling roar behind him. It was a tweaked Mustang V8, maybe the sweetest sound he had ever heard. "Thank you."

"As soon as you stop, roll off away from the windows and the driver, if you can."

"Will do." He closed the phone. The truck did a K-turn and backed up to the delivery bay. The moment the driver braked, Peter scrambled over the edge and, hanging from gloved hands, dropped to the asphalt. Intense shooting pains crumpled both legs. At the covered entrance, the guard missed an almost-naked patient stumbling away.

Talia hit the turn at sixty miles per hour, but seeing Peter stagger toward her, slammed the brakes. The car spun, momentum continuing in his direction. He dived as far as he could, hitting wet pavement. The car skidded closer . . . closer—she was going to run him over!—until the tire grazed his leg. And stopped.

The passenger door flew open, barely missing his head. "Get in!" she yelled.

He crawled into the tiny, dual-bucket rear seats and Talia hit the gas. Hard. Tires squealed, the door slammed with forward thrust and they raced to the exit.

He ducked as low as possible. "You know how to lay patch," he gasped.

"Give me the phone," barked Talia.

He handed it over. She headed for the 99 Freeway north. Once into traffic, she carefully tossed both her and his cell phones out her window, aiming for the most likely place tires would roll. Peter looked out the rear window. Both phones got nailed within seconds.

"No comm tower's gonna ping me and get away with it." She pointed up to the E-Z Pass glued to the driver's windshield before tearing it off the glass and throwing it out after its cell phone cousins. "When are people going to realize these things are information mother lodes for the government, the marketers, and every retailer in the world? Once the unholy trinity know who you are, not only do they follow you everywhere and record your movements, the media companies sell the information wholesale, so everyone can sell you more shit you don't need or have you surveilled by name-your-government-acronym . . ." She took the first exit and reentered the freeway going south.

"You with a militia?"

"That's funny coming from you." She pulled another ancient cell phone out of her wet handbag.

"Jesus. How many do you have?" The drop in adrenaline sped up time again and he shivered with cold and pain. Talia took off the cheap plastic raincoat and ratty sweater she wore over her T-shirt and handed them back to Peter as she cranked up the heat.

"Wish I had more. And it'll be a while. Get some rest." She pulled out a couple of bobby pins, peeled off the blond wig, and stuffed them into her purse. Her red curls fell around her shoulders and she shook them out.

"Where we going?" he asked.

"San Francisco."

"Good," he said. "Take me to Carter. Jackson Avenue at Alta Plaza Park." But even though he fought to stay alert, he fell asleep.

He woke in panic to honking horns near Livermore. He didn't know where he was.

"It's all right . . ." Talia soothed.

They approached the web of freeways that entwined the region, caught in rainy-day rush-hour traffic. He scrubbed at his face with his fists. "You got a makeup mirror in there?" pointing to her handbag.

"Need to fix your lipstick?"

"To quote a one-time friend, 'Such a comedian . . .'" With his new voice and Ruth's accent, he sounded like Rodney Dangerfield's mother after a bender.

She smiled and handed back her entire handbag. The contents only added to her mystery. After the wig and pins, he found three wallets, all black, but each a different style, with a different driver's license, matching credit cards, and personal papers. Half a dozen cell phones remained. Some lip gloss, eye liner. A tiny packet of tissues. A case with a pair of large sunglasses. A bottle of ibuprofen. He opened the bottle and dry swallowed five capsules. He found the metal compact mirror in a small zipper pocket, along with makeup. She must have used the metal case to hot-wire the car. It had engraved on the front, "'If you obey all the rules, you miss all the fun.' Katherine Hepburn." By Hepburn's definition, Talia was a very fun girl. He opened it and took a good look at his face again.

She caught sight of him in her rearview mirror. "Hope you like it. I picked it out, special . . ."

"Huh?"

"Well, I couldn't just hand them a photo of Peter Bernhardt to work from, now could I? I gave them a photo of a guy close enough that a surgeon wouldn't say, 'That's not the guy on the table!' but enough off that you'd end up unrecognizable. Your face was such a mess, it wasn't too hard to put it back any damn way they wanted, but the old-timer plastic doc definitely did a double take at my photo. He understood faces. He knew your cubist mess of flesh and bone and the photo didn't match. The young doc with him didn't know enough to be surprised. That teaches me to only work with the inexperienced . . . they know and ask less. But they did a damn good job in my opinion." She gave him a quick appraisal as she drove. "You look older, more angular, almost ascetic, like some Spanish Grande or martyred saint by El Greco. Not some young, German-American bioengineer. You certainly sound different."

Peter's grimace betrayed a bent ego.

"Hey, don't get me wrong," she explained. "You're attractive . . . really quite striking. Just different."

"When we get to Carter's, park on Pierce. I'll go down the alley . . ."

She snorted with a glance in the rearview mirror. "That's not your first stop. Not yet."

Freeway signs flew by. Peter said, "Then take the 580 to the 880."

"We're not going there, either."

"Yes we are."

"She's not home," she insisted.

"I need to see for myself."

"You really want to get caught, don't you? That's the first place I'd leave a stakeout if I were the club!"

"Stanford Avenue!" he rasped.

"You really are a scientist! You need proof? Great idea. Let's turn you over to the club!" Talia didn't say another word until they turned off El Camino.

Peter ducked as low as he could to still peek out the rear windows. The gray shingled house with the farmstead roof and the zipper fence looked . . . sad. The grass was long. There were no lights on. Talia didn't slow down.

"Four o'clock, navy Crown Victoria," she whispered, lips barely moving.

A guy sat in the front seat, reading a paper. She was right. He was staking it out.

Peter reached for a phone.

"Don't. It's disconnected."

He decided to believe her. He had no choice. "I need to call information. Can I do that?"

"For what?"

"I need a number in Oregon."

She pulled out a phone and handed it to him, then turned down Hanover Street, so she could get back to the 280. He dialed 411. "Madras, Oregon . . . Subhuti Community . . . S-U-B-H-U-T-I Community . . . yes . . ." He handed the phone to Talia. "Ask for Shakti Alvarez. Then ask Shakti if she knows where Ananda is." He said the name like it rhymed with "anaconda."

"Ananda? Shakti? Where the hell is this?" The phone rang several times. Then someone answered. "Yes . . . Shakti Alvarez please . . . Yes, I'll hold . . ."

Peter looked out the window. She was headed toward his dark green oaks and tawny hillsides. They looked different now. They weren't his hills anymore.

Talia whispered while on hold, "What's Subhuti?"

"It's Sanskrit for 'good existence.' She was born and raised on an ashram. Where the groovy and Buddhistly inclined could live together with their guru as though the '60s never ended. Carter thought 'Ananda,' which means 'bliss' in Sanskrit, didn't fit the new person she wanted to be after she fled the commune. So he changed it to 'Amanda.' After his favorite Noel Coward character in a play called *Private Lives*. That was freshman year. He introduced us freshman year . . ."

Talia raised her pinkie. "Yes, is this Shakti? . . . Oh, good. Hi, my name's Angelica Sternwood and I'm wondering if Ananda is around? Uh huh . . . Well, if you hear from her, could you please give her my phone number for me? It's important . . . Well, you might hear from her, you never know . . . Uh huh . . . Sure, I'll hold . . ." When Shakti found a pencil and paper, Talia gave her a number, thanked her, and hung up. In her rearview mirror, Peter stared blankly out the window. "She said she was surprised about anyone asking for Ananda. They haven't heard from her in four years."

He struggled against inevitable tears. Amanda never made it to Oregon. They'd killed her. And her mother didn't know.

"Get off at Woodside," he blurted out.

"Where are we going?"

"Evergreen Nursing Home."

"No. I'm taking you where it's safe."

"The. Evergreen. Nursing. Home."

"Why don't you get I'm trying to save you?"

"I'm sorry you don't 'get' family or love," he shot back savagely, "but I do."

Talia looked stricken, but said nothing. She exited at Woodside, and he directed her with single words to the building.

Overwhelmed with finding Amanda, he couldn't believe he'd forgotten about his own father. He feared the money he had set aside for Pop's care had disappeared. Would they stick him in a public home, a ward of the state?

She pulled into a parking spot across the street. He began to get out of the car.

"Where the hell do you think you're going?" she asked.

"What's your problem, lady? If you couldn't recognize me, do you think a bunch of overworked nurses would?"

"You're wearing a hospital gown. And socks. And you look like a truck hit you."

He sagged back in his seat.

In a gentler voice, she said, "I'll go in and report back. Lie down."

Peter arranged himself as best he could over the floor hump and foot wells until Talia returned. But she started the car and pulled into traffic as though he didn't exist.

After a few miles, he sat up. "So . . . ?" Her silence made him nauseous. "You've got to tell me, Talia. Please."

She refused to look at his reflection in her rearview mirror. After a while, she spoke.

"I spoke to a Mrs. Manela and told her I was a friend of the Bernhardts and heard about the tragedy. Mrs. Manela agreed it was all very sad and assumed since I was there, I hadn't heard about your father. She said the executor of the Bernhardt estate came to tell old Mr. Bernhardt that his son had died and his wife was missing, presumed dead, and that the executor would take care of him from now on. They knew each other, so she didn't think much about it. No one thought he'd understand, but the news hit your father hard. Mrs. Manela spent most of that day and night with him, since he couldn't stop crying. He went into cardiac arrest around 3:20 a.m. They tried to save him, but he was dead before they got him in the ambulance."

Pop's heart had literally broken. How could he have understood? Had everyone, including Peter, misdiagnosed the extent of his illness? And he had let it happen because he trusted his best friend so much, he left his own father to Carter's care. Why didn't Carter just let him live the rest of his life in ignorance? Did he want Paul to die?

Or maybe Carter had meant to kill Paul and eradicate the Bernhardts for good. But it was Peter's fault. He had asked Carter to take care of his family if the worst happened to him. And the worst had. And Carter had done his worst.

It was all his fault. Spindly arms wrapped around bony ribs as he rocked in the backseat.

"She also never believed you were a terrorist," Talia continued. "You were too kind and sensible a young man for that."

After rocking for another minute, he said, "Everyone I love is dead . . . I should have died on the yacht . . ."

"You can't think like that. It'll destroy you," she said quietly.

He wasn't listening. His head ached from overload.

"Peter, who came to see your father?"

"Carter Potsdam. Our executor. And our executioner. I want. To find. The motherfucker. And kill him. Right *now!*" Spittle and tears flew from his face. The same uncontainable rage that had gripped him after Amanda's miscarriage overtook him again. All he knew is he wanted to kill, or be killed. Nothing else mattered.

"That's it," said Talia. She flipped her turn signal, changed lanes to the right, pulling off on the freeway's shoulder, and threw the Mustang into park. She twisted around to confront him. "You can get out right here and let an eighteen-wheeler nail you for all I care. Otherwise, the only place you're going is home to bed. Then we'll figure out what to do. You're in no position to do anything to Carter Potsdam. You couldn't hurt a fly."

But where was home? Peter Bernhardt not only didn't have a home, he didn't exist anymore.

CHAPTER FORTY-ONE

Battered, orphaned, widowed, homeless, penniless, and anonymous, Peter needed an afterlife. Talia took him to a small apartment on Masonic Avenue in the Haight in San Francisco, one block from the celebrated intersection of Haight and Ashbury. The famous neighborhood was ground zero for the Summer of Love in 1967 and its hippie movement and drug culture. But a combination of dereliction and gentrification over the last two decades had thrown upper-class yuppies cheek to jowl with '60s holdouts and the homeless. The Haight did less sheltering of revolution these days than it did the marketing and selling of it.

He looked at the building. The first floor was brick, with arched windows and an arched front door. Above that, the top two floors were classic San Francisco. Queen Anne-styled wood, each floor with four sets of bay windows facing the street. It was painted a sickly flesh tone, with rust-and-blue-colored trim.

"Should I wait for you to bring me clothes?" he asked.

"This is the Haight. You're part of the scenery."

He unfolded himself from the backseat and tried to stand, but his knees buckled under him. He fell on the car roof for support.

Talia looked scared. "Jesus, I've never seen anyone so pale. Lean on me."

The front door had a dozen buttons to buzz apartments, but the apartments didn't have names on them.

"Is it empty?" he asked.

"Nah. People here like their privacy. When they aren't baring their souls to the world."

Of course, she lived on the top floor, only accessible by stairs. All Peter could think of was the song from that Christmas perennial, *Santa Claus Is Coming to Town*, "Put One Foot in Front of the Other." When he started to hum it to take his mind off the pain, she laughed. He rumbled like a tone-deaf Tom Waits.

She opened her door, and one of her many ancient cell phones rang. He staggered to an armchair and collapsed into it.

She flicked it open. "Yeah . . . Look, Steve, I'm sorry, but . . . No . . . Yes . . . No, he's okay . . . I promise I'll tell you everything . . . He's not gonna die on my watch . . . Fuck you! . . . He'd be dead now if he . . . terminate McKinley . . . Make sure you find all the records and match them . . . And I'll need all his meds . . ."

They bickered like lovers. Or ex-lovers. Peter raised his hand. "Ask for D-cycloserine."

"He wants D-cycloserine, too . . . under Angie's at CVS . . . Bye." She sighed and closed the phone. "What's D-cycloserine?"

"Chronic pain doesn't just come from physical trauma. It's also from emotional memory of pain. We have chronic pain because we remember it. D-cycloserine wipes out the emotional part of my pain memory so I won't have pain for the rest of my life."

"Handy." She yanked cushions off the living room sofa to pull out the convertible bed inside.

"Why is Steve Carbone helping me?"

"He owes me favors."

"That's not an answer."

"First sleep. Then the third degree." She grabbed sheets and blankets and made up the sofa bed. "It's a comfortable mattress. The bathroom's over there." She rummaged in the kitchen and came back with a box of crackers, peanut butter, a knife, and a plate. "This'll help. The cupboard's pretty bare, but anything you can stomach, feel free to eat. Now lie down and rest. I'm going to deal with the car and get supplies. You're going to be here for a while."

He just nodded, afraid to speak or he'd blurt out his deepest fear: If she left him and didn't come back, he'd be the most alone person in the world.

Face pinched with concern, she grabbed her bag and left.

It was very quiet, which only made his mind create thoughts to fill the emptiness. Horrible thoughts. About dying wives and fathers. He had to concentrate on something outside his head or he'd go insane.

He struggled to stand and tottered to the bathroom. There was a full-length mirror behind the door. He took off the raincoat, the cardigan, the hospital gown, and the grippy socks to appraise his emaciated, scarred, and ravaged body for the first time. Enormous skin graft scars surrounding cloned skin ran down his right leg and another circled his midsection. Incision and plug scars where bullets had been removed peppered his legs, arm, and side. Today he'd added a new layer of cuts and abraded skin. There was no fat and little muscle. He was all sinew, bone, and scar tissue, like a death camp survivor welcoming the Allies at the gates of Auschwitz.

All he had left was this ruined body. And his mind. And somewhere, Talia claimed she had his Cortex 2.0. He still felt fuzzy without it, like mental connections were severed from some brain injury. Even as a poor kid, he had never felt this deprived and beholden. The only thing more rock bottom was death. But he had a choice. Die. Or do something about it. He wondered what Amanda would want him to do. Amanda . . . she was dead . . . The thought obliterated everything else in his brain, memory chip and all. He curled up on the bathroom mat and wept, and eventually passed out.

CHAPTER FORTY-TWO

P eter woke up, still nude, tucked into sheets and blankets on the sofa bed. Talia was cooking in her tiny kitchen.

"Smells good," he croaked.

"Thanks. Ready in a few minutes."

"How'd you get me in bed?"

"You don't remember me helping you? You're a lot easier to maneuver than three months ago."

"Sorry. I passed out from the sight of me."

"You needed it. It's tomorrow. You slept over twenty-four hours."

"Oh shit . . . sorry . . ."

"No apologies." She plated some penne with meatballs and tomato sauce with generous amounts of garlic and basil. "I guarantee this is better than hospital slop."

A white terry cloth robe was left at the foot of his bed. As he maneuvered it around himself under the sheets, he saw she'd cleaned all the small wounds from his escape and bandaged them. His modesty was irrational, since she had handled his naked body yesterday, but he needed to preserve a little dignity. He stood with the robe wrapped and tied, but the rush of blood to his feet made him stagger.

"Whoa!" She caught and gently guided him to a small table with two chairs. He pounced on the pasta.

"This is awesome . . ." he said with his mouth full. "In some alternate universe, you've got a gaggle of fat, happy kids and a very satisfied husband."

Her mouth smiled, but her eyes were sad. He had a talent for hitting buttons he didn't know she had.

Peter changed the subject. "You know everything about me and I know squat about you." He shoveled another forkful.

"Eat slow. You'll make yourself sick."

"Wrong answer," although he did take time to chew.

"You want to know why you?"

"Start there."

"You were the next wonder boy. You didn't have *one*—you thought up *two* revolutionary technologies. They wanted them, so they went after you with every weapon at their disposal."

He remembered seeing Lobo in the camp amphitheater and the free associations that he couldn't suppress. "Do you think they were behind 10/26?"

"Good question. There's some connection. There are no coincidences with the club. And you're the most important catch I've seen. Brant and his gang were determined to own it and you. I tried to stop you, but I failed, because I . . . I realized you weren't like them, and I felt bad for you . . . So I didn't do everything I could to stop you."

"How did you even know to follow me?"

"I use my job as a business journalist to find out who the next club members are likely to be. You were obvious, because you were a genius. And damaged goods they could manipulate."

He didn't believe her. Only club members knew he was a club target. "What would have happened if I had followed you upstairs at the Hay-Adams?"

"Usually blackmail. Most guys cooperate if I threaten that the media will receive high-def footage of them sodomized by a dominatrix. And loving it."

He was skeptical she could pull that off.

"But you were surrounded like the president," she continued. "Bodies and bugs everywhere. Only you couldn't see them. The mark never does."

"So is the club a complete sham?"

"No. It started for all the reasons they say. But it's morphed since the creation of the military-industrial-congressional complex after World War II into something so . . . callous . . . evil . . . it's hard to get your head around."

"Congressional?"

"That's what Eisenhower meant to say in his farewell speech when he tried to warn everyone about how the country was changing for the worse. By including Congress, he was acknowledging the corruption of the budget process and their creation of a permanent war economy. The Phoenix Club got a hold of his final draft and made him take out the word. Must've had something pretty big on him to make an exiting president and war hero afraid enough to agree."

Dulles's face hovered above Peter's plate while the sauce looked like gore on the Persian carpet . . . He shook his head to rid himself of the visions.

"I know, scary," she continued. "How many people today in any position of real power can honestly compare themselves in motivation, ethics, or accomplishment to the Founding Fathers, who created the club? Zero. Those guys were an amazing bunch of human beings. We've only seen a handful of leaders in this country since then who deserved to kiss their dirty boots. I guess the founders didn't have a lot of power to begin with, so with all their intelligence and idealism, they somehow achieved the impossible—a successful revolution and a relatively painless transition to a democratic republic. But the club changed lockstep with the times. The later power mongers perverted the vision."

She still wasn't telling him what he needed to know. "Are you part of some underground movement?"

"Not like you think. There's no organization or group. I'm really on my own, but there are a couple dozen people I've discovered over the years who are sympathetic and helpful, with their own axes to grind against the club. Or just like to get paid well. Mercenaries have their uses, like dragging initiation survivors out of sea caves. But they've all been loyal so far, and that's what counts."

"But why do all this? What'd the club do to you?"

Talia got up, collected the dirty plates, and took them into the kitchen. "I . . . have reasons. And they're just as valid as yours. But they don't involve you."

"I disagree. I need to know everything. It all involves me now, and the more I know, the better I can plan. For instance, I don't think Talia Brooks is your real name, any more than Angie Sternwood was. What is it really?"

"I'm good at changing identities," she admitted.

"But you're avoiding my questions. Big Gov and Big Biz don't like it when you screw with their antiprivacy matrix. How'd you swing it?"

"Not now. Soon. Now lie down."

"You've got to tell me some time." He stood, feeling slightly less like a beetle crushed under a boot heel, and shuffled back to bed.

She might talk a good game, but Talia could also be a cog in the club's elaborate plan to co-opt him again. Or she might have her own agenda, working for people he didn't know and couldn't trust. Like how did she and Dulles fit? Was she connected to 10/26? Or was that yet another misdirection from the club? What he didn't know could hurt him. Very badly. Like it had already.

If what little she said was true, something terrible had happened to Talia. So terrible, she would spend the rest of her life trying to avenge the wrong. But she only stuck the club with pins, removing a few from their grasp. The club still ran the country. They still plotted. They still killed. If he joined her one-woman campaign and made it an army of two, what could they accomplish?

"So now what?" he asked.

"I have friends who create identities. We can move you to Buenos Aires. Johannesburg. Kuala Lumpur. Pick any distant place and make a fresh start."

He imagined it for a moment: An engineer? In Lima? Drinking coffee in a plaza café, always looking over his shoulder. Waiting for the bullet. And he'd still be him. With the same memories. The same rage. And the same responsibility . . .

And what was in it for her? Was this charity? Or something else?

"I can't. The club's got big plans for my tech," he told her. "They're already using the Hippo 2.0 and Cortex 2.0 for torture, brainwashing. And my bots . . . Carter said Chang worked for the terrorists and the club. That means my bots are a weapon. This is my fault. And I have to stop them."

"Maybe they did it already?"

"I doubt it. Something big would have changed. What I know of their plan so far was very methodical, patient. It took years. And they assumed if I passed the final initiation, I'd help them. It was underway by the time I launched Biogineers. It might still take years to complete. The only way to find out is to get back inside . . ."

"You mean sneak in?"

"No. Join."

She paused at the sink, but said nothing.

"If you're so good with new identities, you can help me create a new person, completely airtight, with all the right hooks loaded with tasty worms to bait them. They'd reel me in again. I know it. They're like an armored tank. You shoot bullets at it all you want and get nowhere, but if you get close enough to lift the hatch, all you need is a single grenade inside and . . . total annihilation. That's what I've got to do."

"You're going to blow up the club?"

"Figuratively. But if I survive, I will personally kill each of the fucking bastards that pretended they were my friends and destroyed me . . . If I don't get myself killed, by the time I'm done with the Phoenix Club, they'll be rewriting the history books."

She looked afraid as she wiped her hands on a dishtowel. Taking it with her, she sat on the edge of his bed.

"I've known these men for years. They're nothing more than con artists with power. They pretend to be one thing, while robbing you blind. Except instead of taking your wallet or granny's retirement fund, they fleece entire countries. To take down a grifter, you have to be a grifter, because hustlers are suckers for hustlers. Their egos are so puffed up, and they think they're so slick, they're blind to their own spin thrown back at them. So you've got to be a better con than they are. You think you're capable of that?"

"I have to be."

"I don't think you can. These guys are big marks. The biggest. You need big guns to even play. You can't offer your expertise. They'll recognize your mind in a second. That means big money and a very seductive, misleading package to get them interested."

"Well, I've got no money and no tech to offer. Good start."

"Know anything about hacking foreign bank accounts?"

"In my misspent youth, I stole cars. Not currencies. And I always returned them."

"Just proves that ethics and a Stanford education are useless in the real world." She smiled wanly. "That's okay. I do. Or I have friends who do. But you need a new identity first, one that can receive the money." She walked back to the kitchen. "But that's way ahead of ourselves. After the earful I got, you're not leaving this apartment, or even the sofa bed, for a long time. Not until Dr. Carbone gives the okay."

"You mean Steve, your lover. Or ex-lover."

Talia's thoughtful smile fell, and her face went blank. She tossed the towel on the counter and without a word, stormed straight to her bedroom and slammed the door.

"Shit . . ." Peter sighed.

CHAPTER FORTY-THREE

When Talia went out the next day to interview a twenty-four-year-old start-up king for *Forbes*, Peter seized the opportunity to do a quick search of the apartment. Disregarding his pain, he rifled Talia's nearly empty desk and tried to hack into her HOME, but it was password and bio-ID protected and nothing he tried worked. She had taken her work tablet with her. He looked in and behind furniture, cabinets, under carpets, checked garbage, but couldn't find anything, not even her blond wig or bobby pins. Her apartment was as clean and anonymous as a hotel room. It looked like this was a setup. But for what? Exhausted, he collapsed on his bed.

When he awoke the next day, the Cortex 2.0 processor lay on his pillow. He pried open the back with his fingernails. Evaporated seawater left mineral and organic deposits, corroding metal. It was useless until he could replace some parts and build a new reader program. And he didn't have the parts or equipment. There was only one world-class lab that could do this kind of work. And sneaking into Prometheus Industries was too big a risk.

He would have to build his own lab, but it would take time. And money. Then he would know what information Josiah and the club believed was so important that people had died for it. Talia didn't know it had been attached to Dulles's head. And Peter had no intention of telling her. Or she might take it again.

One week went by. Then two. Then six. While she nursed him, she kept her emotional and physical distance, only touching him when necessary, not even accidentally, in the little space they shared. As much as he asked, she revealed nothing about herself after that first dinner. He had no idea where her money and contacts came from. He talked to Steve every few days, keeping him apprised of his recovery, and did the physical therapy exercises as best he could without a therapist.

Talia had told the truth about being a freelance journalist with access to club recruits. She was often out on the job or running errands for them both. Peter was alone in the apartment most waking hours.

She gave him access to the HOME, but only for entertainment and general information gathering. Looking up hot-button words was forbidden, like the names of his enemies, friends, or words connected to him, like "Prometheus" or "phoenix." She promised, with permission from Dr. Steve and a good disguise, she'd take him to a public server with her encrypta-key and help him find out anything he wanted to know. Otherwise, he had to follow the rules. But Peter couldn't wait, so he made generalized searches, following hypertext and links, often for dozens of jumps, to get to the websites he wanted. All his searching turned up little he didn't already know. There wasn't much information out there.

It was time for physical recreation. Talia bought protein and nutritional supplements as well as pastured meats, wild fish, and organic produce; free weights, exercise bands, a bench, and a treadmill. The living room was transformed into a tiny gym, with only room for the convertible sofa. With no tissue to lose, he had everything to gain. He kept the fat off and muscle grew steadily.

Mesomorphic German genes paid off, but when muscles hit their natural peak, he went for the heavy artillery: Follistatin, a drug that inhibited myostatin uptake in muscles, creating a twenty-five to fifty percent increase in muscle mass. It was developed for patients with wasting diseases like muscular dystrophy or cancer and didn't have anabolic steroids' side effects. Pro athletes loved it.

Self-transformation covered every aspect of mind and body. When doubts plagued him, he thought about Amanda and Pop, and no matter how much he hurt, how tired or how overwhelmed he felt, he forged ahead with another set of bench presses, another mile on the treadmill. He'd kill those fuckers for Amanda and Pop . . . Amanda and Pop . . . Amanda and Pop . . .

On the second anniversary of 10/26, *60 Minutes* aired a special report commemorating the attacks. Compelled to watch, Peter was mentioned several times by name as a co-conspirator with Chang and ATEAMO, even though they had no solid evidence, except his working relationship with Chang and his alleged suicide attack on the yacht that the government pinned on ATEAMO without explaining why. Carter was interviewed by Katie Couric for a few minutes. He handled her like a master. Serious, heartfelt, never wanting to condemn his friends, he left the audience feeling that Carter, and the nation, had been betrayed by two wicked men who had been as close to him as brothers, but he was too much of a good guy to want to believe it. Amanda was never mentioned, as though she didn't exist. The performance was enough to convict Peter in the court of public opinion forever. Within hours, the blogosphere had placed Peter Bernhardt in the pantheon of evil along with Hitler, Stalin, Pol Pot, and Bin Laden.

Good thing he was dead.

CHAPTER FORTY-FOUR

San Anselmo, California, was the perfect West Coast town, for perfect people with perfect families and perfect bank accounts. Talia drove Peter in yet another car acquired 'from friends' through the picturesque Marin County village filled with chic shops, restaurants, and locals on their thousand-dollar bicycles, to an old ranch-house development from the late '50s, whose once middle-class starter homes now sold in the millions of dollars to middle-aged DINKS.

Peter wore a dark blue fisherman's cap, large sunglasses, khaki trench coat, white button-down shirt and red cardigan, navy slacks, and old-man comfort shoes. With the white hair, he looked like a retiree visiting from San Diego.

They parked in front of a ranch house. White, one story, with a well-designed and maintained front garden, complete with koi pond and tiny Japanese bridge. He expected Pat Morita to open the door. Instead, a short, overweight black woman in her seventies, balanced between two canes and moving with difficulty, stood in the doorway.

"Hey, Talia, honey. How you doin'?"

Talia grinned. "Better, now we're here."

The old woman squinted at Peter with suspicion. She asked Talia, "You sure 'bout this one?"

"Oh, yeah." she replied.

"Then come on in, honey." She waddled away, turning a moment to shake a cane at Peter. "And don't you fuck with me."

The interior of the house continued the Asian theme, with calligraphic drawings on parchment rolls and nineteenth-century Japanese triptych prints hanging on the walls. It was extremely tasteful. Simple, classic furniture with modern lines. Muted colors. They walked through a dining room and into the kitchen. The house was as immaculate inside as out, although he could tell none of it was new. He caught the bright pixels of a HOME unit paused mid–video game through a door to a small den. On the screen, a car was running over an old lady. *Grand Theft Auto IX.* There didn't seem to be anyone else home who could be playing it.

He leaned over to Talia and whispered, "Is she Dr. Who?"

The old woman heard him. "You call me that?" she asked Talia. "You're funny, girl."

"Yeah, I made it up," admitted Talia. "This is the kind of business where using names is meaningless."

"I like that so much, I may print business cards," said Dr. Who.

The dining room opened with sliding doors to a teak deck. Peter peeked out. The backyard was extraordinary. Water features burbled musically over perfectly placed stones and around a variety of Asian plants in meditative compositions. A tiny teahouse was hidden in one corner, with another pagoda pavilion in the other, both reached by exquisite, meandering pathways.

"Wow . . ." For a moment, he forgot why he was there. It was restful just to look at it.

"My husband and I created everything you see, and I've spent at least two hours almost every day for more than fifty years on that garden. It kicks your scrawny white ass wow." She smiled at Talia. "Want some iced tea, honey?"

"Yes, thanks," replied Talia.

Dr. Who pulled a glass pitcher covered in painted sunflowers from the fridge and poured the tea into three tall glasses with matching sunflowers.

"Fifty years?" said Peter.

"I moved into this house when it was new, with my new husband. He'd just come back, stationed in Korea and Japan, and we married, and he went to work as a teacher for the local school system. He ended up a high school principal. Wilber died, bless his heart, about twenty years ago. I worked for the Social Security Administration in San Francisco. And I raised three God-fearin' children here, may I add! I was the only black woman in the neighborhood then. And you know what? I'm still the only black woman in the neighborhood!"

"Was that hard?" he asked.

"Whaddya think, they sent over the welcome wagon? When Wilber was alive, we managed fine. After he died . . ." She sighed. "It got real nasty. Some neighbors tried to 'encourage me' to move on, complete with all that Frisco PC BS and promises of a real estate payday. But I bought this land, and it's mine until I die. They can kiss my black ass—you know what I'm sayin'?"

Talia took two glasses, Peter took one, and they followed Dr. Who back into the hallway toward the bedrooms. There were four bedrooms. A small one had a freshly made twin bed and appeared lived in by the good doctor. One was ready for guests, with two twin beds with trundles beneath them. It could sleep four, but it would be very cozy.

"Got grandkids every weekend. Those rug rats are a handful . . ."

The two rear bedrooms were completely blacked out. She had converted one into a server room, and the master bedroom became her office. It consisted of a large glass desk and midcentury credenza, an ergonomic chair, and a couple of upholstered chairs for guests. A very impressive HOME setup, linked to her server room. And the most advanced security system he'd ever seen in a private house. He didn't know anyone who had a system like this outside paranoid billionaires and corporate or government institutions. A separate monitor covered cameras—both regular and infrared—air movement, and a pressure graph of floors, walls, and ceilings, as well as her fences and pathways outside. If a cat burglar or SWAT team tried to get in here, she'd know the moment their body weight hit her property or their rotor blades fanned her bonsai. But how fast could she move on those canes, for all her prior warning? Dr. Who gestured to the chairs and sat with an audible "Oof!" in her own.

She looked him over once again. "So my girl here tells me you need an extreme makeover."

"Forgive me if this isn't considered . . . proper . . . but I don't know you from Adam, and I do know how hard what Talia's proposing is. Can you really do this?"

Dr. Who's vast bosom giggled with laughter. "Honey, you have no idea! You remember what I did for a living?"

"Social Security."

"The San Francisco office runs California, Arizona, Nevada, Hawaii, American Samoa, Guam, and Saipan. I was there for forty-two years. Worked my way up from a secretary to a GS-15 in information resource and technology management. Even the regional commissioner wasn't my boss. Mine were back in DC. I ran the information flows for the entire region and their connections to the national database. Of course, I was involved with information security, too. Can't have one without the other. But like all bureaucracies, they talk a good game about protectin' your assets and your ass, but they don't deliver, 'cause it costs money they'd rather spend on pork barrel. I made a stink for a long time about that. Not right the government's givin' away folk's financial security to any old ID thief with the right hand, and collectin' their taxes on stolen money with the left! And what it get me? DC made me retire. And that made me mad. I expected to die with my boots on! What the hell else was I gonna do? Just garden?"

"She's also a famous Metaverse avatar," Talia said to Peter. "Ever hear of Foxy Funkadelia?"

Peter's lower jaw went slack. Foxy was a notorious ass-kicking omnisexual dominatrix and pole dancer–cum–web philosopher who had developed a global following. He'd seen her web exploits first hand. "No fucking way," he whispered, blushing from the memory and the disconnect between the brilliant, sizzling hot, X-rated avatar and this righteous grandma giggling in her office chair.

"You think the juices dry up just 'cause you got no one to share 'em with? You gotta lot t'learn, boy . . ." Her bosom jiggled with laughter again. "But you can't be doin' that all day, every day. Fries the brain. Need gainful employment for mental health. So here we are. I got all the connections—both meat and digital—from my previous job in every aspect of governmental identity. That's the easy part. And I got a way with creatin' characters and scenarios. The hard part's makin' you seem like you always been there, everywhere. It's a giant puzzle that needs every piece in the right place. So let's start with the easy part. Talia told me you wanna be the age you look now. Pick one."

She handed him four pieces of paper with a list of approximately 150 male names, their Social Security numbers, and dates of birth. They were all in their late forties to early fifties. A name jumped out on the list.

"Thomas Paine." He handed the pages back.

Talia chuckled grimly under her breath.

"Whatchoo gonna do with a loaded name like that?" asked Dr. Who.

"I'm a one-man revolution."

"Not a one-man nut job?"

"'These are the times that try men's souls. The summer soldier and the sunshine patriot will, in this crisis, shrink from the service of their country; but he that stands it now, deserves the love and thanks of man and woman.' Thomas Paine's 'The Crisis.' It's the quote that began the American—and French—Revolutions. And I'm going to deliver a revolution."

The old woman looked at Talia with concern. "This boy serious or is he still on the oxy?"

"Serious . . ." sighed Talia.

"You really think you're givin' it to 'the man'?" asked Dr. Who.

"Any way I can," he vowed.

"You got delusions of grandeur, but I shouldn't care, long as you got the cash for this."

"It's ironic, really," said Talia. "The quote could be used by those who stand for—and against—the club. Everyone thinks they're on God and history's side."

Dr. Who shook her head. "I think we're livin' in an age of misplaced religious feelin'. And that's very dangerous. Instead of bein' humbled by the unknowable God Almighty, there are a frightenin' number 'a people who think they're the Lord's gun-totin' sidekick. They claim they know what he wants done and how it wants doin'. What's good for God is good for me and vice versa . . . as long as it's still good for me in the long run, which must make it good for God. Imbeciles who don't have two brain cells to rub together comin' up with circular reasonin' for crusades and inquisitions . . . get us all killed . . ." She typed on her keyboard, accessing Social Security's databases. "Please tell me you're not one of them 'Jesus is my ass-kickin'-warrior' types. Or I'll whip your ass with this," brandishing a cane, "as I kick it out my door."

"I'm not. How do you make the hard copy look legit?"

"If you didn't need a lot of background or were only goin' to use it for a short time, I could do it quick and cheap, with a forged birth certificate and a stolen Social Security number. The companies that provide the actual holograms and RFIDs to the DMV and the State Department sell 'em to less authentic companies, like myself, and make a killing. Black-market identification is big business. I can get them through real government departments if you want, but it wouldn't matter. Costs more for the same thing. All that would get you by if you were an illegal looking for work or wrongly accused and on the run—by the way, I also don't work for real criminals, so don't you get any more crazy ideas—because with those two documents, you can get a driver's license, a passport, and start a line of credit. But in the age of Google, you need some serious hacking to create a realistic deep background of someone who never existed. Bank accounts and credit history, IRS and Social Security history, family history, travel and immigration history, education, work history, mentions in the media, family photos on file-sharing sites, and there's so much more. And it's all possible for a price, honey."

"If you're angry the government isn't protecting national security, why are you doing this?"

"I never said it was about national security. I said they were lettin' bad guys steal John Smith's money. And makin' him pay taxes on it first! Problem is, everyone's turnin' out to be a bad guy. Did you know the worst offender distributing your precious identity information to the criminal element is the United States Federal Government? Either through incompetence or on purpose, because we're all for sale, honey. National security is make-believe. They don't follow everythin' you do because they think it's makin' the country safe from terrorists. Yes, they want you to think they are so you reelect 'em. But they aren't. All a body needs to do is look at the budget appropriation expenditures and then compare that to the Transactional Records Access Clearinghouse at Syracuse University so you see where the money and people really go. All that taxpayer dough, buildin' bombers and comin' up with the next harebrained high-tech gizmo that'll supposedly stop a terrorist in their tracks. Only they don't. They pay out to the contractors, who pay in with campaign contributions. Money just goin' round and round. And they ignore basic security, 'cause it ain't sexy, and their donors only make money when bad stuff happens. Not when we're safe . . ."

Impatient, Talia interrupted the speechifying. "We need you to make this your masterpiece and take whatever time you need. This will be the most scrutinized background check you've ever encountered, with every angle at their disposal. So price is no object."

"You serious, child?" Dr. Who's large brown eyes glittered as she imagined the delicious challenge.

"What you've done for me? Square it for him." She handed Dr. Who a long list. "Here's some ideas to start. Deep background. Points we need to hit. What do you think?"

"What she did for you?" Peter asked. He was hoping for real answers to the mystery of Talia.

The two women looked at each other. After a moment, Talia spoke. "I have an avatar of the old me running around the world. I'm supposedly living abroad, on the run from the club. I rent apartments, buy groceries, live a life. They've tried to kill the old me several times, but they're chasing a ghost. And they have been for the last ten years. Where am I now?"

Dr. Who smiled. "You're livin' in Bolivia, under the protection of Evo Morales and his friends. They won't mess with you for a while."

He found it hard to believe it was possible. But he had no choice.

Dr. Who smiled her big, toothy grin and continued. "She's the only other 'price is no object' client I got. I have a ball maintainin' the old her. It's like a game character. Except the stakes are real. Better adrenaline rush than *Grand Theft Auto IX*."

Dr. Who turned to their list, methodically making notes in the margins. Peter didn't know how much "price is no object" meant. But whatever it was, he was willing to pay it—as soon as he had some money.

Peter Bernhardt was dead. Long live Thomas Paine.

CHAPTER FORTY-FIVE

I n contrast to the Stepford perfection of San Anselmo, the Santa Cruz "surf city" shack they pulled up to the next morning was as low-rent and shaggy dog as they came. Gray, weathered wood shingles hung precariously off the sides and the newly christened Thomas Paine was sure the shake roof leaked. A collection of battered surfboards lined the walkway. It was hard to believe one of North America's leading money launderers lived here, but curiosity overrode any concerns he harbored. He needed to know where Talia's deep pockets came from. She had never said this was the source, but he figured it was, or close enough.

Inside was no better. It had nothing in common with Dr. Who's setup, except the awesome computer and security systems. "Tom" sat in the only comfortable seat, an old armchair whose upholstery lost ten rounds with the old calico cat asleep on its shredded arm. Talia perched on the other arm, and Mr. Money sat in the only other seat—a rickety wooden kitchen chair he pulled up to his board and monitor, which sat before an enormous picture window framing the Pacific Ocean. Either this was just his office or Mr. Money was deeply into nonattachment and antimaterialism.

Mr. Money was also deeply into surfing, and his location and boards were not the only clues. He appeared to be in his midthirties, but his Eurasian face was darkly tanned, with wrinkles heavily etched and shaggy, straw-like black hair fried by sun and sea salt. He was very lean, with powerful, broad shoulders and lats from paddling, and strong legs. He wore board shorts and a Hawaiian shirt, which exposed the scars of a gonzo surfer. Arms slashed, legs gouged, a body beaten in pursuit of the perfect ride.

"So Talia never told me what you do exactly," said Tom.

Mr. Money smiled at Talia, but his smile never reached his eyes. Tom's scalp tensed and rippled. The smile assumed a great deal and none of it good. Talia smiled back, noncommittal, her eyes cast down at the tattered carpeting.

"She's a good girl. Knows when to talk and when not to," said Mr. Money, his eyes focused on her bare, crossed legs, languorously stretched out beneath her short denim skirt. "I've checked you out, so it's only fair you get my curriculum vitae . . . I've been doing this since high school. Started out as a peso broker for the drug cartels, before the big banks got in on the action and tried to force small operations like me out of the drug business. I've gotten some business back post Patriot Act, since banks supposedly can't launder money anymore, but some just ignore the act and stick to profit making until they get caught. Most don't care 'cause they've got friends where they need them. Like your club. I have enough loyal clients and work to keep me happy. And I'm loyal in return. Institutions have no loyalty. Can't overstate the need for mutual loyalty. Isn't that right, Talia?"

"Absolutely." Her voice was affectless.

Tom's scalp tensed again. It was disturbing.

"So this can go two ways," said Mr. Money. "If you give me account and routing numbers and banker's IDs into established accounts big enough to rip from the inside, you can have the money today. Five percent fee. If not, it'll take way more dinero to come up with a clean approach based on my own contacts. I charge for both hours and expertise. Ten percent and one thousand dollars an hour until I've cracked it. Usually takes a couple of days to set up if I've got the right contacts. Weeks, if I have to make 'em from scratch."

Talia sighed. "No one has all that information at their fingertips."

"Maybe not your fingertips, baby . . ." Mr. Money's lips compressed in the faintest smirk.

The assumption of intimacy made Tom's internal radar scream. Did Talia use sex to keep Mr. Money and Dr. Steve loyal to her?

"What about the Russian RATs? Could we buy it from them?" asked Talia.

"They'd have to have it for sale already. And I doubt any Trojan's getting this type of account information regularly." When he saw Tom's confusion, he added, "RATs are crackers who write remote-access Trojans that hide their malware as something harmless that appears on the user's system. The Russians are the undisputed masters, and they've raised it to an art form. A very lucrative art form. I guarantee if you've ever had a system hooked up to the Internet, and you've ever made a financial transaction—from banking to eBay to charity to subscriptions—they've had your information for sale to thieves at one time or another."

"So why not them?" asked Tom.

"The key to their business model is taking small amounts from millions of users. Ten bucks times a million accounts is ten million bucks. Banks consider it the cost of doing business, and customers only get angry when the amounts are high enough to matter. This is not our situation. No VXer goes after the kind of cash you need in one bite. It would bring the wrath of governments and corporations down on them. No one wants that if they can avoid it."

Tom had no choice. "I have them." He wasn't sure he did. If the processor was still attached to him, he'd know.

"Really." Mr. Money didn't sound like a believer.

"Try this. Bank of the Caymans . . ."

Mr. Money looked at Talia, who subtly nodded. He turned to his keyboard and brought up the Bank of the Caymans website. But it wasn't the homepage interface a customer would use. It was the internal interface for employees.

Tom closed his eyes and thought of the music he heard reading the memo—Flaming Lips' "Race for the Prize (Sacrifice of the New Scientists)." Music always embedded itself with other memories, but since the implants, he had noticed it more and more. "Manager's name is Octavius Crawford. Hard to forget a name like that. I saw a code next to his name, just once, don't know why, but maybe . . . Try, all caps, C8G5V93JKB7."

Mr. Money tapped on his keyboard. After a minute, the screen changed to an internal user screen. "I'm in. But you won't know his password."

Tom was disappointed. "Right. Of course it's not his password."

"It's his ID. And that was an amazing piece of luck. Also tells me the guy's an imbecile for sending it in a document. Unless he's in the pay of a cracker team already. It's possible. I'm running a password generator. Might take minutes or hours. You might have to come back. Why don't you both relax." Mr. Money got up. As he walked by, he grazed his fingertips lightly over Talia's shoulder.

The computer beeped. "Already?" exclaimed Mr. Money.

"Why the surprise?" asked Tom.

"It goes through proper names, fictitious names, and dictionary words first. Then date configurations. Birthdays and anniversaries. All very popular with the rabble. Then it starts randomly generating letters and numbers. That's what a password is supposed to be, especially at the institutional level, alphanumeric nonsense, and that can take a long time to crack. This doofus used"—he peered at the screen—"oh, Jesus! 'HarryPotter.' They should fire his fucking ass! Then again, if they catch this, he's dead." Mr. Money sat back down at the keyboard. "Okay, dude, you're on."

Tom knew the stakes were high, and he couldn't dwell on Octavius Crawford's fate if he was after bigger fish. He needed to concentrate. The next numbers would fail if he got even a single digit wrong. It was only a fluke that he'd been in Carter's office in the first place. He had asked a question about a club wire transfer and his partner, eager to allay his fears, jumped on a keyboard to access the account himself. He remembered watching him type a number, but even though it came up all stars on the screen, he thought he remembered keystrokes . . . He squashed down his anger and focused on Carter's hands flying over the keys on his mental screen. "Account number . . . 0409856735627585 . . . Routing number . . . 198403849587."

After thirty seconds, the only thing he heard was a male voice say, "Fuck me." He opened his eyes. Mr. Money was staring at Talia and Tom with deep suspicion. For a moment, Tom thought Mr. Money was imagining him dead along with Octavius Crawford. "You been planning this for a while?"

"No. Why?"

"That's the smoothest ride I've had from a civilian. How could you remember that? You some idiot savant?"

"I've got an unusual memory. And I always believed you keep your hands on the flow of funds personally, even if I had a great controller and accounting department. Start-ups suck down money like crazy, so I spent a few minutes every day looking at financials and asking stupid questions since I started my first company at twenty-six."

Mr. Money said nothing for a moment, but stared at Talia again. She nodded, looking as calm as possible, but Tom could feel her fear.

"That's old-school, dude. You only hear that from geezers or Russian mob . . ."

"Guess I'm an old-school kinda guy."

"So what have I just landed in?"

"Talia told you my company was financed by the Phoenix Club. This is the account the last payment was made from on"—he closed his eyes again—"May 28. How much is in it?"

"$1,275,360,032.27. You know this is just one account. I'm sure they've got others. In other banks. In other tax havens."

"I know they do. As far as I can figure, they've got a few trillion deposited around the world." Tom smiled at Talia. "So I did okay?" he asked her.

Talia tried to look relieved. "You did more than okay."

"If you're not the angel of death, you're my new poster client," said Mr. Money. "In my experience, it's delegating too early that gets dudes in trouble with their finances. Before you know it, some accounting grommie's got his hand so far up your butt, you can't see his elbow. And then you can kiss your business—and your keister—good-bye."

"How do you make sure the club can't trace this money back to us?" asked Tom.

"I've got so many rabbit holes, through so many ISPs, in so many countries, most of which are so corrupt, all they want is their cut, and they've got no interest in helping some badass American club or corporation. I give them more money than the multinationals do. The account just disappears without a trace. For my percentage, I make sure there are no loose electronic ends or trails, I backdate everything, with just enough user history to make it seem real enough, but not too much to get questions asked, although I can't guarantee hard-copy issues, like if the bank decides to rectify their hard-copy printout to their computer-accessed information by hand. But no one bothers anymore, and I've never had a problem yet."

"But they've got to realize it's missing," insisted Tom.

"Yeah, but it'll be too late, too hard to trace, and too embarrassing."

"But what's to stop everybody doing this? Why isn't everyone missing their money?"

"First of all, who says money doesn't go missing all the time and the banks just replace it? Banks still make a fortune, even with all the theft. It's the run-of-the-mill ID theft at banks that hurts the most, because even though the amounts aren't huge and not many succeed, the numbers of people giving it a try with all that stolen information are enormous. But it's still cheaper for banks to put in half-assed electronic measures that foil non-pros than to keep the old-fashioned human labor—eyeballing signatures and personally okaying transactions—that made theft harder. Single big takes like this are inside jobs, with the board of directors' blessing to make cleaner payoffs to shady contacts, 'cause there's no corruption line item in their annual reports. And as always, the best way to rob a bank is to own one. But there's the dynamic duo of human interaction that makes sure big outsider grabs like ours rarely happen."

Tom bit. "And that's . . . ?"

Mr. Money smiled. "Loyalty and fear. But in this case, none of us have loyalty to either the bank or the club. And we don't care if we live or die. If we did, we would never have the balls to do this."

Tom shoved the contemplation of "fear" into the mental appendix that held "collateral damage." He hoped he didn't stuff it so full his mental appendix burst. "What's next?"

"I set up five Swiss bank accounts based on the information Talia gave me last night. Even though your accounts will appear old, we also need to back up because of your nonresident status in Switzerland. Swiss attorneys represent non-Swiss residents in absentia to prevent money laundering. Only thing the law does is make lawyers rich. I work with several Swiss attorneys. Thomas Paine has been a client of Zeiss Spiegel for the last decade, and they'll have proof they set up your accounts, which I'll provide. You send that info to your ID maker to build into your new dossier. I'll also give you all the information you'll need to do your own banking."

"Good. Then what?"

"My trade route's all set. Now . . . we transfer." He typed a command into a screen and clicked his mouse.

"Swiss accounts have no names, right?" asked Tom.

"Right, just numbers."

"So what's stopping you from using my accounts later?"

Mr. Money's face went flaccid, his eyes vacant, voice robotic. "I told you. Loyalty. And fear. In my business, if you screw a client, you're dead."

Talia unconsciously shifted closer to Tom. How much disloyalty had she witnessed?

The money launderer's animated affect returned. "Hey, it goes both ways. I'm getting my five percent—and let's face it, $63,768,001.60 is nothing to sneeze at, and it's sixty-three mil more than I had this morning. I'm not greedy. Of course, I share a healthy percentage with my compatriots around the world, but those are my expenses, not yours . . ." That sly, creepy grin that made Tom's skin crawl spread across his mouth. "It'll keep me in bitchin' boards, scorchin' babes, surfside vacation villas, state-of-the-art computing, supreme al pastor burritos with extra salsa at Taco Moreno, and personal security for the rest of my life—and really, what else does a dude like me need?"

Mr. Money was a very valuable friend. Tom Paine walked in a pauper and walked out a billionaire. And he couldn't wait to leave.

CHAPTER FORTY-SIX

Driving back to the Haight, Talia slowly unwound from her rigor mortis-like tenseness. Tom hesitated asking her about her relationship with Mr. Money, for fear she'd clam up again. He approached on another tack.

"So now I'm a Getty, how much do I owe you?" he asked.

"About seven million, give or take."

The uninsured medical bills alone would be millions. Plus mercenaries, ID builders . . . "Well, you tell me how, where, and it's done."

"From now on, it's harder than you think. Every movement of funds, every move in a vehicle, every call, every computer connection is monitored and recorded by surveillance video, cookies, RFIDs, smart cards, and GPS, collected and transmitted by private data-mining companies to their corporate clients and the intelligence community of the United States and therefore, to the Phoenix Club, all to complete the daily dossier of every American. Of course, that's where Dr. Who and Mr. Money get their information, too. Money talks and bullshit walks, especially in the low-paid corridors of intelligence gathering, and there are leakers, moles, and the disaffected everywhere."

"Thank God. We need them."

"And that's where Dr. Who's creation comes in. The Thomas Paine online avatar is your personal agent in the world. And your smoke and mirrors. It'll go places you can't. Have done things you didn't. All to create your electronic dossier."

"But I thought to be a true personal agent, you needed a more sophisticated level of artificial intelligence than exists right now. Human or near-human level artificial intelligence. And that doesn't exist yet."

"It is human level. Dr. Who, Mr. Money, you, and me. You don't need a computer."

"You don't look artificial to me."

"You just haven't looked close enough." Her brows knit together, and she stole glances at him. Finally, she blurted, "Do you really think you're up for total transformation? This isn't some Metaverse role-playing game. Everyone's life is on the line."

He bristled. "You doubt my commitment?"

"I know you're committed, but there's nothing in your background to indicate you're devious enough to pull this off. You've gone through a lot of change since childhood, but you always remain yourself—Dudley Do-Right. Most people change as their circumstances change, and given the right motivations, a human being is capable of any behavior, however horrible, ridiculous, or inconceivable. It's why most people who make a great deal of money mutate into the classic rich asshole. I'm sorry, but Fitzgerald was right. The rich are different."

"And you're saying I wasn't."

"No. And you have to be. To out-club the club."

"I'll change. I have no choice." He sank into the seat. "Carter thought I did already. Amanda, too."

"From the implants?"

"Yeah. I don't think they disliked what I was becoming, just disliked I was changing, period. Maybe Carter was nervous I'd find out what was going on. But even implants didn't make me smart enough. And Amanda . . ." Tom couldn't look at Talia, concentrating on the gray, fire-scorched hills as they flew along Route 17, hillsides dead as far as the eye could see. But fire could bring life. The knobcone pines and cypresses only released seeds after fire. Wildflowers would flourish on the same black earth. "Amanda acted like my change created some disequilibrium and that was enough to trigger a miscarriage. I know I wasn't to blame. I just wish she hadn't died . . . upset with me . . ." He couldn't speak anymore.

Talia watched him, worried. No one spoke for a few minutes. She fidgeted in the woe-filled emptiness.

"You know," she finally blurted, "I don't always agree with Fitzgerald. He also said there were 'no second acts in American lives,' but he died after he wrote it, so what the hell did he know? Must have been the booze, 'cause this country is nothing but second acts. Europe's landless second sons become colonial landowners. Ragmen on the Lower East Side become Hollywood moguls. Poor boys and girls become businesspeople and celebrities, and when their arrogance or crimes trip them up, they write best-selling mea culpas and star in their own TV shows and make even more money. And isn't your memory chip a second act? A second chance for those who lost theirs? In America, we rehabilitate, reform, and rebuild until the fat become thin, the addicted become sober, the plain become beautiful—all so that a nobody-from-nowhere can metamorphose into a celebrity for everywhere. We created Second Life, Web 2.0, Andy Warhol, and Madonna, the patron saints of reinvention. We even cornered the market on being "Born Again." Haven't we proven resurrection and reinvention are American talents?"

"Been preparing your fifteen-minutes-of-celebrity sound bite for long?" he deadpanned.

Talia blushed. She didn't often, but when she did, the pink-peach flush across her cheeks looked remarkably pretty. "You don't get a soapbox when you write puff pieces on CEOs."

As plants grew stronger from fire, so would he. "I appreciate your concern. But I will change. I have the greatest motivation, and I acquired my primary weapon only yesterday: I know who Thomas Paine is and what makes him tick. They don't, and they won't know what's coming. Brant said I lacked the killer instinct, the fire in the belly. He was wrong. I promise they'll get their killer, and they'll get their fire. Wait till Josiah, Bruce, and Carter get a load of Thomas Paine rising from the ashes."

CHAPTER FORTY-SEVEN

Talia led her nascent golem to her hiding place. It was time to teach as many transformation secrets as she could. She shifted a chair and gently removed a slab of base molding in her bedroom. Tom could see where the seams had been, but in such an old apartment, he never thought to pull at every paint crack. A treasure trove of theatrical secrets emerged: colored contacts, hair dyes, wigs, clothing, makeup, body padding, all neatly packaged in clear ziplock bags.

She displayed them on the duvet. He stood close behind and couldn't help flicking his stare between her red curls and the bottle of hair color in Delicious Mango. "It isn't real?"

Grimacing, the muscles of her shoulders rippled, and she moved away.

"Classic male. Get this through your head—nothing is real. I've got tits and an ass God never gave me, and that makes me walk differently. That's really important, because security cameras have been scanning and identifying gaits for ages. I've had facial surgery, and I wear sunblock at all times because I tan easily, and that wouldn't match the new me."

She sat on the bed, regarding him like an insect mounted on

a pin. It was as unnerving as at the inaugural ball. "None of these things are enough for you. My creation of Talia Brooks predates ubiquitous biometric IDs, so when I was finally IDed, I was already Talia. Now they've got your irises, fingerprints, face, voice, vein patterns, DNA, all as Peter Bernhardt's data . . ."

"I don't think anyone has a vein pattern on me."

"We'll see. But we've eliminated facial and voice issues. I've got a guy who can create great semipermanent fingerprints from artificial-skin appliances made from these new organopolymers they use for skin grafts that will read as real prints. Or we may have to stick to polishing off your fingertips. There are people who legitimately have unreadable fingerprints, usually from job wear or accidents. And unless you know differently, I don't think anyone knows enough genetic engineering to screw significantly with your identifiers without unwanted side effects. And we're going to have to be really careful about DNA from here on. If they match your hair, they'll know who you are." She appraised his features. "Your skin . . . it's pale. But easy to fix. Melanotan injections color the skin . . ."

He interrupted her. "Not really. It's an analog of an alpha-melanocyte stimulating hormone from the pituitary gland. It makes additional melanin to create a tan where the skin couldn't produce one before."

"Correct, Mr. Spock. You are a scientist."

"It has a side effect of increasing libido. Like Viagra, but not as controllable. That's why it's off the market."

She turned away and shook out the blond wig in a clear plastic bag, so the hair was all lying neatly in the same direction. "Lucky you."

"I beg to differ. Try being that guy. Not as fun as it sounds."

"Lie back and think of America," she quipped, still fiddling with the wig.

Did she lie back and think of America during the loyalty sex Tom assumed she performed?

She threw the wig back on the bed. "Anyway, there's laser removal of your skin graft scars."

"Don't forget cosmetic and brain surgery scars . . ."

"Right . . . and your eyes . . . unless seriously damaged or diseased, eyes don't change much, and contacts won't work . . ."

A mirror hung over the bureau, and his bright blue Achilles' Heel stared back at him. The arresting azure, and what his male ego always regarded as his best feature, would have to go. So, too, the iris pattern.

"Iris surgery?" he asked.

"Either laser decolorization or slip-in iris transplants. I'd go for the transplants to get the color and pattern you want, and we'll put your new eye-D in the biometric data fields for them to find and match."

"And you have a trustworthy ophthalmologist?" He counted on his fingers. "And dermatologist, prosthetician, let's see, am I missing anybody? Oh, yeah. Urologist."

"Of course. Doesn't everybody?"

He didn't want to know how she kept an army of contacts loyal. In his embarrassment, both at the thought and his discomfort, he picked up one of several pairs of Talia's sunglasses and put them on. In the reflection, the mirrors of his soul were hidden from him. And her. And everyone who might want to know the real Thomas Paine.

"Tell the docs I have acute, traumatic lesions on the striate cortex," he said. "Full-field bilateral scotoma, and we'll need appropriate MRIs of the visual cortex that match up with my new medical history."

"Translation, Professor?"

"I'm brain blind. And I'll have to prove it." And there was someone who would be desperate to know this particular blind man, especially if Paine became everything the man's offspring was not.

There were advantages to a blind man having the Hippo 2.0, although he wished the Cortex 2.0 was up and running. He quickly taught himself Braille, voice-recognition, and screen reading software systems. He could mentally map spaces and navigate a memorized area with ease. He learned to use the classic long, white "Hoover" cane, which became an extension of his body and perceptions. He practiced the behavioral tics of the blind, then practiced suppressing them, like the subtle head weaving, the lack of turning toward perceptual stimuli, the lack of facial reactions and social indicators. His presentation would fail if he were affected by darkness and disorientation like a sighted person.

Meanwhile, he added to Thomas Paine's dossier online. Between his work and Dr. Who's, the virtual golem was shaping up into a person, with a formidable past, shrouded in enough self-created secrecy to be a convincing member of the elite: a fascinating and mysterious present to keep people interested; a fatal flaw to lure the club; and a malleable future.

It was lonely work. He never saw Dr. Who or Mr. Money again, although Talia created a shared information exchange between one of her virtual personas and both crackers for communication. Except for after-hours medical procedures with skeleton staffs, he was a prisoner of Masonic Street until he could pass as a blind billionaire. He yearned to join humanity outside the apartment walls, like a man marooned on a spaceship in orbit around an Earth he could never return to.

Memories gnawed at him, more painful than surgery recuperation. Amanda's death had no closure and he, the man who remembered too much, could not remember she was gone. When would he awake without turning to the right side of the bed, surprised by its emptiness? Nights were worse, plagued by nightmares where she didn't recognize him and refused to take him home. He was abandoned night after night.

There were many dark hours to dwell on the past. When Amanda had been alive, he had noticed how much more he wanted to make love to her after his implants. Even after the miscarriage when she withdrew. At first he chalked it up to a postsurgical survivor's high. When it continued, he wondered if permanent memories made the daily sexual thoughts that floated through men's minds stick more concretely, embed in the Cortex 2.0 as an idea that wouldn't go away. But as the weeks progressed, he realized something else. His mind was occupied by so much more information, he craved the oblivion of sex, the forgetfulness of love. To blast his brain with endorphins and oxytocin and all the other chemicals that made the world fall away and only you and your lover remain. Sex once had the power to do that, if only for a little while.

In daylight, with Talia's presence and possessions all around him, he obsessed about her, complicating his mental state. He knew what toothpaste she used, but not where she was born; what foods she preferred, but not the family who raised her. Every clue could be deliberate misinformation. What precious little he thought he knew led to one conclusion: She was one complex and mysterious woman, and what guy wasn't attracted to that? She was also beautiful, ridiculously so and even though self-consciously designed to entice, it didn't matter. It still worked on his visual cortex and amygdala like nobody's business. And she was smart. And compassionate, when she wasn't trying to put him off. And intense. And under her influence, he saw reality as she saw it—where it was the two of them, back-to-back (if only she'd let his back touch hers) against the world.

As his desire for Talia increased, so did his guilt. He couldn't help but react like any healthy male to female beauty, and until now he had had the self-control to consciously ignore it. But Melanotan injections made it hell. While his skin darkened, he sometimes fantasized about a well-placed nanobomb or laser scalpel destroying his brain's amygdala, the seat of emotions, or the hypothalamus, which produced gonadotropin-releasing hormone. Both regions of the brain responded when given visual and olfactory sexual stimulation, and Melanotan only encouraged his hypothalamus to hitherto-unknown hormonal heights. Talia's sight and smell intoxicated and engorged him. It was extremely uncomfortable. And thinking of America didn't help.

It felt like Talia watched his every move, even after she left the apartment, hoping he would measure up to the transformation necessary. It was smothering. But she still avoided touching him as though her life depended on it. At first, her rejection annoyed him. Annoyance grew into anger, because it wasn't just a lack of sexual interest. He frightened the person he relied on most, as though his touch carried a terrible contagion. He didn't know why. And she wouldn't tell him.

She hadn't been afraid of him in DC, although her planned seduction might be considered taking one for the team. Her fear first appeared in the hospital.

Every so often, he'd catch his reflection, and the stranger looking back surprised him. Tan, muscular, with lean, angular, elegant features and distinguished white hair. His posture and movement was athletic, his voice Tom Waits–sexy. Scars were gone. His Silicon Valley geek-boy antistyle was replaced with clothes that would make Carter envious, and he practiced wearing them until they were part of him. Anyone would think he was 'da bomb.

Maybe it wasn't his looks that scared her, but his brain. He pitied her fear of his improved mind. She had no idea this was only the beginning.

CHAPTER FORTY-EIGHT

After a long day of blindness, he rejoined the seeing a few hours every evening. It was his refuge of normality, when he tried to communicate with Talia as though they weren't freaks living on the edge of existence. Making a bodybuilder's dinner of wild salmon and broccoli in the tight galley kitchen, the oft-stirred combination of proximity, rejection, and cabin fever could not help but result in a chemical explosion.

The HOME was on. Footage from the National Guard played while a newscaster described the disappointing growth of National Guard regiments designed to protect Americans from the "enemy in our midst" and the reliance of state governments on private militias and military personnel contractors to keep peace in the homeland. Being "objective," the journalist voiced no opinion on this development one way or the other.

Standing at the counter, Talia chopped the head of broccoli into small florets with a large chef's knife. To her right, Tom placed two salmon fillets in a dish of marinade. He dipped his pinky and, deciding it needed more soy sauce, reached past Talia for the bottle on the far side of her cutting board.

His left hip brushed up against hers. She gasped and quickly faced him. He was right in her face, transfixed for a split second by her beauty and closeness. He leaned in. Her lips were moist, inviting . . . She reflexively skittered back, but cornered against the door of the pantry, she turned, knife pointed at his chest.

Reality slowed, anger rose, and he couldn't stop either, carried away by a storm surge of emotions that the Hippo 2.0 wouldn't let subside. He lunged, grabbed her wrist, slammed it against the pantry door, and pinned her against the wood panel with his body. She cried out in pain, but still gripped the knife. Before she could push him away, he smashed her free hand above her head to join its mate.

"What's your fucking problem?" he hissed. She shrank from his presence and looked away, as though she could be absorbed into wood through wishing. It only enraged him more. "What disease do I have? Huh? Am I that hideous to you?"

She hyperventilated, eyes wild, jaw clenched, and nostrils flared, and looked everywhere but his face.

"I don't move till you tell me what's wrong," he breathed in her ear. He pressed himself along the length of her body. Her breasts heaved against his solar plexus. His face overshadowed hers and the butcher's knife hovered over their heads, while his brain switched biochemical gears, from the fight-or-flight surge of epinephrine to the neurotransmitter cocktail for sexual arousal. Their position might prove harder to maintain than he thought.

He squeezed the wrist of her knife-wielding hand until she grimaced in pain. "The truth. No more fucking bullshit."

Water pooled in the corners of her averted eyes. Her lips trembled. All he wanted to do was kiss them.

Finally, she raised her face. Expression shifted as though actual cogs turned, her brain a geared steampunk contraption. He wished he knew what she was thinking.

A subtle nod of her head and he relaxed his grip slightly. She slowly lowered the knife, pausing halfway, hovering around his jugular.

"You don't want to hurt me," he whispered, eyes locked with hers. "You're my guardian angel."

The knife clattered to the floor, barely missing his left foot. He let go of her wrists. Her face unreadable, her hand touched his cheek, very gently, like his skin were some forbidden fruit.

Was she seducing her way out of this, using sex as a weapon? Was that Talia Brooks's default salvation plan when threatened by men?

If it was, he didn't care.

He slowly lowered his head to hers. He could smell her perspiration just under the remnants of her perfume, Poison. How could he know her perfume and not know her? The combination of sweat, Poison, and confusion made him dizzy.

Their lips touched, a gentle, exploratory kiss, her eyes squeezed shut.

He pulled away to run his tongue lightly around the edge of her ear and whispered, "Why do I scare you?"

Fingers clenched his hair, crushing his lips to hers.

He fumbled with the tiny buttons on her blouse. She took over, deliberately undoing each. Too slow, he ripped the shirt open. Buttons pinged on china, Formica, linoleum. He slid it off her shoulders and devoured her neck and shoulder, pulled her breasts from their bra and suckled them. The bra was yanked down, then off.

Skirt hiked around her waist, he groped along the counter and grabbed a carving knife, gently sliding, teasing the blade between the silky fabric of her panties and her skin. She stilled her movements, enjoying the game. After a sufficient tease, he sliced one side open. Then the other. The fabric fluttered down her legs to the floor, and his hand replaced it, his fingers probing, caressing.

He wanted to savor her every way, with every sense. Blindness had its advantages. Eyes closed, he became deeply aware of his other senses—and her effects on them.

Her breath quickened, deepened, her hands moved from her shirt to his. It slid off his body and disappeared into the oblivion of blindness. She unzipped his fly and released him, stroking his length.

His teeth dug into her salty, velvet neck. She roared in response. But he didn't relent, teasing the line between pleasure and pain. She dipped her head and returned the favor, biting his neck a little too hard. The pain brought his brain up for air.

"Why do I scare you?" he repeated.

Her nails raked his balls, his cock.

He forgot the question.

A mental map formed in his mind, embedding in the Hippo 2.0. The mountains of her breasts here, the valley of her navel there. The smooth, undulating ridge of her backbone. The smell of her cleavage. The different smell of her cleft. With each place he touched, a different sound came from her throat: gasps, squeals, gurgles, moans, sighs. Each region had special characteristics, held separate fascinations. He was an explorer again, charting a new world. He missed exploration more than he realized.

Blindly kneeling before her, he lifted her up against the door, throwing a thigh over each shoulder so she sat on them. His hands clutching her ass, he buried his face between her thighs, his mouth consuming her. She grabbed the countertop for balance. He heard no songs in his head during their lovemaking. Her rhythmic moans were his only accompaniment. It was a rousing melody.

So much hard-won sensation flooding his brain he never wanted to forget. Where was his processor when he needed it?

"Keep your eyes closed," she said. She slithered off his shoulders. He heard the sound of a zipper, the whoosh of fabric, the thud of pumps kicked to the floor. "Okay, blind man. Open."

Eyes wide, he caught his breath. She was nude. Gloriously lush, Vargas pinup unreal.

She fell upon his remaining clothes. In moments, they were gone.

Tongues twined, her arms reached over his shoulders, raking his back. One leg wrapped around his waist. He cradled her ass, and when he lifted her, she wrapped the other. He turned them around and laid her against the wall. After teasing her mercilessly until she begged, he slid inside, slippery tight, divine.

They rocked and rolled against the wall for minutes, hours, he didn't know. Memory was gone. Only this remained, here and now, no past, no future. A constant present of mutual and overwhelming sensation, unable to stop and, he prayed, never ending. Only when he came did he fathom the depths of oblivion he'd sought for so long.

Spent, he leaned heavy against her, a tangle of limbs and hair, a slick of sweat, saliva, juices. As he surfaced, he hummed a melody he'd never heard until that moment, and his fingers danced and plucked at her red ringlets like guitar strings. When the song was over, he pressed his forehead against hers. Nose to nose. Sharing deep breaths. Her eyes were closed again.

"Why do I scare you?" he asked.

She shivered, sleepily. "It's cold."

After a minute of silence, the dam broke deep within her eyes, and the water came. In torrents. He kissed her cheeks and rocked her. Green contact lenses floated out on the tide, settling on his chest, and with a start, he saw her real eye color for the first time. It was a deep, rich brown. The same eye color she and the ophthalmologist had chosen for him.

It was cold, and his muscles grew stiff. He scooped her up and carried her to bed. Tucking her in, he crawled in, wrapping himself around her. The tears hadn't stopped. He knew once they did, he'd have an answer, but perhaps not *the* answer.

After another quarter hour, her voice, ragged, mumbled into her pillow, "I can't lose you . . . They killed him, but it was me . . . my fault. Oh God, I loved him so much . . . and . . . I . . ." She bit off the rest.

Smartest guy in the room, and he didn't know shit.

If what she didn't say was true.

CHAPTER FORTY-NINE

H e held his breath and listened.

"I know what feeling responsible for your father's death is like," she said. "I didn't shoot him, but he died because of me. And the club. I was sick when the nurse told me about your father. I've been there . . . I am there."

She rolled on her back and stared at nothing. He watched her profile in the darkening apartment.

"He was in Somoza's cabinet in Nicaragua, and he fled when Somoza was assassinated and the Sandinistas took power. He had legitimate businesses here, but he also raised money for the Fuerza Democrática Nicaragüense: contras. He invented a faster way to make money from the cocaine smuggled through Nicaragua from Colombia. He sold a cheap alternative to expand the coke market beyond cash-flush yuppies. Freebasing it, but leaving the base in to cut it . . ."

"Crack . . ."

"Yeah. The Phoenix Club approached him and made him a deal. He joined, cut them in on the action, and from then on, the CIA helped build a trans-American crack pipeline. Within a few years, with well-established markets, he sold guns to the gangs so their turf wars drove up the street price. He had it coming and going, and the money flowed, which made the contras, the club, and the US government very happy." She shook her head. "He thought he had every angle covered. And he did. For a long, long time. Even after Iran–Contra broke and CIA drug ties were exposed and his old network fell apart. He just built new ones. He had it all covered . . . except one little thing: me.

"He tried, he really did. Lectured me, begged me, punished me, had bodyguards tail me, tried to keep me straight every way he could. But I was so smart. By college, I was a junkie. When I got nabbed in a DEA sting and needed his fed friends to bail me out, I wanted a safer dealer. And who was safer than Daddy? When he said no, I told him I knew what he did and who he did it with. I'd met club members and CIA who came to our home. I'd figured out who were financiers, distributors, dealers, users, and I told him I'd find someone who was interested in all that information. I even figured out a little bit about the club. I told him I'd tell everyone who'd listen if he didn't give me what I wanted. But we were bugged. The club heard it all, and they were ready to deal with the problem if Daddy couldn't. The Nicaraguan civil war was long over, and crack had its day, but Daddy was still a cash cow, moving the business into meth and ecstasy and anything else the marketplace wanted. So they ordered a hit on me. I'm sure it was some newbie's initiation. They set up a fake suicide. That's another of their faves. But it was Daddy who walked into my apartment first, looking for me. I'd gone on a binge, and he was worried I aspirated vomit on the bathroom floor or something, and he was the one who walked in on the gunman. The story the DA gave the news was that I killed him, making it look like a fake suicide. When I realized what happened, I freaked. I had to get away. Instead of faking my death half-assed, I ran. My mother had stayed behind in Nicaragua during the war, with my older brother, and had a new life. She didn't want some murdering junkie daughter on her doorstep. And Daddy left everything to me in Panamanian tax haven bank accounts I already signed on. I donated his estate to a charitable trust in Colombia and had J— Mr. Money launder it back to my new Swiss bank accounts. Then he introduced me to Dr. Who."

"So you're wanted for murder?"

"Yeah."

"Where does Anthony Dulles fit? Why were you connected?"

A shudder of held breath escaped her body. "Dulles ran the contra banking operation for the CIA. Daddy and he were close. When he retired from the spooks, he ran a legit bank and still laundered drug money."

"But he knew about the hit on you."

"Of course. He was in the chain of command that authorized it. Years later, I discovered a club member offering information, and it turned out to be him. He was regretful for what he did. I think he was religious in his old age and afraid of going to hell. He confessed his role in my father's death and swore to protect me."

"So what side was he on?"

"His own. He didn't like the club dictating to the country like that. He'd been a rabid anti-Communist and saw the club as increasingly antidemocratic."

"Did he hate nano or just my tech?"

"If it'd been open to the market, he'd have been happier. For a guy with a finger in every black-market pie, he was a big free marketeer . . . But he was afraid what the club might do with it and paid pit bulls like Mankowicz to push through anti-nano legislation."

"Was Mr. Money another of your father's launderers?"

"Yes."

"And your mercenaries?"

"You acquire unusual skills and contacts to do what needs to be done. It's remarkable how many people are willing to help. And teach. Especially for a lot of money."

"And what about Steve Carbone?"

She drew a jagged breath and turned to Tom. "We met at University of Florida. He was in med school. And he was my boyfriend. And then I had to disappear."

"So he helped you."

"Not at first. I was afraid I'd get him killed at worst. Ruin his career at best. So I left the country. Mr. Money found the cosmetic surgeons I needed from overseas contacts."

"What made you think you could take on the club?"

"You wouldn't understand . . ." she muttered.

"How can you say that?"

"No. It's not the same. Your father didn't come to you and say it was your duty to destroy them."

"He came to you?"

"Well . . . yes . . . kind of . . . I know you'll think I'm crazy . . . I was sleeping, and I had this waking dream, at least I think it was a dream, and he was standing in my room and that's when he told me. I swear, he was as real to me as you are right now."

"You know how *Hamlet* that sounds . . ."

"Maybe Shakespeare had a pissed-off dead father, too."

Each stared at their own patch of darkness, remembering the deceased and their unfulfilled obligations.

He hoped her fear of him stemmed from a fear of intimacy and abandonment. He needed to believe that story very badly.

CHAPTER FIFTY

After she left for a *Wired* gig the next day, Tom looked up Talia's father on the HOME. He researched the larger story of the cocaine–contras connection and found a photo of the man described as the mastermind, whose biographical details fit with Talia's account. His name was Ricardo Gonzales. The bio didn't mention the Phoenix Club or a daughter, but didn't contradict anything Talia said, and filled in certain gaps. For a nanosecond, he wondered if he'd ever met the man. He looked so familiar. And then it hit him.

The man in the photo, with his handsome, lean, angular face, short-cropped, thick white hair, rich brown eyes and *café con leche* complexion was his doppelgänger.

It was the first time in his life he regretted acquiring knowledge.

Talia gave his surgeons her father's picture to build her avatar, designed for her revenge. It was why she wouldn't touch him for months. Or look at him during sex. But by telling him her story, she ensured he would eventually figure it out. What could that mean?

The room reeled. He staggered to the bathroom and vomited.

Desperate to clear his head and settle his stomach, he fled the apartment and hit the drizzly streets of San Francisco.

The rain felt cleansing, but the more the pretend-blind man tapped along the streets with his cane, the more he thought about Talia. Was she crazy? Would they recognize Ricardo Gonzales when Thomas Paine came knocking? Analyzing what he knew so far, one question clawed at his mind.

What else had Talia been hiding from him?

Ever since he had regained consciousness in the hospital, Tom had wanted to stalk Carter in person as soon as he was able. Talia told him he was too sick, or later, not convincing enough to pass as blind. But he was more than ready now.

He crossed the street to pick up the 43 MUNI inbound. Doing his best blind impersonation, he felt for the money slot and, stuffing his coins in, asked in the direction of the driver's seat if they could tell him when to get off at Jackson. The driver said yes. A young man's voice said, "There's a couple seats to your right." He gave thanks and found an empty seat, but not before almost sitting on someone. He felt bumps, starts, and stops as they traveled north on Masonic, then Presidio into the exclusive neighborhood of Pacific Heights.

Before he knew it, the driver said, "Jackson." It was six blocks to the center of the northern edge of Alta Plaza Park. The only people out were either nannies, their tiny charges wrapped in blankets and cocooned in plastic-hooded strollers, or tradespeople renovating multimillion-dollar houses. His white cane and dark sunglasses made it clear what he was. No one gave him a glance.

When his cane found the park stairs, he carefully climbed, finding a bench to his right. He sat on wet slats, facing the street, not the park, focusing his hidden sight on the building directly across the street.

His vantage point and the overcast day gave a clear view through floor-to-ceiling windows into the top two stories of a three-story house. A cube of smooth gray concrete and polished steel, it was the street's sole monument to modernity, tucked into a mish-mash of unevenly renovated, century-old Italianates, Queen Annes, and Beaux Arts structures. Like its owner, the house stood in hand-some reproach to those around it.

Lights were on, exposing the house like a fish tank. Carter sat at his desk on the top floor, facing the windows on the park, cheer-fully absorbed in a desktop HOME screen. How could a man like that live with himself, no less look happy? Sting and the Police warbled "Every Breath You Take (I'll be Watching You)" through Tom's head, warning of voyeurism's dangers, as images of death and dismemberment made a fantasy music video in his mind. Light drizzle increased to heavier rain. He had to refrain from wiping his sunglasses off.

A skinny urchin with spiky blond hair, baggy tee, and loose jeans ambled out of the bedroom. He moved with youthful, effemi-nate grace. Most likely picked up in the Castro for a few days' fun, only to be sent packing with a nice fat paycheck, so Carter never had to see him again. That was the usual MO.

The screen held the older man's attention. The boy crept slowly behind, hovering for a second, then lashed out, grabbing Carter's neck. The older man clawed crushing hands to prevent suffocation and lurched from the chair, toppling it. A tussle ensued. Was it overenthusiastic roughhousing? Or some punk stealing the satisfac-tion of killing Carter from him for whatever he could load in a van? Both were tall and slender, but Carter had at least fifty pounds of muscle on the boy. And the way he fought back, it wasn't the first time some kid had tried to roll him.

Empathy spiked adrenaline, as Tom imagined himself in the fight, and time slowed. If the kid wanted loot, he was pretty dumb. Tom would have just hit Carter on the head or slit his throat from behind, giving him no chance to fight back. He threw mental punches and kicks, like he was watching a video game.

They grappled to the window. In profile, the attacker had what looked like female breasts, but it couldn't be. Then the boy's face turned directly toward Tom.

It wasn't a boy. It was a woman.

It was Amanda. Attacking Carter.

Tom leapt from the bench and slid down the wet grass to the pavement, and forgot he was blind, forgot there were steps, forgot to look both ways, running in front of an oncoming car. It honked, slammed brakes, skidding to a stop. An elderly gent behind the wheel of the big, old Lincoln was about to have a coronary, hyperventilating in confusion as a blind man ran across the street. Tom reached the double yellow line in one piece and stood stock-still to look up. Carter pinned Amanda against the window. And kissed her. Deeply.

Raindrops paused in midair.

As slowly as a vine's tendril curls around its support, Amanda's arms snaked around Carter, and she kissed him back. Tom had been those lips and felt that endless kiss, tongues entwined, down to his bones' marrow. Even as cars honked at the blind man glued to the pavement, the lovers didn't notice.

Was this a dream? Was he having a stroke? Had his pain and longing finally caused a psychotic break with reality, a release of subconscious fears? He pinched the back of his hand. It hurt.

If real, Tom didn't know what stunned him more. That Amanda was alive and in love with Carter. Or that Carter was in love with her. Given his love and trust in his wife and his best friend's homosexuality, how was this possible? The idea of Amanda and Carter . . . in love . . . and conspiring against him . . . blew his tenuous reality away.

Any crazy thing could now be possible. How long had their affair been going on? Could Amanda have been a part of the plot against him all along?

Her voice rang in his head. *"We needed his help and that was the payment."* Maybe Prometheus was only the deposit. This was the balance.

Every troubled moment of his marriage's last two years tormented him. Had she planned the miscarriage to unbalance him? Maybe she didn't want his child, since she and Carter had a plan to be together . . . But from when? Had the baby even been his? His head flooded with so many memories, it hurt. Could Carter have introduced Amanda to him as the beginning of the setup? Was that insane thought actually possible?

If so, she deserved her comeuppance more than Carter. Her betrayal was worse than if she died. He wished he had a rifle. He would have shot them both, right through the glass, then and there. Sting warbled in defiance, lonely, crying . . .

Tom would have crushed his head between his hands if it would quiet the taunting music, but it played regardless.

Chang, Carter, and Amanda. All traitors. How much more of his life was a lie? What about Ruth? She seemed loyal, but then they all had. She was also the one who had enabled him to create the technology and augment himself. And that's what the club needed for their plan, even if Carter was conflicted—or pretended to be. Was she involved in the club's machinations as well? He had approached her about Prometheus, not the other way around. Ruth was lots of things, but given her unusual wiring, was she capable of such deceit? If she was a traitor, then every important person in his life since entering Stanford was not what he or she seemed. Only Pop and Nick had loved him. Or maybe not even Nick? Who knew? The notion was so enormous, it seemed insane. One's entire life could not be a lie. Could it?

But one question stabbed at him under it all: Why did Talia keep him away from here for so long?

She must have known.

His mind was so preoccupied running betrayal scenarios, he didn't notice how he got back, although a few riders glanced at him strangely on the MUNI. He must have forgotten he was blind. So much for the Hippo 2.0.

While he fished out the keys, Talia flung open the apartment door. She grabbed his coat lapel and pulled him inside.

"Oh, thank God . . . where were you? I was crazed!" She tried to pull him into a kiss, but he slipped out of her embrace to take off his raincoat.

He tried to control his voice. "You were?"

"Of course I was! You weren't here." She tried to kiss him again, but he sidestepped away. "What's wrong?"

"Why did you hide Amanda and Carter from me?"

She went very still, eyes wide. "What?"

"Did you want us locked at the hip before I found out? Did you think I wouldn't want you if she was alive, even if she was a traitor?" He backed her up against the recently closed sofa bed.

"Amanda's alive?"

"When were you going to tell me?"

"No . . . No . . . that's ridiculous. I didn't know she's alive . . . and I had no idea we'd sleep together . . . I did everything to stop it . . . and I never thought I'd tell you about me. None of this was a plan . . ."

"She's living with Carter, right in his house, in plain sight of everyone!" he yelled. Her knees buckled, and she sat hard on the couch. "You shouldn't be in the revenge business. You suck at contingencies. Or you knew. Oh, her hair's chopped off and dyed blond, but you of all people would have seen through that!"

"But I checked. Several times. Only he was there. Or his house-keeper. No one else. Not even hustlers. She never turned up . . . She was dead . . ."

"She's. Fucking. Carter."

Her eyes watered, and she twitched momentarily like Ruth.

"And when were you planning to let your pathetic creature know who he was modeled after?" gesturing dramatically to himself.

Talia buried her face in shaking hands.

He bent to her ear. "You can see why I find it hard to believe you."

She peeked out, tears on her cheeks. "Please . . . I know you don't . . . but you have to . . ."

"What did you imagine I'd think when I found out I was Ricardo Gonzales's ghost . . . zombie . . . avatar . . . golem . . . none of the words are quite right in this case, are they?"

Her father's name made her gasp, as though he spoke the unut-terable name of God. He supposed for her it was.

"Puts a whole new spin on the Electra complex. Maybe Freud was right about something." Disgusted, he stood to leave.

She grabbed his wrist with her left hand, then placing her right hand on her heart, softly moved her left to the center of his chest. "I swear, on you, on me, on my father, on God, on anyone you want, I only wanted you to be safe. I worked with what I had. I didn't plan on . . . us . . . I mean . . . you looked like my father! I did everything in my power for it not to happen! And if that makes me horrible, I'm sorry."

He stared unblinking at her, making her muscles writhe in dis-comfort and her breath shudder until she held it. Would she pass out before she dared breathe again?

Had she created him for her own revenge, risking him instead of herself? Was she still holding back important information? Ana-lyzing all the possibilities, he decided the questions were moot. He needed her help to accomplish his goals. And if he examined his motives, he needed her for more than that, but he was rarely that introspective anymore.

He knelt in front of the sofa, encircling her in his arms to hold her close. She gasped for air, shivering in relief, and melted into him.

His kisses started slowly at her collarbone and worked their way up her neck to her earlobe. His breath tickled her ear, and she moaned softly.

"If you betray me, I'll kill you," he murmured. "Like I'll kill Amanda. And all the others."

Then he kissed her lips. Her fingers clenched his hair, and she kissed him back hungrily.

CHAPTER FIFTY-ONE

Eight blocks from Carter's college house on Stanford Avenue, Yale Street was quiet. Teachers, administrators, and students who lived in the neighborhood of tidy homes southeast of campus were asleep at 3:00 a.m. The lights inside a particular house went out at 11:00 p.m. sharp, as they had every night for the last three weeks. The owner was obsessive-compulsive about many things, including bedtime.

Tom dressed for stealth. His hands covered in black nitrile-rubber gloves; feet in black smooth-soled shoes curled up at the edges, leaving no hint of size and covered in nitrile-rubber that left neither a footprint, nor a specimen; his body covered in a black nano-pored paper biohazard jumpsuit. He would leave no particles behind and take none with him.

He accessed the property through the back fence of a small, two-story apartment building on Williams Street. The fence was broken, and the untrimmed backyard trees protected him from curious eyes and made it easy to case the house during the day while the owner was at work. According to Talia, club security on Prometheus employees was not as heavy as it was on members, but it was there. The club might have almost-infinite resources, but not infinite patience to monitor needlessly. There was an alarm system, easily circumvented with an electronic patch delivered from the telephone line that generated an all clear, as opposed to a breach signal. The mobile security detail covering local Prometheus homes, confirming occupants were snug in their beds, had already made its nightly rounds. The GO/HOME bugs were set for content retrieval, not surveillance. There was no need for further security with so little to fear from the scientist. The club trusted her naïveté.

Tom still remembered the entire interior vividly. He had spent a great deal of time there, since Nick Chaikin expected him for Shabbat dinner every Friday night, which was weird for a lapsed Catholic the first couple of times, but he adapted, learning the blessings and how to behave properly in a devoutly Jewish home. But above dietary laws and Shabbat edicts, you didn't contradict Nick on his turf, unless it was about work, and then you had to really know your stuff and prove the master wrong. Which didn't happen often.

Nick was a classic Jewish paranoid. His favorite quote was Henry Kissinger's: "Even a paranoid has some real enemies," which might have been the only time the scientist agreed with Kissinger about anything. Given Nick's experience as a Jewish scientist in the USSR and his protracted and painful emigration with his wife and young daughter to the US, as well as the whole of Jewish history, he had good reason. He made sure his most trusted students had keys to his home, office, and lab or knew where to find them, in case something suspicious should happen to him. He had always expected it. When he died in his bed from a heart attack, it was tragic, but strangely anticlimactic for a man so sure he'd be murdered by one government or another's stooges for his research.

Only now did Tom recognize Nick Chaikin as a political, as well as scientific, Nostradamus.

Standing on the back steps, Tom lifted the end of a wooden plank in the floor of the back porch. The old emergency keys were still in a little plastic baggie where Nick had left them over a decade ago. He unlocked the back door and stepped silently inside.

With neither the money, nor the inclination, Ruth had left the interior unchanged since her parents' deaths. Her mother's passing from cancer had preceded her father's by only a few months. Everyone assumed Nick had died from stress-induced cardiomyopathy, otherwise known as broken heart syndrome, just like his own father. That was over a decade ago, but you'd never know it by the house. The remnants of the elder Chaikins were everywhere. A place for everything and everything in its place. Polished wood floors in every room so you could scrub them and keep the allergens and pollutants at bay. Simple pull-down shades, modern furniture of the Bauhaus school—lots of wood and chrome and easy-to-clean leather.

The stairs were noisy, with no carpet. He crept on hands and knees to distribute his weight over as wide a space as possible to minimize creaking. Upstairs were only three rooms: the parents' room, left like a memorial, undisturbed, as though they'd be back from vacation any day. The bathroom. And Ruth's room. Her door was open.

Tom hovered over Ruth's body in her twin bed with the faux colonial frame, star and moon stickers still clinging to the headboard, their phosphorescence long gone. The bed was pushed into the corner, and Ruth shared the cramped mattress with a lineup of stuffed animals along the wall. In the opposite corner stood the leather, cloth, and metal hugging machine.

He withdrew a syringe from an inner pocket, uncapped it and bent over.

Ruth's eyes snapped open. Wide.

She opened her mouth to scream, but Tom was quick. He stuffed a well-worn Snoopy into her mouth and sat on her chest, pinning her arms to her torso. She screamed into the stuffing, his physical proximity more terrifying to her than any notions of assault, rape, or murder. Struggling in hysterics, Snoopy almost popped out, forcing Tom to shove it in just short of choking.

He jabbed the needle into her upper arm and pushed the plunger steadily, until it was empty. Then he waited the forty-seven seconds it took for her panicked movement to cease.

He pressed her limp hands to a letter he pulled from a ziplock baggie. The file was on her hard drive, printed on her paper with her printer and ink in her own house from a previous foray. And now her fingerprints would be on it, confirming she did it herself. For a bit of drama, he even added a bit of her own saliva that had escaped from the corner of her slack lips so they'd have a nice clean DNA sample, confirming she'd handled it.

He ran downstairs and placed it on the desk in the front parlor, Nick's old study, where he was sure the authorities—and the club— would find it. Before leaving, he took a last look around. Ruth was tending Nick's flame here, too. He never knew how she could keep the study so immaculate, when her own office was a disaster. There was his Nobel Prize diploma on the wall, along with photos of the Chaikins meeting a scientific Who's Who of the last few decades. On his way back upstairs, he passed another copy of the photo Ruth had taken from her lab to Prometheus's offices: Nick hugging Carter tightly and Peter less so, with Ruth hovering to the side. The photo had much more meaning to him now.

In Ruth's room, he wrapped the body in a black plastic tarp. His burden was as light as a feather. However, before leaving the house, he neatened the bed and left everything just so. Best to think like Ruth would have.

An hour later, Ruth's old Honda Accord was parked at the Golden Gate Bridge's southwest parking lot. The driver got out into the damp, foggy night, wearing khakis, a ratty turtleneck, and a worn trench coat, her gray-brown hair in frizzy disarray. She pulled an old woman's bike, complete with white wicker basket, out of the hatchback and bicycled to the pedestrian gate. Ruth rode it to her office every day. She waited for security to buzz her into the bridge path that was locked only at night to prevent walkers after dark. It was the walkers who tended to be the jumpers, not bicyclists. She cycled to the middle of the bridge quickly. The guard was busy with the comings and goings at the gates in the dark hours of the early morning and would miss her completely.

She climbed off the cycle, leaning it against the railing, and scaled the four-foot barricade, never raised higher because of San Franciscans' aesthetic and financial concerns for the famed landmark, regardless of the bridge's reputation as the most famous—and oft-used—suicide spot in the world.

A handful of witnesses rushing by in cars and on bikes saw the woman disappear into the inky darkness beyond the orange steel before they could stop her. Like many jumpers before her, she timed her jump with the neap tide, her body dragged down to the bottom of the current and out to sea, never to be found.

CHAPTER FIFTY-TWO

The one-story log cabin was tucked into a pine-covered property on Sequoia Lake, with the only other lakefront-property owner a YMCA camp empty for the season. Talia arranged for the cabin's availability through one of her sympathetic anticlub contacts.

It was clean and spartan: a small living/dining/kitchen with an old leather sofa, a rustic wooden table, and four similar chairs; a bedroom with two double beds, a bureau, and a small closet; and a bath. A handful of old black-and-white photos from the cabin's early days of fishermen and hunters escaping their big-city responsibilities. And the ubiquitous HOME, even here. It uncomfortably reminded him of the club's encampment, but it would suffice.

Tom had stripped off his protective gear and destroyed it in a ranch incinerator outside of Tulare. Once settled into the shack, he cleaned up and made himself presentable and nonthreatening. A blue button-down shirt and Levis. Sneakers. To pass the time, he stretched out on the too-soft double bed and watched cable news on the HOME. President Stevens spoke at the unveiling of a brand-new robotic tank, telling the nation they had to "dig deep for the fortitude necessary to fight the enemy at home. It could be their neighbor, their friend, a member of their family . . ."

Fools, thought Tom.

He knew it'd be at least another day before news of Ruth's death was publicized. Given both her father's and former employer's notoriety, the press would at least grant her a small headline, a few sentences about a brilliant career cut short, a woman deeply influenced by both a Nobel laureate and a terrorist.

On the other bed, a plastic sheet covered the entire mattress. Ruth Chaikin lay gagged and bound on top of it, still unconscious; the army duffel he had carried her in lay at the foot of the bed.

By the time the news broadcast churned enough stomach acid to fill his mouth with its bitter taste, Ruth moaned and tried to move. He gratefully turned off the HOME. She struggled to clear her head as she slowly realized the extent of her restraints. Tom waited patiently until she saw him. The gag muffled her scream.

He rolled off his bed and sat on the edge of hers. She flinched and twitched uncontrollably at his closeness, but he wanted her uncomfortable. Concerned the drugs might not be out of her system enough to understand, he spoke slowly and clearly. "I'm going to take out your gag, and we're going to talk. Don't bother screaming. There's no one to hear. I'll ask questions, and you'll answer and behave. Or the gag goes back in and we start again. If you're good, I'll answer any questions you have after. Understand?"

She nodded furiously. He removed the stuffing.

Taking careful aim, a wad of saliva hit him below the left eye. *"Gai tren zich!"* she yelled.

He stuffed the gag back in, then wiped his face with his sleeve. "Shut that potty mouth. You're alive because I'm a fair man and I need information. Don't push it."

Her eyes narrowed. Even with her foggy, enraged brain, she realized he understood Yiddish.

"If we establish good communication, I'll untie you, and you'll be free to go. That is, if you want to go. You may not by the time we're done. Shall we try again?"

The frightened animal nodded her head. He pulled out the gag.

"Kish mir en toches," she muttered.

"I'm glad your mother can't hear you."

She tried to read into that, but the drugs made her eyes unfocused. "What did you give me?"

"Ketamine and Valium."

"You w-w-want I should be an imbecile? How dare you mess with neuroreceptors like that!"

"Who knows? Might straighten you out." He loosened the buckled nylon web straps around her, and she shook in fright at his hands on her body. She couldn't get away, but could shimmy around. That's all he needed. He could have made a basic lie detector to read changes in galvanic skin resistance, i.e. sweat, from any simple electronics around. The archaic alarm clock on the bureau would do. But he didn't need any scientific instruments, even homemade ones. Ruth was her own giant polygraph.

"I'm going to ask you some questions, and I need you to answer to the best of your ability," he said.

Still shaking, she stuttered, "Wh-wh-who are you? You knew my m-m-m-mother?"

"Did you ever suspect that Chang Eng was a 10/26 conspirator?"

She said nothing, staring him down. When she realized after thirty seconds that resistance would get nowhere, she barked, *"Nein."*

"Never?"

"Only when he ran away. And into FBI bullets."

"Did you ever suspect Peter Bernhardt was a 10/26 conspirator?"

"N-n-n-o! He wasn't!" Her body twitched up, but the straps held her.

"I appreciate your vehemence. Do you suspect any other colleagues were or are 10/26 conspirators?"

Ruth twitched under the restraints. It took a few moments for her to answer. "Not sure about Chang. Didn't know him well. But I know Peter. He would never. Never. They are liars. All of them." Her body went quiet.

"Who are liars?"

"Carter. Government. News. Papa was right! They all lie!"

"About what?"

"P-P-Peter!"

"Why do you think so?"

She rolled twitchy eyes. "He swore!"

"What did he swear?"

"To work with me f-f-forever . . ."

"And how did that work out?" asked Tom sardonically.

Ruth was silent, but her eyelids fluttered angrily.

Tom continued, "Do you suspect any colleagues are involved in conspiracies or projects not directly related to your own work at Prometheus or might manipulate your work for other ends?"

She went very still. "Why should I answer stupid questions? You are an idiot."

He smiled crookedly. "That may well be. But it's not for lack of trying."

"My questions now," demanded Ruth. Tom inclined his head. "Wh-wh-who are you? Why am I here?"

He smiled. "It's a little complicated. My name is Thomas Paine, and that's what you'll call me. But once, you knew me as Peter Bernhardt. And I'm exacting vengeance. For us both."

Her pasty complexion went green. *"Bist meshugeh?"*

"No, I'm not crazy." He loosened one arm from under the straps. Ruth's hand twitched violently as he gently moved it to his scalp. "I'd show you the keloids, but I had them lasered away. You can still feel the Cortex 2.0 receiver under the scalp if you know where to touch. I know I don't look or sound like Peter, but I had to change all that. Or I'd really be dead."

Her fingers felt the small device under the skin, but it was too far a mental leap, and she yanked her hand back. *"Es iz nit geshtoygen un nit gefloygen,"* she muttered.

"It's not bullshit. I would show you some great memory tricks, but the processor's ruined. And anyway, both you and I know the memory tricks aren't really impressive. Any good magician could do it. But I can tell you all kinds of things about me, like the music I hear and the dreams I've had since the surgery, things only a handful of people in the entire world know about Peter, including you. And . . . I can tell you things about you, like . . . how I sat shiva with you in your house after Nick died. How I had to pester a janitor in the experimental physics department to give me a wooden box for you to sit on in the study. How we covered all the mirrors in your house, including the mirror behind your bedroom door, using your astronomy sheets with the constellations on them . . ."

"You know about my house because you kidnapped me!"

"But how would I know about your parents? Like how your mother always complained I was too thin? If she made me eat any more stuffed cabbage, I thought I'd explode. Carter wouldn't touch it, and Amanda didn't eat meat. And you know me. Poor boy can't let food go to waste. And her kreplachs! Jesus, you could crush a toe if you dropped one! Forget about the freshman fifteen, I had the grad twenty. Lucky you forgot to eat, otherwise you'd have been a porker."

Tears formed in Ruth's eyes. She searched the strange man's face for signs of Peter, but couldn't find him. "Are you a g-g-g-ghost?"

"I thought you and Nick didn't believe in ghosts."

"Got in himmel . . ." she gasped. There it was in her eyes: stunned belief. In him. He took off the restraints. Then he handed

her Snoopy. She clutched the ragged, graying dog to her breast. It was the only thing he'd ever seen her hug before, except her father.

"You left me . . . You swore you wouldn't," she said, rocking side to side with Snoopy. She could never have hugged the man, so she squeezed the stuffing out of the toy.

"I know, Ruthie. I missed you, too."

"Where did I go?"

"You left a note. First Chang's death, then mine. You refused to believe we were guilty. You were despondent over our deaths and certain whoever got us was messing with you, too. You didn't know what to believe anymore, what to do, and you were all alone with no one to talk to and it just wasn't worth going on."

"How did you know?" she whispered.

"Because I know you."

"All except the last part. I would never kill myself."

"No one else knows that."

"How did I die?"

"Golden Gate. Neap tide. My friend was hooked to two elastic lines attached to the bridge, set a dozen yards apart hours before. Like double-cord bungee jumping, except at the bottom she unclipped from the drop line to swing across to the ascender line. Then her mercenaries popped the drop line off by remote control. She stripped off your costume in midair, dropped it in a weighted bag into the bay, and came up in exercise clothes. She packed up the ascender, her helpers drove onto the bridge, picked her up, and no one noticed, everyone was so preoccupied with looking at the spot they last saw you."

"Golden Gate. Such a cliché," she sighed. "This friend . . . woman . . . she works for the circus?"

Tom smiled. "No, but Talia does have an unusual résumé."

Ruth frowned. "You . . . have feelings for this Talia?"

Tom cocked an eyebrow. "Ruth . . ."

Ruth tried to purse her lips, but they twitched like a toddler practicing kisses. "Why vengeance for both? Against whom?"

"Carter killed my father and tried to kill me. And he murdered Nick."

She rocked more strenuously. So he patiently told her everything. All the pieces of the Phoenix Club's plans to use their technology and Carter's deceit fit together.

"Carter admitted it. Brant even teased him about it. And given everything I experienced, I understand their motives. Carter joined the club a year before Nick died. And Carter's first company? That he supposedly self-financed, but was actually cofinanced by the club? It was based on carbon nanotubes for prosthetics connections. It was Nick's tech for DARPA, the one he wouldn't let you work on. The club took it, like they took mine. And a favorite method of club assassination is the fake embolism, especially for men of a certain age. That was Nick."

Ruth rocked vigorously to keep from crying. "No heart disease in his family. He had the Ashkenazi longevity gene. With the CETP W variant. I never believed he died that way. But I had no data to deny it."

"Genius and longevity weren't enough to protect him. And then there's Amanda . . ."

Ruth's eyes narrowed.

"Amanda and Carter are in love and living together," continued Tom. "She was in on it, maybe from the beginning."

Every spasm revealed her madly whirling cogs thinking they could finally be together. Then she spat, "I knew! She was bad news! *Paigeren zol sei!*"

"They won't drop dead on their own, Ruthie. I need your help. We have to stop them. Then kill them."

It was as though he spoke Swahili. If for a moment she thought this strange man was Peter, she had a harder time imagining it now. Her shaking head melded into her spasmodic twitching.

"Why not?" he asked.

"I cannot . . . k-kill. My family. We know what it is. To be hunted. To flee your home. To be hated. Just for your beliefs. That you are wished dead."

"But you are dead, Ruthie. You'll have to live underground; you can't go back to your old life . . ."

This brought tears to her eyes. "Death would be better."

"But you just said . . ."

"I would never end the life I was leading. As unhappy as I was. But you did. Without permission. I don't want a new life."

Tom reached into his breast pocket and pulled out two clamped microscope slides, sandwiching a smear of dried blood. He handed the proof of their covenant to her.

"First, I gave you my work. And then my brain. Now I'm offering my life."

Her only response was the shaking of the mattress from her whole-body vibrations.

He sighed. "I guess you don't care if I say 'intravascular nanowire neural enhancement system'?"

She clutched the slides so hard, he was afraid the glass would shatter. *"A broch tzu dir!"*

"I'm already cursed, Ruthie. You can't make it worse."

Tears flowed as her face twisted in a churlish grin. "P-p-permanent? And biocompatible polymers? You'll have problems. With increased platelet adhesion. From long-term blood flow turbulence . . ."

He might have destroyed her life, but she couldn't resist the challenge. And they both knew it.

CHAPTER FIFTY-THREE

Their new lab was a far cry from Prometheus's deep-pocket setup, but it sufficed. Contained within only four windowless rooms onboard a docked ship, one room housed the computing power, with multiple server towers and a seawater cooling system. Another contained an operating theater, with the basics that a cardiac or neurosurgeon might need, including a small fMRI. The third was a small nanofabricator. Talia and her gang stole the "nanofabber" that Ruth heard was hidden in a Stanford basement from government confiscation. Since it was contraband, the university would never report it missing for fear of government penalties. They used it to make bespoke parts. Any large-scale fabrication of wires or other standard nanoparts were purchased from Chinese manufacturers with no interest in tipping off the US government, sent through multiple vendors and addresses to different drop sites and picked up by different mercenary messengers. Ruth and Tom could manufacture the rest.

The fourth room was a tiny studio apartment for Ruth, where Tom, Talia, and a staff provided her with three meals a day, plus a fridge full of whatever she wanted, which usually meant her precious G-3 elixir and NutrinoBars. It suited her. She had few interruptions and could concentrate on taking her R&D to the next level. She claimed she was content, as long as she had unlimited encrypted-anonymous wireless access to any intravascular nanowire neural enhancement research she wanted.

In these small rooms, Tom and Ruth would build improved cybernetic implants that would take him far beyond what Peter Bernhardt created at Prometheus Industries and make him truly more than human.

The new-and-improved Cortex 3.0 would miniaturize the memory system further and make it invisible to the naked eye. Everything would be internal to the body, including the computer processor. It would also be completely integrated to his brain, not just a select area, allowing control not only of thought, but also of brain and body processes. And he'd have Wi-Fi. Building it entailed manipulating electrically conductive needles under a scanning tunneling microscope, a Mini Cooper–sized steel-tubed and steel-bolted machine that looked like a gizmo from Captain Nemo's *Nautilus*.

Hunched in front of the microscope monitor for hours manipulating nanosoldering guns and poking at nanocircuits, his back ached, but Tom couldn't wait to finish and plug back in. Since his supposed death, half his brain was missing.

After a few weeks, the circuits were in place, and he hooked up the Cortex 3.0 to the computer for program downloading and diagnostics. Dr. Who found them the world's greatest cracker, for whom no computer system was inviolate. The cracker broke out all the data and programming from Prometheus under the guise of a scheduled system backup, revealing Prometheus's progress in their absence. The company's Cortex 2.0 algorithm development had slowed. Any new ideas initiated by Peter Bernhardt or Ruth, like the bloodstream nanobots, were dead. Carter held the company to his original plan, with no innovations. Tom was consoled by the fact that he and Ruth weren't as expendable an intellectual resource as the club had hoped.

The cracker broke into IBM and released their Blue Gene brain modeling for Tom and Ruth's perusal. It was either a demonstration of the cracker's genius, since IBM was legendarily impenetrable, or her access to a quantum computer capable of running Shor's algorithm, which supposedly could beat any encryption, except perhaps quantum encryption itself. But that seemed unlikely, since quantum computing was still struggling in its cradle. The third possibility was she, or a compatriot, worked for IBM. Ruth developed an intellectual crush and, puzzling over her identity, named her *Fräuline Ethische*, meaning "Miss Ethical" or "Miss White Hat"—a good-guy hacker, as opposed to a "Black Hat"—a bad-guy hacker. She was so brilliant, Ruth didn't care if she was white hat or black hat, but she was sure she was a Russian Jew. No one else could be so smart. And she spoke Russian and Yiddish. And German, English, Dutch, French, Spanish, and Italian. And a smattering of Mandarin.

Tom believed she wasn't black hat or white. She was Miss Gray Hat. He tolerated the mystery because their digital relationship was so fruitful, but was aware if she was buyable by them, she was buyable by others. Just like Chang.

Then one day, Talia appeared at the clean room's glass door and pointed at the handsome bald man standing next to her, carrying a doctor's bag. It was the first time Tom had seen him without a lab coat.

Dr. Steven Carbone shifted nervously opposite Tom at a small dining table in Ruth's room, transformed into a lounge with her Murphy bed tucked away for the day. Ruth sat on one end of a small sofa, catching her daily dose of Vitamin D under a standing sun lamp. She often stared twitchily at Talia next to her, unable to parse out the code behind her and Tom's mutual attraction.

Talia trembled almost as much as Ruth, her eyes flicking between the two men who knew her better than anyone else.

The doctor finished hovering over Tom, checking surgery sites, taking vital signs, and asking questions about his pulmonary health, which was weakened from the ARDS. Satisfied his patient had healed remarkably well considering all he'd been through, he sat back in a chair and smiled.

That's when Tom dropped the bombshell.

"You're crazy," said Steve.

Tom motioned toward Ruth. "She says that to me all the time. Sounds more insulting in Yiddish."

"How could you think I'd just take an indefinite leave of absence to work for you? For . . . enhancement?" Steve spit the last word like a profanity.

"For experimentation," Tom corrected. "And it's ten million dollars. In return, you bone up on catheterization, cardiac and brain surgery, and interventional neuroradiology. We can teach you the rest."

"If you're here, Steve," said Talia, "you can make sure Tom doesn't go too far. What he's doing is . . . evolutionary, and he needs a balanced, insightful person to gauge just how far the upgrades should go. It's because you're not gung ho like them that you're the right man for the job."

"I am not g-g-g-gung . . ." insisted Ruth.

"If I cared about money," interrupted Steve as he jerked his thumb at Talia, "I'd have taken hers long ago. You're asking me to throw my Hippocratic Oath out the window. Who do you think I am?"

Tom leaned forward. "I think you're someone who realizes that, sometimes, you need to stop bad people before they destroy more lives. You were a victim when they took the love of your life from you, too. You've been marching in Talia's army for a long time."

"I might kill you!" said Steve. "Maybe you can forget about 'Do no harm,' but I can't."

"I've worked the stroke problem out," insisted Tom. "And there aren't other risks."

Ruth twitched uncontrollably. *"A mentsh tracht und Gott lacht,"* she muttered, as her legs shook.

Steve appraised her tremors with a professional eye. "How long have you had that?"

She shrugged as cheek muscles fluttered. Tom shook his head in amusement. "Oh, believe me, she's fine."

"What did you say before?" Steve asked her.

"I said," replied Ruth, "'a m-man plans and God laughs.' And this man? God's hysterical."

"You're not helping, Ruthie," Tom sighed.

"Steve, if you just hung around more, you'd see they've come up with a great idea," insisted Talia. "Not only to do what we need it to, but to cure so many people of other problems . . ."

"Talia, you can't honestly tell me that you think this is necessary . . ." Steve said.

Tom interrupted, "These are some of the smartest, most savvy men in the world. They will be using my brain prosthetics to control the minds of their enemies. And my bots pass the blood-brain barrier. They could use them for brainwashing or killing their enemies on a vast scale. There is no one else but me to stop them—and I'm willing to die trying. The only way to do that is to get inside: join their ranks and become a trusted companion alone on their turf. As a human 'army of one,' I'll fail. I must take all our compatriots and all available human knowledge in with me, virtually, so I need the maximum amount of communication, data retrieval, and cognitive power available 24/7, instantly and secretly, or I'm dead. And so are all of you if I'm captured."

"Even if you succeed, which I doubt, then what happens?" His head kept shaking like a metronome. "You know how crazy you sound? Like two comic book characters . . . Brainiac and the Incredible Disappearing Girl. Do the two of you live happily ever after, on your secret island hideout, after you nuke the bad guys?"

Talia's jaw dropped. "Is that your problem?"

"And he looks just like your father! Why did I let you do that?"

"You didn't 'let' me." Her eyes flashed in anger. "Maybe you're *not* the person for the job . . ."

"Why, because I know you too well?" barked Steve.

Talia prepared for war, but Tom cut her off, right in Steve's face. "You do an awful lot of favors for Talia. Saving my life was a huge risk. I'm very grateful. You could have turned me in at any time. Or just ignored the situation. But you didn't."

"I knew what you both were up against. It wasn't right . . ." mumbled Steve.

"But you blame yourself for what happened to Talia when you were together, don't you? Do you think if you had to do it over, you could have stopped her before she self-destructed, before it all fell apart?"

Steve twisted in his chair. "Yes! Well . . . I don't know."

"You feel guilty. Wish you had been more of a man of action? Now's your chance to play that heroic role . . ."

Ruth snorted at Tom. "You should talk . . ."

Tom drove on. "You couldn't help her before, and you lost the woman you loved."

Steve looked aghast. But didn't argue.

Talia squirmed. "Tom, stop it."

"Don't believe *mein Übermensch,*" said Ruth to Steve. "This isn't nobility of innovation. Or self-sacrifice against evil. T-Tom hates

332

the weak man he once was. He blames himself. He thinks if he is no longer just human, he will overcome his enemies. And his p-past. This will make it all better."

Tom reared back. "Do you have a better idea how to stop the club?"

"No," said Ruth calmly. "I do not. This is the best idea. But Steve needs to know. You are the same men. With the same reasons. And apparently, the same woman . . ." She tried to arch her eyebrows, but they danced a jig.

Both men slumped in their chairs, their body language less combative than before. Their eyes locked.

"How can you guarantee I won't destroy your brain? Or kill you?" asked Steve.

"I can't. All I can do is trust you," said Tom. "And you trust me."

CHAPTER FIFTY-FOUR

Medical personnel in green surgical scrubs and masks packed the tiny surgical suite. In a corner, Ruth consulted with two neurologists, asking endless questions. Steve finished a talk with the remainder of the group, examining a computer-reconstructed image of the vascular system in Tom's brain. In scrubs and mask like everyone else, Talia clenched Tom's hand as he reclined on the operating table after being prepped by a surgical assistant. She kept searching his eyes, but didn't say anything.

"Is it a little late to ask what's wrong?" asked Tom.

"I'm trying to remember you. Like you used to be."

"And how was that?"

She smiled. "Naive. Sweet. Infuriating. Someone who thought my pasta with meatballs was the best in the world."

"I still do."

"You won't. Not anymore."

He smiled. "I'll just be more intelligent and distinguished. I thought that turned you on."

She looked away, concentrating on his brain's blood vessels magnified on the big monitor. He couldn't see her expression under the mask.

Finished prepping his team, Steve came to Tom's side, glancing at the held hands. Fleeting, contradictory emotions flashed across his eyes. "Time to sit in your corner."

Talia dutifully moved her stool behind the equipment.

"Now shut up," Steve continued to Tom, "unless you've got something constructive to add to this shooting match."

Tom obeyed, certain his for-hire medical team would do the best job possible. They had a lot riding on it. The eight new faces were once Cuba's infamous medical mercenaries, four men and four women out of tens of thousands dispatched around the world for goodwill and economic purposes. This interventional neuroradiology group was rescued from Venezuela's medical care-for-oil deal, in which the Cuban government sold over twenty-two thousand Cuban doctors into medical slavery. Venezuela got cheap medical care for the poor, which generated votes, and the Castros could keep their country's cars and generators going, on free Venezuelan oil. The only ones who lost in the deal were the doctors and nurses, prisoners in a foreign country whose own jealous medical establishment and political opposition so loathed their existence that Cuban doctors were murdered to eliminate both the competition and the political advantage free healthcare brought the government. The survivors were locked up, supposedly for their own protection. However, they were not permitted to leave Venezuela to return to their own country. Or any other country.

Through Talia's contacts in Miami, Tom anonymously financed the eight's escape and contact with Solidarity Without Borders, a Cuban American organization devoted to providing asylum. In exchange for their freedom, they would perform this operation in an undisclosed, offshore location, after which they'd be blindfolded until they were handed over to SWB in Florida. His promise of freedom more than paid for their silence. All eight jumped at the chance. A crazy American who wanted experimental brain surgery of his own design? Why not? Their biggest concern was the insecurity of doing a procedure no one had ever done before.

The concept was deceptively simple, but the devil was in the nano-sized details. Like preparation for angioplasty, a catheter was threaded into the femoral artery in the groin and laced up the wide arterial vessels to the heart, but in this case it continued past and into one of the four carotid arteries that led to the brain. The procedure was then repeated in all four carotid arteries to gain maximum access to brain tissue. A cable of one hundred thousand conducting polymer nanowires, narrower than a human hair, was sent through the catheter. It was steerable, bending and contracting like a muscle on a low-voltage charge. When the blood vessel was too narrow for the catheter to continue, the cable continued alone, to bend and subdivide into smaller and smaller bunches of wire at each arterial divide, until eventually a single wire could make its way into a single capillary.

The surgeons manually controlled steering the catheter into the brain. They had performed this procedure many times, since interventional neuroradiology repaired brain damage, such as aneurysms, frequently. They were to the brain what the classic angioplasty was to the heart: high-tech plumbing. However, individual wires went farther than these doctors had ever taken a probe. Based on the MRI map of his brain's circulatory system, the wires were preprogrammed to twist and float on the blood's current into their final position in a capillary feeding a neuron. As electricity flowed through the wire, it would stimulate the individual neuron next to it, and the message would be sent through the chain of adjacent neurons.

Once all the wires drifted into place, the surgeons embedded a wireless microprocessor—the new Cortex 3.0—no bigger than a quarter, in the thigh tissue near the femoral artery, to which the wires were attached. Hooked directly to the neurons, as well as the

Hippo 2.0, Tom could teach different parts of his brain to communicate with the electronic and virtual worlds he would theoretically access with his wireless processor via the Internet.

He also wanted to control his physical systems. Some wires connected to his motor cortex, controlling his muscles. Others to the pain centers. Or fear centers. In theory, with proper programming, he would stimulate or repress brain activity at will or when his processor recommended it, as though his brain had an all-encompassing deep-brain stimulator. Using it would entail trial and error. But the Cortex 3.0 made it easy. Once the connection between his brain and the external source had been established, he would always remember how. Hopefully.

Most interventional neuroradiology catheterizations were done while the patient was under general anesthesia, but Tom insisted on being mildly sedated to watch the fluoroscope, a combination live X-ray and video system, and observe the progress of the catheter himself.

Tom mentally thanked Dr. Werner Forssmann, the man who had first self-experimented with venous catheters, as his catheter glided up his neck, tingling arteries. At the base of the brain, wires blossomed through blood vessels like time-lapse photography of a growing plant.

Several hours later, after the final set of wires found their home, Ruth tested the system with mild current, recording the neural stimulation. Then she sent basic data to small neural groupings. Beginning with the thalamus, which integrates sensory input, and using the same algorithms used with retinal implants, she sent colors, shapes, and symbols to the visual cortex. To Tom, it felt like seeing with a transparent overlay of double vision. The Hippo 2.0 and the Cortex 3.0 processed the extra information, unlike a solo brain, which dumped information when overloaded. Tom would learn to separate each out to see them simultaneously, like the spectacular savant Kim Peek, the original "Rain Man," who could read the left page of a book with the left eye and the right page with the right eye simultaneously and never forget either page for the rest of his life. In Tom's case, one visual feed would be internal, and the other his eyes, so he could process and manipulate the Internet and databases directly in his brain.

Then Ruth sent sounds to his auditory cortex with an audiometer, something reminiscent of the old gray box and headphones used in his childhood. He raised a finger each time he internally "heard" a tone, but this time he vocally reproduced the tone if he could, or named the note, so they could see if the tone they sent was the same as the one his brain received. It was. Then Tom heard the impossible.

A clear tone. But he certainly couldn't sing it.

"Ruth . . . fifteen octaves above middle C. I have dolphin hearing!"

Amazed, the Cubans whispered among themselves.

For the next test, Ruth combined visuals with sound. She piped through a montage of images, some black and white, some color, with different actors from different decades, but each fundamentally the same scene: Wyatt, Virgil, and Morgan Earp, and Doc Holliday, confronting the Clantons and their men in the mythic gun fight at the OK Corral.

Tom closed his eyes. The contrast between the images his eyes saw and his brain perceived made him seasick, although he would adjust in time. "Very funny, guys. If I'm Wyatt, does that make Steve Doc Holliday?"

"I'm a lover, not a fighter," said the doctor. "How are you?"

"Still woozy, but I think my senses are just . . . overwhelmed. And tired. But all on target."

"My God, Talia, Superman admits he's human," snorted Steve.

"Who said Superman's hu—" Internal vision pixilated to white static. "Hey, where's Burt Lancaster?" He opened his eyes. External sight was pixilating, too, into a twinkling, starry sky. Nausea surged as the chest pain hit. Before he could say another word, the stars supernovaed and merged into a field of white.

From a great distance, Talia's panicked voice was cut short by Steve ordering a nurse to take her out. Spanish voices yelled out heartbeat and blood pressure. Even as the sound floated away, he knew the numbers weren't good.

A voice across a chasm yelled, "Clear!"

Cold, gooey paddles thudded hard below his right clavicle and his left ribs. The shock seared like branding irons. But his heart did not return to a normal sinus rhythm. The nanowires shouldn't have tripped a heart attack, since they had no contact with autonomic parts of the brain stem, which regulate respiration, heart rate, or blood pressure. So why was he dying? Was it the surgery's cumulative shock or the implant's effects? A rogue electrical charge he didn't account for? There was nothing unusual in the outputs before it hit.

He struggled to keep one track of his mind on the medical team, but the other fell into a dream state, which engulfed him.

He lay alone on deck of a thirty-foot sloop. A life preserver attached to the railing had the name *Pequod* printed on it. The only sounds were of the breeze and lapping waves, the sheets tapping against the metal mast, birds calling to each other overhead. A bald eagle dived, and swooping with claws extended, landed on the deck near Tom. It waddled toward him, talons clicking along the teak, circling his head, ready to attack. Tom tried to swat it away, but he didn't have the energy to lift his arm.

A voice boomed, "Peter! . . . Peter!" like a tuba blast. With great effort, he turned his head. Pop was on shore of the rocky breakwater of Matthiessen Park at the waterfront. It was the park he had played in as a child and only a few blocks up the hill to their apartment.

"Come . . . home . . . now!" bellowed Pop.

Three more eagles arrived: a female with a spasming bass in her beak, gills and fins flapping in death throes; and two scruffy brown juveniles, most likely her offspring. Mama tore pieces of fish flesh with her claws, passing them to her children. They swallowed them hungrily.

His chest felt hammered by a chisel and split asunder. The blue sky went translucent, and he could see the medical drama that lay beyond the azure ceiling of his little floating world, like God and the angels above peeked down wearing surgical masks.

He was desperate to communicate, but his body in both worlds was unresponsive. He searched the new wiring in his brain, but was confused. What went where and which channels had Ruth opened on her computer?

If the same neurons worked when you saw a thing, remembered the thing, and imagined the thing, then his imagination was all he had to create words to contact Ruth. He concentrated as hard as he could and searched for a network to access, to send one word painstakingly spelled out—"R-U-T-H"—back through the system. But he got nothing back. The channel wasn't open.

Then it hit him, and he blamed sedation and lack of oxygen for his stupidity. Of course words didn't work. The system was testing picture and sound channels, and in the panic, she didn't open any others. He needed sound. He'd use his hallucination to communicate.

He summoned the largest bird. "Can you sing?"

Its yellow eyes flashed. "Any requests?"

"'Help.'" Getting bailed out by a Beatles song was becoming a family trademark.

Papa Eagle turned to his Partridge Family, lifted a wing, and on the downbeat, the Fly Four broke out in four-part harmony.

A heavenly voice that sounded like Steve barked, "What's that?"

"I th-th-think it's m-m-music!" stammered Ruth.

The chief neurologist, Dr. José Irizarry, swore, "*Mi Dios . . . El Beatles . . . !*"

Ruth tapped the audiometer at a frequency of 261.626 Hz, or middle C, dot-dot-dot, dash-dash-dash, dot-dot-dot. After a pause, she repeated it.

Tom interrupted the eagles' serenade. "How about 'Message in a Bottle.'"

Papa Eagle rolled his lemon eyes. "You're very literal, aren't you?" The foursome sang and sent his message . . .

"He's still with us. Hang on, Tom!" said Steve.

Dr. Irizarry muttered in a thick Spanish accent, "He's very literal, isn't he?"

"What can I d-d-d-d-do for him?" wailed Ruth.

Tom eyeballed the birds. Papa Eagle sighed. "Yeah, yeah, I know . . ." Without prompting, they began to sing R.E.M.'s "Let Me In," with appropriate grimaces at Tom's lack of creativity.

Ruth sent a repeated message to a small subset of wires in Tom's cortex. Closing his eyes to the burning sun over the boat deck, he imagined following the signal to its source, like a spelunker grabbing a rope hand-over-hand in the dark. At the end of the figurative tunnel, he reached a rushing river.

It was information energy. The Internet.

Connecting to the Internet was like diving into the infiniteness of an ocean. Afraid he'd be swept away, he dipped his toe in. His brain filled with data, images, sounds. Seismic readings from China. The *New York Times* front page. Children singing "Free to Be You and Me." Radar of a hurricane in Haiti. Spreadsheets tracking currency fluctuations. Lolcats. Migrating wildebeests. He pulled out of the data stream.

He was a tiny, but integral part of an enormous, complex system. Earth was as much a cyborg as he was.

His heart jumpstarted, drumming two hundred beats per minute. The chisel sunk in his chest once more, and he gasped for oxygen like Mama Eagle's caught bass. The bright sky peeled away and he discovered his eyes were open. The medicos crowded over him with slack mouths covered by surgical masks.

"What happened?" he mumbled through his oxygen mask, lips still numb.

Flushed, disheveled, and stunned to be talking to a dead man, Steve sputtered, "Not sure. Wasn't a myocardial infarction; there's no real blockage. Could have been a blood-flow irregularity from the wires. I know they're nano-coated to prevent clotting, but man, embolism and thrombosis still worry me. There's no sign of either or any permanent damage. Maybe a complication from the ARDS . . . oh, who the hell knows! My medical diagnosis is you're one stubborn asshole who needs rest. And if this happens again, we're yanking it all out. And I don't care what you say."

"Don't like ambiguity, do you?"

With a huge exhalation, Steve deflated into a question mark, head shaking back and forth like a recalcitrant bull. "No. I like knowing. Knowing's good. I can do something with knowing."

Now that Tom had touched the void, he was sure if he told Steve about the unknown to come, he'd blow the young doctor's mind.

PART THREE

CHAPTER FIFTY-FIVE

For two hundred million dollars, Thomas Paine purchased one of the most famous sailboats in the world and rechristened it the *Pequod*. A modern interpretation of a clipper, she was a great white whale of a ship: 290 feet long, 43 feet wide, and 192 feet tall from the waterline, and her vast and very literal whiteness blinded observers on a cloudless day. Three enormous, computer-controlled, hollow white masts carried five giant white sails, each of which unfurled from the inside along her yardarms, allowing them to appear and disappear at the touch of a button with no visible rigging. They could rotate and adjust their sails for maximum wind efficiency, which was a revolution in the art of ship design. And like clippers of old, she was long, sleek, and fast, regularly beating any sailboat in her class. The group of competitors with sailboats this large was a small, elite club, dominated by mega-wealthy American owners out to best the international yachting pack with leviathans and other oddities.

Standing on the prow, his hands gripped the metal bars of the forward pulpit as saltwater sprayed and drizzled on his face, like the aspersion of baptism, with each dip of the bow. Behind him, footsteps climbed to his platform. Talia came to keep him company. She sighed at the sight. Santa Monica Bay sparkled in the summer sunlight. In his blind-man role, he shouldn't have enjoyed the view, but no one on his crew thought twice when the blind owner wanted to experience the wind and water in his face from the prow. He could look with focused eyes at his objective: Malibu, America's Riviera, from the open water of the Pacific Ocean.

"Want me to tell you what you're missing?" she teased, as she pressed herself against the back of him.

"Don't need to. I've got everything I need right here." His fingers tapped his head. A GPS icon on his internally visualized screen told him exactly where they were. He patched into a live video feed and surveyed the crowd on the beach. "I know he's there," he murmured.

"Of course he is. He lives there. Can you see him?"

"No. I know it . . . I feel it."

Worry creased Talia's eyes behind her sunglasses, and Tom pretended he didn't notice.

"But will he come to you?" she asked.

"Of course. I'm pissing on his territory, and he can't resist the challenge." He smiled. "And he thinks I'm damaged goods, so he'll tell Brant he's got a live one."

It was Fourth of July weekend, and the housewarming-birthday party of the decade was in full swing on Carbon Beach, Billionaire's Row. Thirty-million-dollar homes, many left empty for weeks and months, were filled with the flotsam and jetsam of renters, weekenders, and staff, and crammed cheek to jowl along the beach's length with hardly an arm's length between them. Relentless competition for attention was reflected in the try-hard or location-deaf architecture.

The town hosted Los Angeles's best Independence Day parties, and everyone turned up, from the most powerful to the most beautiful to the most talented to the most ballsy. If you were none of these, you still came. A need to belong to the in-crowd brought some.

Curiosity or voycurism brought others. Many could talk their way in, but it was simpler for the hoi polloi just to walk in—via the beach.

The birthday boy invited all his Carbon Beach neighbors, as well as those from the neighboring, star-studded beach enclaves, encouraging them to fold their own parties into his if they wished. In a community where narcissism was a survival trait, many neighbors complained, "Who the hell is this guy who thinks his party is more important than mine?" But as rumors circulated months in advance, one by one the neighbors conceded, "Well, maybe this year I'll let someone else shoulder a big blowout . . ."

Only one neighbor refused to cooperate.

The host (or at least his party planners) thought of everything. Amazing food and drink, served by beautiful, scantily clad young people; fantastic music performed by world-famous bands—including Garth Brooks out of retirement for the umpteenth time to sing the National Anthem. The host didn't hire a barge of fireworks; he hired dozens of barges to light up the Malibu coastline two nights in a row prior. He rented adjacent houses for spillover from his own enormous house, a Richard Meier beauty crafted from golden teak, concrete, and glass.

Tom was eager to arrive at this over-the-top party.

Because it was his.

The captain of the *Pequod* furled her sails to pull up her huge keel's centerboard and motor to Malibu Pier. Waves and a light breeze gently rocked the masts, and a string of brightly colored signal flags danced from the bow along the tops of her masts and down to her stern, as though to say, "The party's here!" In fact, each flag represented a letter of the alphabet and spelled out a discreet message only professional sailors could decipher: "In every well-governed state, wealth is a sacred thing; in democracies, it is the only sacred thing. Anatole France."

If the massive, otherworldly ship pulling up to the dock didn't garner enough attention, the owner's next stunt did.

On the aft deck of the *Pequod*, Tom stood in the center of a shiny silver disk only eight feet wide and three feet thick, wearing an elegant white suit and T-shirt, setting off the dark tan of his skin and the matching shock of pure white hair atop his head. Like Michael Rennie from *The Day the Earth Stood Still*, his hovercraft rose vertically like a Harrier jet. It hung for a moment above the deck before it took off to the east along Carbon Beach. Tom remained balanced atop. The music stopped, and the sounds of the party faded to silence as people watched in amazement. A musician turned to an odd box with two antennas and waved his hands around them. It was a theremin, invented in 1919, and one of the earliest electronic musical instruments. Eerie sci-fi sounds poured from its speakers as the musician controlled the pitch and volume with graceful gestures like a magician conjuring doves from thin air. As Tom's craft settled on the sand in front of his beach house deck, a huge crowd formed around him, people yelling, "Whoa, man!" and "What's that thing?"

"People deny the acceleration of technological progress by demanding 'Where's my jet pack? Where's my jet pack?' I don't need no stinkin' jet pack! I got a flying saucer!"

"Who are you?" someone yelled.

He threw his arms open wide. "I'm Thomas Paine, the birthday boy!" The crowd cheered.

Standing next to the craft, Talia took his extended hand, and he stepped onto the sand to be led to his guests. A line formed of those ready and eager to try the floating contraption themselves.

The theremin's hum dissolved into a rousing cover of the Beach Boys' "Good Vibrations," complete with theremin solo and Brian

Wilson singing. He segued into another theremin-inspired hit, "I Just Wasn't Made for These Times," but only Tom and Talia appreciated the irony.

This was the mystery man's official debut. His avatar had been very busy until now, creating a googleable presence and persona without having to be in Los Angeles. Guests became instant reporters and trotted alongside the couple with recording GOs extended in front of them. One guy yelled, "How the hell can a blind guy pull off a stunt like that?"

"Magic," replied the host.

"That was fuckin' Kodak courage, man!" a surfer dude screamed, fist pumping the air.

Hundreds of videos were posted on NarcisCity's and Youniverse's portals within minutes. Tom mentally surfed them as the party continued. Overnight, Thomas Paine's arrival on his flying saucer was the most viewed event on the planet.

Everyone on the beach sober, intelligent, or old enough to understand focused on Paine, the handsome, cool, blazingly intelligent, yet controversial billionaire, who happened to be blind. And there was no denying the guy was a star. His mojo was palpable, with something for everybody: mature good looks for the daddy lovers, style for the metrosexuals, and brains for the sapiosexuals. Projecting their physical insecurities, rampant in the SoCal body-conscious culture, onto his disability, women were instantly attracted to his comforting blindness as something they could simultaneously capitalize on and mother. Men were not immune to the billionaire's charms. He was as bi-sexy as Brad Pitt. One look at Talia, his arm candy, and his sexual market value went sky-high across genders. Every guy wanted to be him.

A prickly feeling set the hair on Tom's body erect. "He's coming," he murmured to her. He let Talia decide whether he had technological evidence or not.

Within a minute, Bruce Lobo limped barefoot along the sand in rolled-up khakis, an untucked French-cuffed shirt, and blacked-out aviator sunglasses, arm in arm with Vera, the prostitute from camp. Her presence was unexpected. Was she just his expensive chew toy? An über-pro to screw on a regular basis? Or more? The beauty wore a gold bikini top and gold-embroidered sarong with at least a million bucks in diamonds dripping from various parts of her. Lobo's two de rigueur bodyguards discreetly hovered behind. So did two dozen others, dressed like wealthy partygoers. But they were clearly in Lobo's posse.

With obvious calculation, Lobo and his gang stopped directly in front of Talia and Tom, a standoff in the sand. Lobo stared in surprise, seeing Talia arm in arm with the mystery man. He had no love for the journalist, who had bashed him repeatedly in print. He puffed up his stance and bristled, a pit bull ready for a jaw-locking fight.

Talia said quietly in Tom's ear. "Bruce Lobo and . . . friend . . . and more friends."

Tom's face lit up. "Hello, neighbor!"

"You didn't get my attorney's letter?"

Tom's smile only dimmed slightly. "What letter?"

"The cease and desist regarding this party?"

"What needs ceasing and desisting?"

"Your party's too big. It's on my property and interfering with my own event."

"How is a public beach your property?"

"I own a dozen houses here. It's mine."

"I believe you never ask permission. Only forgiveness . . ." Tom smiled broadly.

Vera contained a laugh.

"Please," continued Tom. "Come inside and have a drink, relax, and let's talk about this. Your friends are certainly welcome."

Talia ignored the mogul and reached across to offer her hand to Vera. "We've never met. I'm Talia Brooks. Welcome to our party."

"Hello. Vera Kostina," she purred.

Surfing his mental Internet rapidly, Tom found a Russian phrase book and audible pronunciation guide. *"Menja zovut* Thomas Paine," he replied with a slight bow and his hand extended toward her voice.

She shook it, delighted. "You speak Russian!"

"Vyochen' dobry. Ja nemnogo govorju po-russki."

"What's he saying?" demanded Lobo.

"He's making excuses for his Russian. But he's being modest. His accent is excellent."

A server with waist-length blond hair, a body to compete with Vera's, and wearing a stars-and-stripes bikini, appeared with a tray and offered champagne. Bruce grabbed a glass, turned his back to Talia and Tom, and gestured to his group. They walked with determination toward Tom's house.

Tom hid his concern, but turned to Talia. "I hear people leaving?"

Before Talia could answer, Vera took a glass and changed the subject. "I've been aboard your yacht with a previous owner. She's extraordinary. But she had a different name. So I must ask, what's *'Pequod'*?"

Bruce's minions climbed the deck stairs into his house. Tom wanted to follow them, but couldn't ignore Vera's question without raising Bruce's suspicions. "It's the name of the whaling ship in *Moby-Dick*. She's three-masted like the one in the novel."

"But what does the name mean?"

"The Pequot were a tribe of Native Americans who were destroyed by the New England Puritans only seventeen years after the *Mayflower* landed. Smallpox killed most of them. Then the survivors fought the Puritans . . . and lost. When Melville wrote his story, he thought the Pequot were tragically extinct. But they weren't . . ." Paine grinned.

"Instead, they got their revenge. They sued the government in 1976 to give them back their land in the middle of Connecticut—and won in 1983—and they have one of the largest casinos in the world. They're rich. Used our own avarice against us."

Meanwhile, he directed his internal connections to the in-house security cameras. Bruce's horde was spreading through the house like a plague, looking for electronics and discreetly placing bugs. With staff and guests around the house, they worked carefully not to be discovered. Two made it into Tom's office and surreptitiously placed a tiny device on the rear of his HOME screen. He and the mysterious Miss Gray Hat had noticed an unusual number of cyber attacks on his HOME system in the last month. No one had penetrated his firewalls, but it was obvious now who was prepared to get his information from the inside. If he reacted in panic and shut down their access at once, they'd know he'd discovered them. He hailed Miss Gray Hat through the brain implant and alerted her to the intruders so she would not fall into their traps and could secure their networks from further trespassers. Two more operatives made it upstairs to the master bedroom. They were wiping for skin cells, grabbing hair from brushes.

It was a good thing Tom had never stepped foot in the house. The cells and hair they collected were planted, having been previously procured from a foreign national not found on any biomarker database. The data would reveal a ghost. Tom had prepared for that.

"But you don't find *Pequod* a depressing name for a pleasure craft?" Vera purred the word "pleasure" like caramel dripped from her tongue.

"No," replied Tom. "When everyone thought they were dead, they won. I admire their tenacity. It took three hundred fifty years. High-quality revenge takes time."

Lobo stepped forward. "I'm tenacious, too. And I'm not letting this go, Paine."

"I understand, Bruce. Please, let's go inside and discuss this," said Tom.

"I'd prefer to stay outside. So I can monitor the situation."

It was a funny choice of words. Tom studied Bruce's face more carefully. Bruce was actually monitoring the situation from contact lenses in his eyes that had a feed from his security staff.

As a garden-variety cyborg, Bruce was more like Tom than he realized. That gave Tom and Miss Gray Hat something to hack. He sent her another message. And she replied.

"Darling," said Tom, "why don't you give Vera a tour of the house while Bruce and I chat? You don't mind guiding me around the party, do you, Bruce?"

"Actually, I do," Lobo growled.

"Come now, Bruce. I'm at your mercy, am I not? You could drown me in the ocean if it gets out of hand," he jested.

Vera sighed. "Time for boys to smoke cigars and girls to do needlepoint."

"It's easier than ignoring their macho mind games," grinned Talia.

"I like her!" Vera said to Bruce. He snorted in return.

"Talia?" asked Tom. "Would you get my GO-B out of the office? I want to confirm we received Bruce's letter."

"GO-B?" asked Bruce as he blinked repeatedly. Something was wrong with his feed. Miss Gray Hat had successfully attacked him.

"A GO-B is for blind people. Braille keys, voice recognition, dictation, and playback, verbal and aural GPS. All the disability bells and whistles. I call it the third lobe of my brain. Almost makes blindness irrelevant."

Bruce grabbed the GO in his pocket. "Almost. Excuse me, I've got a message." But he didn't. He was sending one. Within thirty seconds, his team was leaving the house. But the damage had been done.

"Shall we?" Tom asked Bruce as he extended his hand. But Bruce was at a loss. "May I put a finger under your left elbow? That way you're guiding me, but not leading me." The two bodyguards, alert with nervous energy, moved a foot closer to their boss.

Bruce slowly raised his right hand, then handed back his champagne flute with his left. "Uh . . . okay . . ." Every macho cell inflamed with Tom's physical proximity.

Gently touching Bruce's elbow made Tom's neurons replay their fight in the Biogineers conference room. His ribs ached in memory. He turned down his internal mental volume. "Now go ahead. Walk around."

Bruce moved with caution across the sand, towing his host.

"You've caught on quickly how to lead me," said Tom.

"I have?"

"Yes. Some people want to control the disabled. They think that a lack of independence is more helpful. But your discomfort and, if you'll allow me to say, your not wanting to help me is more helpful than someone determined to help more than I need. Coercion is the most disorienting aid of all . . . for a blind man."

"Where the hell do you come from?" blurted Bruce.

Tom played confused. "I live four doors down from you."

"I never heard of you before the last few months. And I didn't see you until today. You're not from California."

"Ah. Well, I haven't lived in the States for a very long time. When I went blind, twenty years ago, my world became very small, only to the end of my fingertips and my cane and as far as I could hear. Since my work is in no way location dependent, it was simply easier to run away from my problems and live on a boat. Go anywhere, do anything. Or not. No one knew me and I liked it that way. Granted, the boats got bigger over time . . ."

Lobo eyed the yacht enviously. "Yeah, you'll need an aircraft carrier and a teleporter next."

"And why not, if I have the means? Don't we all create our own little worlds?"

"So why plant your flag here?" Bruce asked.

Tom smiled. "On your beach?"

Bruce did not smile in return. "Yeah."

"You can only run away for so long before it screws with your head. And I've got a lot to offer. I've gained a great deal of objectivity from decades of globe-trotting, and I'm arrogant enough to think I know what's wrong with our country. And the world. And I'm in a position to make a difference. Others have done the same. Why not me? And as we both know, advertising works. Carbon Beach is a billionaire's Schwab's Drug Store, and I'm Lana Turner."

"That's not what I heard."

Tom's face pinched in concern. "What do you mean?"

"I heard you're in trouble with some Russian oligarchs over water rights in Central Asia. I think you're here to hide out from your nasty pals, kiss up to your former countrymen, and get a bailout. What makes you think anyone wants to help you when we can buy you out for pennies on the dollar? Hell, that boat costs so much in upkeep, I could get you to pay me to take it off your hands."

Tom stiffened. "So you think you've got me cornered?"

"I think this is one hell of a show, and you need help. And I might be able to provide that. For a price." Bruce smiled broadly to a passing neighbor who owned a media empire.

The fish bit the hook. Tom sent Miss Gray Hat a message: *Disinformation Phase I successful. Time for Phase II. Search/destroy/co-opt plan for bugs ASAP.* Hopefully, Bruce and the club found nothing inadvertently useful in Bruce's bold attack. But Tom and his cracker would never be completely sure.

CHAPTER FIFTY-SIX

I n the week between the party and his summons to visit Josiah Brant, Thomas Paine underwent the most thorough background check in history. He had no idea if his creation passed the test. Miss Gray Hat could only say from her analysis that the information had been gathered. But not how it had been received.

He also underwent the gauntlet of public opinion. From the party to planted PR stories in a variety of outlets, it was clear to the mediaverse that Thomas Paine was a star. Everyone wanted to know more about the mysterious blind billionaire.

Tom did his own background checks and, in the process, found David Brant. The blind son of Margaret and Josiah Brant had a minimal Internet profile, mostly chatrooms on old video-gaming-for-the-blind and role-playing sites and alumni fundraising lists from Yale University. Miss Gray Hat uncovered his whereabouts through insurance and Social Security records: an easy drive from Phoenix Camp in Carson City, Nevada, at a special long-term addiction rehabilitation facility called Evermore. He'd been an inpatient there for video-gaming and Internet addiction for the last fifteen years. Hacked medical files indicated that his continual immersive escape in a virtual world, so unlike his own, made him irrationally angry at the real world and the people in it. And the more the Brants had tried to get Davy to live up to familial expectations, the more the young man rebelled. The Brant family had encouraged the facility to keep him there indefinitely (with the help of fifty thousand dollars a month) due to his "violent hatred of his father." That was enough to get a Nevada judge to sign away David Brant to medical imprisonment for as long as the Brants desired.

It was time for Thomas Paine to become everything Davy Brant was not.

Tom's chauffeured car pulled up to the fifteen-acre compound on Crest Lane in McLean, Virginia. He rode past many mansions, every one of them owned by a member of the Phoenix Club. McLean, the wealthiest community in America, had been home to almost every major political operative for the past three decades, and Crest Lane was the epicenter of federal power brokers. It was fitting that the kingmaker lived here among his vassals. Blocks away loomed the Central Intelligence Agency's fabled Langley headquarters.

When he checked the local Internet network, he found governmental blocks and firewalls at every house. Miss Gray Hat had warned him Internet countersurveillance would be fierce, forcing him to shut down his internal system. He was Internet blind with no data or backup for the first time since surgery. It was as unnerving as if he were actually blind, having come to rely on the constant stream of information with just a thought.

A tall red brick wall was topped by an ironwork grill and razor wire. Automatic gates swung open only after two checkpoints with private armed security. Josiah's army walked the property and a counterassault team was available just out of sight. No one went in or out without permission of the owner. It was the lion's den here as much as the clubhouse in DC or camp in the Sierras.

Once inside, the illusion of bucolic splendor and peace was maintained throughout, especially when Josiah walked Tom around the graciously designed landscape. "I wish you could see it," said the proud owner. "It's more than a dirt-farmer's son from Alabama needs, but Maggie loves it, and I love her, so, you know how it goes . . ."

Tom sniffed at the air. "I smell . . . honeysuckle? And roses?"

"Yeah. Guess what my nickname for my wife is." The older man chuckled. "Sometimes my wife ain't the most subtle. But she's mighty sweet." He breathed in the scent. "Yes, I'm a lucky man. From a farm to the army, to Washington, to here. Sometimes have to pinch myself."

"And I smell and hear a waterway over there." Tom gestured to the east. "A river?"

"Yep. The Potomac. Other side of the garden ends on a cliff over the river. Nice view of Maryland, I wish you could . . . Oh well." July in Virginia was steamy. Brant pulled at his sweaty polo collar with his free hand. "Ooh boy, the sun's gettin' to me today. Let's take a load off inside and have a drink."

They walked along a brick path toward the large verandah that overlooked the river. Josiah studied him.

"I've had a lot of personal experience with the blind," said Josiah, "and you don't have those obvious physical quirks that can alienate people."

"Like . . . ?"

"Oh, you know, the head bobbin' and weavin,' or the unfocused eyes or lid droop. I'll be honest, I see 'em a bit, but they're very subtle. Your head even follows people's voices. Frankly, only the sunglasses and cane are dead giveaways."

"Thank you. Were your parents blind?"

"No. My son, Davy." He studied Tom's face more closely. "You look so much like someone I knew many years ago . . . Any Central American or Spanish in ya?"

"No, not a bit."

"Guess everyone has their double somewhere . . ."

Tom hoped Josiah didn't think too hard about Ricardo Gonzales. "Well, I went blind as an adult and practiced seeming unimpaired, because you're right, it does make others more comfortable. Part of it may be because I have a peculiar side effect to my blindness called blindsight. Have you heard of it?"

"Can't say I have . . . We're goin' up three stairs here." They walked onto the large brick patio and inside to an enclosed sunroom at the rear of the house.

"Thanks . . . It's specific to my kind of blindness. I damaged the optic centers of my brain, not my eyes or optic nerves. That means my eyes work and the image goes to my brain, but there's nothing there to pick it up. That stop on the vision express is gone. But the next stops that take up the message are still there. And no one really knows how the message jumps over the missing part and why it's only a few messages and not the rest. At some level, my brain recognizes things I can't see. So I . . . know things . . . Well . . . 'know' is the wrong word. It feels more like a guess. And I would swear to you that I can't see the thing I supposedly know about, but I must sometimes, because I react to it. It's almost like knowing I'm blind gets in the way of seeing. Does that make any sense?"

"Sure does," said Josiah. He took Tom to the back of a comfy, down-filled chair and placed his hands on the top, so Paine could feel his way down the arms to take a seat.

On the glass-and-metal coffee table, family photos stood five deep, with pictures of Josiah, Maggie, and their children and grandchildren. A photo from the '90s of an unhappy young man, about twenty-five years of age, took center stage. He looked like a genetic amalgam of the Brants, wore no sunglasses, and his eyes were half-closed and unfocused. He was blind.

Josiah sat down with an audible "Ahhhh . . ." in a matching chair, his eyes catching the sad boy's picture and momentarily reflecting the same sadness. He broke the minitrance, yelling, "Two beers, Octavia!"

"Yessa, Mr. Brant."

"How did your son deal with his blindness?"

"Lost his sight as a boy, so knowing what he once had, always felt sorry for himself, but never got the gumption to make the best of it. I suppose bein' the son of a famous person is difficult. But Davy never cottoned to the idea of a legacy. Fought me all the way. What kids never realize is you do these things partially for them. But he didn't want any of it . . . or me. Wallowed in time-wastin' and destroyin' his mind with online garbage. Gave him the best therapies and education money could buy."

Tom smiled. Josiah didn't reveal to him that Davy was his father's prisoner. "He's lucky he has you as a father. I didn't have one, and it made a tough situation even harder. I'm sorry to hear he had such difficulties. It didn't have to be that way."

For the first time, Josiah gave Tom a covetous stare. A glance back at Davy's photo brought a disturbed sigh. "Such a waste of skin. You two could not be more different. You got more charisma than a dozen revival preachers put together. Wish I had a son like you . . ." Josiah shook his head to stop the memories and coughed. "I'd appreciate your discretion in this. It's a skill sorely lackin' nowadays. But Bruce filled me in on what motivated your break of silence . . ."

"He seems to think you might be able to help. And here I thought he hated me."

"Hate's a strong word, Tom. Let's say he's jealous of your ability to draw positive attention. Hell—any attention!" He chuckled. "You made a mighty big splash very quickly. And that means you're somethin' special." The old man's smile gleamed. "What made ya so willin' to come out in the open in such a way?"

"I've had two attempts on my life already. That's why I live mostly on the move, with bodyguards and staff. I was hoping becoming a public figure might provide some protection from certain former business associates."

"That's debatable," said Josiah. "If the Russians want you dead, you're dead, if for no other reason than to send a message they are not to be crossed. And don't keep up a brave front just for me. I know you're in a heap of trouble! Who do you see as the key player, who'd call off the dogs?"

Tom looked appropriately frightened. "Vasily Grigorii." Miss Gray Hat and Dr. Who had created a paper trail to the shadowy, hermetic oligarch that would stand up for at least a month of investigation. If Tom needed more time than that, he would have failed in his attempt to stop the club. "Do you really think you can do this?"

Josiah laughed. "Son, I've done a lot more difficult things in my time. I don't know Grigorii personally, but I've got a handful 'a young bucks who deal with these Russian thugs daily."

A middle-aged black woman in a housekeeper's uniform carried two frosted mugs and two lagers on a tray. As she poured the first glass, Tom asked, "Octavia, would you just hand me the bottle, please? It's easier that way."

"Of course, sir." She passed the full glass to Josiah and a bottle to Paine. His hands and lips were covered in artificial skin that would mimic his avatar's own for longer periods of time than the acrylic gloves the 10/26 terrorists used.

"Thank you," said Tom.

"I'm happy to help in any way I can. But we got a problem . . ."

"Beyond my problem?"

"Well, son, it's more a lack of a problem. I've learned it's important to leave as few skeletons in one's closet as possible. Everyone has 'em, and they jump out and squeal 'Boo!' at the most inopportune times. With the exception of your Russian friends, I can't find any of your skeletons, which is unusual, or even a hidden closet, which is downright bizarre. Everything we've found on you adds up. It's what we haven't found that concerns me. And I don't like surprises."

It was time for Paine to dance. No matter how well or deeply one built a false identity, there were some things that couldn't be recreated if people dug enough, like the web of friends and family that provably went back to childhood. And Josiah could dig as far as it was possible to go.

"There are things I decided the world didn't need to know about me. I've had to walk away from a lot of my life to get free of the garbage."

"And that garbage is . . . ?"

"No one becomes a billionaire following the Golden Rule. You of all people know that. Most people in my position don't care what others think—look at Bruce—but I always did, because I understood the ramifications. The fact you found nothing means I've succeeded. If you couldn't uncover my past, there's no reporter or government that will. I'm a free man in an age where information exposure is slavery to the IT gods and those who serve them."

"So when do I get your story?"

"Whenever you want. But it'll have to be to you alone, on my boat. I don't want a recording or witnesses. I know you have to be careful, Josiah. So do I."

"Where's your school teachers and transcripts?"

"I was homeschooled and skipped college for the school of hard knocks."

"The girl whose teenaged heart you broke?"

"I was shy. Didn't really date until much later."

"You got it all figured out, don't you?"

"Nope," Tom laughed. "Just a lonely, late bloomer."

362

"Well, you sure caught up." Josiah scrutinized the steamy lawn outside as a guard patrolled past with an automatic rifle. "You spent an awful long time away for a man who claims to love this country."

"Blindness was a great shock for me, as it was for your son. I needed time to run away. But I overcame that. I want to come home and be of service. And I can't think of anyone better to guide me."

"If we can help you avoid your Russian friends."

Tom grimaced. "Yes."

"You got plans?"

"Please don't take this the wrong way, but it's plain to me that, with the exception of yourself, there's a vacuum of smart and effective political leadership in this country. You say I've got charisma. I've been told that a lot. I'm thinking of running for office. Maybe governor, senator. California's up for grabs either way. I'd base my campaign on Teddy Roosevelt, a man not afraid to stand up for his constituents, but seen by the people as above corruption. A protector of their interests. Intelligent, but fun. Outrageous in an aspirational way to reach young people. I can do all that, if they can get over my blindness."

Josiah sat quietly for a moment, nursing his beer. "What do you think of our great nation's electorate?"

Tom sighed, "Well . . . I've seen this all over, not just here. Our world's changing so fast, we can't leave the big decisions to an undereducated populace anymore. They aren't up to the job, especially if our dialogue with them has no relation to reality to begin with."

"You're a wise man, Tom. Let's toast. To a new world," said Josiah, lifting his glass.

"To a new world," replied Tom, lifting his bottle.

They both took a sip.

"But no one said politics was wise," said Josiah. "And charisma isn't enough. Do you think you can set aside your wisdom to do what needs to be done?"

"Wasn't it Will Rogers who said, 'A fool and his money are soon elected'?"

Josiah roared his trademark laugh. "I like a man who shoots when he sees a turkey!" Then he guffawed louder. "If you'll pardon the expression!"

"I don't think I'd give me a gun anytime soon. But I understand your metaphor," said Tom, grinning. "And, please, allow me to help you: I may not make him everything you hoped he'd be, but I think I can help your son."

Josiah looked at Davy's photo again and stopped laughing. Tom could see the tumblers click into place inside the older man's head: Tom was his second chance at fatherhood. He went pale and shaken, this meant so much to him, and tried to conceal it with graciousness. "Thank you. That would be the greatest gift of all. In the spirit of new . . . opportunities, I have a few in mind. Bruce and I are members of a very special club that might help you find your place in life. I know you'd just love it. Great bunch of fellas. Really the best and the brightest. I promise to save your hide from those pesky Russians, but you've got to make me a promise, too."

"Anything," said Tom, breathlessly.

"Just promise to trust me and do what I tell ya. You can ask any member of the club. I'd never steer you wrong."

"It'd be an honor to be guided by you, sir."

"We don't have much time till the club's next powwow. I've got to go to a PAC fund-raiser in your hometown tomorrow night, and I'd love you to meet some 'a my boys. A few might even be neighbors. Could I entice you and your lady friend to be guests at my table?"

"Of course. And what's the name of your club?"

"The Phoenix Club. Ever hear of it?"

CHAPTER FIFTY-SEVEN

T om and Talia cut striking figures as she led him around dozens of ten-seat tables in the Crystal Ballroom of the Beverly Hills Hotel. He, distinguished in a sleek, minimalist tuxedo and she, exquisite in a floor-length halter gown and killer jewels. Josiah stood and waved from his seat front and center to the stage. Tom checked his system of ear jacks, patching into the wireless system of government microphones set in the centerpieces of each table and around the room's periphery. He recorded all conversations through the course of the evening, just like the government.

Josiah pumped Tom's hand and slapped his back with great enthusiasm. "Can't wait to introduce you to everyone! Hon? Come on over!"

Tom and Talia shook hands with Maggie Brant, an imposing older woman who stood at least six inches taller than her husband in a Nancy Reagan-esque red dinner suit, less steel magnolia than Teflon southern pine; and David and Danielle Davis of Beverly Hills and Malibu, a petite and perfectly toned couple of indeterminate age and most-determined demeanor. Lobo and Vera outblinged the room.

Between Lobo and Tom, two empty seats loomed like ghosts. He knew who would fill them, like he knew lots of things lately without evidence. But could he pull off his act if the people who knew Peter Bernhardt best sat next to him?

Bruce leaned sloppily over the empty chairs after three straight vodkas. "That was some soiree, Tom. You made every tabloid and soc-net-site this side of Mars."

"Thank you."

"Still waiting for my invite to your rust bucket."

"It's a mess since the party, at least that's what Talia says. Soon as it's shipshape, you'll be the first to know."

A steady procession of people paid tribute to Josiah and said hello to the others at the table. Most were eager for an introduction to the media's latest sensation, Thomas Paine. Everyone's subtle alienation of Vera indicated that the men had either slept with her or knew her profession, and the wives and girlfriends envied her beauty and despised her unmistakable courtesan air.

Lobo flagged down a waiter for another drink. He stared for a blurry moment at Talia. "Hey, Brooks, better watch my mouth, huh? Or you'll try to make me the laughingstock of the Valley. Again. Don't know why you bother. No one gives a shit. You turn off your interviews. You're too pretty for analysis, anyway. Puff pieces are more your speed."

"No need to bait me, Bruce," said Talia. "I'm retiring. No more stories."

Tom interjected, "Talia's changed my life so profoundly that I refuse to be without her. And since I can afford to take care of her, why should she ever be a journalist again?"

"That's a great idea!" exclaimed Josiah. When other men murmured agreement, Danielle Davis burst out laughing.

Amazonian Maggie Brant couldn't help but chuck a spear at the downed fawn. "I'm real surprised a woman of your generation, so clever and independent," saying the last words like she was any-thing but, "could become so old-fashioned and embrace family val-ues so quickly."

"I admit," said Talia, "my working life was extremely hard and gave me few tangible rewards. But it wasn't until meeting Tom that I realized how fulfilled I could be just being there for someone else."

Danielle leaned into her husband and stage-whispered, "His money didn't hurt, either. Welcome to the club, honey."

Talia stared Danielle right in the eyes. "His money was the only thing that made me hesitate becoming involved with him. In my experience covering the rich and famous, too much money makes most people very ill-mannered, and sometimes, even a little morally suspect." Her eyes twinkled. "One of my favorite proverbs is, 'With the rich and mighty, always a little patience.'"

A nervous titter sprung up around the table.

Josiah barked, "Even though Talia is more than up to the task of defending herself, I'd suggest we stop if others might be less entertained." His look demanded obedience. Danielle smirked, Maggie sulked, and Bruce regarded his defense with surprise.

Vera caught on to the mood, and suddenly legitimized by the others' censure, gently asked, "Tom, how did you lose your sight?"

"Thanks for asking, Vera. Most people think it's impolite and end up concocting stories that are invariably wrong. I had brain lesions in the optical lobe from an accident," he said, touching the back of his skull.

Dave asked, "Why don't you get one of those retinal implants?"

"Those replace the retina. That's not my problem. It's my brain, or lack of it."

The band struck up a reasonable cover of the Police's "Every Breath You Take (. . . I'll Be Watching You)" and a sly, ironic grin covered Paine's face. He placed a hand on Talia's arm. "Would you like to dance?"

Her hand covered his and squeezed hard. "Yes, please."

Tom bowed his head to the group. "Please excuse us," he said as Talia led him to the dance floor.

"Let's get closer to the band," said Tom. It would be harder for microphones to hear them.

Tom's left hand held Talia's right and his right palmed her tiny waist. She leaned her forearm and head on his chest. They could see the members and their women watch enviously.

The halter-topped gown left her back bare to the waist, and he appreciatively ran his fingertips down the silky ripples of her spine. "I can read you like Braille."

"What do I say?" She moved sinuously under his touch.

Tom's fingers danced for a moment more. "Still a mystery. Better brush up on my Braille."

"If you're a good boy, I've got something to show you. And tell you later."

"Mmmmmm . . . I like show and tell. If I guess now, will you tell me if I'm right?"

"Nope. You're too good at guessing. You'll just have to wait."

They danced silently for a moment, then he whispered, "They're almost here."

Talia buried her anxiety-filled face against his chest.

When they returned to the table, Vera commented, "You two are very romantic together. Couples should dance more often. They'd probably be happier if they did."

"If I'd known you were sentimental, I'd have bought a corsage," Bruce flung back.

Vera's face fell.

"Restrain yourself, Bruce," growled Josiah.

Even Bruce took notice through his veil of inebriation.

The empty seats haunted Tom. When filled, a world of hurt would engulf him. He had to keep dancing. "I agree with Vera," said

Paine. "I think a man hasn't done his job if he doesn't try to seduce his lover at least once a day."

The wives regarded Talia with envy, Paine with desire, and their husbands with contempt for their lack of initiative.

Lobo cracked, "It isn't the once-a-day part that's a problem for me. It's the one lover . . ."

Vera moved his fresh vodka to her place setting.

"It's about time!" exclaimed Josiah with relief. "Thought only New Yorkers and Los Angelenos believed in bein' fashionably late!"

Unable to turn around because it was senseless for a blind man, Tom stood carefully. Talia tensed and squeezed his hand. Hard. When the new guests stood next to the seats, Paine surreptitiously glanced at them from behind his dark glasses.

He held his breath as the world disappeared beneath him. Carter pulled out a chair for Amanda right next to Tom.

CHAPTER FIFTY-EIGHT

Tall, slender, tan, and blond, they reminded him of fraternal twins. With their beauty, posture, and effortless elegance, they could be the twin gods Apollo and Artemis, descended from a Bay Area Olympus to dally with the all-too-mortal Angelenos.

This was a traveling political fund-raiser run by a political action committee. It was going to San Francisco later that week, so there was no reason for Carter and Amanda to come to Los Angeles, unless Josiah wanted Carter's opinion about Thomas Paine that evening. Carter must have been forgiven for his misjudgment regarding Peter Bernhardt.

The chiffon from Amanda's dress brushed up against Tom's pant leg, and he was afraid to move it away. He was prepared for her gamine, white-blond hair. But her face seemed softer, and her breasts filled out her cream-colored silk gown, covering her thickening waist with its empire cut. He recognized her body's changes.

Rage bubbled up. He wanted to kill them.

His former partner was giddy. "Everyone? I don't think you've met Amanda . . . well maybe Josiah!"

The old man nodded, smiling with tepid benevolence.

"Sorry I've been so hard to reach, but we wanted to keep the secret until now, until her debut . . ." Carter squeezed Amanda's shoulder lovingly. "We eloped last weekend . . ."

Eight glasses were lifted in a chorus of congratulations.

"Wait!" interrupted Carter, laughing. "Because we're pregnant! Can you believe it? I'm going to be a father!"

Everyone else rushed the couple to kiss cheeks, slap backs, and shake hands. Brant's knowing calm meant Carter had cleared it with the old man first. Maybe it was Josiah's idea.

"Carter's so busy making sure I meet everybody before I can't travel anymore," apologized Amanda, "that you'll have to tell me all your names again. Since we got pregnant, my memory's shot." She was not virginal, chaste Artemis. She was Ariadne, wife of Dionysus, god of fertility. All that wine, women, and song had consequences.

Danielle asked Amanda, "How long have you known Carter?"

Amanda took her husband's hand. "Since freshman year at Stanford, and we've been best friends since. It was Carter who picked me up and took care of me after . . . my late . . ." She sighed heavily. "I guess it's not surprising we already loved each other, but when we turned to each other in grief . . . we fell in love." The couple gazed adoringly into each other's eyes. A chorus of "Awwwws" rang around them.

It was a play, and everyone knew their lines. They would all pretend they knew nothing about her and her past.

Paine leaned toward Amanda. She smiled at his attention, and her glowing eyes, so close to his, shot through him like a bullet. "Please forgive me, but I'm a stranger in these parts." His voice was shaky. He sent a signal to his brain's limbic system to calm down. It wasn't working. "Who was your late husband and what did he do?" Talia dug her lacquered nails into his thigh, hard enough to draw blood. He ignored it.

An odd, aloof look crossed Amanda's face. "He was a bioengineer and entrepreneur."

"And what was his name?"

She waited until attention had moved away from her and whispered, "Peter Bernhardt."

He was grateful his eyes were covered. "I'm extremely sorry for your loss," he said quietly.

Amanda stared at the napkin covering her expanding belly. "Thank you." After a moment, she stuck her hand out.

But Paine didn't respond.

Talia interjected, "You'll have to forgive him. He's blind and can't see your gesture." Talia lifted Tom's hand and placed it in Amanda's.

His ex-wife's soft fingers felt fragile in his sweaty palm. "Please forgive me. I'm Thomas Paine. It's a pleasure to meet you."

"Amanda Potsdam. Nice to meet you, too." Her face clouded over, and she stared quizzically at their mutual grip.

At the piano's attack of the first G chord, he knew the song instantly. His minimal composure evaporated. Carter stood, one hand out to his wife, the other on the back of her chair. "Please excuse us. This is our song. Darling?" Amanda released Tom's hand and joined her husband to walk to the dance floor.

The golden pair danced to "American Pie." Why did they play this damned song at every club-infiltrated function? The first time they danced, it was the puppet master moving a pretty marionette around the floor. Now having shared bodily intimacies, Amanda moved against Carter as if Ginger Rogers had had wild, passionate sex with Fred Astaire. Tom wasn't the only one to notice. Maggie and Danielle stared dreamily at them.

Had the music died for Tom, along with everything else?

During dessert, Carter changed seats with Amanda, settling in with chummy camaraderie. "Excuse me, but I wanted to introduce myself again. I'm Carter Potsdam. So what do you think of our little cabal?"

"Tom Paine. And congratulations again on your happy news." Smiling, he was grateful the wait staff had removed the steak knives. "But why call this a 'cabal'? Doesn't that word imply a conspiracy?"

"Well, I'm sure Josiah's gone over the club with you. We promote people who deserve promoting and effect positive change in the country at a level politics and the market can't reach. If that's not a nondemocratic conspiracy, I don't know what is!" Carter took advantage of Tom's disability to scrutinize him closely. Aspects of his presentation registered their importance in Carter's subtle facial movements: the immaculately tailored, bespoke tuxedo and shirt, his handmade dress shoes, his custom-made sunglasses, his haircut and manicure, the expressions he made at Carter's words. This was a common reaction, but Carter's systematic, ruthless appraisal was the closest he'd felt to undressing in public since Talia. While Tom passed the physical inspection, there was doubt in Carter's eyes. Why did Josiah want this blind man so much? "Josiah's told me you'll be looking for a new gig . . ."

"You mean after my initiation?"

The Cheshire cat grin gleamed. "He told you that? He must really like you."

"But others may not . . ." whispered Tom.

Carter glanced back at Lobo. The tech titan had passed the point of social drinking, leaning back in his seat, unfocused eyes with lids at half-mast. Given his dilated pupils, it was probable he had taken a stronger substance, as well. Having jettisoned her wasted paramour, Vera was deep in conversation with Talia, the only woman who would talk to her. Shifting his chair closer to Tom, Carter leaned in and said, "Take it as a compliment."

Tom laughed. "So I've been told. Now tell me, Carter Potsdam, what do you do?"

Carter gave him the rundown on Prometheus Industries, the Hippo 2.0 and the Cortex 2.0, minus the participation of Peter Bernhardt or Ruth Chaikin. "The bioengineering we do at Prometheus could benefit someone like you, but it might be years down the line. Right now it's aimed at correcting cognitive disorders, but perceptive disorders are an area of interest as well." He explained how parts of the cognitive prosthetics might solve the connection problem at the root of his blindness by acting as both a replacement for the first rung of damaged neurons and a neural bridge between his optic nerve and the visual neurons that were still active.

If he knew about the blindsight, Carter was briefed by the club on more than the basics of Thomas Paine's background.

"If what you say is true, I'm fascinated by your work. Do you have any interest in taking on a partner? Are you the type who's had partners in the past and finds you can take advantage of what they offer?"

Hearing a double meaning, Carter pulled back, spooked, and said nothing.

"I'm sorry, did I make an improper assumption? Forgive me, but you strike me as extremely socially adept. Social types like partnerships. It gives you a mirror to gauge your impact and appreciate the difficulty of your accomplishments. It's hard to be proud of your work when you lose your perspective or outsiders denigrate you for having it all come so easy. Am I right?"

Carter's right eyelid fluttered as he struggled with the instant psychoanalysis. "It is hard to be proud of what you do sometimes . . ."

"You'd be surprised how common that feeling is among entrepreneurs. I've learned how to overcome it. Even when the work doesn't pan out."

Tom could see the cogs turning as Carter glanced in Josiah's direction.

"Well, hypothetically," said Carter, "if someone like you became involved in Prometheus, you could motivate research toward your ends."

"True, but my motives are simpler than that. I missed out on the ground floor of the computing revolution. If I miss out on bio-tech, especially when it might benefit me, then I'm just an idiot, aren't I?" Tom laughed. "I apologize, I didn't mean to invite myself into your company, Carter. You don't know me from Adam! I'm just excited by your prospects and, as you know, I have a lot to offer, especially with my knowledge of global markets. We could keep each other on the straight and narrow, couldn't we?"

Carter took a very long time to swallow.

The rest of the evening was interminable with self-congratulatory speeches by people who couldn't be elected dogcatcher endorsing those who should have remained dogcatcher. Women chattering about plastic surgery for pets, men holding forth about golf hand-icaps and measuring the size of their genitals by comparing tax shelters and transportation. Carter and Amanda were the center of attention, except when Carter and Josiah had a quiet conference in the corner of the ballroom about Tom. The hidden bugs picked it up: Carter told Josiah about Tom's offer of partnership. Josiah not only encouraged it, he demanded it. And he told Carter of Lobo's unacceptable behavior during the dinner. Carter was surprised at the vehemence of Josiah's reaction.

It wasn't until Tom and Talia prepared to leave that Josiah pulled him aside.

"I just took an informal poll of our members. If you enjoyed who you met, barin' that little display on Bruce's part and some catty women, who, if you don't mind my sayin', are simply envious of your beautiful and clever lady, I'd like to plan your initiation in DC."

"Please don't worry about it," said Tom, smoothing the waters. "I don't take it personally, and it made for an amusing evening. I'd be honored to join."

"The sooner, the better to get you safe from your . . . problems. You don't want to miss camp. It's too much fun to wait a whole 'nother year."

"I'd hate to wake my pilots from their beauty sleep. I could leave in the morning."

"Good." He pumped Paine's hand. "I've ordered an accelerated process. Initiation tomorrow night or the night after. Gotta scare up a quorum in the meantime." He patted Tom's back. "See ya soon, son."

Alone, Tom reached out and found a chair back to anchor to until Talia could tow him to the car. A hand touched his shoulder. A hand he knew.

"Hi . . . it's Amanda Potsdam again."

How could her touch make him love her and hate her at the same time? Did emotions have quantum states of nonlocality and entanglement like subatomic particles, flipping from one emotion to the other with observation? Resisting the impulse to clasp his hand on hers and kiss it, he turned, and her hand fell. She took up his to shake.

"I wanted to say good night. It was a pleasure to meet you . . ." She paused, regarding their gripped hands, her fingers subtly rubbing his skin. Slowly, she turned his palm up. Her face paled like that only once before: when she lost their baby. Would she believe her feelings or brush them off as impossible?

"It was a pleasure to meet you, too," he replied. Her grasp triggered a twenty-year rush of memories that suffocated his critical faculties. Was she feeling the same, or was her troubled face guilty? The room spun to catch with his whirlwind of thoughts. She was so close . . . he could snap her neck in an instant . . .

He slid his hand from hers and clung to the chair back for dear life.

"I still have morning sickness," she said. "Please excuse me . . ."

"I'm sorry. Of course. Good night . . ." Amanda stood there a moment longer, chewing her thumbnail, not sure if she could leave him. She caught a glimpse of Carter, laughing loudly with Josiah at the exit. Then she hurried away.

After a minute, Talia rushed up to him. "What's wrong?"

"Don't ever leave me alone like that again," he hissed.

CHAPTER FIFTY-NINE

Their chauffeured car drove along Sunset Boulevard and up Pacific Coast Highway, past darkened homes illuminated by security and streetlights. No one said anything. Talia tried to speak, but Tom shook his head, unable to speak freely in transit. While he'd bug-proofed the car, they might be tailed, or a new bug could have been introduced that evening. He'd developed a code with the driver, a security expert hired by Talia. If either of them tuned the music to "Galileo" by the Indigo Girls, it meant they were being followed. If they tuned it to Johnny Cash's "Man in Black" it required evasive action. He had already played "Galileo" once tonight.

Closing his eyes, Tom tried to meditate, but only his synthetic cortex concentrated on the flow of breath. The organic cortex fantasized various revenge scenarios. It wasn't calming in the least. Frustrated, he played back the party's jacked recordings, culling them for clues.

Talia led Tom into their Malibu home in silence. While eavesdropping was always an issue, Tom had taken many steps to secure the building even before Lobo's gang infiltrated it during his party. Their enormous windows were made of two layers of glass with nanowire mesh and, in the space between panes, music was piped in to garble detectable sound vibrations. He chose the playlist with irony in mind, alternating selections like Tchaikovsky's "1812 Overture" with John Fogerty's "Bad Moon Rising" and Elton John's "The King Must Die." In addition, the windows were covered in clear counterintelligence film that blocked wireless radio frequencies into and out of their home, so hackers couldn't pick up transmissions or attack them with electromagnetic interference. The film bounced laser mics, infrared sights, and even photography. Likewise, aluminum-iron oxide paint covered the walls, blocking and absorbing airborne data. He installed a signal scrambler to neutralize "house-fly bugs" flown through open doors and windows and "barnacle bugs" discovered attached to the building's pilings. He mentally ordered his security system to increase randomized, distracting signals appropriate to each room, hoping the club's spy personnel were as disorganized and cocky as the government's, which would buy some time.

It was high tide, but the waves were louder and more powerful than usual. Tom mentally checked the weather. A rare summer cyclone far off in the Pacific was making its presence known. With the moonless night and their lights on inside, only his devastated reflection showed.

"We need to talk about this . . ." murmured Talia, but she couldn't finish. Tom stopped fifteen feet from the glass, ripped the sunglasses off his face and threw them at the windows. They shattered and fell to the hardwood floor. Striding back to Talia, he grabbed her upper arm and dragged her into a spook-proof walk-in closet.

Huddled among the coats and hand luggage, he spit out, "How do you think I'm feeling right now?"

She twisted in his grip. "Tom, you're hurting me . . ."

He let go. "She was in on everything . . ."

"How do you know that?"

"Couldn't you see how happy they were?"

"So? You were dead, and she needed her best friend's support. She may not know any more than you did about him. Even if she was suckered into a conspiracy, it could be self-preservation."

"She's too happy for self-preservation."

"I know you think that stuff in your head gives you some special insight, but I'm telling you, as a woman, you're on the wrong track."

"Right. Your female intuition trumps my implants. That's a joke. Look at the evidence. They didn't kill her!"

"There's more than one motivation for that."

"Of course. It was an idle threat regardless. But I can't be sure of the motivation and neither can you." He couldn't admit he needed to hate Amanda to keep revenge's flame burning bright. "And she knows I'm alive."

"How can you be sure of that?"

" 'Cause I've got a husband's intuition from spending more than half my life with her and knowing her better than I know myself! She held my hand. She knows it's me. And I have no clue if she's going to tell Carter or not. Do I kill her now to protect my identity . . . ?"

Talia paled.

"Oh! So now you're sensitive all of a sudden?" He turned away from her and leaned his head against the smooth teak door. "My God, how bizarre can this fucking world get when Carter Potsdam goes straight and impregnates my wife?" He didn't want to cry, so he beat his head against the door. Maybe it would shake some wires loose.

"Your ex-wife . . ." She tried to stop her own tears.

He tried counting breaths, counting numbers, counting sheep to the point of obsessive-compulsive disorder. Like a sibling's endless taunts, nothing shut up Amanda-thoughts on the Cortex 3.0. He wished the prosthetic were still attached to the outside of his head. He would have thrown it back in the ocean. If he could have ripped open his femoral artery with his fingernails and yanked out the wires tickling his brain, without bleeding to death, he would have. Tom had to stop the impulse to run to the kitchen for a knife. Suddenly, the closet was suffocating. Or was it Talia's presence? He flung open the door, hard, cracking the wall's plasterwork.

In the foyer, he took a huge breath, struggling for oxygen to clear his brain. Goddamned Amanda . . . If he analyzed her motives dispassionately, which he couldn't, she might maintain the status quo for now. She was pregnant, rich, and happy, and wasn't the type to rock the boat, for fear of losing it again. But he couldn't trust her to keep secrets from Carter for long. If he couldn't kill her now, he'd have to avoid seeing her, so she had no more reasons to doubt herself and ask her new husband's opinion of her sanity.

Talia was behind him. Desperate for more air, he moved to the windows again. "I'll get more evidence before I kill her, if it makes you happy."

"Is this about making me happy?" She squatted on the floor, picking up pieces of broken sunglasses.

"Amanda is the enemy. Isn't that enough?"

"And what if she isn't?"

"But she is!"

"But what if she isn't?"

Breaching his fortification, he threw open the glass doors to escape onto the teak deck that ran the length of the house. He closed his eyes, as the wind whipped drops of seawater onto his face, and the crashing waves drowned out sound. He gulped salty air, pungent and bitter.

Talia's voice at his shoulder overwhelmed the ocean's roar. "No. I need to know now. Where does that leave us? Before I go any further, I need an answer."

"Us?"

"If you find out she's innocent. What then?"

"What do you expect me to say?"

"I expect you to stop being a coward!"

Whipping around faster than she could see, he backhanded her face.

She landed on her backside on the wet deck. Stunned, she crab-crawled back into the living room and staggered to her feet to run upstairs.

"Talia?" Tom stumbled in, but his second cortex had the presence of mind to make sure he closed and locked the doors behind him. "Talia? I'm sorry!" This was inconceivable. He'd never hit a woman in his life. He could clearly remember how it happened, but why? He needed to contain his rage and delete the file. As he imagined it, a crushing pain gripped his chest and he gasped, staggering. Was it another cardiac episode?

The pain crested and subsided. He tried to catch his breath. Slowly, he followed her upstairs. She wasn't in the bedroom or bath. Red hair gently fluttered over the back of a chaise lounge on their bedroom deck. She huddled in a wool throw like a lost child.

He knelt next to her. "Talia." He reached out to gently touch the red patch of skin on her left cheek, but she pulled away. Keeping his hands at his side, he said, "Talia. Please believe me. I'm sorry . . . I don't know what happened. I reacted without thinking . . . I know that sounds impossible, but . . . I don't want to hurt you." Talia stared at the black ocean as though she were deaf. "You said you wanted to tell me something. What did you want to say? I'll listen. I promise." But he was a ghost. He withdrew and, after a minute, returned with a more substantial blanket, tucking it around her body. She did not thank him.

An attache and suitcase stood by the front door. Out front, the limo and driver waited on Pacific Coast Highway. The storm passed and it was overcast at dawn, Malibu's annual "June Gloom" still around in July.

Tom crept onto the balcony, perching on the edge of her chaise to stroke Talia's damp hair. He kissed her forehead. Even with her closed eyes, he knew she wasn't asleep.

"I'm sorry . . . you have no idea how sorry . . ."

She didn't stir.

"To answer your question: It leaves you with me. You won't lose me—as long as you want me. Because I won't leave you. And I promise I will never hurt you again."

Her eyes opened, as pained and vulnerable as the night before. "If we don't stand back-to-back . . ." She stopped, for fear of being overheard, and mouthed, "they'll destroy us."

"Is that the only reason you're still upset?"

The look of disappointment in her eyes said that, for all he thought he knew, he still didn't understand. Or he wouldn't be foolish enough to ask.

"I'm sorry I'm such an idiot. I'm trying . . ." He kissed her forehead again and stood, but she reached out and pulled his torso down to her.

"What is it?" he whispered.

Her voice was muffled against his sports coat. "You might not come back . . ."

She was right. At least her concern was something. He kissed her again, gently removed her arms, and headed for his limo that would take him to his Gulfstream VI.

CHAPTER SIXTY

I hate to tell you all the history you're missin'. It's a mighty impressive lookin' place we got here!"

Thomas Paine tapped his way down the central hall of the Phoenix Club in Washington, led by Josiah as his nominating member. Lobo claimed his schedule was too tight to assume responsibility for Paine's nomination and membership.

"Sometimes, ignorance is simpler."

"Amen, son!" guffawed Josiah. "Speakin' of which, we've tried to keep the initiation ceremony as traditional as possible for you. We're tryin' to respect your wishes to treat you like you're not blind. But it's all a formality anyway. I'm really lookin' forward to camp this year! It's the most important one in generations. Can't miss it." Josiah leaned a little closer. "You'll bunk with me and President Stevens. That way, I can guide you around and make sure you get the most out of our proceedin's. Just stay away from the president's Long Island Iced Teas. They'll peel the stomach linin' outta you!"

"I wouldn't miss it for the world."

Eyes barely open behind his sunglasses, he glimpsed a portrait he missed last time. Balding and mustached, the subject resembled the actor and film director Ron Howard. A gilt plaque nailed to the gold frame said, "Horatio Alger Jr.," the nineteenth-century dime novelist whose rags-to-riches stories of young boys throwing off the shackles of poverty through industry and integrity to place their foot on the middle-class ladder immortalized the American Dream. Of course, none of the boys became wealthy like the men who walked these halls, because neither honesty nor simple hard work got its members there. However, the club was happy to encourage Alger's fairy tales, motivating the worker bees to construct the empire for them. Tom knew Alger had exposed the terrible conditions homeless youth lived and worked under in American cities, but decades later it was revealed the American Dream's mythmaker had been a molester of the very boys he claimed to help.

They descended into the building's bowels and made their way through the horror-movie antechamber to the dressing room, where Josiah put on the red-and-black member's toga, then helped Tom dress in the white initiate's toga. He guided Tom into the cave.

The painted walls vibrated with ancient energy, and the cries of terrified men it encircled for centuries echoed. But was it all his imagination?

The anonymous, hooded figures stood as they had before. None of them felt like Carter.

Sampled over whispered subfrequencies of the past, Todd Rundgren's "Initiation" played in his head as it had the last time he stood here. Painful experience shaded the lyrics with a sinister cast. Power *did* change hands, hidden from view . . .

Josiah handed Tom the drugged goblet, and he knocked it back without a second thought, handing it over only after licking his lips clean.

From the moment the Praetor Maximus uttered, "Step forward, candidate!" Tom was sure the Praetor Maximus intoning the initiation rite was the president of the United States, John Stevens. He should have felt honored. As the Praetor Maximus asked questions and Tom answered clearly and correctly every time, hooded figures gave sidelong glances with greater frequency. The humiliation-of-a-drug-addled-initiate script was not being followed, because Tom was unaffected by the hallucinogenic elixir. President Stevens stumbled in his performance, realizing his anger was inappropriate. How could he demand obedience like a drill sergeant with a clueless recruit if the recruit wasn't clueless?

After a flawless Pledge of Allegiance, Stevens sagged, shrugging shoulders at Josiah. He couldn't scream Paine wasn't worthy. Brant plunged ahead without his cue, halfheartedly swinging the wooden stick at Paine's shins. Tom parried with his Hoover cane, deflecting the blow, but snapping his cane in two.

There was silence in the cave, then the Praetor Maximus burst out, "How did you see that?"

"What happened?" Tom asked Josiah.

"You blocked a blow!" shouted a hooded Decemvir.

"Sorry if I messed up . . . it's automatic . . ."

"Just answer the question!" yelled another.

Tom turned to Josiah. "It's blindsight . . ."

"I checked his medical records. He has it," said Josiah.

"What the fuck *is* it?" asked yet another.

"Can we just get on with the show?" boomed Josiah. The scolded schoolboys went quiet. It was clear who the real Praetor Maximus was. There was a shuffling of feet, the Decemviri reluctant child actors. They parted to reveal the altar and the eagle.

"We're walkin' to a table. Follow my lead," whispered Josiah. At the stone platform, Josiah moved Tom's hands to the altar and then, ever so gently, to the eagle tethered to its surface.

His fingers jumped with shock at a living creature. "What is it?"

"Bald eagle," whispered Josiah.

The eagle seemed more lethargic than last time, but Tom couldn't trust drugged memories. Even on Valium, the bird was nervous and capable of attacking with its beak. Tom gently stroked the bird's back, until he could measure its length with each stroke. The enormous bird calmed at his steady touch.

"Amazing," muttered Tom, a huge grin on his face. Fingers continued to explore. He tugged at the leather strap that imprisoned the great bird to the altar.

The Praetor Maximus took Paine's hand and placed the ceremonial knife in it. "Kill it."

Tom carefully felt its circumference, identifying the object and finding the cutting edge. Satisfied, he raised the knife high, paused for dramatic effect . . . then brought it down hard, slicing the leather strap. Free at last, the relieved bird rose on great wings. Men ducked to avoid a face slapped with feathers. It perched on the top of the American flag hanging over them.

No one spoke, but the members' hoods fell back as they watched the bird's ascent and forgot to pull them up as they stared in silent amazement at each other. Tom recognized every bare head from the previous year's camp. Carter and Bruce were definitely not among them.

"What the fuck is going on here?" yelled President Stevens. Attempting his own improvisation, he grabbed the front of Tom's toga. Disturbingly, the walls' painted warriors danced, whooping and hollering in Tom's ears.

Surprised, Tom defensively twisted the president's wrist while holding his knife high. The leader of the free world fell to his knees, no match without his Secret Service, who paced nervously in a parlor upstairs.

"Gentlemen! Please control yourselves!" barked Josiah. "Tom, let go of the president!"

"Oh dear . . ." he gasped, and released his grip, stepping back apologetically. "I'm so sorry . . . I didn't know . . . Mr. President!"

Josiah snatched the knife from Tom's hand and leaned in, asking with quiet menace, "Why did you release the bird?"

"It was clearly a test. No true American would sacrifice such a creature and symbol of our great nation. Wouldn't our job, as the best and the brightest, be to protect it and what it represents?"

No one bothered to look to the president, who sat on the cave floor nursing his wrist, for a final decision. They all stared at Brant. After a moment, he said to the initiate, "Of course."

To a man, their expressions broadcast disbelief.

Stevens whined from the ground, "What about him suffering the fate of those who break the oath of obedience?"

"Forget it," snapped Josiah. He took the blind man's hand and shook it. "Congratulations. Welcome to the Phoenix Club, son." Then he glared at his Decemviri. "And perhaps, gentlemen, we've all learned a lesson to not underestimate a blind man!"

It was a cue for the Decemviri to laugh at themselves. But the laughter was strained. Tom made initiation history by circumventing the burning man ritual. It was silly to hope he'd be as lucky in his second initiation.

Painted warriors howled in congratulations as bison bellowed and horses whinnied. And Todd Rundgren sang. The new world would be revealed.

Tom approached his beach house's front gate with trepidation. Was she home? Was he forgiven? The chauffeur hadn't reached the doorbell when the door flew open and Talia threw herself into Paine's arms. He was never so gratefully hugged in his life. She started to speak, but he gently shushed her, and they entered the foyer. The chauffeur deposited his cases inside and left. They were finally alone, and Paine still hadn't said a word.

"So tell me . . ." she said quietly.

Paine put his fingers to his lips and held her close. He missed her so much. His lips kissed her cheek, and he barely whispered, "It's begun."

CHAPTER SIXTY-ONE

The nantidote worked perfectly. Stone-cold sober." Tom didn't tell Ruth about the wailing natives and cavorting megafauna.

"*Ach*, thank Carter. He was schmuck enough to hint the recipe. And you always had a good memory. The rest was easy."

Ruth sat hunched over a monitor in the lab running algorithmic translations of Dulles's final memories from the sea-damaged Cortex 2.0. Tom applied tremendous pressure on her to work beyond her expertise and do neural network modeling. Pilfering Prometheus's data made it easier, but the system was far from perfect, and Ruth was frustrated she couldn't speak to their engineers to fix their mistakes. She didn't understand how she had taken their data so much further, while Prometheus's research had stalled.

He pulled up a chair and studied the monitor, teasing out a story from an enormous flow chart, with thousands of interconnections covering just the brief amount of thought-time the chip contained. Ruth had assigned only a handful of thematic thought flows with different colors to make graphing easier. Its complexity demonstrated how tagging the thoughts in an entire brain, even with a supercomputer, would be overwhelming.

"Tell me what I'm missing, Ruthie."

"You see? In yellow?" she pointed. "Fear of death. Dominant concept. Takes up lots of space."

"Not surprising."

"This red," she pointed again, "is the Phoenix Club. Lots of conflicting emotion. Then over here. In green. 'P-Peter Bernhardt.' This is both old access and new information at time of recording. He knew you before you met. Like he studied you."

"I felt it at the time. But I don't know how or why."

"This purple is '10/26.' Terrorism. A conspiracy. Some nodes are events. Some people. Haven't untied or identified them yet. But see? They all lead back to these . . ." Her fingers traced the links to "Peter Bernhardt" and "Phoenix Club."

And a third section, in orange. Tom couldn't help but watch his own finger point to it, tracing the surprising number of connections, as though everything eventually led to it. All at once, the map came alive, and the connections ceased being theoretical. They were real relationships. A story emerged.

Ruth nodded grimly. "T-T-Talia."

"What else haven't you told me?"

Talia hadn't seen him standing quietly at the door, studying her. But his strangled voice shot panic through her. Abandoning her HOME controller, she scrambled to the far side of their bed, looking for escape.

He leapt on the bed and caught her shoulders, shaking her. "Why do you keep things from me? Don't you get you can't lie anymore?"

"How did I lie?"

"Dulles! And the club! And me! What are you hiding from me?" Her entire demeanor changed in subtle ways he could now see as clearly as skywriting. "You're lying now!" He grabbed her wrist and held it to her face. "Your raised heart rate, your quickened breath." He gripped her jaw with one hand. "Dilated pupils. Cool skin. Flushed cheeks. I used to think it was pretty. Now I see microexpressions of distress across your face. I'm a fucking polygraph!"

She wrenched her head away to climb off the bed. He lunged for her, pulling her to face him.

"Talk to me! Why is everything a fight with you?"

"Why do you keep digging? It doesn't matter anymore!"

"Just tell me what you know! I'll find it out from Dulles's recording soon enough. Unless you want me dead."

Expressions shifted like sand through a tangle of thoughts. After some time, authentic grief swamped her. "I didn't think you'd get this far! If they caught you and found out about me . . ."

"If I hadn't taken the processor off the yacht, they would have read Dulles's thoughts. And you would be dead! After everything that's happened, how can you not trust me?"

"I've lived a lie longer than you. It becomes your reason for being!"

He studied her face. "That's not the only reason. You didn't completely trust me from the beginning, and it never changed."

She wouldn't look at him.

His own rage was harder to contain, and he focused on manipulating his neurons to relax. "Answer me: Did Dulles ever say the club was involved in 10/26?"

"No, but after the attack, his attitude about the club changed. Dramatically. He'd been against them before, but after the attacks, it was personal."

"Against who?"

"He hated Josiah Brant."

"Were there others inside the club, working with him?"

"He claimed he had a reliable informant. That's why I knew you were correct about bigger plans. The informant told him that."

"A mole! You were afraid of compromising a mole if I failed?"

"Yes. It'd be one less person I could tap through Dulles. Tony said that every spy network is eventually uncovered. I was protecting mine."

"He's right," said Tom with sadness.

"He also said you'd have your second initiation at camp and told me to let you go. He thought his informant would be able to help and, with both of you inside, maybe he could turn you to work with him . . ."

"But you tried to stop me . . ."

"I didn't think you'd carry through the second initiation. And they'd kill you."

"And if he'd known he was the victim, he wouldn't have stuck around . . . So did his informant fail him? Or betray him?"

"I don't know. But Josiah sets up the loyalty initiations. Maybe the informant had no clue."

"Let me get this straight. Someone inside the club may be my ally. Or may betray me to my enemies if I reveal myself." The parallels with his ex-wife's situation were unnerving. "I need to find him. He may know what the club is planning and help me stop it."

Talia rolled away from him and leaned over the side of the bed and yanked open her nightstand drawer. Fishing around, she found a prescription bottle, uncapped it, and dry swallowed at least one, if not more, of its contents.

He reached over her shoulder and snatched the bottle. It was a prescription for Xanax. Ordered by Steve. "How could he let you take this shit?"

"Excuse me? You can alter yourself beyond recognition, but I can't even tweak me?"

"You're a former addict."

"Gee, that thing in your head really works. I'd completely forgotten." She grabbed the bottle back and threw it in the drawer.

Tom stared her down for a long moment. "I want you to change. And be better. Like me."

She turned her head away. "Why?"

"Then maybe . . . you'll understand me."

"I can't be like you . . ." she said, shaking her head and looking at the ocean.

"Why not? You can't imagine what it's like . . . I was a child until the surgery, and now, I'm finally an adult. It's not a change, actually. It's a maturation. If you did, we could communicate with just our minds. Share each other's thoughts, feelings . . ."

Terror of such intimacy filled her face.

An improbable medley of monsters by Aimee Mann, Rob Zombie, Fantômas, and Mr. Bungle rang through his head. "That's why you don't trust me? I'm monstrous?"

She wouldn't meet his eyes. "All your changes . . . you're running away . . . as much as me."

"I don't want to run from you." Pushing her hair off her neck, he kissed her skin, making a trail to her ear, where he whispered between kisses. "I'm sorry . . . I've been betrayed . . . so many times . . . makes me crazy . . . forgive me?" She nodded, not bothering to hide her fear anymore. His fingers threaded her frenzied curls and he kissed her mouth to shut off taunting lyrics of golems, Frankensteins, and their tragic revenge the only way he knew.

Daylight flooded their windows. The bedspread was heaped on the floor, linens rumpled in postcoital disarray. Talia slept languorously on her side, naked back to him, sheets pushed off to bask in the warmth of the summer sun. He reimagined her back's curvatures and lush tangle of hair as the cherry-red and flaming-maplewood curves and strings of a 1958 Gibson Les Paul Sunburst—as though he was Man Ray, she his Kiki de Montparnasse, and her body his electric *Le Violon d'Ingres.*

Through it all, he wished he knew what she was thinking.

Her breathing deepened as she awakened. After a moment, she rolled to face him and studied his face. Her own betrayed fear. Or was she reflecting his own? Since the boat explosion, he felt chained to his horrible past. Traumatic moments of Carter's betrayal, Dulles's last minutes, and his own near death played like Muzak in the background of his thoughts, unease creeping through his body. He wanted to erase the fear, even if that meant erasing the body.

"I can't stay here," she said.

"I have work for you here. Ruth needs help."

"No. I want to be nearby camp, in Yosemite."

"Don't worry. I've got nothing to offer the club this time, except Thomas Paine. I guessed right: They need whatever popularity or celebrity I represent. I'm the product, and they won't mess with that."

She coiled her limbs around him. "Don't go."

He buried his nose in the tendrils of her hair. There was a sweet freshness to her body that conjured a younger, more innocent girl. "I need to be with them. Or I can't stop them."

"But I see you in the sea cave . . ." Her look implied this could be their last morning together. She kissed him, then pulled her lips away. "Remember the PAC fund-raiser?"

Humiliated, he closed his eyes. "I can't forget . . ."

"I want to tell you my secret. Just in case."

His eyes opened. Her expression was raw, vulnerable. Her lips moved, but little sound emerged. "I love you."

She hadn't said those words since her father had died. He wanted to believe her.

"I love you, too." He'd never said those words to any woman other than Amanda. Not even his mother, who left before he could speak.

"Hard to say, isn't it?"

"Oh, God yes . . ." He forced his wiring to clamp down on his amygdala, to stop emotion overtaking him. Emotion was the enemy. Rationality was the key. Even though he knew he needed the first to have the second, it was too hard feeling so much. "And you're telling me now, in case of what?"

Her face twitched as imagination seethed with tragic possibilities. He flipped her aggressively on to her back, and grabbing both her hands, pinned them above her shoulders and laid his legs heavily across hers, as though he could immobilize her mind as easily as her body.

For all their declarations of love, he knew after today there would be a letting go between them. Whatever he left behind wouldn't be the same when he returned. Whether he would be changed or she was the mystery. The greater question was why he simultaneously knew things that came to pass, yet rejected the notion that implants could create something beyond improved pattern recognition, like ESP. He stubbornly refused to believe intelligence might be more complex than science accepted.

"You can't get rid of me that easily. I love you, and I'm coming back. And I always keep my promises." His lips found hers and wouldn't release them, as though force of will could make his conflicted mind stop spinning.

They made love like it might be the last time. He was certain it was.

CHAPTER SIXTY-TWO

T homas Paine took his place in Cabin 1 at the center of the Phoenix Camp next to the main lodge, along with Brant, Carter, and Lobo—and the president of the United States. Lobo had yet to arrive.

Apparently, the president held no hard feelings from the initiation. This was the first time Tom studied President John Paul Stevens up close. A tall, lanky frame accompanied his Lincolnesque visage, making historical comparisons inevitable. Many presidents crafted an image the American people could easily grasp. Cowboys were perennially popular; however, Stevens's role was president-as-stern-but-loving-father. The country was a screwed-up teenager, and the former marine was going to discipline us until we were worthy of his love again. But in private, he was a polka-playing accordionist, rock climber, and horticulturist, with a hybrid pansy species, *Viola tricolor stevensii*, named in his honor.

They were waited on by the president's personal Filipino American naval valet, from the same corps of Filipino American valets that had faithfully attended American presidents, generals, and admirals since World War I. As the valet made drinks, Paine listened to Brant and the president chitchat about recent Chinese investment in American illegal immigrant labor. The president joked that he wouldn't know what to do without his *consigliere*, Brant.

"We make a good team, don't we, John?" nodded the secretary of state.

"The best. I'll be sorry to see it end."

"Good teams are important." Brant's eyes flicked between Carter and Tom several times. Carter got the old man's message loud and clear: This is your new partner. And take notes.

The president motioned to the valet. "Tom? You like Long Island Iced Tea? This one's my secret recipe."

"Yes, thanks," said Tom. Josiah quietly sighed in spite of himself.

The valet poured a highball with ice full of amber liquid, garnished with a slice of lemon and placed it on the table in front of Paine.

"Sure you don't want some, Josiah?" teased the Bartender-in-Chief.

"I'll stick to coffee, thanks. Coffee?" Josiah asked Carter.

"Not the way you drink it," grimaced the younger man. "I'll take the liquor."

"How's that?" asked Tom.

The old man cradled his creamer like it contained liquid gold. "With breast milk."

Tom cocked his head in amusement. "May I ask why?"

"Tradition and self-preservation. Our brothers John Jacob Astor and John D. Rockefeller Sr. popularized it. They died of extreme old age, especially for the times they lived in. Rockefeller was ninety-eight! That'd be like one hundred twenty now. This stuff's full 'a antibodies, amino acids, easy to digest. Young fellas like you should be doin' this every day. Along with your Omega 3s and Vitamin D. The future's comin' when it might be possible to circumvent death itself. If we drink enough of this stuff, we might make it there in time."

"Not if I have to drink that," shuddered Carter.

Josiah poured a little more milk in his coffee. "Well, I may be too late, but no harm tryin'."

"And you get it from . . . ?" asked Tom.

"World's second-oldest profession: wet nurses."

The president sipped his cocktail while his valet discreetly wiped condensation rings off the rustic table and placed Phoenix Club coasters in their place. "Tom, I have to know how you've managed to stay out of the public eye for so many years. And what makes you so special that you've become my *consigliere*'s new boy here? We thought we had tabs on everybody who'd ever be anybody!"

"Going blind is a traumatic experience and self-pity would drive anyone under a rock. It took me years to figure out my liability might be an asset. If I compare my life before and after, I'm more successful and complete now than I ever was as a sighted man. I've finally got a good woman who loves me, and she's helped me see my way clear, if you'll pardon the expression, to participate in the world in ways I never imagined. My blindness gave me 'insight' that sight never did. As to why I'm sitting here, in God's own wilderness, talking to the president of the United States and surrounded by all the men who really matter in this country? I have no idea, except to guess blindness was a blessing."

"Until we cure it," said Carter.

"Yes," said Tom. "And that would be a blessing, too."

"Blessin's all around," toasted Josiah. He raised his coffee cup to them. "To all our health." Tom carefully felt for his glass and raised it.

The other men raised their drinks. "To our health."

Tom sipped his cocktail. It tasted as innards-peeling as Josiah had warned. "Delicious, Mr. President."

His plan to be everything Davy Brant was not was working.

Dionysus stood center stage once again, whipping his acolytes into fevered anticipation of limitless freedom. Carter Potsdam knew a dependable gig when he saw one. No one else in that amphitheater could control and guide this audience's emotions as stunningly as the man strutting on stage in nothing but a lion skin and grape leaves. Tom's déjà vu couldn't rightly be called déjà vu—this was a replay of his past, however distant he felt from it. Crosby, Stills, Nash & Young had said a mouthful about being here before . . .

The vice president of the United States, an affable, malleable man named MacAlister Buchanan, escorted Tom to the amphitheater. With a full head of white hair, his primary skill was to look and sound patriotic no matter what he did or said.

With Josiah and Carter busy preparing their roles, the president felt it wasn't appropriate to be seen leading a blind man around the camp. It was, however, the perfect job for the vice president. Tom was impressed with President Stevens's sense of self-conscious irony.

It was hard to ignore Buchanan's whipsawed emotions during the play, from anticipation of the Praetor Maximus's and Dionysus's arrival to his fear of the phantom voices riding the wind to his frenzied joy at Dionysus's endorsed debauchery. He and his fellow masters of media supposed they were so sophisticated the basic tools of stagecraft could not manipulate them. But if the rabid crowd was any indication, they were more affected, perhaps from the simplicity of the techniques. Or maybe Talia was correct: Con men were easily conned. Regardless, being human meant emotion trumped logic every time. Even Tom was moved to nod when Dionysus beseeched his followers to "Cast off the civilized masks you wear and realize your true nature! Human and animal! Citizen and anarchist! Alive and dead! Here, in this sacred grove, you are born again, to live how you wish to live, to be how you wish to be!" Tom understood more than anyone both the thrill and the price paid for living such contradictions.

Camp attendance this year was mandatory. The invitation

claimed classified intelligence would be conveyed to the membership, but only in person. The last compulsory attendance had been during the darkest days of the Cold War when an unexcused absence was akin to Communist sympathizing. In truth, it was for members' own protection, in case of nuclear war. Old-timers often joked about mines underneath the camp converted to bomb shelters in the '50s. The tunnels were supposedly converted to food and wine cellars after the Berlin Wall fell. But was that true? Did he really know what was going on, out of his sight and just under his feet?

As the crowd departed the amphitheater, Mac Buchanan pulled ahead like a dog straining to break his leash. He hurriedly described the fun on offer, jerking the blind man's arm this way, then that.

"Mac, why don't you drop me at the nearest bar stool? Really. Go have fun."

"You sure?" the VP asked, as though the president or Josiah might spank him for not following orders.

"Absolutely. I'd be happy with a drink."

It took twenty-eight minutes for Dionysus to find Tom nursing his whisky, a bottle at his elbow ready for refills. By that point, most of the drinkers had fortified their egos and scurried away into the night.

"A man after my own heart," the god said.

"God of wine, women, and song?" inquired Tom with a smile.

"You bet. Another glass," he said to the bartender, pointing at Tom's glass and sitting on the stool next to him. "So, what'd you think?"

"Whatever you do must work. And you sound like you can act, though I'm no judge. The wind and sound effects worked for me."

"Yeah, those are good."

"And everyone's doing what you told them to do. So congratulations. You're a hit." He emptied his glass, and his hand went in search of a refill.

"Please, allow me," said Carter, grabbing the scotch. Their hands met at the bottle at the same time, Tom's hand covering Carter's for a moment.

"Thank you," said Tom, and he withdrew his hand.

Carter filled both his and Tom's glasses.

"What's your chosen poison tonight?" asked Tom.

"Other than whisky?" Carter held his glass aloft. "By the way, cheers . . ."

"Cheers."

After he took a swig, Carter sighed, and his tense shoulders dropped an inch. "You know? After all these years, the one thing I've never done is experience a Bacchanalia straight." He raised his glass. "Or as straight as I can be." He snorted at his private double entendre and took another sip, unable to resist a wistful glance into the darkness.

"Please don't hold back on my account."

"No," said Carter. "It'll be interesting to be an observer this year. Maybe it'll teach me restraint. I'll need that as a new father." He seemed earnest in his desire for self-improvement.

Could Carter's sociopathic guiltlessness know no bounds?

"Did Josiah ask you to babysit?"

The Cheshire cat grin illuminated the night. "Can't get anything by you, can I?"

"Where'd you find Mac?"

"Headfirst between some Amazon's thighs and not up for air anytime soon."

"To each their own," said Tom, grinning slyly as he raised his glass and sipped again.

Struggling to read into Tom's words and gestures, Carter lobbed a ball back. "I've given your offer at the PAC dinner some thought. And I think you're right. I'm better with a partner. Let's spend this week exploring if a relationship between us will work."

Tom smiled broadly. "Great. I'm really looking forward to getting to know you better."

Without eye contact, Carter found it frustratingly difficult to infer his meaning. Was this guy "family" or just obtusely straight?

Fantasies of a different sort ran through Tom's mind: a blow to the throat, crushing Carter's trachea and suffocating him was pleasant to imagine.

"I hear you've got problems in Russia that need more than the usual help . . ." poked Carter.

Tom breathed in sharply. "Unfortunately, the problems . . . have left Russia."

"And if the Russian mob comes after you, I don't want to be collateral damage."

"That's fair. But Josiah seems to think he's got that covered. I hope to God he's right . . ." Tom shivered at the thought of assassination. "We've got lots of time to discuss my head on a Russian pike. Come on," said Tom, grinning again. "Let's cruise camp."

Drinks drained and refilled, Dionysus led his blind Tiresias through the wilderness. Tom grasped Carter's elbow as they visited the bonfire by the lake, where groups of older men gathered. With Josiah's favor now public, Thomas Paine was Celebrity of the Week. Many engaged him in conversation, eager for his opinion, or just to meet the mystery man. He made sure to give each man the introduction best calibrated to put him at ease. He had to be sure not to physically mirror them, because that would make it clear to a third party he could see. But he could vocally and conceptually copy them. He must have said and done the right things, because even alpha dogs who bristled with territoriality and challenges ended conversations wanting him as their special friend. Several times, Carter couldn't help smiling at Tom's smoothness.

Since Tom arrived at camp, every man whose hand he shook was given a gift: while his right hand grasped theirs and his left patted an arm or shoulder, both deposited RFID tags, small as powder specks, on their person. He held them in a tiny, impermeable nanoplastic pocket built into his larger khakis' pocket. Then he mentally IDed the tags and put them in a database, acting as the primary receiver and transmitting the information back to his lab for backup. It didn't matter if they washed their hands or changed their clothes. He just kept shaking hands and depositing more. He tagged and released hundreds of men in one night to see where they went and with whom they associated, and he continued throughout the week.

He hoped it would reveal Dulles's mole. And the club's plan.

Dill Kenilworth made a special effort to make Tom's acquaintance. "I want to congratulate you, sir, on being a role model to millions of disabled Americans," said Dill, pumping Tom's hand strenuously.

"Thanks very much, Dill, but I'm not trying to be a role model to anyone."

"You may not be trying, but that doesn't mean the good Lord hasn't made you one. If He doesn't see fit to heal you because you don't truly believe in our Lord Jesus Christ as your personal savior, the Lord is still making you his example of how living—and dying—with whatever affliction He's seen fit to bestow is ennobling and empowering. It's the best of what makes us human. You're not some namby-pamby running to every Dr. Frankenstein for some . . . robot cure . . ."

As they walked, Tom built a detailed map in his Cortex 3.0, searching for what couldn't be seen, like bomb shelters, as well as amassing a complete list of every brother and staff member attending. There were more men here than during his previous visit, filling every bed available.

One of them was Anthony Dulles's mole. Any of the more than three thousand men could have a piece of the puzzle, whether they knew it or not. He scanned all transmissions into and out of camp and ran background checks on everyone. Given the thousands of people involved, Talia, Ruth, and the mysterious Miss Gray Hat helped collate and complete electronic dossiers in a database on the most likely candidates. As more and more members were processed, patterns quickly emerged. Some had married into each other's families. Many had businesses or projects together. For instance, a group of six ran a company most Americans considered as American as apple pie. However, digging revealed their headquarters was physically based in Singapore, with intellectual property rights filed in Dubai, financed by Koreans, staffed by Australians, with no accountability or taxes to anyone. Dozens of members protected the company from the media, government, and consumers. What American interests were members protecting other than their own? Or did it reveal the growing irrelevance of nation-states and their economies that rendered currency—any nation's currency as long as it was solid—as the only thing worth allying to?

No one he met seemed to know or was willing to say why the members were all summoned this year. Josiah was playing it close to the vest.

When Tom and Carter ran out of liquor, they headed to a bar for refills and sat down gratefully. Schmoozing was exhausting work.

After they were served, Carter regarded Tom intently, eyes darting, searching for something in his face and manner. "How much do you know about me?"

"Which answer do you want? The philosophical or the informational? And do you really want my answer?"

Carter hesitated. "Touché. But . . . yes."

"Well, philosophically, we can't know anyone. We present each other our well-constructed masks, which are no more real than Plato's shadows on cave walls. I would argue most people don't even know themselves. And they avoid self-knowledge with good reason. It's painful to see our frail, scarred psyches. Makes us feel inferior. Informationally, we uncover layers of history, behavior, and relationships and piece it all together into a rag doll of a personality. Anticipating a possible business deal, I've uncovered everything that can be publicly found about you. As I'm sure you have of me. But the simulacrum's a poor zombie creature in comparison to the person before you, isn't it? Isn't there far more subtle information to glean in person if you know what to look for? Even with the masks? I may not be able to see, but I'm getting all kinds of information about you, and how people behave around you. It's very hard to decipher a true identity, and not everyone's up to the task. But I believe you might be."

Carter had the stunned look of a skeptic who has met a flawless psychic. Or his match. "I agree. But you realize most people here wouldn't understand a word you just said."

"Of course. Which is why you're with me. And not Dill. Being the smartest guy in the room in a group like this can get lonely, can't it?"

There it was: the slight puppy-dog wideness to his eyelids and pupils, the relaxed and open posture, the deepened breathing. Carter was hooked. He wanted to believe that a man like Tom, physically and economically immune to his more obvious enticements, could understand the "Carter" under the veneer. So far, no one had come close. Until now.

But hooked didn't mean stupid.

"You're good . . . very good. I could take lessons from you. Fuck, I'm thirsty." Carter upended his glass. He stared out at the revelers.

Tom leaned in. "Now let me ask you a question: What are you most proud of?"

Carter struggled with the word. "Proud?"

"Yes, and not some cliché like 'my service to my country.' That's a load of crap. I want to know what gets your motor running."

"I . . . I don't know . . ." Carter mentally ran through his life, but anything positive he had built he had also destroyed, and his drooping expression betrayed it. "Umm . . . becoming a father? I was a . . .

I don't know, I'd guess you'd call it a playboy . . . but I've changed. I really have. Marrying Amanda and getting ready for this baby . . ."

"But you're not a father yet. You might fail miserably at it. And pregnancy is usually the mother's job. Come on, there must be something you've earned all on your own . . ."

"Prometheus . . ."

Tom smiled at the lie. "Good answer. Then I'm even more honored you'd consider me for a partner. I hope I do nothing to lessen your accomplishments."

"And what are you most proud of?" asked Carter.

"Making it this far. With everything against me, I wasn't sure it was possible."

Tom could feel Josiah approach them from behind, along with Bruce. Sensitive to the low tones of the two men chatting, Josiah cleared his throat loudly.

"Carter, son? I've been lookin' all over for you. I got a problem with two gentlemen that I think you might be the only one diplomatic enough to handle. You know 'em, and you'll know how to diffuse 'em. If I have to hear their nonsense one more minute, I swear I'll shoot 'em right where they stand. Tom, do you mind if I break up your conversation? This might take a while."

It was obvious Josiah was lying, not only by his physical tells and the fact that Crichtons were also security personnel, but from Carter's low-grade panic he fought to suppress. And Josiah's RFID tags revealed he was most recently near the mines, then his signal had disappeared for a time, until he resurfaced.

"Of course not," said Tom.

"What are you drinking?" asked Bruce, his voice already slurred.

Carter held up the whisky.

"Mind if I join you?" But facial twitches revealed Bruce wasn't a willing babysitter.

"Guys, it's not necessary. I won't fall in the lake or anything. One of the staff'll steer me back to the cabin when I'm done."

"Nah. Happy to take you," insisted an unhappy Bruce.

"Now you take care of our boy, Bruce," said Josiah. "We'll be back late, Tom. Don't wait up. Have a good night."

"Wanna walk?" asked Bruce.

"Happy to."

"Good." Bruce took Tom's arm and they started down a tree-lined path. "I got someone you should meet."

Within minutes, the RFIDs did their job, tracking Carter and Josiah to the mine entrance, where they disappeared.

Tom stood on the front porch of a prostitute's cabin, and framed in the doorway was Vera, hands braced high up both sides of the door-frame, displaying her scantily clad body to its best, backlit advantage. But her intended audience couldn't appreciate it. She quickly adjusted her game plan, stroking Tom's arm. After she introduced herself, he acted surprised.

"What are you doing here?" He turned to Bruce. "Where are we?"

"Come inside, Tom. We'll talk," Vera purred.

"Have fun, man!" Bruce pounded his back and limped into the darkness.

She guided him inside and closed the door behind them. The quasi-Victorian room was simple, neat, clean, and utilitarian. There was a canopy bed without fabric (suitable for bondage and hanging toys, restraints discreetly out of sight for now), an over-stuffed recliner, and a hard, upright chair. There was a bureau for the escort's clothes and accessories. One wall was mirrored, as was the ceiling, which had strong hooks embedded for additional toys.

There was a bathroom, with a sizable tub shower just beyond the only internal door.

"Bruce didn't tell you I work here Camp Week?"

"No. I'd remember that."

"He's a naughty boy. I specifically told him to tell you first. Well, now you're here."

"But why are you?"

"This is what I do, Tom. And I'm very good at it."

"I'm sure you are, but . . ."

She ran her fingers through his hair. "You know, I've been with blind men before. I really enjoy it. You use your other senses so much more, so sensual, like a woman." She whispered in his ear, "Very sexy . . ."

Tom gently pulled away. "Why are you letting yourself be used like this? Is Bruce your boyfriend or your pimp?"

"He can be both . . ."

Reaching out, his fingers searched for a seat. He bumped into the hard chair and sat with a sigh. Vera crouched at his feet. "You'll have to forgive me, Vera, but you've really . . . surprised me. Please believe me, I'm not judging you. I've been told of your beauty, and I know you're highly intelligent. I like you and I just want what's best for you. And I guess I'm old-fashioned enough to think this isn't it."

Vera sat back on her heels for a moment. "Thank you. Most men don't bother to question the impropriety of the situation and just enjoy taking advantage of it."

"I've never been that kind of man."

"No. You're a gentleman. I thought they were extinct. When you came to my defense at the dinner, I was impressed, although you had no notion of my occupation and felt free to back me . . ."

"I could tell something was wrong, and I was surprised at their bad manners. And I would still come to your defense."

"We Russians have our own sense of bad manners—*Nyekul-turny*—but few in Russia understand being a gentleman in the European sense, of having consideration and deference to those who are less fortunate than themselves, because they can afford to. After centuries of czars and commissars and Mafiosi and oligarchs, it's a trait that couldn't survive. Lobo is just like a Russian. Maybe that's why I'm with him. We understand each other . . ."

Tom wished Vera could hear Elvis Costello's tortured singing "A Man out of Time." Maybe she'd realize she was living a cliché.

"You're lucky you have Talia," Vera continued.

"I know."

"She shares your values. And she's very kind to me. I never forget a kindness." It was pathetic listening to one of the world's most beautiful women describing her life as if she were a tormented, feral puppy.

"How do you put up with this?"

"With what?"

"The abuse . . . the degradation . . ."

"Degradation? I make more money than most people in the world. And what is the value of my life? Isn't it culturally relative? I am treated much better here for what I do than if I stayed in Russia. Here, I am exotic, rare, valuable. In Russia, I'd be dead, because I am disposable. There's always another pretty body to warm a mattress and relax a customer. And death can be a relief. Why do you think Russians smoke and drink so much? We want to have as fun, pain-free, and short a life as possible." She touched him, stroked him. "Here, I make very good money, live the life I want with who I want. I don't want to die when I live here. But how can you understand? You're a rich, white, American male. What do they call them? A Master of the Universe? You're accustomed to believing the world is there for the making and taking."

What had Vera and Bruce concocted that linked them together? Bruce had been too eager to introduce him to Vera at camp both times. And what about the others who used her services? Could Bruce have arranged something as old-fashioned as a pillow-talk scam among his own "brothers"? And were the men nowadays dumb enough to fall for it?

Surfing the net in his head, he scanned data on men he surmised were involved with Vera. Cross-referencing their corporate histories with camp dates, patterns emerged. In some cases, within months after camp, Bruce bought or sold shares, made moves on companies, created or dissolved business relationships with these men. Several times, he made moves on companies before CEOs revealed they were retiring or turning over the reins for health reasons. While some deals were open, some appeared clandestine, through holding companies that appeared benign to corporate officers. Investigating the fronts revealed Bruce controlled them.

He could not let his DNA expose him. But did Bruce use DNA to reveal other secrets? A semen sample would expose not only genetic propensities for diseases, but active diseases. He didn't need an insurance company to release this information. He could collect it himself.

To Vera, all the analysis on the second track of his mind was invisible. He could carry on the conversation without missing a beat. "I appreciate your efforts to make me feel good about myself. But I'm deeply in love with Talia. And I would never do anything to betray her love. Not when we finally found something so real and important to us."

"Every man says that right before he gives in," she purred.

"I'm not every man." He gripped the chair and stood up.

Her hands and lips fell away. She sighed. For the first time, it felt like the real Vera rose to the surface. "You have no idea how rarely they mean it. It's sad. Here are men who have everything. They could have love, too. But they deny themselves, always thinking something better is around the corner. They want to be free, thinking freedom is a commodity you buy and sell. You seem to understand there is no such thing as freedom, unlike your fellow countrymen. And we Russians have known it for centuries. Freedom is an illusion, except maybe in love. Life is servitude to others, those who have power over us and those whom we are in obligation to, and that means suffering. We are only free in our hearts when we love and are loved. And that makes you a truly free man. You must cherish and protect that."

"And you, my dear, are the quintessential philosopher whore, both intellectually and physically stimulating . . ."

"Thank you." She preened at the compliment.

". . . but I don't agree. Love is servitude, too, but it's the kind where you welcome the chains. Because to be free means to be alone. And that's suffering."

Elvis Costello's anguished scream and thrashing lead guitar rang in Tom's head. He lowered it away as if Vera might hear the tortured howl escape his ears.

"Is something wrong?"

"I have a headache."

"Isn't that what the woman is supposed to say?" she teased. "Let me find Bruce. He will take you back." A brief GO call, and less than a minute later, Lobo arrived.

A look passed between the two, signaling her failure. Bruce's eyes narrowed. Suddenly, he acted more intoxicated than the moment before. He grabbed Tom's arm, the blind-drunk leading the blind. Staggering down the porch stairs, Lobo tripped, pitching forward. He grabbed Tom to right himself, but dragged him down, too. As everything slowed, Tom did his best to cushion himself, but Bruce shoved him extra hard to make sure Tom crashed on the rock-strewn ground. There was nothing Tom could do to stop the laws of physics or Bruce's plan.

Lobo bellowed like a child, "Vera! He hurt himself!"

"What did you do to him?" she cried. Bruce lifted Tom's cut hand.

She ran inside to emerge with a cloth handkerchief. It was embroidered with her initials in Cyrillic lettering. Who used handkerchiefs anymore?

Tom pushed them away. "Please, I'm all right."

Bruce grabbed his arm with a strong grip while Vera forced the handkerchief around the wound. She turned on Lobo. "Bruce, you are a clumsy oaf."

Trying to squirm free, Tom grabbed some RFID particles in his pocket and touched the bloody cloth, tagging it, sending Talia the ID coordinates. Bruce snatched away the handkerchief and tossed it to Vera. "Bleeding stopped. Can you get the stain out?"

She rolled her eyes in disdain. "Are you sure you can get him back safely?"

"Yes, yes, yes . . ." Bruce waved her away. "You'd think I just had my training wheels removed." He waved to Vera. "Nighty-night."

Vera stood on the porch as Bruce led Tom into the night. The woods were dark and the sounds of enthusiastic lovemaking surrounded them until they left the red light district.

Bruce had him. One of Lobo's companies owned the patent on a DNA sequencing machine that could decode the entire human genome in hours. Tom had to ensure it was intercepted any way necessary before it reached Lobo's lab. If Talia didn't catch it, the lab would find the RFIDs, as well as identify him. But if Bruce discovered Thomas Paine was Peter Bernhardt, it didn't matter what else Bruce knew.

CHAPTER SIXTY-THREE

The RFID tags never left camp. They and the blood sample remained in Bruce's cabin, under the watchful eyes of Crichtons ordered to guard his effects with their lives. Talia never intercepted the couriers, because there were no couriers to intercept.

The DNA was Bruce's advantage and Tom had to wait for him to play his hand.

During the remaining six days of Camp Week, the rhetoric flowed thick and fast from all quarters. Josiah Brant was in total control, whipping the ideologues into a frenzy of hypothesizing and planning about the future of the country—and the world. Through camaraderie and cocktails, policy lectures and pissing contests, dramatics and drinking games, Tom expected to be uncovered all week. He waited, wondering if it would come as kidnapping and torture or a bullet to the back of the head.

By week's end, professional lobbyists and political operatives of all stripes had spent time with Tom, as though they could sniff the shifting wind. But camp wound down and Josiah hadn't revealed any secrets.

After meticulously tagging every member of the Phoenix Club, his background analysis revealed almost everyone had a relationship of some sort with Anthony Dulles. However, no one stood out as the mole, and his few clues did not expose the club's plan. In the meantime, meta-analysis revealed the club consisted of a handful of generators, those deserving of the label "best and brightest" who produced work at a high level, but most others were sycophants, schemers, operators, and hucksters, men of mediocre minds and little talent except for self-promotion and survival who congregate around the extraordinary. Their backgrounds and connections betrayed the price they paid to live at the top of the food chain. They didn't get this ride of a lifetime for free.

Surveillance data revealed Josiah, Carter, Bruce, and a handful of staff made regular visits to the mines. Tom tried a few approaches to the shaft entrance, his Hoover cane tapping the way, but was intercepted by staff every time. He knew one entrance was an industrial-sized double door, made to look like rough-hewn wood on the outside, but it closed with the low, breathy thud of solid steel. From his shepherds' behavior, not only was he being watched and reported on at all times, it seemed certain people had been ordered to keep others away from him. And he couldn't just stuff his pajamas with a pillow and sneak around Ninja-style in the night. The camp rocked 24/7. Even if he manipulated their electronic security, the risk of live security was too great. While he knew the entire membership's whereabouts at all times, that didn't mean he knew why they were all there.

He felt certain the technology he had invented was nearby and would be used to kill or brainwash a large number of people soon. But he had no idea how to stop it.

On the last day, Josiah Brant asked Thomas Paine to take a stroll. Josiah guided him as they chatted about the week's events while

circling bonfires' ashy remains and skirting the dark forest's edge
until they arrived at the mine entrance.

"If you don't mind, I have someplace mighty special to show ya,"
said Josiah.

The icy chill of déjà vu suffused Tom's brain, even though he
had never passed through the mine doors before. And he was right
about the steel. They were atomic-blast shields, fitted with a rustic
veneer. Some of the underground was still Atomic Age. The first ret-
rofit occurred in the '40s for a World War II bunker to avoid possible
Japanese bombing. The second in the '50s expanded it as a Cold War
nuclear-bomb shelter, should mutually assured destruction break out
during Camp Week. But more was Nano-Bio-Info Age, which indicated a recent renovation. The steel doors opened into a white foyer,
bare except for a doorframe surrounding a second set of steel doors,
recessed lights, biothreat sensors, fire sprinkler and decontamination
caps on the ceiling, and a biological identification system next to
the door. It simultaneously measured multiple biometrics of iris, retina, palm, and voice. Josiah stepped up to an ID station and leaned
his chin and forehead against a padded brace, positioning his eyes
properly, while placing his right hand on a scanner, spoke his name
into a tiny microphone in the headpiece and added, "Guest: Thomas
Paine," to prevent the alarm sounding if two bodies passed through
the doorway. The console displayed both names, and the door slid
open. Josiah took Tom's arm and guided him through the door.

It slid shut behind them, and his internal wireless blinked out.
The walls were too thick, the facility's internal computing system
hardwired and not networked to the outside to avoid discovery or
tampering. Cut off from his constant information flow, he was running blind. So close to knowing, and suddenly unconnected! The
Internet was a lobe of his cortex, and this was brain collapse.

It was a different world on the other side of the door. The original mine tunnel was transformed into a long hallway, off of which

numerous doors led to unknown chambers beyond. Instead of the sterile environment of the foyer, it was beautifully appointed with subtle, creamy paint, lush and thickly padded carpeting, detailed wood moldings and excellent oil-and-canvas reproductions of great works of art. At least he hoped they were reproductions. Otherwise, the real *Nighthawks* was in a mineshaft and a copy of Edward Hopper's iconic painting hung in the Art Institute of Chicago. It looked more like a hallway in the Ritz-Carlton than a bunker to house civilization's survivors at the end of the world.

Each handsomely paneled door had a number on it, beginning with 1-1 and 1-3 on the right side and 1-2 and 1-4 immediately across and so forth. Some doors were open. A closed and multi-locked door was labeled "Armory." As they ambled past, Tom could see, with his peripheral vision, meeting rooms, exercise facilities, an opulent and spacious dining area.

"It smells and feels like a hotel. Where are we?"

"If it all went to hell tomorrow, odds are you'd end up here. Mount Phoenix is part of the Continuity of Operations Plan, which includes locations replacin' necessary governmental operations in case catastrophic events endanger or destroy DC. There are several facilities around the country, includin' Cheyenne Mountain, which is on warm standby to house NORAD, Site R in Pennsylvania, which contains a mini-Pentagon, and Mount Weather, which organizes FEMA and houses Congress in extremis. When 10/26 hit, we shipped all the politicians there, just in case. You shoulda heard 'em squawkin' all the way to West Virginia. We also got several aircraft, like Airforce One 'n' Two, Nighthawk," which pinged the painting's pun, "and Lookin' Glass, which takes over for NORAD, and others that act as travelin' command bases."

"Which department is based here?"

"Not a specific department. A type of person. Phoenix people. Those who can rebuild a society from the ground up. We're well aware that society isn't a bunch 'a generals and politicians runnin' around. The foundation of society is the people who bind us together and can envision and create change. That's what you and all your brothers are. The engine of society. Think of this as the home of the ultimate think tank for humanity."

"Well, it's nice to know I'll have somewhere to go if it all goes to custard. What about spouses, families?"

"We can get our membership and staff down here, but that's a few thousand already. No more room or supplies."

"I'm sure there'd be a lot who might turn you down in that case."

"Maybe. Maybe not. Survival is a powerful imperative."

"Could you leave Maggie and your kids and grandkids behind?"

Josiah was pricked for a moment by his private thorn. "If the future of my country depended on my survival, yes, I could." He looked to Tom expectantly. "But it might be easier than I think."

They entered an elevator. It, too, had biometric devices, and Josiah was IDed before the elevator would move. They went down eight levels out of a possible nine.

The door opened onto a very different floor. Painted flat white, with a concrete floor and lit by utilitarian LEDs. Their movements made noisy echoes down the hallway.

"This feels different. Where are we?"

The old man moved quickly for someone his age. He raised his elbow, detaching Tom from him, and slipped behind and into an open door. His sports shoes made no sound. To a real blind man, he would have disappeared.

"Josiah?" Tom turned in a circle, like a dog chasing his tail, as he tapped out the perimeter with his cane and hit the two corridor walls. "Hello? Josiah!" he yelled louder.

The initiation test had begun. Acting frustrated, he felt his way with his hands and cane to the closest open door and passed through. Then Tom felt a wall of fabric, which he batted his hands along until he found an opening.

"Josiah?"

With the fabric acting like a light shield in a photographic dark room, the room behind it was completely black. The space felt small, confined; he could hear the short reverb of his movement's sounds. There was quiet breathing. He supposed one was Josiah, but it sounded like three others, one in the center and the rest on the perimeter. His cane tapped to the middle, then hit the leg of a heavy wooden chair . . . then something soft, fleshy. His fingers found a body duct-taped to the legs and back of the chair, with a cloth bag over its drooping head. It smelled foul, like old excrement. Tom found the victim's carotid artery and checked for a pulse. It beat slow, but steady. The limp body indicated unconsciousness.

Tom heard the switch of an electrical circuit microseconds before the room flooded with a blinding interrogation light hung from the ceiling. He made sure his lids were shut to stop his body's involuntary jerk from dilated pupils.

Josiah, Carter, and Bruce stood in the room.

"Sorry to be constantly testing you, son. I know you must be sick of it. But that nifty defensive move you made at your first initiation was too surprisin' not to double-check."

"Bet you couldn't see this coming," snorted Bruce.

Carter flinched at the bad joke.

"Who else is here?" asked Tom, weaving his head to hear their presence.

"Carter and Bruce, son. It's all right. We just need you to meet the man in the chair." Brant, posturing with drama lost on a blind man, whipped off the black bag from the torturee's head.

It was Chang Eng.

The blinding light woke Eng with a start. Dazed, he squinted blankly at Paine, not recognizing his former employer. Chang's mouth was duct-taped shut, his ears taped over, most likely covering earplugs. Eng could speak no evil and hear no evil, but they allowed him to see it. His once-immaculate white button-down shirt and pressed chinos were torn and stained with sweat, blood, urine, and feces. His feet were bare and bruised, three toenails ripped off with bloody scabs in their places. His hair was no longer a number two buzz cut, but an inch long and shaggy. They'd been torturing him a long time.

"His name is Chang Eng. Ever hear of him?" asked Josiah.

Tom thought for a moment, then said, "Wasn't Chang Eng an employee of Carter's? And I thought he was killed by the FBI for 10/26."

"Yes . . . and no. The FBI weren't really FBI. They were our private security team. And they pretended to kill him. Fired some blanks here, some squibs and fake blood there, just a bit of theater, so the world would think he was gone."

Which meant Peter Bernhardt was chased from the hospital by the club, not the feds. Was all surveillance on him run by the club and not the government?

"And he wasn't really a member of ATEAMO," continued Josiah. "Eng worked for the club. We arranged for him to disappear so he could continue his work for us." He circled Chang, regarding the man with no more consideration than he would an irritating pile of manure. "But we checked his loyalty recently and found it wantin'."

"How?" asked Tom.

Carter stepped closer. "He came to work here after 'dying' at Prometheus. Initially, all was well, but we needed him to be more productive, so we installed the Hippo 2.0 to increase productivity and the Cortex 2.0 so we could read his chip, and therefore, his mind. It's always good to know what your most important researcher is thinking."

If Chang was involved with the club now, he was probably involved in 10/26, along with the club. That meant Biogineers was indeed responsible for mass murder. And Peter Bernhardt never knew . . .

They'd also broken the algorithm for reading thoughts before him. Carter developed the processor from a theoretical to a practical device. How did Miss Gray Hat and Ruth not discover that? Unless it had been done here, in the mine.

Tom's transmitter could contact Chang's receiver on his processor. They could communicate, but it would reveal his augmentation. Certain there was no Wi-Fi receiver in proximity, Tom sent a message.

Chang? Why did you do it?

Chang's head swiveled in panic, neck joints clicking, searching for the source of the transmission.

whoareyouwhoareyouwhoareyou . . . ?

It's Peter.

Eyes widened and panic intensified, his head weaving and clicking, back and forth. *wherewherewherewherewherewhere . . . ?*

Calm down! ordered Tom. He needed Chang to relax, because the torturee's panic was swamping his own wiring. He struggled to push Chang's terror back.

Peter is dead! Chang wailed in Tom's brain.

Tom asked Carter, "And what did you find when you wired him up?"

"He didn't want to participate anymore," said Carter.

"Chang's been dead for some time now, even if he didn't realize it himself," said Josiah. "You're just finishin' the job. Please understand I would never ask you to do somethin' like this if it wasn't crucial for you to grasp the stakes by which our country will rise or fall."

Chang, did you work for the Phoenix Club? transmitted Tom calmly.

You're not Peter . . . you're not Peter . . .

Peter is dead. Your brain is coping with helplessness by creating him. Answering the question to an alter ego will bring relief.

No! It's from my processor!

You're so far gone you don't even realize you're psychotic. Talking to me, the Peter manifestation, will assuage your guilt and bring you peace. Did you work for the Phoenix Club?

Yyyyyeeeessssss! Chang visibly relaxed. So did Tom.

Doesn't admitting things to yourself feel better? What did you do for them?

Designed bots.

Which bots?

10/26. And new bots.

"How many others have this system in their heads?" asked Tom.

Carter replied, "Chang was the first person in the world to receive the full two-part unit."

That was a lie. Carter knew Peter Bernhardt was the first person.

"It's too unstable a device at present," continued Carter. "We've alpha- and beta-tested it with the Pentagon on military personnel. About a dozen to date. So far, there's too high a percentage of post-implant military psychosis to mass-market it yet."

What are the new bots designed to do? Tom asked Chang.

Like Hunter/Seeker virus. Permanently bond with serotonin neurotransmitters and receptors. Happy pills . . . happy pills . . . happy pills . . . giggled Chang's mind. Tom held Chang's madness at neuron's length. It was too easy to fall into, like an ice-cold lake on a stifling hot day.

"Military psychosis?" echoed Tom to Carter.

"Post-traumatic stress disorder, postcombat dissociative behaviors, hallucinations," replied Carter. "We think that quick-onset, induced hyperthymesia—remembering too much—makes them regain moral autonomy, which military training is designed to eliminate . . ."

"They're not wantin' to kill anymore, or we can't control their killin' when they do!" complained Josiah. "What good's a soldier like that?"

What club members were involved in 10/26? Tom asked Chang.

Brant organized technoterrorist synergy. Lobo ran it. But was only a practice run . . .

Practice run for what?

7-28

Happy pills on July 28? It was July 24. *How will the bots be released?*

Water. Happy water . . . Happy . . .

"We need selective memory features we can control," corrected Carter. "Chang demonstrated the same behavioral change of increased moral autonomy."

Leaning against a wall and bored with psychobabble, Bruce checked the time on his watch. "He refused to take orders. End of story. Can we get on with it?"

Tom understood. The implant expanded Chang's mental context and allowed the whole world to make an impression. Not just the parts his brain chose to select. Knowing more meant he understood more, which meant he realized he was wrong. And he wanted to stop.

It was like murdering his twin.

Why did you do it, Chang? What could you possibly gain?

Gain . . . gain . . . gain . . . gain . . . nothing ventured, nothing gained . . . gain . . . gain . . . gain . . .

"Nothing ventured, nothing gained": the words technologists live by. He wanted to be angry with the man who had created the tech to murder thousands, but how could he? Hadn't he done the impossible just to see if it could be done?

Would Peter have wanted you to do that?

All Tom could perceive inside Chang's brain was laughter. He was laughing at Peter.

"So what am I here to do?" Tom asked Josiah.

"Good for you, son. I knew you'd catch on." Josiah carefully placed a 9mm Glock in Paine's hands. "You need to aim at the heart to preserve his brain implants. And there's only one bullet, so make it count."

Gingerly fingering the object to identify parts and not accidentally pull the trigger, the inescapable repetition nearly flattened him.

"You realize since I can't see the man, I don't know if this person is really Chang Eng. Not that it would matter. I didn't know him anyway." Tom sighed. "Brings a whole new meaning to the phrase 'blind trust.'"

"Excellent observation, son. Think of this as one of many times you'll have to trust your brothers to do the right thing. You've come this far with us, haven't you?"

Chang shook at the sight of the gun. *Peter? Where's Peter? Help me, Peter!*

I'm holding the gun. Tom regretted it the moment it came out of his brain.

Eyes rolled back, his body spasmed stiff, catatonic with fear. Chang tried to scream, but the gag muffled him. Inside his head, Tom could hear, *AAAAAAAAAAAAAAAAAAAAHHHHHHH HHHHHHHHHHAAAAAAAAAAAAAAAAAAAAAAAAHHHH-HHHHHHHHHHH . . .*

Tom lurched from the mental anguish, almost dropping the weapon.

Josiah was sympathetic. "Tom, son, I know how hard this is. But we need to know you would do anything for club and country. Especially since I've got big plans for you. You can do it, son, I know you can."

Chang still screamed. *AAAAAAAAAAHHHHHHHHHHH-HAAAAAAAAAAAAAHHHHH . . .*

Tom tried to concentrate: Chang was just another traitor, a necessary sacrifice to his enemies' destruction. Pull the damn trigger . . .

It was a lesson that it paid to forget, because he couldn't turn off his own processor. The fear he'd remember this scene gripped his gut, twisting his bowel in knots. Holding the gun toward the floor, his left hand fumbled the bloody shirt, unable to locate Chang's heart.

But he had to destroy Chang's processor, because now recordings of Peter Bernhardt *and* Thomas Paine were on it.

"I can't find the spot." He reached his left hand out. "Carter, I need your help."

The blond man blanched, but stood next to Tom and placed his left hand on Tom's right wrist, guiding the barrel to press hard against Chang's breastbone. They were close enough to see blood surge through Chang's strung-out neck veins as he hyperventilated in terror.

Tom hyperventilated, too. He had to pull the damn trigger . . . Their hands wavered under the victim's heaving chest.

"Hold it steady," urged Carter.

Carter's fingers slipped around Tom's, two hands making one double-handed pistol grip. Physical contact amplified Carter's conflicted feelings. He wanted to be here. And not. He wanted Tom to succeed in this. And not. Tom was sure Carter shared some of his own déjà vu, unable to forget the last moments he had spent with Peter Bernhardt. But did he feel as sick as Tom did at this moment?

Unable to look at Chang, Carter watched Tom. "Ready?"

"On three," replied Tom. "One . . ."

Chang rhythmically shoved his breastbone against the barrel to dislodge it. It was harder to hold it steady. *No! No, Peter!*

"Two . . ."

Chang pressed down with his feet onto the floor, bouncing the front two legs of the chair off the floor. *Please, Peter, noooooo!*

"Jesus . . ." muttered Carter.

The chair bashed against Tom's legs, tipping back . . .

"Three . . ."

Tom leaned in with the gun, tipping the chair farther back, aligning for the kill . . .

Noooooooooooooooooooooo, Peeeeeeeeteeeeeeerrrrr!

. . . and together, the men squeezed, the large gun kicking as they pulled the trigger. Chang's chest fell away, the bullet flying in a direct line to his head.

Noooooooooooooooooooo . . .

Chang's skull burst, and the chair toppled onto the concrete floor.

Bull's-eye.

But the connection wasn't dead. Not yet. There was a spasm of electrochemical activity, a churning of neuronal waves, images Tom fought to resist, and didn't understand.

Then the room went dark. Sound was sucked into the void. Agony transcended to oblivion. The gun floated to the floor. Tom staggered and Carter caught him.

Fighting to keep his eyes open and not black out in a dead faint, Tom could see the tiny hole on Chang's forehead gave lie to the viscous eruption of gore in the back. Blood pooled and flowed in rivulets to a floor drain. His recurring dreams of red and blood the night after Chang's first death rushed back. The fake blood's color and liquidity was more movie blood than what a bioengineer would have witnessed in the OR. His implants tried to alert him to the lie the rest of his brain accepted without question.

"Oh, shit," muttered Carter, bowing his head to cover a tremor of fear, his hands holding up Tom's sagging body several adrenalized heartbeats longer than necessary.

Noticing this, Josiah's bushy eyebrows raised slightly. Carter lowered Tom to sit on the floor and retreated to the wall.

"What happened?" gasped Tom.

"You killed him, son. But in the wrong place. It's unfortunate. I do hope we haven't lost all that information."

"Fucking retard!" erupted Bruce, rushing to examine the bloody pulp. "Can't you do anything right?"

"Bruce . . ." warned Josiah.

"Guess we know who the next Praetor Maximus is . . ." Bruce snarked to Carter.

"Enough!" barked Josiah.

Lobo glared, annoyed at Josiah's outburst, as he poked at Chang's skull with his sneaker toe to look in the back, never flinching at the bits of brain. "It'll take a few days to figure out what's lost." He bent down and raised the skull by Chang's hair to look more closely. "I'd say a week to piece it together."

"I'm so sorry . . . I really am," said Tom as he groped the floor for his Hoover cane. "But I warned you, I wasn't the type to give a gun to anytime soon."

"I know, I know. We'll get it all sorted . . ." Josiah reached down to take Tom's arm and helped him stand. "Regardless, I want to thank you, Tom, for risin' to the occasion and protectin' your country from those who would harm her. I knew you'd be the kind of man I'd be honored to call my brother, son." He took Tom's trembling hand and shook it.

"Thank you, Josiah," said Tom.

"I do believe it's time to continue the tour." Josiah placed Tom's hand on his elbow to be led. Josiah didn't give Chang Eng a backward glance. Carter and Bruce dutifully followed.

Captured in Tom's Hippo 2.0 were the final minutes of Chang Eng's interior life. It would transfer that data, to be saved forever in his Cortex 3.0. He had never excised data before, but he was desperate to figure out how to do it now.

CHAPTER SIXTY-FOUR

The four men took the elevator down to the ninth floor. The doors opened on a similar, bare-bones corridor, which they followed for fifty feet.

"What I wish you could see, Tom, is an extraordinary nano-manufacturin' facility built by Carter and Bruce. Right after the attacks, we successfully reprogrammed nanomanufacturin' for a specific mass use, as well as explorin' protective technologies against potential terrorist groups. We got floors of nanofabricatin' machines churnin' out our own little nanobots."

Josiah didn't exaggerate. They walked past a dozen labs and factory floors behind clean-room glass, each holding dozens of nanofabricators. Since nanovirus and nanorobotic work was illegal in almost every country on earth, they had collected all that hardware and put it to work.

"For what?" asked Tom.

Josiah sighed, looking all of his seventy years. "You know, Tom, it's hard out there for a leader. You said it yourself: The uneducated masses aren't fit to direct their leaders. And the public doesn't like our messages anymore. I guess if we're honest with ourselves, they can only stomach so much media-cooked fear with generous helpin's of mind-numbin' bread and reality-show circuses before they get sick. That combination was enough to control 'em over the last century, but it isn't enough anymore to create the consensus politics we need to move in the direction we must go in the future. We tried surveillance, watchin' over them from the top of society to find the troublemakers, but the people countered with sousveillance. That's them watchin' us from the bottom. And let's face it: Transparency's a bitch! Societal consent has got to be created in more permanent ways to get us out of this annoyin' loop of snoop or be snooped. Let's, for a moment, call it 'compassionate coercion.'"

Compassionate coercion . . . Chang had said, *Hunter/Seeker virus. Permanently bond with serotonin neurotransmitters and receptors.* That meant the bot would pair and bind permanently, like a key in a lock, with specific proteins in the brain to increase the uptake of serotonin. Like a one-time-only, permanent dose of selective serotonin reuptake inhibitors—antidepressants. The neural location and the proteins involved with decision making and contentment were well known. If you bound the bots to neurotransmitters that fuel discontent or dissent, the victim would be complacent. Forever.

"And there's a bigger problem on the horizon: the democratization of everythin'," continued Josiah. "What people don't get is if everythin's judged by individuals, social media takes over from traditional media, and the public decides what's important, what has value. Not us. That's never happened in the whole of human history. The people at the top have always told the rest of the tribe what to think. It's how we've survived as a species.

"But even more important is what happens when you add these mighty clever nanofabricators, here. If they can snap together bots with their little atomic buildin' blocks, what's to say they can't make other stuff? Your clothes, food, shelter. Make a big enough machine, add the right chemicals, and it can make . . . anythin'.

Even another machine. And what if everybody has one 'a their own? Supply and demand disappears. If markets don't exist, what happens to corporations? Currency? Energy? The world's economy crashes. That's anarchy, Tom. Soon, we won't have control over anybody or anythin' and our entire economic system is based on that. Make somethin', tell 'em it's important, then sell it to 'em. Keeps factories workin', people in jobs, schools full, money flowin'. What do you do when all that could come to a screechin' halt?"

"Make sure they can't do it in the first place," said Tom.

"Exactly. We were given a golden opportunity to gather all the machines, so we did. And now we're puttin' 'em to good use creatin' our compassionate coercion. Just think. No more conflicts. No more wars . . . never thought I'd live to see the day."

"And when will this happen?" asked Tom.

"Soon," said Josiah vaguely.

Chang had said July 28. In four days. And in water, which meant the water supply. They would release nanobots in the country's water supply to brainwash the populace.

"And how do you all fit in?"

"Prometheus oversaw the R and D," said Josiah, "Lobo Industries will oversee the implementation, and I will oversee the information content, and help with any implementation problems that might arise."

"There won't be any," said Bruce, scowling.

"And what about the rest of the world? They're not exactly complacent," Tom said.

Josiah smiled. "All in good time, son."

Of course, Tom understood it meant a political administration that could do anything it wanted: pass bad laws, elect crooked legislators, appoint cronies, start wars, become a totalitarian state, enslave its people, all in the name of protecting the nation. With no backlash.

And if they released it overseas . . .

In rooms all around him was the transition from one method of control to another. From *1984* to *Brave New World*, replacing Orwell's fear and propaganda with Huxley's engineered complacency. He had always found Huxley's vision far more terrifying and realistic than Orwell's. At least in *1984*, people realized they were slaves to the government. In *Brave New World*, they were too stoned on contentment to care. It was the ultimate weapon of mass distraction.

"How is the club protecting its members?"

Carter replied, "Attendance this year was mandatory. Our food and water was already laced with protective, permanent bots that render these useless. The others get flushed from our systems. Don't worry. You're fine."

"Gentlemen? What can I say?" said Tom. "It's brilliant. The world will be grateful they have you to take care of them. But why am I here?"

Josiah smiled and took hold of both Tom's hands. "Because, son, you're goin' to be the president of the United States."

Tom hadn't expected that. "But I've never even held political office!"

"Don't worry. I've worked with several presidents in my many years on God's green earth and while the more ignorant or malleable have been well suited as Figurehead of the Western World, that just won't cut it in this game. Politics has always been zero-sum, but now it's for keeps. Whoever wins now wins forever. But my stumblin' block with this entire scenario was who to put in the driver's seat. Every potential candidate was either needed elsewhere in my plan or temperamentally unsuitable." He eyed Carter and Lobo knowingly, acknowledging Carter's indiscretions and Lobo's vicious demeanor were obvious to all. "I was only missing one thing: an heir. I was afraid I'd never find someone with all the qualities I needed. I'm no youngster, and I need an equal participant with the charisma to lead, hold his own, and cover our backs when I'm gone. I'm done with mouthpieces. Every man wants to leave behind a legacy. And you will be part of mine."

Beyond the stunned looks, cogs in Carter's head were visibly turning to twist his new partner to his advantage.

Lobo's face reddened, puffed with barely contained rage. "Are you fucking nuts, Josiah?"

Josiah regarded Lobo like an insect. It was the same pitiless stare he had given Chang. "Bruce, you are not indispensable."

What would a mere mortal do when offered the kingdoms of the world by the devil himself? Part of Tom reeled even as he knew he'd never be commander in chief. The world would change course in a few days.

"But I have no experience!" he said.

"You're a brilliant and perceptive manager who sees the big picture and excites the population. That's all you need. I'll be there to teach you. And how long, Carter? Two years for your new implants to give him sight back?"

"If we focus on it, two years at most," Carter replied.

"Just in time to take office. And we've done all kinds of pollin' over the years and even without the bots' . . . encouragement . . . Americans want a straight, white, Christian male, 'specially someone as photogenic, articulate, and glamorous as you, if you tell them what they want to hear. Your Russian problems were hard enough for us to find. We'll make sure they disappear. You're such a blank slate historically, we can make you anything we want. You had the right instincts before when you referenced a Roosevelt, but we'd position you as a combination of the two Roosevelts: above corruption, protective of your constituents, with enough smarts, life experience, diplomacy, and backbone to defend them from the rest of the big bad world out there and who's overcome his disability to the extent that it's meanin'less. Demonstrates character. Your disability is a metaphor for the psychic disability our nation must overcome, and you'll lead the way. Of course, the bots will make sure of it."

"You really think I'm the one?"

"I do, son."

"Then . . . I'm your man. It'd be an honor, sir."

In deeper than he ever thought he'd get, Tom wasn't sure he'd be able to get out.

CHAPTER SIXTY-FIVE

They emerged topside in time to hear a bugle sound. Camp Week was over. A stretch limo sat at the mine entrance, and Josiah gave the chauffeur a look. The driver nodded back.

"Time to go, son. Hope you don't mind, but I took the liberty of having the valets pack up our things. I'll drop you at the airport."

"I'm flying with Carter."

"I know. We're all set."

Tom felt impotent as their car joined a caravan of limos, town cars, and SUVs on their way to the airstrip. Everything regarding the club and Thomas Paine had gone far too smoothly, as though they had dumped him onto a conveyer belt headed for a cremation furnace. A phalanx of Humvees ripped past toward the airfield.

"I noticed you invested a heap in aerospace, defense contractors," said Josiah.

"Yes, sir."

"Smart man. We love our war economy. Gives the country a big economic and emotional hard-on. Guaranteed profits. But if our plan comes to pass, take out that trash, boy, and dump it. They're obsolete."

Tom couldn't suppress a smile at the irony. To end war, they would drug the world.

"I'm so happy you've accepted the call, so very happy. It's a mighty big relief. I've watched a real degeneration of high-level political candidates over the years. They get dumber, more plastic and vacant every decade. I haven't felt I had anyone I could pass the leadership on to in years." He leaned in to whisper, "Really, I know it sounds like a senile old man talkin', but I consider you like my son. Well, who knows . . . you don't have a pappy anymore. Sounds like we got the makin's of a fair trade. Can your new pappy give you some advice?"

"Absolutely."

"Marry Talia."

Tom laughed nervously. "Why? Are you my father concerned about my personal happiness? Or is it the Bible Belt?"

"Of course I want you to be happy! And unmarried, she's a cultural detriment, even in a country stoned on bots. But married, she can't be forced to testify against you, should we all ride to hell together. Gotta cover every base, son."

"I hope she'll have me. She doesn't think she's the marrying kind."

With a very straight face, Josiah intoned, "Wait a couple of weeks and make sure she drinks plenty of tap water. She'll be more amenable . . ." Then he burst out with a belly-deep guffaw. "Seriously, son, you're a very confident man, but you gotta watch out for cracks in the sidewalk. Even if you can't see 'em."

"Any others?"

"Well, I know you're makin' deals this week. Keep a handle on your partner. He's a brilliant operative and valuable in your corner, but has a tendency to dissipation and moral ambiguity."

"You're saying he's what? A gay drunk?"

"No. I'm sayin' he sits on every side of a fence, 'cause he don't know where his house is. With Carter, you gotta make sure he remembers *mi casa es su casa*. Speakin' of '*su casa*' . . . Lobo . . . watch your back."

Tom hesitated. "There might already be an issue . . ."

"What?"

"It seems like he's got a game on the side. And he tried to suck me in."

"Go on . . ." ordered Josiah, no longer jovial.

"Like you've checked me out, well . . . I've checked you all out. And he's had a series of deals that seem . . . suspicious. I'm not so naive as to think there's no insider trading here, and I don't care if there is, but this is strange. Like he knows what's going to happen and capitalizes on it to the detriment of his brothers. I think he's got a scam going, and he's putting his self-interest over that of the club."

Josiah's face set like stone. "Consider it checked."

"To change the subject, if your plan comes to pass and I get elected, what position would you take in the new administration?"

Josiah relaxed. "I don't want somethin' with too much responsibility. Secretary of state's exhaustin'. It's a younger person's job. How about VP? I'd look like the old man of the mountain sittin' behind you durin' the State of the Union address."

Both men laughed.

"Actually, deputy chief of staff would be perfect. Don't have the pressures of a real day job, but I'm officially on the inside. And I'm there when you need me."

"How can you be so sure about outcomes even with the bots? Wouldn't complacent consent depend on the loudest and most consistent voice getting through? How can you be absolutely sure you're that voice?"

"You still don't get it, son. I've been a student of human nature all my life, and as the tools that expose our minds become more sophisticated, my job becomes easier. We already have technologies that change how we view and manipulate popular opinion. In the old days, they were called 'The Media,' but then we used brain scans to see what parts of the brain react to different kinds of information, and we tailored a message directly to the part of your brain you can't resist. And now, we have the most powerful technology ever created available for our exclusive use, and you're investin' in it—Prometheus's Cortex 2.0. Someday we can upload and download memories. And what do we base all our decisions on except memories? They guide us to make the choices we do. People'll think they had experiences they may not have, but those 'experiences' will color their decision makin'."

"Clever to control the means to keep you in office. Like if you invested in vote-counting machines."

"Been there, done that." Josiah smiled contentedly, like a happy, plump Buddha as the car pulled into the airport. "But I'm not the right wing or the left wing. I'm the whole damn eagle. So I always win."

CHAPTER SIXTY-SIX

Cars and vans lined up, directed by staff to the gaggle of Gulfstreams littering the tarmac, ready to ferry owners around the country. Switching his internal vision to a satellite view, Tom monitored which members entered which planes and linked their destinations to his databanks.

As they drove by Bruce's G750, Josiah lowered his window, his smiles and goodwill at complete odds to the conversation moments before. Lobo offered Tom a lift back to Malibu in his jet with Vera, but Tom explained that Carter was waiting for him.

A different Potsdam jet held pride of place in the center of the tarmac: a revamped Boeing Super 27, it was a supercharged 727 small enough to land and take off from shorter, private runways like this, but big enough to sleep ten in comfort, with large fuel tanks to fly anywhere in the world quickly. It was his family minivan, more suitable for his growing household than his old G750. He waited at the bottom of the stairs for Tom and helped him from the car.

As they hit the first stair, Amanda appeared in the doorway. She wore a plain white linen shift that skimmed her thickened body, and she was barefoot. Her short blond hair was growing out, black roots showing. She watched the two men climb the stairs. Tom concentrated on Carter until she revealed herself.

The jet's interior was a study in sybaritic sophistication. Rich leathers, fur throws, soft silk carpeting for bare feet, fresh, aromatic flowers in crystal vases. In flight, the engines' noise was so well baffled, the only sound was air speeding by the window at six hundred miles an hour. The cabins were arranged like a luxury penthouse with wings, including two lounges, a dining room, full kitchen, three bedrooms, and crew quarters. Full-wall HOME units entertained in every room. Who needed earthbound accommodations with mobile ones like this?

Tom was extremely polite to Amanda, but directed his attention to Carter and their business during the short hop back to San Francisco. Due diligence had begun while they were still at camp, with accountants and attorneys from both sides to converge at Prometheus the next day to dot i's and cross t's. Contract drafts sat on a table, and Carter and Tom concentrated on debated provisions, while sending amendments back to their lawyers via their GOs. Amanda took the hint and curled up at the other end of the lounge, long, bare copper legs tucked under her, snuggling into a fur throw and pretending to read an e-book on her GO. Tom could feel her involuntarily staring at the back of his head.

After takeoff, he asked a pretty flight attendant to escort him to the bathroom. Alone inside, he ripped a plastic bag off a disposable razor and tossed the razor in the trash. Then he urinated, splashing a small amount of urine onto some toilet paper and wadded up the wet paper inside the plastic bag. He pocketed the plastic-covered clump and returned to his seat. After the men finished notations on the documents, Carter slid them into the file envelope they came in. Suddenly, Tom spilled his drink, and while Carter mopped his pants and the flight attendant cleaned the floor, he slipped the tiny cellophane bag between the pages and into the envelope. Amanda appeared not to notice.

"Would you do me a favor and fast-courier the papers to the boat tonight?" Tom asked. "The lawyers have their notes, but I'd like to keep track of our original ones, and Talia's helping me process all this information, if that's okay."

"Of course. We can turn the plane around as soon as we land." Carter asked the attendant to courier the envelope back to the *Pequod* personally.

Twenty minutes after takeoff, the S27 landed at NASA's Moffett Field.

It was Tom's first time back in San Francisco since emerging on the world's scene several months before. As they drove city streets, he felt sympathy with the thick grid of electrical lines crisscrossed over roads to power streetcars and buses, lights and communication. He was a single neuron in the hyperconnected network brain of this world, in one of the few cities left where the network was so visible.

The limo pulled up to a large brick Tudor revival sprawled across two lots on the corner of Broadway and Broderick, two blocks from the Presidio, and only five blocks from Carter's former Pacific Heights home. Broderick was a pedestrian walkway along the property's eastern boundary, so the home's three sides were open to space, light, and views, all of which were at a premium in this city. The moment the car stopped, a man and a woman, both in their fifties, exited the baronial oak front door. Their functional, neat clothing and attitude of cheerful deference indicated they were staff. Introducing themselves as Rosinda and Tony, they disappeared with the luggage. Amanda slipped by, claiming a headache, and wandered inside.

Carter guided Tom. "Welcome to Xanadu. Sorry if you still smell paint. Amanda insisted my bachelor pad was a baby death trap. Gotta love nesting," he sighed. "But we keep 'em happy any way we can, don't we?"

The interior was brighter than Tom expected. Dozens of lead-paned windows flooded high-ceilinged rooms with light. Huge glass doors opened north onto a flagstone veranda overlooking the Golden Gate, giving the illusion of having San Francisco Bay all to themselves.

Carter continued, "The executive summary is: It's not too big and not too small and I'm sure you'll be comfortable. We're in the hallway, walking into the living room . . . It's already baby-proofed, so don't worry, you can't hurt anything, either, even with your cane. Rosinda and Tony run this house like a nanofabricator, so anything you want, just ask and it appears . . . This is the dining room . . ."

The furnishings were museum quality. With the exception of some enormous, overstuffed sofas and armchairs that sloppy, twenty-first century bodies could slack across, there were no pieces less than two hundred years old.

It was a radical change from the previous Potsdam temple to hard-edged modernity, as though genealogy suddenly mattered. Carter's child would inherit the family name and heritage of over twenty generations of American history. But what might have been a stuffy historical hodgepodge was instead fresh, irreverent, and consummately stylish, and it had to be Carter's doing.

He recognized pieces from Carter's parents' house. As though he could read Tom's mind, Carter grinned slyly. "My parents are so ecstatic I'm finally becoming a father with a proper home, they shipped half their furnishings to me. Unfortunately, my dear sister thought she'd be inheriting the ancestral pile, lock, stock and termite-ridden barrel. She's spinning."

Dinner was agony. While the food Rosinda prepared and Tony served was delicious, the hosts' behavior was excruciating. Carter doted on Amanda, massaging her shoulders after he held her chair, kissing her forehead, asking her if she was all right every ten minutes. Amanda was subdued, even as she basked in Carter's attention.

However, she avoided acknowledging her blind guest. Every time his head swiveled in her direction to listen, an electric current seemed to flow through her, and she'd look away.

Her mood did not improve when Carter mentioned he would be traveling after he finished the deal with Tom.

"Where are you going?" she whined.

"New York. Then DC. Might be a few days. Maybe a week. It'll be very dull for you—all work. You'd be better off here."

After dinner, Amanda excused herself and disappeared upstairs. Carter escorted Tom to the library, where the two sat enveloped by a pair of enormous upholstered wing chairs, a Baccarat decanter of Louis XIII Black Pearl cognac and two snifters between them on a Philadelphia Chippendale piecrust tea table worth as much as the neighbor's house.

They drank half the decanter's contents and got quite chummy before Tom said, "I feel we have a certain rapport and . . . I trust you to tell me the truth."

Carter's eyes widened slightly and he leaned forward. "Anything . . ."

"What do you think of Josiah's plans?"

That wasn't the question Carter hoped for. His glass was almost empty and he took his time refilling it before answering. "I think he's optimistic. While the outcomes are possible, there's no experimental data to prove it will happen the way he thinks. This is the ultimate behavioral science experiment, and he's not anticipating unintended consequences."

"What consequences?"

"Like what happens when you emotionally neuter a person? Or a nation? Are we dead weight? Sitting ducks? Does the population go up? Or down? Does productivity go up? Or down? And I think anyone he makes captain of this ship . . . better be very careful."

"Did you expect Josiah to offer me the presidency?"

"Well, there's definitely been a lack of viable candidate material lately. And he certainly doesn't think I'm up for it." Carter snorted. "Not that I blame him. But I was surprised today. He has . . . unusually strong feelings for you."

"I've noticed. But you think anyone who takes that position is fooling themselves?"

"I didn't say that. But you're going to need help, or you could end up taking the rap for the biggest crime against humanity since Mao Zedong's purges."

"Whom would you suggest?"

"Well, certainly not Lobo."

"No, certainly not. But I'd value your help, Carter. With Lobo. And the plan. And the presidency."

Carter eyed him warily. "I could do that."

"So if you have doubts and fears, why are you involved in this?"

"Being on the inside is always better. More likely you'll end up on top and the side you need to be on when it all hits the fan."

"You can be on top and the wrong side?"

"Have you met Bruce Lobo?" snickered Carter. "He's going to screw himself royally one day . . ."

Tom wondered how much Carter knew about Bruce's scam.

"You asked me this week what I was proud of," continued Carter. "Well, I know this: I want my child to be proud of me. The only way to do that is to make sure mistakes aren't made that we can't undo."

Tom had to repress his disgust at the notion of Carter and Amanda's child, growing in her belly upstairs. "Is that where Prometheus and its biotech comes in? So you can have your social experiment and correct it, too?"

Carter smiled at Tom's quick mind. "If necessary, yes. That's why it's so valuable. And why I need more than just me at the top of it. If anything happens to me . . ." He stared moodily into his snifter. "I want you to know I value our friendship. I haven't been able to talk to anyone like this in a long time. I had a friend . . . but he died . . ." He sighed and his eyes unconsciously darted up to where Amanda was—the master bedroom. But was it because he sought her out or was hiding something from her?

"Is something wrong?" asked Tom.

"No. Josiah's brought you in deep. And it's good to have you here. It gets lonely at the top." Carter stared long at Tom, perturbed that so much couldn't be conveyed to a blind man through the silent eloquence of body language.

Carter's last statement had multiple meanings. Had he made the Peter-Tom connection? Or was he falling for Tom's head game? He believed Carter at this moment. Or at least felt sure Carter believed himself. It was hard to decipher a pathological liar. These guys believed their own bullshit.

"Thank you for your honesty. It helps me see my way clear, if you'll pardon the expression." Tom stifled a yawn. "You know, I think I've hit the wall. Would you help me upstairs?"

Carter hid his disappointment. "Of course."

They climbed the grand staircase, Carter's left hand firmly on Tom's right elbow. They passed the master bedroom door, and Carter glared at it, as though he tried to see through the polished mahogany. Fifteen feet away and outside Tom's door, Carter paused, wrestling with some great dilemma.

Tom smiled. "So what are you waiting for?" he whispered.

Carter faced him. He gently touched Tom's face, searching it for an answer. "I don't know . . ." he murmured back. He grasped Tom's bicep and pulled him close. Then his lips met Tom's.

Tom kissed him back, as every cell in his body yearned to disembowel Carter. His kingdom for a shiv.

The master bedroom door creaked slightly as it opened. Carter pulled away, but not quickly enough.

Amanda poked her head out. "I thought I heard you . . ." She paused at the sight of the two men standing too close. Stricken, she lowered her eyes and slipped back into the room, shutting the door.

"Shit . . ." muttered Carter.

"We both have a lot to lose in this scenario," said Tom gently. "Good night."

In his darkened guest suite, Tom appeared to sleep in an enormous eighteenth-century four-poster bed. Since he had left camp, Miss Gray Hat had hacked for inside information on 10/26 through known ATEAMO and Phoenix Club members' e-mail accounts, financial records, and computer histories. She transmitted it now to Tom—travel plans, communications history, corporate involvements and business transactions—confirming the secret leader of the ATEAMO cells was Bruce Lobo.

After reviewing her data on his mind-screen, he mentally cracked into the Potsdam home-surveillance system. Its security layers were not as deep as he expected. From their video feed, he observed all the occupants in the house from hidden cameras in their bedrooms. Rosinda and Tony slept in their quarters on the third floor. But the huge master bedroom contained only Amanda, tossing and turning, unable to sleep. Carter slept in another bedroom down the hall. He wondered how often the couple slept apart and was pleased he had sown distrust between the two.

When he cycled back to the master bedroom camera, Amanda was sitting up in bed, HOME remote in hand. The room's only light came from the security camera feed on her bedroom screen. He watched her as she watched him, apparently asleep in his bed. Was she wondering about her husband's new friend and partner?

Her worried expression filled his mental screen for eighteen minutes before she turned over and closed her eyes. However, she kept her monitor on, his virtual image sleeping in the room with her.

She unbalanced him. If he didn't deal with her soon, he'd make a fatal mistake.

CHAPTER SIXTY-SEVEN

Amanda snuck out of the house before sunrise for a gentle jog down Broadway west into the Presidio. Tom dressed quickly to follow, with his own excuse of an early morning stroll and armed with his GO-B's GPS, audio-earbud in his right ear and Hoover cane, allowing him independence and an ability to find his way home unsighted. Having RFIDed her the night before, he followed her GPS mark on his mental map.

She took the Presidio woods trail as Tom closed in behind her. Alone and hidden by the trees, Tom folded and pocketed his cane, then broke into a run-off trail through the underbrush to intercept her. He scooped up a broken branch with a thick, sharp, jagged point. Holding it tight, he hid behind a tree, watching her virtual blip come closer to his location . . . closer . . . closer . . .

Lightning quick, he made an upward jab into her solar plexus. She doubled over, gasping for breath, as he threw her over his shoulder and carried her into the trees while holding the sharp stick to her temple.

"Be quiet or you're dead," he hissed.

There was a hillside depression where no one could see them from a path or road. He slid down the incline and nestled her in a

V between two large boulders and knelt in front to block her escape. She was still recovering from the hit. He had to make a final decision quickly. San Francisco was waking up.

Gasping for breath, her eyes scoured his face for something, anything she could understand. "I knew you'd follow me . . ." she whispered.

His voice sounded reasoned, but it took extreme control to stop trembling. "Listen carefully. I can replace security footage with anything I want. No one will know we've been here. When they find your body, they'll assume some transient psycho killed you. And if I don't kill you now, I can kill you at any time, even if you turn me in. I'm not alone in this, and you'll never see it coming. Do you understand me?"

She nodded her head furiously.

"Why are you watching me?" he demanded. In his rage, he shook her shoulders harder than he meant, and her head thudded on a boulder. She yelped in pain.

"Please, Peter . . ." She tried not to cry. "You've hurt me every way you could . . . and I probably deserve it . . . but don't hurt the baby."

The leaves on the branches overhead ceased their rustling to wave slowly through the air. He watched two ants in a titanic struggle over a piece of dead beetle on the boulder's face.

An eon later, she continued, "Yes, I know who you are."

"When?"

"When I said good-bye in LA. But I don't know how. Or why . . ." Her eyes became watery. "How can I be afraid of the man I'm afraid for every day? And I don't know why!"

"Afraid for me? You did this to me!"

"*What?*" Months of fury burst to the surface. "*You* did this to *me*! You left me! I thought you died! And now you're . . ." she looked at him in confusion. "I don't even recognize you! Why did you leave

me? I thought you loved me! And what are you doing to Carter?"
Tears cascaded down her cheeks. "I did everything you said. I took
the cash and ran . . . I hid . . . I cut my hair, bought old clothes,
lived in a motel outside Bend . . . but you never came to find me.
Then they said you were a terrorist!"

"You know it's a lie."

"I thought so. But you hear it so often, you think, 'Maybe I'm
the one who's crazy . . . '"

"So your only recourse was to fuck Carter?"

"I waited for months for you, but the money ran low. And I
didn't know what to do. So I turned up at his house one night . . .
He took me in. Promised to protect me from them . . . whoever
'them' is; I still don't know, he won't tell me. I don't know what to
believe anymore; everything's turned around. You can't blame me
for thinking you were dead. The whole world thinks you're dead."

"They also think I'm a terrorist."

Her face betrayed doubt.

"Mandy, we were together since we were nineteen years old.
We worked with each other every day for ten years. You would have
known."

"But Carter thought . . ."

"No! He wants . . ." But he stopped. He wasn't ready to destroy
everything with the truth. "He wants you . . . He wanted you to
love him. And maybe he thought tarnishing your memory of me
would help."

Amanda squinted in disbelief. Who needed a polygraph or
increased cybernetic intelligence to tell the truth from a lie? An ex-
wife would do just as nicely. "And what do you think you're doing
with him?" she spat.

The words tumbled out before he could stop them: "Do you
even sleep with him?"

"Yes!"

"I mean, you have sex?"

"Yes! We do!" She choked on sobs. "We love each other . . ."

"The guy wants to fuck me! How can he love you . . . like that?"

"How can you love . . . a woman like Talia?"

"Talia?"

"She looks like . . . a bimbo. A plaything . . ."

"I thought *you* were dead! We looked for you everywhere I could think of. And then, when I found you living with Carter, I assumed you . . . you wanted me dead." It sounded ridiculous when he said it aloud. He tried to get back to the subject at hand. "And Talia's not a lesbian!"

"Carter's bisexual. There's been an attraction since freshman year."

His right palm slammed the boulder an inch from her head, killing the two ants. Conflict averted.

Shocked by the violence, she choked back tears again. "It's the truth. We were destroyed when you died. We had no one but each other. We're together because we loved you, Peter. It was always about you."

"Carter wasn't destroyed . . ." he snapped between gritted teeth.

"Yes he was! You weren't there. You don't know . . ."

"Mandy, I know things about him . . ."

"STOP IT! JUST STOP IT!" she screamed in jagged, ugly sobs, clamping her hands to her ears.

He stopped. She'd have time and reason to cry over Carter soon enough. They didn't speak for a minute while she hiccupped, trying to stuff her grief inside.

Gently, she took his grazed hand, bleeding from slugging the rock, and kissed the wound. Then she placed it on her belly. The fetus was still tiny and yet a mental roundhouse kicked Tom. He was lucky to be on his knees or it would have knocked him over. Barely breathing, he covered his face with both hands and rocked back and forth in the dead leaves and brittle pine needles.

"It's mine?" he choked out.

Shocked, she nodded her head and whispered, "I used your sperm, left over from our last IVF. Carter doesn't know. I'm naming him Peter."

She was innocent. And having his son. Peter.

He had almost done something too horrible to contemplate. "Peter? Dear God, what am I doing here?"

An urgent internal message arrived from Talia. She had only succeeded in stopping three out of four couriers that left from the camp as directed by Bruce, and there may have been others unidentified. Bruce was suspicious and had created multiple decoys. Therefore, they had to assume at least one of the couriers had made it to the DNA lab.

The odds had spoken. Peter Bernhardt was revealed. And Bruce would decide who would know.

He staggered to his feet and lifted Amanda to stand with him. "You have to go home. Now. None of this happened."

"Where are you going?"

"Just remember this: I'm doing the best thing for everyone. Anytime you don't understand, remember that."

Then he ran, calling a taxi to meet him at the corner of California and Lyon and take him to North Field, where Talia had a jet waiting. He sent apologies to Carter—an emergency had come up, and he had to return to LA immediately. He requested that the Prometheus meetings proceed without him. He'd attend them virtually.

Carter was the least of his problems right now.

CHAPTER SIXTY-EIGHT

Thirty thousand feet above the California coast, plugged into flowing data, Tom had an hour to consider scenarios, with no interruptions. All of them necessitated dealing with Bruce immediately, as opposed to later, when enemies might gain the upper hand. But his other mind-track obsessed about his encounter with Amanda and the unborn Peter. He had almost killed them. How did he become so unhinged? Was he like those poor soldiers, too aware of the bigger picture to kill, too emotionally crippled by their memories not to? And could he focus on the task at hand with the knowledge of his son's existence?

Knowing he lacked objectivity didn't release Carter, Josiah, or Bruce from responsibility for 10/26, or their future plans. By grasping the big picture, it was impossible not to be staggered and enraged by the enormity of the club's plot against America and the world.

But at its core was a bewildering political dilemma that would only increase in complexity: If, as Josiah believed, the world was progressing faster than most humanity could comprehend, was democracy something that could still work if the populace didn't understand the changes and their ramifications? Was Josiah's opinion—that people were unable to grasp their problems or solutions—wrong? While

Josiah's solution was immoral, what alternative could Tom, or anyone, give that allowed progress to continue in everyone's hands and not leave social decisions to a ruling elite? To deny humanity the benefits of progress, improvement, and growth was immoral as well.

But did people want to make up their own minds? Or was the majority's secret desire to be ruled by a benevolent dictator, even though a dictator would never be benevolent? If he destroyed the club, at least one dictatorial force would be gone.

But he had more immediate problems than how to govern. If the Phoenix Club knew he was Peter Bernhardt, they could stop him easily. Every moment he lived was a moment they didn't know his identity. And he couldn't ask Talia, Ruth, or Steve to endanger themselves any longer. The only way to succeed was to transform into something the club could not anticipate—and eradicate 'Peter Bernhardt' for good.

He had to return to the *Pequod* as soon as possible to see just how far Ruth and Steve had gotten on their experimental nanobots. The three different injectable treatments would make him even more superhuman than he was now. And he had to have them—immediately. He would deal with the consequences afterward. If he survived.

He was in the backseat of his limo at Santa Monica Airport. A woman's fist knocked on his passenger window. It was decorated with two ice cube–sized pavé-diamond rings and holding a solid-gold-and-diamond-encrusted GO, known as a GOld and very popular in Moscow.

He told his chauffeur to lower his window, and Vera stuck her head in.

"Hello, Tom," she purred, an ironic smile on her glistening lips. "Bruce and I just returned from Silicon Valley, and he took the car to some silly meeting. I was calling for another, but now my white knight has arrived. Do you mind dropping me home?"

"My pleasure," replied Tom.

Vera climbed in, slinking along the seat close to Tom. As the car pulled away, Vera fingered the controls, closing the passenger-driver divider.

"How bug-proof is this car?" She spoke quickly in Russian, and it took all of Tom's dual concentration to translate via Internet, process the spotty aural translations, and reply back instantly in Russian, all while learning the language on the fly.

"Good enough for government work." It didn't sound as funny in Russian.

"Do not joke. Bruce knows you're Peter Bernhardt."

The name hung in the air. He quickly sent a message to Talia to tell Mr. Money and Dr. Who to disappear. The club would find out the money was missing and be looking for them.

"When?" Tom asked calmly.

"This morning. He analyzed the DNA sample last night."

"Has he told anyone other than you?"

Vera shook her head. "He's waiting to see what he can gain with it. You men and your stupid games. This is what got Tony killed."

"Dulles?"

"Yes."

"How did you know him?"

"After Tony left the CIA, he worked on the US aid to Russia scheme. It was really just money laundering with university economists and the World Bank. That's what created the Russian oligarchs—money the US gave Russia in the form of economic shock therapy, which Yeltsin handed to former apparatchiks to privatize state assets. The Kremlin supports the oligarchs and the oligarchs support the Kremlin. And the club supports them both through the back door. And since no sane person reinvests profits in Russia, they buy the occasional European football team to give them somewhere to go on the weekends and send the rest to China or the US to buy influence or invest in your companies. Club-controlled companies."

Tom never thought to look at the Russian angle to the club story, because it didn't seem relevant. But was he missing something? Was Vera his mole? "What game got Dulles killed?"

"He knew something he shouldn't and was trying to influence events. He wouldn't tell me, but he did try to leverage information in the Russian sphere for information in the other."

"Information?"

"Yes. He thought the Russians might be as unhappy with this turn of events as he. So he was going to give them information to do something about it. And I was to be the conduit. But he died before he could give it to me."

She appeared to be telling the truth, as far as she knew it. But what was Dulles giving the oligarchs? The nanotech? The bot plot? A way to stop it? Peter Bernhardt? "And how did you fit in his strategy?"

"The oligarchs think I work for them because I provide information about all of you. Tony felt confident I worked for him, because I did the same for him. And really, there was little conflict of interest—they both want the same things—to make sure their money is well spent and to make more. So proving useful to both has kept me alive and given me my cut. And Bruce . . ." She sighed. "What we have is his version of love. And as your nation's cultural hero says, 'He made me an offer I couldn't refuse.'"

"Was anyone else working with Tony on this?"

"That's like asking how many ride the Russian president's coattails. It is a large, fluid, and unknowable number."

"So if Dulles is dead, who's your American contact?"

"Justin Dardanelles. He supposedly passes the information to Secretary Brant, but I have no proof. Dardanelles's specialty is Russian mineral futures, so he might have his own game going directly with the oligarchs."

Dardanelles was the steroidal financier who had shared Peter's cabin at the first Camp Week.

"And what's Bruce's deal with you?"

"A piece of his action in his own scheme. More than I could ever make working for Russians and Americans."

"But what is it?"

Vera hesitated for the first time. She had not wanted to go there if she could help it.

"Why are we having this conversation?" he pressed.

"I need to get out. Of everything. And no one, including Bruce, will like it."

"I can't help if I don't know all you know."

She sat demurely for the first time, hands folded in her lap, and violet eyes downcast, making her look a decade younger. Sadly, the rare display of modesty suited her.

"I also siphon information to Bruce."

"What kind?"

"Whatever the johns say to me . . . and . . . leave behind."

Information left behind. Tom wasn't the only person from whom she had tried to harvest biological material. "DNA."

"Bruce bases business decisions not just on pillow talk, but on the health prospects of my customers. We have a full genetic analysis of hundreds of club members, as well as oligarchs."

"I assumed Bruce played the futures market with lives. What else?"

"I can infect them with genetically engineered viruses when necessary, for which I have been made immune . . . if, of course, it proves financially beneficial for us."

"You kill members with a sexually transmitted disease for money?"

"Not kill, necessarily . . . but incapacitate. Make them step down from boards, sell shares, withdraw from cartels and consortiums for their health . . . things like that."

"And Bruce gives you a percentage of his profits?"

She nodded.

His head shook in amazement. "And you think I have the ingenuity to help you?"

"I can't do it anymore. I just know something bad is going to happen."

"How?"

"Bruce is acting oddly, and it's not just about you. I'm not sure why. But I haven't survived this long to ignore warning signs from men."

"If he's identified me, how do you think I can help? Just riding with me might get you killed."

"He sent me here for information. He needs to believe I've done my job."

"What more could he want?"

"He can track you all he wants, but he needs to know your next move. He feels you damaged him in Brant's eyes. Never forget, everything leads to Brant. And Bruce has always been jealous of Carter Potsdam. He represents everything Bruce is not, and his close relationship with both versions of you makes him suspect, as if Carter's been on your side all along. Bruce wants a . . ." She struggled for the phrase, jabbing an imaginary opponent with both fists.

"A one-two punch," he suggested in English.

"Yes! One-two punch. But to destroy you both and curry favor is a complex move, especially without Brant killing the messenger. Bruce needs to be as fully armed as possible."

"He'd destroy Carter just out of jealousy?"

"He's done worse for less." The depth of pain in her eyes said she had witnessed it personally.

"So when will he make his move?"

"When he returns to camp in two days. He'll have you all there. At least, that's what I've recommended."

He smiled in admiration. "You play an open game."

"Chess *is* the Russian national pastime."

"Are you planning to disappear when we return to the camp?"

"Yes. I've contacted a powerful friend, who will hide me in Europe for as long as it takes." She gave a Slavic shrug of her thin shoulders. "To him, it will be like a honeymoon without marriage, so he is looking forward to it."

Outside, the air was unusually crystalline, and from Pacific Coast Highway, he could see across the sparkling ocean to Catalina Island and the Palos Verdes Peninsula. With the same clarity, he knew Vera wasn't Dulles's mole and could not stop 7-28.

"Tell Bruce we'll meet tomorrow. He's in danger, and he's fighting the wrong adversary. His real enemy is Brant, and a Phoenix Club takeover should be his goal. And I can help."

CHAPTER SIXTY-NINE

After dropping Vera at Lobo's house, the car continued to Malibu Pier, where Tom picked up his launch to the *Pequod*, anchored a half mile off shore.

As crew members helped him climb aboard, the *Pequod* seemed forlorn, as if Tom had stayed away too long. He noticed the longer he lived on her, the more personality he imbued into her, and he no longer wondered why sailors had called ships "she" for millennia.

His other mistress waited on deck, her curls whipped by westerlies that originated off the coast of Asia. Talia had never looked more beautiful. One part of him wanted her more than ever, and another knew the more he wanted her, the more painful the future would be.

He brushed past as though he were really blind. Confused, she followed him below deck. His most important near-term goal was not their mutual comfort or love, but to inject himself with the little nanobots Ruth and Steve had created.

Tom had less than two days to destroy three of the most powerful men in the country and stop their plan, while keeping himself,

Talia, Ruth, Steve, Amanda, his unborn son, and now Vera, alive. In fanciful moments, he wished he could just expose the entire plot for the world to see. But Talia told him, from her journalistic experience, the public didn't want to believe bad stories about their leaders, because they couldn't imagine doing the same heinous things themselves and didn't like knowing they were suckers for buying a sociopath's song and dance. And by the time the media fact-checked the story, it might be weeks and far too late.

There was no time for a sexy plan, so brute force would have to do: he, Talia, and a team of foreign-national mercenaries she assembled would surround and infiltrate the Sierra compound after the three ringleaders—Josiah, Carter, and Bruce—all arrived. Talia's platoon would wait in Oregon for a signal to leave their motels, campsites, and tourist attractions and head to the Phoenix Camp.

Ruth and Steve worked feverishly to prepare the nanovaccine for their team based on Tom's urine sample hidden in the Prometheus partnership agreement contract. Led by Tom, Talia's team would kill the ringleaders, immobilize their security team, and destroy the nanomaterials before they could be deployed. Everyone involved in the campaign would flee the country immediately after, including Amanda and his unborn son, whether she wanted to or not. None of them could return to the US again.

The only way Tom might survive the next several days was through radical personal change. In two other rooms, a dozen nanofabricators that eluded the Phoenix Club had manufactured tiny nanobots. These were collected in vials, prepared in a serum, and stored in atomically precise containers. Previously, they had tested samples on a handful of animals. All experimental data said Ruth's designs worked.

But he would be less "human" than ever before. If he survived the treatment.

As Talia opened the lab door for Tom, the loud clatter of metal trays echoed inside. His appearance in the doorway made Ruth's face quiver. She was not happy.

Like a rag doll in scrubs propped against the wall, Steve was floppy with sleep deprivation. "You're"—he searched for the word— *"meshugah."* He tried to smile, but even his face muscles were flaccid. "Ruth taught me that one."

"Regardless, I'm ready for the bots," he said. "And I need a chemical or bioweapon to use against the club as backup. In two days."

"You don't mean that," said Steve, his olive skin blanching a sickly puce.

"I need something to knock out everyone at the camp for good—just in case. You don't have to engineer it from scratch. Buy it off the shelf from an arms merchant. Talia can hook you up. Anything that breaks down quickly when released to air and is not patient-to-patient contagious will do."

"I . . . I can't do that." Staring vacantly like an Alzheimer's patient, Steve grabbed the intercom handset and dialed the bridge. "Hi. I need a copter to take me to . . . I don't know, anywhere on the . . . Okay, Sacramento . . . Thanks." He hung up.

"Don't leave," whispered Talia, as she gently touched his sleeve.

He squeezed her hand. "You almost convinced me you were on the side of the angels, and I shredded my Hippocratic Oath to get you here. His goal may be necessary, but you're going somewhere I can't follow." Steve got in Ruth's face, or as close as she'd let him. "You can't stay and do this, can you?"

"I-I d-d-d-d-don't kn-now," she stammered, backing away.

Tom said nothing.

"Look at him," said Steve to the women. "He knows he's gone too far, or he'd be plying me with arguments."

Talia crossed to the door. Steve asked hopefully, "You're coming with me?" But she didn't answer and disappeared into the bowels of the ship.

He shook his head at Tom. "I'd say you're a lucky man to have women adore you so much. But you're not lucky. I feel sorry for you."

Ruth's entire frame spasmed, and she leaned against the worktable to steady herself.

"I'm sorry, Ruth," Steve said, facing her, "I don't want him to make you do anything you don't want to. If you need help leaving, I'm there for you." He hefted a messenger bag over his shoulder. "I'd wish you good luck, Tom, but I'm not sure that what you want will bring you any." Steve looked around one last time, then trudged out of the room.

After ten seconds of silence, Tom soothed Ruth. "It's okay . . . We don't need him anymore."

"We do," muttered Ruth, her shoulders twitching up to her ears.

"Ruth . . . I need the bots."

"Such foolishness. You cannot make me watch. I'm no doctor. If it goes wrong . . ." She pointed at the refrigerator and fled the room.

Tom opened the fridge and rummaged around a tray of glass vials. Next to them was the antidote for each that would flush them from his system if necessary.

He quickly filled three syringes from three different vials. The red-tagged vial marked "Respirocytes" contained artificial red blood cells that held a thousand times more oxygen than a standard human red blood cell could. With these, he could swim underwater for an hour without a breath; walk through a burning building without dying of carbon monoxide poisoning; appear to die and yet, not.

The yellow vial, labeled "Microbivores," was his daydream's brainchild, when the Flaming Lips and moving clouds inspired tiny machines consuming foreign invaders like microscopic Pac-Men—artificial white blood cells. With these, he would never be affected by foreign bacteria, viruses, or pathogens. He would be immune to disease and in the best health of his life.

The final blue vial, labeled "Macrosensors," held tiny machines to send new and enhanced signals from his sensory organs to his brain and increase connectivity and speed between neurons within the brain. They could also interrupt the nerves' signal transmission, neutering pain at will. With these, his brain cells would also be hyperlinked. He hoped to make intellectual connections that he had not been smart enough to make before. He loaded a smaller dosage of these than the others, since he wasn't sure how powerful the effect would be.

Tom tourniqueted his left arm, alcohol-wiped the median cubital vein site in the crook of his elbow, and quickly plunged each of the three needles in turn.

After fifteen seconds, he stopped breathing. But he wasn't concerned. The respirocytes were working, and his brain had more-than-adequate oxygen. He felt crystal clear, cogent, if not a little giddy, as though hyperventilating. The medulla oblongata ceased signaling the lungs to inflate and radically slowed his heartbeat. It would pick up again when it registered a drop in oxygen. That might take a while, especially if he remained at rest.

The microbivores in the second vial had a delayed and subtle affect. Twelve hours later, he felt in the best health of his life. Energized, no aches or pains. Any pathogens his body fought were gone. And any he might encounter would be neutralized, because the microbivores knew to keep alive and whole only the organisms and chemicals his body needed, and were programmed to destroy everything else.

It took a minute for the macrosensors to come online. First Tom initialized contact. His processor sent out a general radio call to each of the hundreds of thousands of little bots to wake up and smell the frequency. Soon, macrosensors talked not only to each other, but to nanowire connections already in his head. They relayed signals while providing additional hookups between his senses, emotions, and therefore, his thinking.

On the worktable, the vials sat upright in their holder, meta-morphosizing into crystalline vessels shimmering in the fluorescent light. Inside, nanoscopic bots, that he shouldn't have been able to see with the naked eye, twinkled like diamonds.

A book beckoned on a small shelf, its paper cover gone. The cloth binding was a vivid, luminous vermilion, so luscious in its overwhelming redness, he felt compelled to reach out and hold it. It was Dutton's *Nautical Navigation*. Ruth must have been bored one night. At his touch, the smell and taste of Chinese chili sauce assaulted his senses. His tongue even tingled!

He slid off the stool and sank to the floor to consider the table's leg, admiring its cylindrical tubularity. He stroked the chrome, which shone like a mirror lit from within. Even minute bumps in the finish that marred the smoothness like the tiniest Braille letters rang like bells to remind him everything was as the Japanese said, *wabi-sabi*, as it should be and perfect in its imperfection.

He needed fresh air. Not breathing made the room feel stuffy and cloying. Tom tried to heave himself upright, but even though the Pacific was glass, he weaved like an inebriated sailor on a storm-tossed deck. He caught his hip on the corner of the worktable, jig-gling the vials in the metal tray. Tinkling glass made him duck and cover as a shower of tiny meteorites fell on him. And the pain in his hip felt deep green and tasted of mushrooms.

To compare, he pinched a pressure point on his ear. It was a vivid violet, stinking sulfur, shattering glass. Digging nails into his palm brought navy-blue steak sirens.

He was higher than a space shuttle. It felt like the crosswired hallucinogenic effects of hashish or LSD. Now he knew why the animal subjects were subdued after the injections: They were stoned! There were people born with crosswired senses—synesthetes—who seemed to function normally, although usually it was only a cou-ple of senses that fused. Like taste and touch. Or sound and color.

Some people perceived letters and numbers in colors or flavors. He had heard of no one who had every perceptive input crossed with every other one all the time. But synesthetes didn't have the processing power his brain did.

Feeling it was safer near the ground, he crawled on all fours out of the lab, down the corridor to one of three spiral staircases surrounding the masts through all four decks. As he crept up steps like a baby, he could feel his security cameras watching. People would come to check on him. He hoped he could speak coherently.

Breaking free through the deck door and into the air and light, he climbed onto the top deck to curl around the foot of the mast. Platinum-blond tangy lemon sun washed his body and he let himself 'be' as he awaited his concerned crew. He knew who would come and when. The sun sang to him in a high-pitched vibrato like an atonal celestial choir. If heaven sounded like this, surely the atonal musical masters Arnold Schoenberg and György Ligeti were up there.

The mast's six spars stretched above like the limbs of a great tree that gently raked the sky. Their song was deep, hollow, resounding. Teakwood under his body cradled him, and the mast urged him to consider its strength as his own. He felt at peace, wholly connected to every animate and inanimate thing. Was this what the Buddhists called bodhi? The awakening that brought unification and understanding of all things as one? And was the mast his bodhi tree, the tree Siddhartha Gautama sat under until he achieved Buddhahood?

As Tom predicted, Garrett, the New Zealand-born captain, ran on deck with a female steward, another young Kiwi named Keri-Ann. They carried a first-aid box, complete with defibrillator.

Even before they touched him to check his pulse and pupils, he felt sensual familiarity with them, as though they were all appendages of one being and not separate beings. The intimacy was embarrassing, yet oddly comforting, as if humanity really were united. He would never be alone again.

Feet pounded on deck. Talia and Ruth. Talia was deep purple bittersweet chocolate that sounded like the 1958 Gibson Les Paul Sunburst electric guitar that only a week and a half ago he had imagined in their bed. Ruth was gun-metal gray, scratchy, like steel wool across a vinyl record, balsamic vinegar. They were an interesting combination. Like a sharp, purple Mexican mole sauce. His brain spun with jokes, references, analogies, but he didn't share them. They'd be sure he was insane. He looked deeply into Talia's eyes. He brushed glowing swirl-foam of bright orange curls from her face and tried to calm her with his thoughts, then took her velvety hand.

"Hi," he said.

"Hi." Ultraviolet terror quaked her body. "Are you okay?"

Her voice sounded lower, yet higher. His brain had lost its usual interpretation of frequency and modulation. He giggled at the sounds. "Never better." He took a deep breath to speak and turned his head toward the captain. "Garrett? We'll call for you if we need you. Thanks, mate."

Captain and steward exchanged concerned looks. "No worries, sir." They left the defibrillator, but headed inside.

"Shulgin was right," said Tom. "If everyone did this, it would be the end of evolution and the human experiment. We'd achieve nirvana and sit on our asses, contemplating infinity."

Talia looked to Ruth, confused.

"Alexander Shulgin," grimaced Ruth. "Biochemist who experimented with psychedelics." Twitching in disgust, she glared at Tom. "He's high."

"From bots?" said Talia. "And you let him take them?"

"Possibly the combination. Of all of them," said Ruth. "And I'm n-n-not the one manipulating him. To go too far! With my wiles! *Eyn imglik iz far im veynik! A meshugener zol men oyshraybn, un im araynshraybn!*" She stomped loudly down the deck and into the stairwell.

"What was that?" asked Talia.

"One misfortune is too few for me. They should free a madman and lock me up." Then he giggled. "She thinks you're my Mata Hari."

"What have you done?"

He was less concerned with actions and more intrigued by predictions. The fact that he knew when and who would come should have surprised him, but it felt inevitable. Macrosensor effects were not like psychedelics or hallucinogenics, creating false perceptions. They were real premonitions. Neurologically, whatever the brain constructed as reality was never the whole story. We could only hear, see, smell, taste, and feel within a certain limited bandwidth of information, just enough to keep us fed and safe, and encourage us to reproduce. By increasing his bandwidth, was his amped-up consciousness creating this reality? Or was he seeing a reality that was there, but until now one he had been unable or unwilling to perceive?

His prescience had the same mental weight as 1 + 1 = 2, the sun rising in the east, and gravity making objects fall. These were heavy certainties in people's minds, heavy enough to base their lives on. However, his newly gained prescience felt equally reliable, as concrete as the alphabet or numbers. But weren't the delusional just as certain they were Jesus or Cleopatra?

ESP was antithetical to everything he was trained to believe. Like most scientists, it was easier to reject paranormal experience than consider it consistent with laws of the universe, even if scientists knew they didn't fully understand the universe yet. It had been easier to ignore what might help him succeed than consider the implications.

"You should tie me to the mast. Maybe if Captain Ahab tied himself to the mast, he wouldn't have died and the *Pequod* would've been saved."

Fear grew in Talia's eyes. "Shhh, baby, shhh . . . it'll stop soon."

"This isn't a drug trip, babe. This is me. And I like me." Surrendering to multireality made him feel better about everything. Somehow simple complexity and rational irrationality loosened hatred's grip from his mind.

But forewarned curiosity (what else could you call curiosity when a brain sensed the future?) got the better of him. He closed his eyes and stuck his fingers in his ears to dampen sensory input and mentally searched the lab's database for Ruth's research on Anthony Dulles's download. Prometheus's algorithms proved incomplete and Ruth had to put the project aside to work on the bots. And what better way to decode thoughts than with a real, augmented neural system, like his brain? He opened the program and downloaded and processed data faster with his newly hacked 'n' jacked intellect than any purely electronic computer program could.

It was like swimming through thoughts as information. One moment, he floated above and around, treading data while looking for patterns. And the next, he was submerged within it. He was Anthony Dulles, his skull splayed open in the *American Dream's* dining room, terrified equally of dying and revealing anything that might get Peter Bernhardt killed. He wasn't sure how those implants in him and the boy worked, but he had hoped Peter could read his mind, silently conveying Josiah's dreadful plans.

The irony was painful. If only Dulles had realized how far Peter was from real telepathy.

Josiah's questions were clever. They exposed the spy's knowledge of Josiah's role as architect of the most deadly terrorist plot in history and sought Dulles's mole.

He dived into the data again. Dulles's mole . . . Dulles's mole . . . The person had to be here, somewhere. Dulles could never have known so much about Peter Bernhardt or the 10/26 plot without a mole. Tom swam deep to find it. He discovered Vera data and Dulles's thoughts about her were pragmatic, Machiavellian. She had served her purpose, and while he'd regret her death, believing it was inevitable given the geopolitics, he wouldn't lose sleep about it. She was a big girl who got in with her violet eyes wide open.

But there was someone else, deeper still, even more involved, but hidden. He dived down further. And found the mole.

Carter Potsdam.

CHAPTER SEVENTY

Tom?" Talia shook his shoulders in concern.

Certainty flooded him again. Carter knew he was doing wrong, but couldn't stop. Instead, he'd do wrong and then tell Dulles in the hopes someone could stop it for him. Carter tried to have it both ways, just as Josiah had warned. Tom assumed the CEO of Prometheus planned to delete his own starring role as Dulles's mole from the cortex download and Josiah's prying eyes. And Dulles's extensive Peter Bernhardt dossier was exposed. It wasn't from Talia. It was from his best friend.

As Dulles's download suffused his brain, he lived the dying man's hopes, fears, regrets, anger—thoughts filled with the family he left behind, final moments of resignation, as well as the associations that made those final thoughts possible. Children and grandchildren Tom never knew felt as intimate as his own. Even physical sensations of anesthesia, restraints, and pain flooded back, causing similar torture in his body. It felt like spirit possession. Or channeling.

"Tom?" Talia shook him again.

He opened his eyes. "The mole is Carter Potsdam. And Dulles thought about you before he died. He was sorry for what he did, and he prayed you'd be all right."

She jerked back as from electrical shock. "How?"

"I'm Anthony Dulles."

Terrified, she pulled farther away.

"You don't understand . . . I've cracked his processor data. It's in my head now, as my own memories. I'm him. And I'm me. At the same time."

"Please, enough . . ."

"But he wanted you to know this. He thought he could communicate to me telepathically and hoped I might tell you some day. You were right. He regretted everything he did to you and never forgave himself for your father's death." His eyes narrowed with new sorrow. "I was worried about you and yet I still dragged you into this all over again. Some Cold Warrior. Pathetic old fool, aren't I? What was I thinking?"

She recognized the expression. Her eyes filled with tears. "Stop it . . . please . . ."

"Can you ever forgive me?"

"Who am I forgiving?" she exploded.

"I thought Dulles was your friend. I thought you might want some closure . . ."

"Shut up!" She slammed her right hand on the deck.

His right hand ached sulfur green, and he cradled it, stunned.

"You're not even human anymore," she cried. "I don't know what you are . . ."

"Not human? I just felt your pain. And if that doesn't make me human, I don't know what does."

But how much longer could he consider himself completely human, if by "human" she meant as intellectually and empathetically hobbled as everyone else? Maybe this was what Nietzsche meant by the *Übermensch*. Was he really a separate species now, *Homo excelsior*, as different from the *Homo sapiens* around him as the *Homo sapiens* were from the Neanderthals? Or was it more like

470

Homo sapiens versus australopithecines? They were all "human," so the definition would have to expand to fit him.

"How do I describe what I see?" said Tom. "What I know? Can you understand I see spinning helixes of DNA not just connected, but part of the spinning of the planet, the spinning of the solar system, the entropy of the universe? Each spins in its own frequency, creating a tone, a note. Together, it's music. And I hear it. Our intelligence is not unique. There's intelligence in everything. And it's growing. We're made of stardust and it's not a metaphor or scientific theory. I see it. I feel it. I am it."

She tried to hide her terror in disgust and spat, "No, you're some newbie Lucy . . ."

"This isn't LSD . . ."

Dulles's thoughts continued to churn. The more Tom discovered, the more Carter had to be stopped. And only Tom could do it. Carter begged him to.

Talia was determined. "We have to get you help. We have to fix this."

He reached out to touch her face. Her purple chocolate strummed velvet across his body, and he closed his eyes to wallow in the sensations for a moment. "I need these changes. Otherwise, it won't be the same world a week from now. And you won't want to live in it."

Psychedelia and enlightenment distracted him from his task and could no longer be tolerated. He would steel his heart and mind to tend his fire, fuel it to burn bright, no matter how in love he had fallen with the universe. He concentrated on culling the bot's effects down to just the information he needed and kept club memories running on an endless loop. Talia grew less velvety purple chocolate, but he kept a little bit for his own enjoyment. He looked out at the coastline, sparkling champagne in the lemon sun.

"In the land of the blind, the multi-eyed man is God," he said. "And it's time to do my job."

"If you think we're blind because we're not like you, you're kidding yourself. And if you think you're God . . ."

His head felt clearer, and he hauled himself up the mast to stand. "I know I'm not God. I'm just a sheriff with a mighty big gun."

The sound of crying was muffled behind Ruth's door. Tom knocked gently.

"Arein!"

He peeked in. "Ruthie?"

She rocked back and forth on the sofa and raised her head to glare with twitchy eyes. Books, papers, and clothes were strewn all over. She found a plastic garbage bag and dumped a few pathetic things in, half spilling everything on the floor.

"A mentsh tracht und Gott lacht," she barked. "Which are you?"

"A man plans and God laughs? I'm a man."

"Too bad. I would like to talk to God. Finally someone smart enough to answer my questions."

He gestured to the room. "I can see you're packing . . ."

"Ziss greena tzu arein az vy aroys gekimmen."

"It's easier to go into something than to get out of it? And that includes me?"

"I don't answer rhetorical questions. All your questions are rhetorical, now you are an *Übermensch.*"

She didn't say *"mein Übermensch"* anymore.

"But you know I have the best of reasons," he said.

"Everyone has their reasons," she spat.

He crouched at her feet, but not too close. "I understand. But what can I do for you, Ruthie?"

"I want t-t-to go to China. I have friends there. They'll t-t-take me in."

"Done. A helicopter will take you to a Chinese ship. They'll be paid handsomely to make sure you get to your contacts." He mentally made the arrangements and paid her as well, transferring fifty million dollars to her Swiss account, created for an emergency such as this.

"I never wanted your money . . ."

"I know, Ruthie. I'll miss you . . ."

Her lowered head swung back and forth and incessant twitching flung tears from her face, falling on the carpet like raindrops. One fell on a clipped glass slide that had fallen out of the plastic bag. It joined two blood drops into one.

"Vos vet zein, vet zein," said Ruth.

"What will be, will be." Tom knew that better than anyone.

CHAPTER SEVENTY-ONE

There were two messages on his mental GO. The first was a text from Josiah:

Thanks again for your words in the car. Mess will be cleaned up once and for all. Will send travel details.

The second was from Bruce:

El Señor Presidente—*my place, eight tonight.*

Meanwhile, Tom downloaded martial arts techniques, floor plans, and staff schedules from Lobo's house, and anything else that might come in handy. But was all of this learning at his neuron tips worth it? Especially when disturbing images of things to come kept flashing through his mind?

The Malibu Pier was built in 1905, but refurbished over the decades. Many people of all ages and races walked along its white-and-marine-blue length in the setting summer sun to fish, enjoy the view, or eat at the restaurants near its entrance.

Tom's launch from the *Pequod* delivered him to the pier. His limo waiting at its entrance would ferry him to Bruce's home nearby.

But he saw more than the visitors enjoying a California landmark. He saw it freshly built, unpainted, and empty of buildings. Cattle grazed in the hills above. Sweaty stevedores loaded pallets of hides, fruit, and barrels of milk from a private railroad terminus onto a steamship.

At the same time, Malibu Pier didn't exist. Tom floated above the water lapping twenty feet below. Two young Chumash Indian boys, skin ruddy bronze like Amanda's, and wearing only a net at their waist that held tools and rudimentary weapons, played tag with a driftwood stick.

The dislocation from a tangible reality made him queasy. He stopped, afraid of taking another step. Suddenly, not only was the pier gone, so was the beach. He was submerged in water, although he didn't feel wet. The shoreline consumed the coastline's cliffs. But was this a distant past or future?

He tamped down his visual-stimulus pathways and concentrated on the weather-beaten pier and its tourists, the one he felt sure was the present. The other scenes fell away like pages in a book he could flip at will.

Was he witnessing the truth of time? That it was nothing like the linear story we experience, but instead simultaneous and elastic, like cosmologists' mathematical formulas implied? Or was he hallucinating, his mind bored with too much processing power and not enough to process? Was multireality a phantom limb made by his imagination to keep neurons stimulated and happy?

As he approached Lobo's house, the ghost-feeling was stronger than ever. One moment, he felt grounded in the here and now, the next he free-floated in cyberspace/unreality. Was this what God (whose existence he still doubted) felt like? The convergence of worlds would be too much for anyone, no less him.

And what if he was simply insane?

He focused hard on the present, but couldn't help wondering if he was dead or alive.

The door opened automatically, and Bruce's voice came through a speaker.

"*Compadre!* Please come in and allow us to examine you."

Inside the front door, Tom's Hoover cane tapped the walls of a see-through foyer made of two-inch-thick bulletproof Plexiglas, which made it impossible to pass into the house without permission. The front door closed and locked behind him, and he felt a tickle through his body. He was being scanned for weapons.

After a minute, Bruce's voice returned. "Well, you're certainly loaded for bear. But as far as I can tell, not for me. Welcome."

The clear doors slid open, and a burly black security guard approached. He wore his hair in a modified 'fro, with sideburns and 'stache, very Shaft.

"Sir?" Shaft took Tom's arm and led him into the huge living room. Inside was as relentlessly white and oversized as outside. White walls, white polished marble floors laid in a geometric parquet of right angles and boxes. All the sleek furniture's upholstery was white. Ceilings strained past sixteen feet to contain art, some of it white-on-white. Everything was big. Beachside was one-way glass, and the setting sun on the water painted walls in shimmering gold that crooned Billy Idol's "White Wedding" to Tom's hot-rod brain. The sun had sunk low enough to irritate eyes, so Bruce pulled a small remote from his pocket and pressed a button, shifting electrically charged polarized glass to translucent white gold. Tom felt the energetic buzz of an unusually large number of electrical wires. They were hidden in the floors, ceilings, and walls, but seemed excessive for even a smart house such as this with every bell and whistle. Also, the floor's parquet pattern tweaked his brain like puzzle boxes, interesting enough to analyze. He hacked and searched the house's IT system to see what the fuss was about.

Bruce stood, arms crossed in appraisal. He nodded to Shaft, who disappeared behind a white door. "I'd like to apologize for my behavior. If you're going to be president, we better get off on the right foot." But he did not proffer his hand and his eyes were as dead as they had been in Biogineers's conference room. They studied him, searching for Peter. "Nope . . ." he shook his head. "*Nada* . . . Whoever it was did a great job. Or maybe you did it, somehow. I don't see Peter anywhere."

Vera reclined on the sofa, a satisfied, enigmatic smile curling her lips. "Neither do I."

"I'd prefer not to talk about this in front of anyone else," said Tom.

"She knows everything. Why else would you be here?"

Tom tried to contact her telepathically, but he wasn't sure he could. Vera didn't move, although she did look at him quizzically. Perhaps he wasn't the master of time and space he hoped. Meanwhile, Lobo's security system was enormous and multilayered. He continued analyzing.

"I'd really prefer . . ." said Tom.

"It doesn't matter what you prefer. My turf. My rules. And Vera doesn't want to leave. Do you?"

"No, love," she purred.

"Please sit." Bruce gestured to a large white oversized armchair. Tom didn't move. "Chair to your right. So how am I in danger?"

Tom searched with his cane, groping the chair before sitting. "Josiah knows you've been double-dipping."

"How?"

"I told him."

"And you want me to keep your identity a secret? After that?"

"Yes. We both need to stop Brant. And you must take over the club."

"What about your boy toy, Carter?"

"Leave him to me. He's history. Like Brant."

"And what's wrong with Brant?"

"He's making a terrible mistake. One he and the world will regret. If they have sense enough afterward to regret it. It has to end now. And as he said, you're not indispensable."

"You're sure you don't want to be president?"

"This has nothing to do with politics."

"You're wrong. Everything is politics. Just like taking advantage of brothers' weaknesses is politics. It's all about who ends up on top. That's all politics has ever been. We may have a rotten system, but it's the only one we've got, and I'll be damned if I'm not at the top of it."

"So being the biggest predator is it?"

Bruce glared as though Tom was an idiot. "Of course. For instance, what do you offer that I don't already know? Why should I let you leave?"

"This is not about information. Josiah is going to kill you. Very soon. Take my help to beat him, or die. But either way, I'll stop him."

"I think you overestimate yourself. And why do you care about them?" He waved his hands toward the large, opaque windows to indicate an unseen populace. "You know you're as much like them as you are to sheep."

"Is that how you see people?"

"It's hard to believe a man like you doesn't. You of all people know the world is divided into two groups. Leaders and followers. If you're smart and ambitious enough to pull yourself up by your own bootstraps to the top of the heap, you get to be a leader. The rest . . ." He shrugged. "I spent my childhood working on sheep ranches. People are a lot like sheep. They flock around leaders, follow them, and depend on them to get them where they want to be, even if they have no idea where that is. The key is they want to be led. Some of the animals I tended were smarter than the farmhands I worked beside. Both got slaughtered eventually, one way or another. And I swore I'd be neither. Has the world ever been any different?"

"It could be."

"You, *Católico*, are still a softhearted dreamer. I thought you finally got smart."

"Are you smart enough to realize it's either Brant or you left standing? With my help, it will be you."

Bruce gestured to Vera. "And what do you think?"

Don't speak! Anthony Dulles yelled silently to Vera in Tom's head.

"I think Tom's right," Vera replied.

"You do?" Bruce stood and paced the room, limping behind the sofa. He wandered back and forth three times in thought, and finally asked, "Do you know what I hate about technology?"

Tom snorted, "Ironic, coming from you."

"I hate that illusions we create about our lives are revealed by technology to be lies. When you can data-mine so much information and uncover things never known before, you find out what you thought is, really isn't. And vice versa. That can be very upsetting. Even for those of us who wield data for a living."

"How do you know the data isn't an illusion?"

"It can be. But luck reveals the truth." Bruce paused behind Vera and leaned over her, slipping his arms around her shoulders like a shawl. He traced a pattern with the tiny remote along the skin of her cleavage and his other hand ran up her neck, fingers raking her hair at her scalp. He pulled her head back and kissed her neck as she snuggled into his embrace. "And I'm a very lucky man."

Tom saw the flash of emotion in Bruce's eyes. The light around their bodies darkened and cymbals crashed in Tom's head, silencing Billy Idol. As Bruce pressed a button on the remote, Tom sprang from his seat and threw himself at the couple. Time slowed to an extreme. But Tom wasn't Superman. His mind might manipulate time and space, but his body could not defy the laws of physics and human anatomy, however optimized and augmented.

A wall of bulletproof Plexiglas rocketed from the floor, two inches thick and ten feet wide. The top edge caught his chin like an uppercut with a ton of force behind it, tossing him to the marble floor. Four walls rose instantly around Bruce and Vera, thrust into the air from hidden, explosive hydraulic lifts under the marble parquet. The open top met the ceiling and sealed them in.

The floor patterns made sense. Each marble rectangle was an instant, mini panic room.

With a sharp jerk of the arms and a loud grunt, Bruce snapped Vera's neck. Unlike the ease depicted in movies, the action took effort and was exaggerated in Tom's slow-time. She sagged, head lolling to the side. But she was still alive. Her eyes flicked violently, panicked at witnessing her own death.

As Tom struggled to his feet, he hacked the house computer, looking for the panic room's files.

Bruce's voice was modulated through a speaker in the ceiling, "I'm lucky because I'm in complete control of my world." He laid her down, caressing her head as she twitched, then came around to sit beside her. "I did love you," he said to Vera. "But data is data." He turned to Tom. "Like you were never blind." Putting his hands around her throat and squeezing, he ruminated thoughtfully, "You know, sometimes I think we're all 'The Man Who Knew Too Much.' Information is equal parts power and curse. No one ever thought of that when we decided we needed to know more to maintain control. Sometimes I wonder if all the control is worth it. Oh, well. What's that song the wife sings, you know, in *The Man Who Knew Too Much*?"

Vera lapsed into unconsciousness.

Tom found the commands for the panic room as he muttered, "Que Sera, Sera."

"Right. 'Que Sera, Sera.' Whatever will be, will be."

And the walls came plummeting down.

Bruce's face froze in shock, and he stabbed at his remote control without effect as Tom dived over the falling wall in a forward roll. Tom's second command to the house server sent the wall racing back up to the ceiling behind him. Shaft and a white security guard rushed the room and fired senseless bullets at the Plexiglas.

Tom opened up his perceptions to check on Vera. Her fading mauve/suede/cinnamon vibration meant she would be dead in seconds.

Bruce's reflexes were excellent, but not good enough. While he leapt up, ready to attack, Tom, with the luxury of slow-time, could find the right vertebrae and hit it, hard. Bruce's body (coal-black, acrid, and stinking of sulfur) went limp, and Tom caught him, but staggered. His own vertebrae hurt coal-black-sulfuric, too.

He felt Bruce's pain, just like he felt Talia's.

"Thought you might like to know how Vera felt," hissed Tom. Turning to Vera, he didn't need to check her pulse. Her vibrant colors and flavors were gone. There was no vibration. She was dead. Anthony Dulles's prescient memories mourned for her.

Then Tom triggered the wall to retract once more and lifted Bruce in front like a shield.

The bodyguards fired while Tom repositioned Bruce to take the hit. One bullet hit Bruce's thigh and Tom's thigh hurt. Another bullet passed through Bruce's shoulder and Tom felt the pain. Changing tactics, the bodyguards rushed Tom, who tossed Bruce aside like a toy and fought the two men. It was no contest. He could anticipate every move, dodge their bullets, and using some recent Internet videos, executed a swift punch to Shaft's neck vertebrae and another to the white guard's temple, leaving the men motionless at his feet.

Tom's own body felt lesser trauma to the same places. Distance learning over the Internet had its advantages. Supersensory synesthesia did not.

It was time to end this.

Cruelty grew in his synapses, suffusing his being, but he wasn't sure he wanted to stop it. It tasted like Bruce. Grabbing Bruce's broken, bleeding body by a foot, Tom dragged him to the enormous white-marble gas fireplace and placed his feet onto the grate. Then he went into the all-white kitchen and returned with a fire extinguisher and a bottle of cooking oil.

"So here's how it's going to be," said Tom. "I ask questions. And you answer. As you may have noticed when I paralyzed you, I made sure that I didn't damage the spinal cord too much. Need some of those nerves for the pain. So let's get down to it. Who trained the three 10/26 kids to become terrorists?"

"Fuck you," Bruce spat between gritted teeth.

Tom turned on the gas, then pressed the ignition button. Lobo's expensive driving shoes with the ridiculous black nubby bits on the soles (ridiculous since he never drove himself, much less a manual-shift two-seater) seared and cooked in the blue flames.

"Fire seems so miraculous," mused Tom, as the rubber melted like licorice chips, and the leather soles ignited. "It's the ultimate technology. It turns sand into glass and ore into metal, water into vapor, and raw food edible and disease-free. It's been used to fight wars since the dawn of civilization, forever altering the balance of power. No wonder the Greeks had their stories about Prometheus. Bringing fire to mortals was the ultimate creative act: In fire's crucible, men became like gods, evolving ourselves and everything around us."

The burning man whimpered. Tears of pain rolled off his cheeks onto the cold marble floor.

Tom's feet stung as though standing on lit coals. His eyes watered, too, but he had to keep his systems open. He was too vulnerable in Bruce's territory to ignore any hint of danger. "Am I being too philosophical for you? I'll turn it off if you tell me."

"Motherfucker!" Bruce gasped. "Turn it off!"

He got down low to Bruce's face and whispered, "But you haven't told me anything yet . . ."

"We made our own terrorists. So we could destroy them! Terrorists make everyone afraid!"

Tom rose gingerly, walking with difficulty. He turned off the flame, then blasted the burned feet with a quick squeeze of the extinguisher trigger. The fire was out, but the sting remained. "Who ran the cells from the club?"

Bruce was aware enough to notice. "You feel my pain?"

Tom nodded. "With great power comes great affliction."

"Fucking retard." Bruce closed his eyes. They popped open at the sound of the gas hissing. "You don't get it! We had to control bots. Not the market. If we hadn't, some terrorist group might have done it on a global scale . . ."

". . . and not controllable by the club." Tom sighed and turned off the gas.

"Could have been a lot worse."

"Well, they were just a bunch of entertainment people. You're right. Coulda been worse." He grabbed the bottle and poured oil on Bruce's feet, up his legs to his chest.

"Whaaaaat?"

"The big problem with your story is the lack of a central character. And no one is more sorry than me." He flipped on the gas and hit the ignition button once more. The oil caught quickly, flames traveling up its trail. "You see, since torture can't be relied upon to work, I have to already know, or at least have a damned good suspicion, about the answers. The rest is just the illusion of causal effect. In this case, I already know you ran the cells. You financed them, you arranged the training and the plan. You chose the children. And you and the club had them killed. You killed everyone on 10/26."

"Why do this if you know the answers!"

"Torture isn't just about information. Anyone who says that is lying. It's about retribution. You can't destroy all those lives, including mine, and not pay. And it scares the sheep. As excruciating as this is, I'm enjoying it." Bruce's pain traveled quickly up Tom's body. His legs too painful to stand, he knelt down and rocked near Bruce's head to whisper, "Who's the sheep now?"

"Inhuman fuck!" Bruce spat through tears.

Tom laughed through tears. "Great choice of words! No, Bruce. This is the most human part of me. It's the most human part of all of us. Even a mouse feels empathy for his fellow nesters. Only humans torture and hate for no appreciable gain, except that it feels so good."

Flames engulfed the oil-soaked clothing and flesh burned in earnest. The stench was metallically-sulfury-sweet.

Tom curled into a fetal ball of hurt. "It's the same dopamine response our brains get with sex, food, and drugs. And music. You of all dopamine junkies should know. So we do it again . . ."

The burning man's screams echoed endlessly in streamers of charcoal spikes around the huge room.

". . . and again . . ."

Smoke rose, billowing to the ceiling, darkening the perfect white paint.

". . . and again . . ."

He had to admire Bruce's fortitude. If he had felt the torture's full effects, Tom would have passed out long ago.

Bruce's eyes flittered in panic from one immobile ceiling sprinkler to another.

"I shut them down," confessed Tom.

Bruce stopped screaming long enough to grunt out the words, *"Kill . . . me!"*

"No. Time to live a little in my shoes. To know what your future holds, unable to do anything except watch it all end in agony. Lucky for you, your future is very, very short."

From far above the house, a high-frequency vibration ran through Tom that felt like aluminum foil chewed by the metal blades of a food processor. It sent shivers up his spine. The house was being scanned. Unlike the lobster in the proverbial pot, he could feel his core body temperature rise incrementally.

"Good-bye, Bruce."

"Don't . . . !" The dying man gasped for breath.

"I'm sorry. The gods have found you. And you're my burnt offering."

Talking Heads' "Psycho Killer" chased a limping Tom through the house, accusing him of mental illness and atrocities, past, present, and future. Rummaging in the foyer closet, he grabbed Vera's floor-length dark-chocolate Imperial sable.

"Peter!"

In the garage, two black Mercedes looked shiny and new, fresh from the detailer. It was a shame to leave perfectly good getaway cars behind, but the eye in the sky watching the house would track them. He opened the garage door a couple of feet, threw the fur over his head, and crouched down on all fours, scooting out under the garage door at the farthest corner of the property. It was twilight. He continued to scuttle on all fours along Pacific Coast Highway's sidewalk, hoping he looked like a neighborhood dog to the eye in the sky. He avoided crossing lines in the road, for fear spy satellites would wonder what the black blotch was that interrupted the painted line's continuity.

Cars sped by. He dashed through the crosswalk, dodging cars, and scampered into McDonald's. At the counter, he stood and arranged the coat around his shoulders like a cape.

"A Big Mac. To go." He shut his eyes tight and ratcheted down his amped-up senses.

Blinding light enveloped the beach. It was much brighter than the light that struck the young terrorists' cars in Vegas, because it was destroying a larger target. Patrons screamed, hands flying to stricken eyes. The sounds of cars breaking, skidding, crashing, blinded drivers honking horns.

After the light died away, Tom was the first to see the result. Lobo's house was gone, vaporized, just like the 10/26 terrorists. And Bruce's phantom pain was gone from his body. But the memories remained, and the flavor of the man's personality suffused his mind. Like Dulles had.

In place of Bruce's house was an ashen, glassy pit surrounded by beach sand on the ocean side, melted asphalt on the street, and the singed, smoldering walls of the houses next door. The technology to destroy a target with such precision was remarkable. It also proved once and for all the 10/26 terrorists were not suicide bombers. A laser weapon in orbit high above earth had killed them—a weapon the government regularly denied existed.

The question remained: Did those who vaporized the house know Tom was inside, or would he have been collateral damage? STTW sensors had existed for years: sense-through-the-wall radar that could identify people through feet of concrete.

So Josiah knew he was there, assuming he was on Bruce's side, otherwise he would not have sacrificed so valuable an asset.

But it didn't matter what they knew, because he knew their next move.

Leaving the restaurant employees and patrons struggling to regain their vision, he walked to the parking lot. There stood Pop in an empty parking space next to an early '60s Volkswagen Type

2 Bus. With Tom's 3.0 senses, Pop appeared absolutely real, dressed in his comfy cardigan, sweatpants, and sheepskin slippers.

"Do ghosts see other ghosts?" asked Tom.

Pop didn't speak, but he held out his hand to Tom.

"I don't have time for you now, real or not," said Tom.

His father disappeared. In his place stood Talia, her hand out to him. "Baby? I'm real." Once again, she had found him with his GPS nano-RFID, still embedded in his leg from long ago.

His father might have been a hallucination, but he didn't have time for her, either.

"Tom!" She chased after him. "What happened?"

"Keep your voice down . . . They're dead. Bruce killed Vera. And the club killed Bruce. And they know enough to want me dead, too."

"You let her die?"

Hundreds of people swarmed the street, trying to grasp what fresh cataclysm had befallen a community accustomed to fires, floods, landslides, earthquakes, and celebrity DUIs. The sirens from nearby Carbon Canyon Station's fire trucks blared. Despite Tom's clothes stained with oil, blood, and smoke, no one paid any attention to him. "I tried to save her, but there was nothing I could do. And she was a big girl." Some part of Dulles's jaded spymaster spoke for him.

Talia knew those words and looked at him in shock. "That's not you speaking."

"No, it's . . ."

"And I'm a big girl. So you'd let me die? Or Ruth?"

"No! Why are we fighting about this?"

"Why?" She looked frantic. "Everyone's gone! You've driven everyone away!"

He didn't answer. Within a block, they were at their front door.

"Won't they vaporize this place, too?" she asked.

"No. If they know I got out, they'll want to take me alive now.

Josiah will want the satisfaction. I'll go to camp. You and the mercenaries will still attack from the outside."

Talia unlocked the door, and he went upstairs to strip his filthy clothes and shower.

Hot water coursed down his face and body, and for a tiny moment, he relaxed, his mind's floodgates opening a crack. But a crack was enough to loose the deluge. Vera and Bruce's suffering, with all their pain, shock, fear, in all its Technicolor, smell-o-taste-o-touch-o-hear-o-vision glory, felt like his own. His knees buckled, and he crouched, huddled and shaking in the corner under the expensive showerhead that simulated the broad drizzle of falling rain.

Through the steam, a familiar outline stood on the other side of the shower door, his hand outstretched once more.

"Peter. Let me help you." The voice rang clearly in his mind, even though Paul's lips didn't move.

"Leave me alone!"

But it was Talia who jerked back a towel at the open shower door.

"Not you . . ."

"Who then?"

His chin drooped on his chest. "Pop." Her look of pity angered him. "What? Your dad can howl for blood, and I'm crazy if I see mine?"

Her livid violet bitter cocoa–ness, dilating pupils, and wan cheeks all embodied fight or flight. He knew she couldn't stay. But she was trying.

"You don't understand what it's like to be me," he continued. "It's . . . lonely."

"I can't be like you," she murmured.

"I know."

"What's the price you pay to yourself? To me?"

"You think I don't know?"

"Please, baby. Just stop. Ruth said she made antidotes. Take them. We'll follow her to China. Her friends can figure out how to get rid of the crap in your head. We'll get back at the club another way."

"You're crazy. Not me. There's no next time. One enemy's gone. There's two to go. And am I supposed to let everyone become mindless automatons who only think they make their own decisions and live their own lives, but are really happy slaves of the Phoenix Club? I thought you wanted to stop them, too."

"I can't save the world! Only me!"

Faintly, he heard her counterargument in his head, and repeated it aloud. "'These augmentations . . . they're brilliant as therapies, in isolation, but all at once and together, without testing, they're too much, too fast . . .' You really think I'm losing my mind."

Talia hiccupped in shock, eyes wide with fear. "You . . . read my mind? Noooo . . ." She dropped his towel and ran from the room.

He didn't ask why. Her thoughts sent the signal loud and clear. *No love, no matter how strong, can withstand this pressure. This lack of privacy. I love you too much to watch you destroy yourself. And me.*

The garage door rumbled open and closed below him. He wanted to know where she was going, but she had no idea, so reading her mind was pointless. And her piece of the plan, the private army she had raised to fight alongside him, went with her. The farther she drove, the less he could hear her agonized thoughts, until she disappeared off his radar.

It was Tom's turn to cry. Didn't she know he was terrified to be alone? He turned off the rain shower and grabbed the towel off the floor. As he dried himself, he couldn't help but compare himself to another difficult character: the historic Thomas Paine. He, too, had alienated everyone around him in his single-minded obsession to succeed at his righteous revolution.

His GO rang. It was Josiah.

"Hello . . . son." His strangled voice could not feign nonchalance. "Have ya heard from Bruce?"

Josiah's anguish meant he knew Tom's identity. He knew everything and was trying to play it cool while cleaning up loose ends. His game was the only reason Tom was still alive.

"I live nearby," said Tom. "It's chaos here."

"Damned shame . . . I'm sendin' a copter at oh-six-hundred. We're ready for you."

And Thomas Paine had to be ready for them.

CHAPTER SEVENTY-TWO

The Jet Ranger hovered over the Phoenix Camp tarmac. A soldier sat beside him in the second row, casting jittery looks out the window at the ground before returning his gaze to Tom. Private Jefferson was a huge black man—six foot seven and at least 275 pounds. He looked twenty-five and vibrated without the copter's movement, like an amphetamine vet. Most soldiers preferred less reactive psychostimulants like modafinil to keep awake and alert, but Jefferson wasn't on drugs at all. He was hopped up on experience, probably with an undiagnosed traumatic brain injury sustained in battle.

Below them, summer camp was transformed into a military installation, thanks to the club's private army securing the landing strip and perimeter, except, instead of C-130s and tanker trucks, it was personal jets and SUVs. No one needed traditional armaments or war vehicles to subdue a population anymore. Carter's Boeing Super 27 was off to the side along with Josiah's C-32, Air Force Two. There were ten other planes with registrations in club members' names or corporations, with pallets of shrink-wrapped crates loading. These were not nanobots. They were drone aircraft, broken down for transport, to distribute bots.

A computer backpack lay at Tom's feet. He made it clear to Private Jefferson that Secretary Brant would want to see the contents, and he was happy to have it examined. It had been scanned for explosives before they boarded the craft.

Before takeoff, he sent an encrypted e-mail to an anonymous address, apologizing to Ruth for ruining her life. He asked that she please let Talia know he loved her very much, if they were ever in contact again.

As he and Private Jefferson exited the copter, they were joined by a nuggety-muscled, tough-as-titanium sergeant named Antonelli. He whipped out a pair of steel handcuffs, pulled Tom's arms behind him, and quickly snapped them on his wrists. Then Antonelli grabbed the backpack from Jefferson. The pair of soldiers flanked Tom as they crossed the tarmac.

The cabin door to Carter's Boeing opened. Amanda ran down the stairs and across the tarmac, screaming, "Tom!" She looked unkempt, like she hadn't slept since he last saw her.

Before she could get near, Sergeant Antonelli yelled in a thick Chicago accent, "Ma'am, stop! Do not come any closer!" Jefferson pulled a gun, but neither stopped their march to the gate.

Amanda chased them, keeping her distance. "What happened to Bruce?"

"Amanda, get out of here," said Tom.

"Why won't anyone tell me anything? Carter's afraid . . . Is Bruce dead? Was it you?"

"Listen to me. Go home. What was Carter thinking letting you come?"

"Please . . . Spare Carter."

He lifted his handcuffed arms behind him, but Antonelli yanked them back down. "As you can see, it's probably not my call."

"I think it is. I don't know what they've done, but . . ." She unconsciously held her belly.

"If you want him to be born at all, you have to leave." Didn't she know he fought against the tentacles of love and kinship that grew from the baby and wrapped around every part of him? Did she have any idea how much he wanted to be a part of this child's life? A part of hers? "Remember what I told you: I'm doing this for the best reasons."

"I could call Carter and tell him what I know."

"But you don't know."

"I won't let you leave me alone like this!"

"You're not alone. And if you value our child's life, you'll take the jet and leave." Her eyes teared up, but she kept shadowing them. "I can't save you, Amanda. You need to save yourself."

They were near the front gates. She ran up to kiss him, but soldiers dragged him harder.

"Go!" Tom yelled at Amanda.

She bit her quivering lip, unsure what to do, then turned and ran for her plane.

A sentry at the gate took the backpack from Antonelli and handed it off to five different, specially trained antiterrorist personnel. The first soldier, with a jagged scar that bisected his face, visually and mechanically scanned the contents and passed the bag down the line for examination. The clueless overkill was amusing. Five men wearing rubber gloves opened, turned over, swiped, wiped, and mechanically sniffed many objects: a GO-B, a water bottle, a seven-day pill organizer filled with supplements, a copy of *Shibumi* in Braille, an extra set of clothing, including underwear and socks. Two remote control cars were the oddest items.

"Why do you have these?" asked Scarface.

Tom felt Amanda and his unborn child retreating from his consciousness. He told the boy he loved him one last time as the tentacles slid away. "I hoped I'd see my son today."

The toys passed through an X-ray machine and were examined

493

under a magnifier for tampering. Scarface got chemical analysis readings he didn't understand. "We'll have to keep these with us. This may take a while."

"Fine with me," said Tom.

"Send them in when you're done," said Sergeant Antonelli.

The club knew his identity, and the closer he came to those who knew, the more certain he was of their knowing. Like he knew Private Jefferson would sneak up behind to stab a pressurized injector full of dantrolene, a powerful muscle relaxant, into his buttocks. His legs buckled under him, and the two men hefted Tom under each arm and dragged him into the mines. It made him sad. The only reason he was in conflict with these brave, obedient young men was that both sides loved their country with equal passion. They just didn't realize what side they were on.

Before the steel doors closed behind them, he sent several messages to satellites overhead.

The soldiers dumped Tom onto a sofa against a wall near Josiah's dining table and stood on either side with hands on weapons.

Josiah stiffened. "As my Mama used to say, boy, you were too much sugar for a dime. You only fooled us 'cause we were desperate for somethin' sweet."

"The Potsdams' pilot is requesting permission to take off. Mrs. Potsdam's on board," interrupted Josiah's aide-de-camp, a geeky young man with round glasses who sat at the next table, working a small HOME screen and satellite hookup.

"Permission granted." Josiah shook his head at Tom. "I learned the hard way Carter's best handled by holdin' a light leash on somethin' he's not willin' to lose. Too tight a leash and he panics to the other side."

"Affirmative tower. Permission granted," repeated the aide-de-camp.

"Guess he was willing to lose me," Tom mumbled, his lips and tongue loose and numb.

"Now he knows you're Peter Bernhardt," Josiah spit the name with disgust, "he sure is."

"And how long can he still be your boy?"

"Who knows? Protégés come and go. And they never live up to expectations. Sometimes, they're just plain ol' idiots! Or dissemblers. Like you. Like all children, I guess." His sigh rumbled in his chest. "Son, you break an old man's heart."

"You know, it's tough being the smartest guy in the room."

"I don't feel smart. I feel old. And used up. And you will pay." He thrust out his hand to his aide-de-camp. "Cyrus? Those updates?"

Cyrus handed Josiah a GO. He cursored quickly through it. "We were fortunate to interview Jake Hirano regardin' the theft of our money. Even though it's a pittance, did ya think a billion dollars could go missin' and no one would notice? But don't worry. We know where it is. And we have no more concerns about Mr. Hirano and his unorthodox methods of bankin'. Apparently"—he looked down at the screen to read—"he died while surfin'. We'll have our remainin' money back soon—Switzerland always cooperates when it comes to cash—and we'll confiscate your physical assets and set our books right . . . I've always wanted to sail on that boat of yours."

His fingers tapped the GO keys. "Let's see . . . Dr. Ruth Chaikin. If you're the next step beyond Prometheus's research, I'll assume her suicide was staged and not a coincidence. Apparently, someone fittin' her unusual description is on their way to China, but we'll get her eventually. Chinese'll have to play ball after this week. This here's the new A-Bomb, and they don't have it.

"And we finally know where the real Marisol Gonzales is, and I can stop sendin' morons to chase her through every flea-bitten Latin

American hellhole. She'll be dead by tomorrow. Shoulda figured it out as soon as I met you. You do so look like her father."

"People only see what they want to see."

The old man nodded sadly. "That's the God's honest truth. Well, I know there's more helpers. But don't you fear. We'll find 'em. Cyrus? The decoder?"

"He's wireless, Mr. Secretary. I'm hooked up already."

Josiah shook his head in chagrin. "And I bet we share the same addiction—information—right? Worse'n nicotine. Never get enough."

"There's a limit. Trust me."

"But I'd love to get that far, like hittin' rock bottom, so I could get scared straight and sober up. Maybe when I get to know what's inside you, I'll feel satiated."

"I am today what you will be tomorrow."

"You will be dead today, and who knows? I might die tomorrow. But we're not the same."

"When you know what I know, you'll understand. It's a rush at first. You're *Homo excelsior*. But I also did horrible things, because of what I knew. Perhaps you understand the guilt, the pain of that?"

"What do you know about pain? Ah. . . ." Josiah snorted at his realization. "You may be right. We might have more in common than I'd like to admit."

"My memories, my thoughts, are a torture I hope I can share with you," said Tom.

Josiah noticed giant Jefferson staring at the floor, biting his lip, and quivering more than usual. "Private? You got a problem?"

It took a moment for the question to register. The soldier looked up in surprise. "Uh, no, sir."

Loud voices erupted in the hall. A young corporal burst in, all wide-eyed and fresh faced; too much so to have ever seen action. His badge said, "Cpl. Santiago." "Sir, all the ground vehicles are dead. And some of the men seem to be acting . . . weird."

Josiah swiveled. "Cyrus?"

But the aide-de-camp wasn't listening. He was counting the fingers on his left hand, over and over. Except he kept getting different answers. He giggled.

Josiah's gaze turned to the soldiers. Jefferson knelt on the ground and patted the carpet, crying softly. Antonelli swung his head in wide, paranoiac arcs, both Glock 17s in his hands and deep in enemy territory. He spotted a threat, shooting ten rounds into an artificial ficus tree.

The boy was too confused by the bizarre scene to understand.

Antonelli's shaky aim swung toward the corporal, and Tom rose in a flash from his couch. In a fluid motion, he bent over, dropping his hands to the ground, and stepped behind them, putting his cuffed hands in front of his body. Then he stepped behind the sergeant and, while kick-sweeping the legs out from under Antonelli, wrapped handcuffed arms around his torso and yanked upward, while thrusting his knee into the sergeant's back. There was a mighty crack. Spasms gripped the soldier's hands, guns firing into the carpet. He dropped them as his body twitched.

Microbivores had consumed the muscle relaxant the moment it hit Tom's bloodstream. He had not been incapacitated.

Tom tossed the sergeant to the carpet, but the soldier tried to rise, even with a broken back. A swift kick to the temple stilled him. Tom snatched up his gun. No one but wide-eyed Santiago noticed. Trying to be heroic, he pulled his sidearm and aimed at Tom, but a moment later, his handgun lay on the floor. Tom had shot it out of the young man's hand.

"Bug out!" bellowed Tom.

The boy tore out as fast as he could.

Tom searched Antonelli's pockets until he found handcuff keys and freed his hands to grab the other gun.

Fixating on the empty chair next to him, Josiah swatted the air in a panic. "Get away from me! Get away . . . ! It wasn't my fault, Tony! I had to neutralize you!"

Typhoid Tom walked among them. Having filled his pockets, backpack, and possessions with the invisible powder of macrosensors, all who came in contact breathed them in. The tiny robots played havoc on unprepared brains, triggering hallucinations. The two remote control cars confiscated by security were plague-carrying rats, programmed to accelerate off the table once he entered the mines to race around the compound, spreading their psychedelic bounty. As each infected person came upon the uninfected, they spread the bots.

Tom opened his mind and let the macrosensors' tiny voices in. What a din of insanity they shared! Josiah thought Anthony Dulles was coming to get him. Since the tortured part of Dulles resided inside Tom's processor, maybe he was.

Fingers still a delight, Cyrus didn't notice Tom take his console. Searching the site menu of building commands, he cut off the system from outside contact, shut down sprinklers, deactivated security systems, closed doors, turned off sirens, but made sure the fresh-air ventilation system remained fully functional. Then he shut down all elevator shafts, except one.

"No, Bruce! . . . *No!*" Josiah cowered, trying to crawl under the table. "What's happening?" In Josiah's thoughts, a Lobo apparition stalked him from behind the blasted ficus tree. Maybe that was Antonelli's target.

"Reality bites, doesn't it?" Dragging the old man by the collar to his feet, Tom whispered into his ear, "Welcome to the club, Mr. Secretary." He hefted Josiah over his shoulder. The squirming, kicking weight felt annoying, but not heavy. Tom carried him into the hallway, heading directly to the door marked "Armory." Digging around Josiah's pockets, he found a lighter and cigar cutter, which he pocketed, and a large set of keys. One of them unlocked the closet filled with firearms and ammunition, incendiary and fragmentation grenades, and communications devices. With his free hand, he grabbed gun magazines and a couple dozen incendiary grenades to stuff into pockets and hang off his clothing like Christmas tree ornaments.

One element could disassemble a nanobot's diamondoid nanostructure at an atomic level and change it back to harmless carbon atoms: fire. How convenient he had so much practice with it now. And fire rises as it burns, looking for fuel, so the building had to be consumed from the bottom, where the labs were located, and up.

When they reached the elevator, he stuffed the old man's head and hands against the biometric readers.

"Say your name."

Josiah babbled, ". . . fucked up . . . Who do you think . . . ? I'm not bailing . . . What kind of child . . . ? What did I do . . . ? You embarrass me!" Davy Brant wasn't happy with his father, either.

"Say your name or I'll give you to Bruce and Tony!"

Terror snapped him to momentary lucidity. "J-j-josiah B-brant."

It was good enough for the machines. The doors closed and Tom pressed every button, all the way down to the lowest floor, "9."

As they descended, Tom focused on Josiah's frequency. He wanted his mental and vocal message to get through. "The real tragedy is the old saw—'If you think you're going insane, you're not'—just isn't true. We're both proof of self-aware insanity. Sucks, doesn't it? Much worse than physical pain or even death to men like us, who rely on mental control for everything."

The elevator opened at "2." Tom dumped Josiah, bracing a door with his writhing body and holding him there with his hiking boot on the old man's chest. Brant was reimagining his battle with JFK . . . *Well, he was an idiot with the Soviets and the Mafia, wasn't he? Too busy listenin' to the wrong fellas and chasin' skirts . . . what a hullaballoo that was . . .*

Pulling the grenade pin, Tom wound up and pitched the explosive as far down the hall and as close to the emergency stairwell as possible. It was a good throw, over eighty feet and just under one hundred miles an hour. Who needed steroids if you had nanobots? He dragged Josiah in, punching "Door Close" before the explosion rattled the building. Josiah screamed, curling up in a duck-and-cover pose. His terror made Tom want to scream, too.

The car continued its descent until the doors shuddered open at "3." Fire burned around the edges of a ceiling hole down the corridor.

He threw again, hoping the grenade landed far enough away to keep them moving to their final destination. As Tom dragged him back in, Josiah's eyes rolled up into his head, remembering . . . *Had to keep the FBI and the CIA distrustful of each other, not sharin' information. Otherwise, they'd have found those terrorists and 9-11 wouldn't have happened! And we couldn't have gone to war in the Middle East to grab oil and influence . . . Had to do it or the country'd been lost!*

"No, you don't understand yet, do you," said Tom. "I apologize, that's my fault. I can only hold a fraction of the web of existence in my mind, and it's difficult to explain even that small part to you. But I'll try. People think the world's growing more complex, but it's only because they're growing more connected that they finally see and fear the complexity. It was always there. But all the complexity, all the connections, confuse and distract them. They can't see the big picture, so they can stop being afraid . . ." Another toss on "4," another explosion.

"Funny . . . humanity's great at the tiny patterns. We can find quarks in an atom and Jesus's face in a tortilla. But that big picture is so elusive, so overwhelming, people refuse to believe something as obvious as their life in Des Moines affects lives in Delhi. That's big picture lesson number one: Mutual need unites us. You can't get away behaving like a rampaging mountain gorilla if you're concerned about those outside your troop. Evolution didn't wire us to see the big picture—yet. We hunker down in our narrow primate lives with our little brains, only capable of close association with about a hundred and fifty others: the size of a tribe. Our tribe."

The grenade at "5" hit a hanging fluorescent fixture and bounced, lying halfway to its target. "Shit . . ." He punched the door button as fast as he could. *BOOM!* The elevator rattled on its rails for a moment, then continued. "Goes to show, anyone can get sloppy. Anyway, there's always someone around who thinks big. Socrates, Gautama Buddha, Jesus, Copernicus, Galileo, Darwin . . . At least by the time humanity got to Einstein, no one wanted to kill him for thinking up relativity. But because we're now so enmeshed with technological networks, we all get a glimmer of the big picture. And we need to see it more than ever. Unfortunately for you, the more who do see, the more enemies you and your friends will have.

"Can't you see everything's connected, Josiah, but you don't feel the strings? Life's web is not a spider's web with you in the center, but a hugely dispersed web with many centers all interlinked. Or imagine it like the network of neurons in the brain. You might think your little neuron is indispensable to the system. But it's not. Even though your acts were not chaos theory's piddly butterfly wings—but dragon wings whipping storms into hurricanes—history will continue gratefully without you."

Another toss 'n' tremble at "6" and this time, he took care to aim. "Removing you, Carter, and Bruce simply stops your goals from infecting us. If I removed the entire Phoenix Club from the system, there'd be a slight hiccup, a moment of needless panic as society reassesses priorities and jobs are refilled, and then . . . we'd go on and grow without you. Because the future is change and change is the future."

The universe craved equilibrium. The concept of karma, the effect of one's deeds on their past, present, and future, was a physical law of the universe and Tom could see it as plainly as Josiah squirming under his hiking boot.

At "7," his grenade toss was unnecessary. The hallway was

already alight, chunks of burning wood and plaster having fallen from the floors above. He threw one anyway. "Karma reflects the interconnectedness of everything. And it doesn't apply to some next, reincarnated life, it applies to this one. Of course evildoers are eventually vanquished. Their denial of interconnectedness, thinking they can do what benefits them and hurts others, lays the groundwork for their destruction. Newton's third law: Every action has an equal and opposite reaction—whether you're a bloodthirsty dictator or a saint. No deed, good or bad, goes unpunished."

He tossed a grenade on "8" and the building groaned bitterly, fed up with violence. "The fall of empires is karma, because if leaders screw the system to their benefit, denying interconnectedness, the system will screw them. And everyone who let them get away with it. How many empires have to fall before we realize that?"

Tom paused. "I am today, Josiah, what you will be tomorrow. Do you understand now?"

Rheumy eyes glistening with tears bore into his. Lips tried to voice a thought, then stumbled, failing, . . . *but that's not the ball you use, Davy, that's not the right one . . .*

Tom sighed. "Didn't think so." The doors rattled open. "The ninth circle. Final home for the worst of the worst: traitors." He tossed Josiah over his shoulder and followed the concrete corridor about forty feet, halfway to the last fiery ceiling hole. Tom felt the intention before Josiah's hand crept down his back for a grenade dangling from Tom's jeans. He slapped the old man's wrist. "Don't even think about it. I got eyes in the back of my consciousness." Josiah tucked his hand under his chin and whimpered.

The glass-enclosed lab appeared empty, but banks of fluorescent lights were on. Inside were a hundred steel tables lined up in neat rows, each with a nanofabricator on top. The clean-room door was locked. The blast of Tom's Glock reverberated down the empty hall, and he kicked the demolished door open.

He could feel Carter hiding inside.

Tom dumped Josiah on the hard linoleum floor, the old man sliding on his ass to a corner like a terrified child cowering under his towering shadow. Tom popped the Glock's magazine out, pocketing it. That left one bullet chambered. He presented it, bowing with a ceremonial flourish.

"Mr. Secretary, your way out is one bullet. Make it count."

Head bowed away from the bogeyman, Josiah tucked his hands under his armpits and pulled his knees under his chin as far as arthritis allowed. Disgusted, Tom tossed the gun at Brant's feet. Soon enough, the old man would play. It would be the president of the Phoenix Club's only salvation. And they both knew it.

"Carter!" He could feel his partner's presence, crouched behind a supply cabinet against a wall. "White metal cabinet, fourth sprinkler from the door. You can't hide anymore."

A surprisingly calm voice said, "Why not, Peter? So you can gun me down? Or infect me?"

"I know the future. You're going to die regardless of what you or I do. And I can't help but infect you. I could sing "The End" like Morrison, but I don't think you'd like it."

He stood in front of the first line of fabricators. Each had a silver emblem on the front: "Biogineers." His first company seemed several lifetimes ago.

It was time to get to work. Tom made a pile of anything flammable on a fabricator table in the center of the room, then poured a bottle of cleaning solution on top of the pile. "You know why the Catholic Church burned heretics at the stake instead of giving them a much more merciful beheading? 'Cause they were fucked up, sadistic sons of bitches who wanted to make the poor, free-thinking bastards suffer as much as possible. I understand that now." He took a piece of paper, rolled it up, and lit it with Josiah's cigar lighter. Ceremonially touching the pile like a torchbearer at the Olympic flame, he waited for it to catch. "In fact, burning alive is dead last on my personal ways-to-go list, but sometimes, it's the most appropriate choice, especially when you have to destroy bots." When it was good and hot, he threw nanobot transportation packages (bundles of shrink-wrapped plastic bottles) onto the pyre. The burning plastic made a noxious stink, but it was a roaring fire in no time.

Carter scuttled, diving under one of many steel tables holding the nanofabricators, but not before he aimed a Beretta M9. If Tom had not had the luxury of slow-time to move, it would have struck the center of his chest. Instead, it clipped his shoulder. Jerking back with the impact, he instantly cut the pain receptors to his shoulder, sent extra nanoplatelets to the wound site to speed blood coagulation, and kept coming as though nothing happened. He had to stop being so cocky.

"I can feel you in my brain, Carter. You're a big, bright red flag that sounds like cymbals crashing and tastes and smells astringent, like . . . scotch. I feel you on my skin, like a tingling I want to gouge out with my fingernails and in my muscles, like a sharp ache. I can even feel you in the continuum of time."

"Davy!" cried Josiah, still huddled in his corner. "Please come back, Davy!" When Davy didn't come, Tom could feel Josiah pick up the Glock and aim at its confused, disturbed, heartsick target . . . It exploded, and darkness fell on a small part of Tom's mind named "Josiah." The old man's whimpering ceased.

Tom reeled in the dying vortex, but he urged himself forward. "He caught my drift."

Screams of insanity, causing bloody chaos, erupted on the intercom. Carter had left it on to monitor the floors above. By the noise level, every soldier was infected, shooting anything that moved, including each other. It sounded like the end of *The Wild Bunch*.

"How could you do this to all of us?" asked Tom.

"That carnage's not my fault. It's yours."

"You're in such denial, you don't know all that mayhem is to stop you?"

After a moment of silence, Carter said, "You wouldn't believe me if I told you why."

"Why?" Tom flung the closest steel table aside like cardboard. It crashed into fabs, plastic and metal shrapnel flying.

Carter took aim again. Moving quickly, Tom dodged the bullet by a foot.

"I was lazy the first time," chided Tom. "Not anymore."

Carter leaned against his table's leg, thick smoke causing chest-crushing cough spasms. Careless, his gun hand leaned out in the aisle.

BANG!

Carter's gun skittered across the linoleum, ten feet away. He dived to retrieve it, and Tom shot again and again, pushing the battered firearm down the aisle, too far for Carter to reach without exposing himself to a bullet.

Carter was silent for a few seconds, then finally croaked out, "I may not know the future like you, but I know the world enough to know someone's got to control everything people like you create. I didn't want it to be the government. Or we'd have *Brave New World*, like Josiah wanted." Coughs racked his body again. "And I didn't want corporations or the rich to control it because of the price. I wanted it to be us. I thought between you and me, we could manage it and be fair and let everyone evolve. If they wanted to. With my . . . persuasive abilities and your . . . fucking moral imperative . . ." Another fit gripped him. "We just needed help. So I danced with the devil. I was dancing with him already. Worked it from the inside. Got the backing and support. When I found out what Josiah planned, I tried to keep his support and undermine him at the same . . ." He coughed uncontrollably.

"You arrogant motherfucker . . . you can't dance with the devil without learning the steps. And then you're a devil yourself. I know better than anyone. Josiah would have succeeded enslaving the world for its own damned good. And you would have helped. And what about Dulles? Why did you let him die? He was trying to stop all this and save us!"

Carter snorted. "Fuck it. You do know everything."

"And what about Nick? You killed Nick!"

"They were going to kill him anyway. It was all planned before I joined. They were going to develop Nick's research in a way DARPA wouldn't have allowed for years. If I hadn't done it, they wouldn't have given me the patents, and they would have given them to Lobo. Better I killed him and let him . . . go humanely. Lobo's a fucking animal."

"A *dead* animal. And what about me?"

Carter scrambled to the door. Tom dashed to intercept him, but Carter was still quick and slipped past. Tom slowly aimed at the back of Carter's left knee. The joint exploded and spewed a slow-motion floral spray of bright red blood like a small firework burst. Each blood drop was a mini-mirror of Carter, a tiny bead of mercury divided through vigorous shaking from its greater whole. Tom saw a multitude of Carters in the spray of blood as he screamed, tripped, and stumbled to the floor.

Tom shook the meditation from his thoughts. They were running out of time. Limping forward with his now-painful left knee, he yanked Carter up and grabbed both upper arms from behind. He squeezed them back just hard enough to dislocate both shoulders with an extra tug. Carter squirmed and panted in agony. Tom had to dampen his own pain receptors so his own shoulders would not fail him.

"I know you hate me," growled Carter. Squeezing harder, Tom teased the line just before connective tissue tore. Carter struggled to get the words out over the pain. "But you would never have accomplished . . . half as much . . . if I hadn't pushed you . . .

either by ignoring . . . or driving you. I made you, Peter. I gave you dreams. I gave you a life! I made you reach for things you didn't believe you'd have. And look what you've done! It might have got out of control . . ."

"Out of control? You're insane! You almost enslaved the world, asshole!"

"I could have freed it! It would have been as easy."

"Easy for whom? You? Or me?"

Carter didn't answer. Enraged, Tom threw Carter facedown on the steel table. His nose blew open, blood gushing. Tom held his head down, crushing his neck with both hands.

The bloody man sputtered, spitting out a tooth. "Not leaving a beautiful corpse," croaked Carter. "Please . . ." he wheezed, desperate for air. "Don't kill . . ."

"You've got to go. Like the rest of them. But you wanted me to do it for you, didn't you? You're the most lazy, self-absorbed, self-destructive, narcissistic sociopath I've ever met."

"Not . . . yet. Going to have . . . a kid. Let me at least see him . . . be born. And then I'll know . . . I did something worthwhile."

Tom had looked forward to the moment all morning. A wide, white and toothy grin split his soot-darkened face, and he practically sang the words, "He's not your son, Carter."

Furious, even savage, for the first time, Carter's body jerked madly under Tom's grip. "What the fuck's that mean?"

"He's my son. My sperm samples. Not yours. Amanda fooled us both. She wants to name him Peter for more than just sentimental reasons."

Carter sagged under Tom's grasp, a small snigger escaping his blood-soaked face.

Tom released him. The fire spread, engulfing fabricators and nanobots. Flames licked at natural gas lines above the workbenches at the wall. They had only moments.

"Why don't you just kill me, hold your breath, and get the fuck out?" asked Carter.

"I'll never make it. I told you, I know the future already. Radical evolution has its disadvantages."

"Shit."

"Yeah. I wonder who it'll be worse for. You or me."

"You. You'll think about it more." He snorted, "Some Superman. I never even saw you in tights."

Tom smiled. "Asshole."

Carter grinned back, bloody and gap-toothed . . .

. . . as their world exploded in a white miasma of energy.

The blast hurtled everything in its shattering path spinning through the air. Tom overturned the blood-smeared steel table as a shield and threw himself over Carter. He couldn't say it was without thinking, because he was thinking of eight things at once, like the shrapnel's trajectory and the timing of the blast wave's impact and what effect it might have on a steel table protecting them. But clearly, his automatic impulse was to save Carter. Not kill him.

As much control as Tom thought he had over his mind, his unconscious was incorrigibly independent, no matter what the upgrades. Pain in the ass.

As the blast retreated, the person below him felt different than before. Like a network came online and linked to his. Tom heaved himself off Carter. The hyperreality bots Tom had unleashed on the Phoenix Camp and covered his body with had been inhaled and absorbed and had reached Carter's brain. But instead of insanity and fear, Carter locked eyes with him.

Is this it? thought Carter. This question swirled on top of the fear of mental exposure, death, and the unknown territory of Tom's mind. But he wasn't afraid of his visions, unlike Josiah and the others. He was in control as ever, fighting to keep a lid on his secrets.

"Welcome to the Occupation," thought Tom.

They both heard the R.E.M. song play in the background.

I have to die listening to that alt-shit, too?

Even if I forced you, it won't be for long.

Carter coughed hard, gasping for oxygen that wasn't there. Tom opened his mind to share Thomas Paine, *Homo excelsior.* Between coughing jags, Carter regarded his friend for the first time in boundless wonder and mind-tripping awe.

I am everything you wanted me to create. And more, thought Tom. *Then forgive me, Pete. Please.*

R.E.M. ceased, and a lone acoustic guitar strummed an opening riff in a flowing legato as a pleasing, light tenor sang the Beatles classic of love, loss, and the need for connection, "While My Guitar Gently Weeps."

Finally, a decent song, thought Carter, fighting the pain of his broken body, a brutal carbon monoxide–induced headache and useless panting from the smoke inhalation, which would only bring his end sooner. *Good taste occasionally breaks out in you, Bernhardt.* A sonorous string section picked up the bass lines. *It's really good. Who's covering it?*

Me.

As Tom sang of their love lost in exchange for control and betrayal, he asked, *Why? I need to know.*

Carter's mind released its tight rein, and Tom relived his memories, fragmented and subjective like all recollections: Peter refusing to cheat with Carter on an organic chemistry test; Peter humiliating an arrogant Stanford professor with his accurate prediction of biotech's future, which he then helped bring about; Peter's simple, heartfelt wedding to Amanda; Peter working later nights than anyone at the fledgling Biogineers; Peter refusing to partake of the club's camp prostitutes; Peter refusing to murder Anthony Dulles . . .

The memories had one theme: Carter could never have done those things. His perfection and grace masked the frightened, jealous boy who both admired and hated Peter for his ability and honesty. Carter recognized Peter's desire to become an aristocrat like himself. But self-made men make aristocrats insecure. After all the years and travails they had endured together, only with this technological link did they share the understanding of how fundamentally different—and similar—they were.

Soot-and-blood-smeared eyes closed, Carter listened to Tom's accusations of diversion and perversion, but he colored the lyrics, assuring Carter it wasn't a perversion of sexuality or even morality. These were malleable and subject to cultural conventions. It was a perversion of something more fundamental: his soul. Carter's oxygen-deprived brain accepted the judgment. There was no energy left to argue against truth. Confusion set in, and the dying man's mind free-floated in a subconscious dream state of past and present, which Tom meandered through with him.

Drifting to the top for a moment, Carter begged, *Please, Pete.*

Tom took one last breath of lung-singeing air and held it as the world burned around them. The heat was unbearable. He shut down his skin's nerve receptors to ignore the pain. Carter couldn't, and Tom felt his agony of skin bubbling and burning.

I forgive you, Carter. Tom hoped he could forgive himself. Before the end.

With the song finished, and forgiveness granted, Carter's mind quieted. Tom felt the moment Carter fell unconscious, like his mind's mute button clicked. There was still peripheral activity, but no one there to care. Tom cradled his old friend in his arms and kissed his bloody lips. He was no longer the beautiful man admired, respected, envied, and desired by all. He was a mutilated mess, with only a little seed of humanity remaining in his diminishing brain. And soon, that would be gone, a lump of useless flesh devoured by flames. And what would be left of Carter Potsdam, the Sun King?

Or Thomas Paine? Peter Bernhardt was irrelevant to him. Another species, he had been consigned to watery oblivion a lifetime ago.

Life flickered in Carter's mind, stretching out into the darkness of the universe with Tom there to catch him. Suddenly, in a burst of pure energy, everything that was ever Carter Potsdam exploded outward, a psychic atomic blast, beyond heat, beyond light, beyond power. The wave reverberated through Tom, and he shuddered in shock as it rolled past.

The fleshy shell he clutched to his chest was no longer just limp. It was empty. He gently laid the body on the floor. Was this what death was for everyone? Or only for those who had been nano-enhanced? He hadn't felt the shockwave when Josiah or the soldiers died. Was it because he was inside his friend's mind? Or that he simply cared?

The contents of Carter's mind clung to his, like hurricane debris stuck to a vast chain-link fence. He scanned the jetsam and was surprised by its completeness: It suffused his own thoughts, having absorbed Carter's essence. It coexisted with pieces of Anthony Dulles, Bruce Lobo, Josiah Brant, and his own multiple selves. It was crowded in there . . . and yet not. He heard music . . .

The song told him the answer: To forgive himself, he had to forgive the human urge for power and status, which Peter himself once craved, and Tom had used as a weapon. He had to forgive humanity and embrace the universal consciousness.

Only the practicalities remained. He could hold his breath longer than it would take the fire to consume him. Might as well just hyperventilate and let the carbon monoxide do its job, in spite of the respirocyte's efficiency. It wouldn't be bad. It would be like drowning, and he had practice in that, too. Better than watching himself burn to death. Or maybe just a bullet to the head, like Josiah and Chang . . .

"Want some cheese with that whine? Get your ass outta here!" His father stood astride the flames, arms akimbo before him.

"But . . . Pop . . ." he sputtered.

"Am I talkin' to the wall?" complained the old man to no one. "I am! I'm talkin' to the Goddamned wall!"

"Pop, I'm dying here, all right? What? You gonna nag me till I'm dead? I still don't even know if you're some fucking hallucination."

"Watch that mouth!"

"Sorry," he mumbled. "Or an honest-to-God ghost, but whatever the hell you are, it's too late. Have you taken a look around me?"

Faintly, he heard something beyond his father's carping. The flames' roar was loud, but Tom's sensitive auditory cortex picked up the thin sound.

"Tom? Tom, are you down there? Answer me . . . please, God . . . Tom!"

Talia? Was this part of the hallucination? He wished he could see her, like he saw his father.

The screaming continued. But it wasn't in his head. He felt the external, electrical source near the door. The intercom. Even though the blast should have demolished it, there was her voice. He was sure of it. He had shut down so much of himself preparing to die, he couldn't hear her. He opened up his senses and let layers of the world flood in. Talia stood in the foyer between the blast and security doors. She would have them opened in a minute because he had disabled the security systems, putting her in terrible danger. Could it be possible she still loved him? That she might want to save his sorry ass so they could be together?

"Got the smartest Goddamned boy on the planet, and he still don't know shit. Go get her, idiot!" ordered the old man.

Sheepishly, he rose, muttering, "Yes, Pop . . ." Carter-thoughts said, *Take the shirt,* so he stripped the bloody cotton shirt from his friend's body and wrapped it around his waist. Staggering through the flames to the door, Josiah-thoughts said, *Take the jacket.* Tucked in the corner, it had escaped the flames, so he pulled off the bomber jacket and tied it around his waist, too. His skin's pain was intense. Bruce-thoughts said, *Shut it down,* so he dampened the agony, except for his fingertips, each stinging like a lit candle.

Emergency stairways were engulfed and impassable. He ran to the elevator. There was no electrical power, but it wasn't too hot to touch. He forced his fingers into the crevice and pried open the doors. Inside the dark car, he jumped and pushed open the emergency trapdoor overhead, disguised as a light panel. Hoisting himself through the hole, he crawled onto the ceiling of the car. It was very dark, except for the faint light of fires seeping through the minute gaps of the doors. Being a modern shaft, there was no emergency ladder on the wall, only metal tracks to guide the car up and down. Ever the engineer, Chang-thoughts imagined the government architect's incredulity: *What could possibly go wrong in a modern elevator to need a shaft ladder?*

It was eight floors straight up with only large steel crossbars every four feet. Grabbing a crossbar at the bottom of the eighth level, he hoisted himself up each section, one at a time. Although the distance between rungs wasn't hard, the bottoms of his boots were caked with grease, making feet as slippery as hands. A good grip was impossible.

One mind-track concentrated on not falling, while the other tried to make contact outside the building. But he was in too deep for an outside line.

Hands slid away from metal . . . He quickly bear-hugged a guide rail. Left arm hooked around steel, he carefully untied Carter's shirt with his right hand and wrapped the shirt around each rail as a harness, releasing it only to tie it around the next rail and pull himself up.

BOOM!

An armory explosion on the second floor rocked the structure. Steel elevator doors plummeted down the shaft. Tom braced himself, head tucked to his chest, grabbing the guide beam with both arms, but a hunk of steel hit his shoulder like a speeding bus. His feet slid out and he dangled by Carter's five-hundred-dollar Egyptian-cotton button-down five floors from the bottom, grateful for the well-made seams. Scrambling for a greasy foothold, he climbed the remaining three floors, passing the blasted opening, the hallway nothing but flame.

Tottering on the first level's two-inch-deep ledge, he touched the doors. They were hot. Apologizing to his volunteer fireman father for all the broken safety rules, he pried at the doors, gripping the edges as hard as possible to prevent falling backward down the shaft from the heat wave's force. He pitched forward, throwing Josiah's jacket over his head, and stumbled into the fiery hallway that led out of the mines.

Talia had opened the inner security doors, but held back by a tunnel of flames, stood there uncertain. Dozens of weapons' discharge rang out in the distance behind her.

Dulles-thoughts urged him, *Faster, faster, save her!* Thirty feet away and closing the gap, he screamed, "Stay away from everyone! Away from me!"

"Tom!"

"Talia! Get everyone away. We're all infected!"

"Ruth protected us! We're here for you . . ."

Ruth, his darling, brilliant Ruth, had figured out what he'd done in her absence, using his protective bot vaccine on them. Surprise piled on top of surprise, none of which were in his future script.

Wishing beyond hope they were home free, Tom yelled, "You *are* my guardian angel!"

R-R-R-RUMBLERUMBLEBOOM!

Erupting from the belly of the mine, the explosion poured out the only vent: The blast doors. Even with superhumanly fast reactions, there was no way to escape the fireball.

"Run!" he screamed as the first flames engulfed him.

Fire flowed over, under, around him like water, consuming cloth, hair, skin. He was thrown to his knees, then face. There was intense pain, and then none. The continued cooking of flesh and bone wasn't so awful. He cut off his pain receptors, but even so, there was a place past pain, where pain wasn't a word anymore, it so overwhelmed the brain and made flesh immaterial.

When the tide of fire retreated down the shaft, he heard Talia and a rescue team dash in, extinguishing what blaze they could to carry his body out.

He only heard them because he was blind.

The bang of rifle shots grew closer, then exploded around him, but because he couldn't see, his brain filled in the missing perceptions, creating a kaleidoscope of color and sound in his head. He checked his internal connections. Even after the holocaust, they worked. He frantically searched for a wireless network that would allow him to see. A camp security line let him log into cameras, which he swung around until he could find himself in the action. A front and rear detail of armed men surrounded a stretcher bearing a black-and-red mass that only vaguely resembled a human in size and shape. They picked off the few remaining security guards who threatened them.

"Ru . . . sssss . . ." he whispered to Talia, who was near him. "Ruthsssssssss?" He could feel the ultraviolet panic in her vibration; taste her hot chocolate effort to stop her tears.

"She thought you wanted to kill yourself, so we came back, shot ourselves full of stuff, and . . . we're here. She's on the *Pequod*."

That's all he needed to know. He sent Ruth a message only she would understand. When she responded in seconds, he sent two streams of data to download and process.

One was the digital recording of everything Peter Bernhardt and Thomas Paine knew or had experienced about the Phoenix Club.

The second was his lifeline.

Talia was on one of her infinite cell phones. "Yes!" she screamed above the roar of the rotors. "But, Steve, he's . . . ! Yes . . . ! At the pad!" She ordered the copter pilot directly to the roof of Sacramento General.

After heli-medics wrapped Tom in blankets to put out his smoldering body, hooked him to an IV, and stuck a breathing tube down his trachea, he finally relaxed. Knowing he would finally die was oddly freeing, and he accepted the karmic irony of his fate with calm. There was nothing for him to do until he saw Ruth again, except continue transmitting. And not die. Not quite yet.

Assuming he was unconscious, Talia released her tears as she huddled next to his still body. "Is this what you wanted? Did you think your . . . revolution . . ." she spat, "would succeed?"

Yes, thought all the people contained within him. *And we'll know for sure soon enough.*

CHAPTER SEVENTY-THREE

Hooked up to life support; both kidneys on dialysis; cross-wired sense organs either destroyed or turned off for comfort; burns over eighty percent of his body; mummy-wrapped in artificial skin to keep bodily fluids from leaking out and dehydrating him to death. All this existed in one reality, but the only reality that mattered anymore was the one contained in his group-mind's memory. As the entity still known as Tom lay waiting, he couldn't help but compare his own end to Pop's. Whereas his father, through forgetting, had made peace with the vacuity of time and space and past and future, he clung to his memories, because it was all he had left. If his father had gained just enough recollection to kill him, Tom had too much to die. Had he learned nothing from Pop? And what further lessons would Pop convey before the end? He hoped for one more visit.

As he waited for something to happen, he played "Yesterday" in his head and decided he agreed with Pop on at least one thing. It was a very good song. A very good song, indeed.

The second track of his brain plucked out a verbal bass line: "I think I can, I think I can, I think I can . . ." He could only quit his marathon at the finish line, but it was a race he ran alone, a mind floating in a virtual world of his own making. When they put him on morphine, it was even worse. At first, he didn't care about anything. Then, as they upped it to a palliative dose, the combination of drugs and wiring made for deeply disturbing dreams, and the lack of outside stimulation made them more than real. His brain created a phantom body and sent it through the flames . . . Tony lay in the yacht's dining room, his skull splayed open . . . Amanda ran from Tom to the plane . . . Josiah tormented by Davy Brant . . . Carter dying, held by Tom . . . Bruce burned alive . . . Talia leaving Tom . . . These new memoryscapes were too real. Was he fated to relive only nightmarish pasts and not the moments he cherished?

After two hours and eighteen minutes, he heard his door open and people push something large on wheels into his room. One voice stood out.

"Got in himmel . . ." she gasped. Her GO buzzed. She had been ordered by Tom to keep it on, regardless of hospital policy. She read her message and quickly typed back.

"He w-w-w-wants I should set it up. Right n-n-now," said Ruth, spastically tapping a fingernail on a metal case. He felt bad he was causing her such distress, but she agreed it had to be done. Heavy metal cases were shuffled and scraped across linoleum.

"Thank God I got the board to agree to this," said Steve.

"For a new wing? Manna from heaven," replied Ruth.

"Considering Thomas Paine doesn't even exist officially, I guess it is. I just hope he doesn't set fire to this one."

The fourth person in the room didn't speak. He supposed Talia had nothing to say. But he was very glad she was here. He wasn't sure he could do this without her, even though he regretted surprising her. It wasn't fair, but if she had been made privy to all his plans, if anyone but Ruth had known what he was developing, she might have stopped him. And he had come so far, suffered so greatly to achieve so much, it would have been a great waste not to at least try.

After never feeling so alive as he did fully functional, plugged in, and switched on, the absence of any connection, be it to flesh or silicon, made his loss more acute. He ached to reach them. If Ruth was successful, he would be able to.

Linked to Ruth's GO, he scanned the media feeds as he waited. BBC World had the best update on the explosion outside Yosemite. A male reporter wearing a hazmat suit pointed to a huge hole in the ground surrounded by dead soldiers, intercut with club members' interviews, emergency personnel tending to the living, and a diagram of the blast. As of now, Carter and Josiah were missing, but no one dared presume them dead. Would they ever excavate far enough to find their final resting place? Given the intensity of the fire, they'd be ash. He could see the club's hand in the downplayed spin, which raised more questions than it answered.

None of it mattered. The world would know the truth soon. He would make sure of it.

After one hour, seven minutes, and forty-three seconds passed (he didn't need to track it anymore, but his wiring couldn't help it), Steve asked, "What next?"

"Did you prepare the site?" asked Ruth.

"Yeah, but isn't he wireless?"

"F-f-f-faster this way. Plug in."

When Tom arrived by helivac, Steve opened the receiver in his leg and attached a special plug per Ruth's orders. Rubber-gloved fingers fumbled groin bandages as Steve plugged in a special broadband nanocable.

There was a delicious surge of mental energy from the electrical connection at boot-up. At last, a reason to be . . . Software programs entered like thoughts. He wasn't alone anymore; he had a direction, a goal, even if it was only an electronic one. Soon the link would be more than that; it would be the human connection of communication. He had quashed his emotions so long and so hard that now they overflowed, unhindered by the need to survive.

Reaching out his thoughts to Ruth's computers, he could "feel" them, "smell" them, "taste" them, even though none of these were the right word. Language had failed him throughout his transformative process and even more so now. He decided his lighthearted choice for the name of their computer program—Major Tom, the hero of David Bowie's "Space Oddity"—was sadly predictive.

Ruth spoke into a microphone jacked into his wiring so it was easier for Tom to hear. "R-r-ready?" Her voice was as intimate as could be, having come from inside his brain, as if she had crawled in, twitching, to join him.

Tom took a deep breath off his inhalation tube and spoke with his mind: "This is Major Tom to Ruth. I'm outputting through the audio." The voice sampling they painstakingly took months ago worked, coming through Ruth's speakers loud and clear, sounding spookily like his bourbon-and-smokes tone.

There was a gasp from across the room. It was Talia.

"Commencing download. Servers on," replied Ruth.

"You do have a sense of humor!" said Steve.

"What humor?" she scolded back.

The same wires that had moved information into his brain were now moving it out as the nanopipeline simultaneously recorded the hundreds of thousands of neurons his intravascular nanowires touched, and the impulses traveled along synapses to the thousands of neurons they contacted.

His idea was simple, yet supposedly impossible: reverse-engineer Tom's brain by mapping the neurons' signal locations, stimulating and recording all the data they contained, and storing those thoughts in the newly mapped virtual brain, located on hundreds of computer servers. If it worked, it was way cooler than some role-playing avatar. Tom had little hope of success. The structure he conceived was too simple, too limited to contain him. But if he didn't try, he was crazier than he thought.

And then came the greatest moment of simultaneous awareness he had ever known.

If he thought he was connected to the far corners of his brain before, now it was a waterfall, a never-ending rush where each drop of water was a memory, emotion, point of view, action, perception, surging past with all the others. Life passing before your eyes had nothing on the unearthly exhilaration of tsunami-surfing your very essence. Especially when it was pieces of six other mental landscapes! And it contained more than that. It included everyone he ever knew. He located the three women who made up his lovescape. Each seemed to emerge from a distinct part of his brain: Amanda from his hypothalamus, where hormonal regulation governed sex, the body's rhythms, hungers, and the need to parent; Talia from his amygdala, where fear, emotions, and rewards were processed; and Ruth from his frontal lobe, where the higher cognitive functions of intelligence, language, and problem-solving took place.

He tried to focus on one moment, one feeling, but reeled, dizzy with effort. What he sensed couldn't be labeled sensation at all, but rather a reinterpretation of all perception ever experienced, the white noise of a lifetime in synchronous playback.

And the music! A fraction of a second of sound identified tens of thousands of songs flying by too quickly to enjoy. Somehow the rush did not create discord, but made its own beautiful music.

For a moment, he wondered if this was a taste of what a creator might feel perceiving the entire universe at once. The vastness of his mind and life astonished and humbled him. But a leitmotif of love of family and friends could be heard above the noise. And what was more humbling than that?

If all went well, he would enjoy the show one last time, hoping all their work would take him from this endless pain to a better place. But what would that place be like?

Ruth rocked back and forth on her stool. "I think your output is . . . all right. B-b-but what is all right supposed to look like?"

"Time to spacewalk," said Tom's voice. "Turn the camera to the room." Ruth did and Tom's inner vision saw Steve at the foot of the bed, shuffling his feet with a tired, nervous expression, and Talia, legs crossed over and under, arms crossed, back curled into a question mark, as though she could pretzel-twist herself away. "Steve? Thanks, man. I owe you."

"Just make some history today, will you? My job's riding on this." He smiled halfheartedly. "Now, as your doctor, I need to know how you're feeling."

"There's pain, but I can handle it. I've dampened what nerves are left, and the last dose of morphine wore off an hour ago. But no more drugs. They'll affect the upload."

"Got it."

"Tal? What's wrong?"

Her head turned away. She mumbled, "What's wrong? Leave it to you to reduce your . . ." she paused, unable to say the word. ". . . to some glam-rock ballad." She buried her head against the back of her chair.

"Tal, I'm sorry, but there's not much time. I've left you Prometheus Industries. Carter's death transferred his part-ownership to me in an automatic cash buyout to Amanda. It was his posthumous gift to us. You are the full owner, with Ruth and Steve as trustees. I believe the three of you together can best guide such a world-changing technology in the future."

"We . . . ?"

"Let me finish. Talia, I loved you, even though I knew there was never any hope for us. Hate made me a monster, not the technology.

I was less than human the moment you saved me . . . and you deserve better. And I think you know where to find him."

Steve concentrated on Tom's monitors, checking vital signs. Talia caught his eyes, and the doctor stared back in pained hope. He walked over and whispered in her ear. Luckily, Ruth turned up the input volume. "Regardless of how you feel about me, he's hanging on by a thread for you. It's taking enormous effort. Make it worth it."

For once, Talia saw the man Tom saw. She stared at her fretting hands, ashamed.

"Ruth," said Tom, "I've left you the Swiss bank accounts with Thomas Paine's money. That should take care of us . . ."

"Us?"

"We have a deal. I promised you my work, then my mind, then my life. Forever. Do you still want me? Even if I'm not quite 'me' anymore?"

Ruth simply rocked and hummed in reply.

A window popped up on the monitor and his internal screen: "Upload Complete."

"T-T-Tom . . ."

"I know, Ruthie. I know . . ." Even though he was still connected and transmitting thoughts, his rushing essence no longer flowed, and the energy surge's delicious flavor tapered off. As the loneliness crept back, a wave of fear gripped him. What if the upload failed? Would it be the ultimate isolation? If his memories were gone forever, would that be the end? Or would the dead remain a part of the memories of the living, as long as they had memories, and then disappear for good once they were dead and gone? Or was there an afterlife, as the priests always promised? Was his father there?

It was time to find out.

"Steve, turn off the life support," Tom said.

The doctor looked stricken. "Tom, I can't . . ."

"You're not betraying your oath. You're expanding it."

Steve shook his head.

If Tom could have made the computer speaker sigh, he would have. "Ruth?"

She rocked more strenuously. *"Nein . . . nein . . ."*

"Talia?" he asked.

She rose from her chair and perched on the side of the bed, reaching down to hold the bandaged remains of his right hand. She leaned toward his face, mostly obscured by gauze, searching for the man she knew. "I'm here."

"Turn it off. Please."

Without a word, Talia leaned over and shut off the respirator. The room was quiet.

"Wish I could see you," he said. "With my eyes."

"Your memory of me is better than the reality," said Talia. "It always was. And it doesn't matter, baby. It's over. It's all over. And I'm here. With you. Now all you have to do is just let go. Let go of everything."

"I'll be alone . . ." said Tom.

"Oh, baby, you won't be. You know what I was thinking, coming to get you? Remember how you wanted to take the *Pequod* up the Hudson? To show me where you grew up? And how you swam in the river? You said it always made you feel like a new man. Remember?"

"Yes . . ."

"Let's go there."

"Can . . . ?"

"You know we can. It's a beautiful night. There's moonlight playing on the water. It looks so cool, so inviting. Doesn't it? You know you want to go in. Just jump in the water, Tom. It's right there, waiting for you. Jump in and swim. And keep on swimming, baby."

"You . . . swim . . . ?"

"Soon, baby. Soon."

Talia stroked his wrapped hand as the mechanical voice fell silent and Tom's rattling breath stopped. The heart monitor, having maintained its steady rhythm until now, beeped erratically. She squeezed his hand. "Tom?"

He was swimming. And the water felt wonderful.

A snippet of music played on the computer's speakers. Bowie's Cool-Britannia voice cooed the journey had begun and he loved his wife very much.

"I know," replied Talia. "I love you, Thomas Paine."

She knows, thought Tom. Just as he saw Pop standing on the river's shore, he took one last, agonizing breath . . . and his chest collapsed with a sigh and stopped.

All eyes turned to the heart monitor and the drone of the flatline. Tom's body shook for a moment, then was still.

Talia rose, shaking with repressed tears. She held her hand out to Ruth. The scientist tried to reciprocate, but could not. Instead, she passed Talia and removed something from her breast pocket to place on Tom's body: two clipped glass slides containing two blood drops. Then she gently pulled the bottom of her pink button-down shirt out of her chinos and tore the hem a little, murmuring, *"Baruch Dayan Emet."* Her eyes met Talia's. "B-b-blessed is the one true judge."

"Can you bring him back to you, Ruth?" whispered Talia.

"I d-don't know," Ruth bleated.

"Where is he?"

"Not in there." Ruth pointed at the computers she had brought with her. "Too small, too little processing power. He's out there. In a server farm."

"Where is it?" asked Steve.

"He n-n-n-never told me," said Ruth, frowning as she logged back into Project Major Tom. "Miss Gray Hat knows."

"But you still don't know who Miss Gray Hat is?" asked Talia.

"*Nein* . . . Tom believed he'd know by now . . ." When the connection was complete, she asked the microphone, "Ground control to Major T-T-Tom? You there?"

"This is Major Tom to Ground Control."

Ruth bowed her head and under her breath said a prayer her father had often repeated: "*Baruch Atah Adonai Eloheinu Melech ha'olam oseh ma'aseh vereshit*"—We praise You, Eternal God, sovereign of the universe, source of creation and its wonders.

"The computer looks bigger . . ." murmured Talia.

Ruth and Steve glanced at each other and then at the body in the bed. They left unsaid that the body looked proportionally smaller. Rationalists didn't dabble in such anecdotal, subjective observations.

Tom stepped through the door. One moment, he had been in his dying body, feeling nothing but love for Talia, Ruth, and Steve, grateful these people were with him, the only ones left who knew him for what he had been and would be. He wasn't alone and felt their love completely, no barriers between them. They were one. That was all that was left of him at the end. Nothing else mattered.

And then, for a period of time both infinitesimal and endless, he seemed to be everywhere and nowhere. For that moment, he finally grasped what Buddhists meant by universal consciousness. But just as bodhi, the awakening of total awareness, was dawning . . .

He was back. But where?

It was the ocean-sized computerscape he had sensed when first connected to the Internet. Reaching out to the topography's edges, his home felt finite and yet potentially infinite. Time, space, and matter had no meaning here. Only energy. It was certainly a unique sensation, if he could use that word. But how do you describe sensation without senses? And what could he perceive with such limited means? There was a video camera and microphone in one world and nothing but information in the other. He knew that by asking these questions, he qualified as a form of consciousness. That was good news. But what kind? At least the music that flowed was really playing Bowie, not his brain processing a digital version or a memory, but an actual, digital recording. And what's more, he wasn't hearing it, he was the music, riding every note and percussive vibration. The tin can of his cybership gave him a radically different view of the universe.

"Ruthie? *Cogito ergo sum*," said the computer.

Talia and Steve looked confused, and Talia unconsciously grabbed Steve's hand.

"René Descartes," Ruth explained. "'I think, therefore I am.' The ghost in the machine."

"My revolution," said the ghost.

"But what happens to you now?" asked Talia.

"I'm sending my story to every website, e-mail, blog, and chatroom in the world. And Ruth will take care of me. *Tsum glik, tsum shlimazel?*"

Ruth's smile twitched at the corners. "'For better, for worse?' *Ach*, you're the perfect mate. Toilet seat stays down. Toothpaste stays capped. Never needs a hug."

But was he Thomas Paine or Peter Bernhardt or a group-mind of Bernhardt-Paine-Dulles-Eng-Lobo-Brant-Potsdam—or something else? He wasn't human. And he contained multitudes.

He was Major Tom, the friendliest ghost he knew, the first human-born artificial intelligence.

Talia hadn't let go her iron grip on Steve's hand while she scooted close to the computer, dragging him with her. "What's it feel like in there?"

Thus began the revolution.

ABOUT THE MUSIC

(R)evolution was born listening to a song, "The Boy in the Bubble," which Peter recalls during the first Phoenix Camp. Paul Simon's classic sums up the eternal dichotomy of society's grappling with technology. It's a miracle in the right hands. And a curse in the wrong ones. All those lasers and signals and millionaires and billionaires. Simon got that so right.

Many more songs influenced *(R)evolution* than the approximately forty that remain. I have a personal playlist of seventy songs that are in this novel one way or another, and there are dozens more on tap propelling the sequel. My MP3s get a workout.

The music and writing formed a feedback loop. A song inspired the story, which inspired another song, which inspired more story . . . and so on. It was a symbiotic, organic relationship much like Peter/Tom experiences, even within a strict story structure. Some songs felt deeply serendipitous, like listening to Todd Rundgren's "Initiation" and "Born to Synthesize." I had the bones of the club initiation scene before I found Rundgren's album. And those thorny issues of how Peter would survive? Todd helped. A lot. But finding "Born to Synthesize" was a revelation. In 1975, Rundgren wrote about the intersection of consciousness, thought, and sound. He intuited brain processes long before philosophers or neuroscientists were anywhere near the truth, and I could see a brain-computer interface in his lyrics. Todd, you rock.

My daughter was my muse for Peter/Tom. Her memories are laid down against her internal and external soundtrack of constant humming, singing, playing piano or guitar, and listening to her recordings. Everything relates to a song. Watching how she processes the world amazes me daily. My friend and artificial intelligence researcher, Dr. Benjamin Goertzel, was another inspiration, explaining how he solves problems musically both to encourage my daughter to realize her potential and to inform my hero.

Collecting and listening to this music in your own music library will provide a richer experience than my interpretations can convey. I encourage you to decipher Peter/Tom's musical motivations. You'll also have more insight into the inner life of his multimedia hacked 'n' jacked brain. That might be your brain someday, so take notes. I'll let you decide what songs you like best. Enjoy!

(R)EVOLUTION PLAYLIST

(in order of appearance)

"American Idiot," Green Day
"Tiny Dancer," Elton John
"Mother's Little Helper," the Rolling Stones
"Bad Brain," the Ramones
"The Star-Spangled Banner," Jimi Hendrix
"Once in a Lifetime," Talking Heads
"Born to Synthesize," Todd Rundgren
"With a Little Help from My Friends," the Beatles
"Norwegian Wood (This Bird Has Flown)," the Beatles
"Yesterday," the Beatles
"Hail to the Chief," United States Marine Corps Band
"American Pie," Don McLean
"Initiation," Todd Rundgren
"Suddenly Everything Has Changed," the Flaming Lips
"No Surprises," Radiohead
"School's Out," Alice Cooper
"What is the Light?" the Flaming Lips
"Welcome to the Occupation," R.E.M.
"Boy in the Bubble," Paul Simon
"Dead Man's Party," Oingo Boingo

"Put One Foot in Front of the Other," Miami Relatives
"Race for the Prize (Sacrifice of the New Scientists)," the
    Flaming Lips
"Every Breath You Take (I'll be Watching You)," the Police
"Help," the Beatles
"Message in a Bottle," the Police
"Let Me In," R.E.M.
"Good Vibrations," the Beach Boys
"I Just Wasn't Made for These Times," the Beach Boys
"Every Breath You Take (I'll be Watching You)," Karen Souza
"American Pie," CDM Rock Project
"Galileo," Indigo Girls
"Man in Black," Johnny Cash
"1812 Festival Overture, Op.49," Tchaikovsky
"Bad Moon Rising," John Fogerty
"The King Must Die," Elton John
"Initiation," Todd Rundgren
"Frankenstein," Aimee Mann
"Revenge," Rob Zombie (a.k.a. "Make Them Die Slowly,"
    White Zombie)
"Der Golem," *Fantômas*
"Golem II: The Bionic Vapour Boy," Mr. Bungle
"Déjà Vu," Crosby, Stills, Nash & Young
"A Man Out of Time," Elvis Costello
"String Quartet #2 in F# minor (final movement)," Arnold
    Schoenberg
"Requiem," György Ligeti
"White Wedding," Billy Idol
"Que Sera Sera," Doris Day
"Psycho Killer," Talking Heads
"The End," the Doors

"Welcome to the Occupation," R.E.M.
"While My Guitar Gently Weeps," the Beatles (Cirque du
   Soleil LOVE soundtrack)
"Yesterday," the Beatles
"Space Oddity," David Bowie

ACKNOWLEDGMENTS

As in all things, my mistakes are my own.

To the experts who generously gave their time to guide my research, allow me to express my gratitude: Jef Allbright, Jonathan Axelrad, Damien Broderick, James Clement, Michael Chorost, George Dvorsky, Benjamin Goertzel, Todd Huffman, James J. Hughes, Paul Karami, Eugen Leitl, Zack Lynch, Albert "Skip" Rizzo, Russell Rukin, Christine Petersen, Anders Sandberg, Lewis Seiden, John Smart.

I wish these brilliant scientists all possible success in the future, because their achievement is humanity's achievement: Dr. Theodore W. Berger and his colleagues' work on the prosthetic hippocampus; Dr. Rodolfo Llinas, the lead scientist on the endovascular nanowire system; Dr. Robert Freitas and Dr. Ralph Merkle, authors of "Nanomedicine" and conceivers of medical nanorobots.

Much thanks and admiration to the songwriters and bands who inspired me and my hero, but most especially Todd Rundgren, the Flaming Lips, R.E.M., Elvis Costello, David Bowie, and the Beatles. You ROCK!

Thanks to my friends for use of your names: you know who you are. I know I fulfilled at least a few parents' career wishes. And killed one of you.

Moral support and readers: Jef Allbright, Karen Austin, David Brin, Damien Broderick, Charles Burkhalter, Michael Chorost, James

Clement, Maria Del Rey, Craig Foster, James J. Hughes, Michael Hurst, Eric Gruendemann, Jo Gruendemann, Paul Gruendemann, Vickie Holland, Amanda Marks, Donna Plank, Eric & Kathryn Savitsky, Amit Shalev, John Smart, Arne Svenson, Laura Faye Tanenbaum, Jonathan Westover. Thank you!

To the team who got it out to the public: Patrick LoBrutto, editor and Goldilocks who made a too-big thing just right. Wanda Zimba and Jeff Zittrain, my copy editors. Joe Quirk, writer extraordinaire who gave the most wonderful story notes a writer could ever ask for. Attorneys Michael Donaldson, Dean Cheley, David Hochman, and Neal Tabachnick. Daniel Edelman who introduced me to the wonderful people at Amazon. And the enthusiastic Jason Kirk, my editor and fellow pioneer at Amazon/47North.

I'd like to especially thank:

Jonathan Westover, who gave me notes, held my hand, slapped my wrist, stood me up, wiped my tears, and shoved me out the door. And Karen Austin, who then kicked me in the ass.

My parents, Richard and Gloria Manney, who instilled a love of science fiction and fact and believed I had this in me.

My husband, Eric, who serves more functions in my life than I can count: editor, conscience, guide, soul mate, lover, and partner in all things professional and personal. I could never have written this without your unfailing help and support.

And finally, I thank my children, Nathaniel and Hannah, with all my heart. They tolerated their mother chasing things to come, then had to hear me yak on about it! I wrote this book for them, hoping they would never be afraid of what the future has in store, but instead face it wide-eyed, clear-minded, and with compassion.

Malibu, California
2015

ABOUT THE AUTHOR

PJ Manney is a former chairperson of Humanity+, the author of *Empathy in the Time of Technology: How Storytelling is the Key to Empathy*, and a frequent guest host and guest on podcasts including *FastForward Radio*. She has worked in motion-picture PR at Walt Disney/Touchstone Pictures, story development and production for independent film production companies (*Hook, Universal Soldier, It Could Happen to You*), and writing for television (*Hercules—The Legendary Journeys, Xena: Warrior Princess*). She also cofounded Uncharted Entertainment, writing and creating pilot scripts for television. Manney is a culture vulture and SF geek, and the daughter and mother of them, too. When not contemplating the future of humanity, she is a mother, wife, PTA volunteer, and education activist in California.